For all the Black kids drowning in the sunken place, desperately trying to claw their way out, this book is for you.

And for my mum, who believed in me first and gave me my love of fables.

This edition published in 2022. First published in the UK in 2021 by Usborne Publishing Ltd., Usborne House, 83-85 Saffron Hill, London EC1N 8RT, England, usborne.com.

Usborne Verlag, Usborne Publishing Ltd., Prüfeninger Str. 20, 93049 Regensburg, Deutschland VK Nr. 17560

A CIP catalogue record for this book is available from the British Library.

ISBN 9781803706351 05386/10 JFM MJJASOND/22

Printed and bound in Great Britain by CPI Group (UK) Ltd, Croydon, CR0 4YY.

MIX
Paper from responsible sources
FSC® C171272

FARIDAH ÀBÍKÉ-ÍYÍMÍDÉ

USBORNE

"They say life is full of surprises. That our dreams really can come true. Then again, so can our nightmares…"
– *Gossip Girl*

"All I know is sometimes, if there's too many white folks… I get nervous."
– *Get Out*

TRIGGER WARNING

ACE OF SPADES is a work of fiction but it deals with many real issues including racism, homophobia, bullying and suicide ideation.

For further information on these content warnings, please visit: www.faridahabikeiyimide.com/ace-of-spades-content-warnings

---

PART ONE:
THE IVORY TOWER

MONDAY

First-day-back assemblies are the most pointless practice ever.

And that's saying a lot, seeing as Niveus Academy is a school that runs on pointlessness.

We're seated in Lion Hall – named after one of those donors who give money to private schools that don't need it – waiting for the principal to arrive and deliver his speech in the usual order:

1. Welcome back for another year – glad you didn't die this summer
2. Here are your Senior Prefects and Head Prefect
3. School values
4. *Fin.*

Don't get me wrong, I'm all for structure. Ask any of my friends. Correction – *friend.* I'm pretty sure that, even though I've been here for almost four years, no one else knows I exist. Just Jack, who generally acts like there's something seriously wrong with me. Still, I call him a friend, because we've known each other for ever and the thought of being alone is much, much worse.

But back to the thing about structure. I'm a fan. Jack knows about the many rituals I go through before I sit down at the piano. Without them, I don't play as well. That's the difference between my rituals and these assemblies. Without these, life at Niveus would still be an endless drudge of gossip, money and lies.

The microphone screeches loudly, forcing my head up. Twenty minutes of my life about to be wasted on an assembly that could have been an email.

I lean back against my chair as a tall pale guy with dull black eyes, oily black hair slicked back with what I'm sure was an entire jar of hair gel, and a long dark coat that almost sweeps the floor, stands at the podium, staring down at us all like we're vermin and he's a cat.

"My name is Mr Ward, but you must all address me as Headmaster Ward," the cat says, voice liquid and slithery. I squint at him. What the hell happened to Headmaster Collins?

The room is filled with confused whispers and unimpressed faces.

"As I'm sure some of you are aware, Headmaster Collins resigned just before summer break, and I'm here to lead you all through your final year at Niveus Academy," the cat finishes, his lips pursed.

"So, the rumours *were* true," someone whispers nearby.

"Seems like it... I hear rehab is super classy these days though..."

I hadn't even heard anything was wrong with Headmaster

Collins; he seemed fine before summer. Sometimes I feel like I'm so lost in my own world, I don't notice the things that seem so obvious to everyone else.

"And so," Headmaster Ward's voice booms over everyone else's, "we keep within the Niveus tradition, starting today's assembly with the Senior Prefect and Head Prefect announcements."

He swivels expectantly as one stiffly-suited teacher rushes forward and hands him a cream-coloured envelope. Silently, Headmaster Ward opens it, the paper's crinkle amplified to a blaring shriek through the speakers. He removes a small card and places the envelope on the podium in front of him. I start to zone out.

"Our four Senior Prefects are…" He pauses, his pupils flicking back and forth like black flies trapped in a jar. "Miss Cecelia Wright, Mr Maxwell Jacobson, Miss Ruby Ainsworth and Mr Devon Richards."

At first, I think he's made a mistake. My name *never* gets called out at formal assemblies. Mostly because these assemblies are usually dedicated to the people the student body know and care about, and if Niveus was the setting for a movie, I'd probably be a nameless background character.

Jack elbows me, pulling me from my shocked state, and I push myself out of the chair. The creaking of wooden seats fills the hall as faces turn to glare at my attempt to shuffle through the rows. I mumble a "sorry" after stepping on some guy's designer shoes – probably worth more than my ma's rent – before making my way to the front where the senior teachers are lined up, my sneakers squeaking against the almost-black wood beneath. My heart pounds and the light applause comes to an awkward stop.

I recognize the other three standing up there, though I've never spoken to them. Max, Ruby and Cecelia are these giant, pale, light-haired duplicates of each other, and next to them, my short frame and dark skin sticks out like a sore thumb. *They* are main characters.

I stand next to Headmaster Ward, who is even more terrifying up close. For one thing, he's unnaturally tall and his legs literally end at the top of my chest. His pupils move towards me, staring, despite his head facing the front.

I look away from him, pretending that the BFG hasn't got a scary emo brother called Ward.

"I've already heard great things about our Head Prefect this year." Ward's voice drags, making what I'm sure was meant to be a positive, somewhat lively sentence as lifeless as a eulogy. "And so, there should be no surprise that the Head Prefect is none other than Chiamaka Adebayo."

Loud cheers fill the dark oak-walled hall as Chiamaka walks forward. I notice her army of clones seated at the front clapping in scary unison, all as pretty and doll-like as their leader. There's a smug expression on her face as she joins us. I almost roll my eyes, but she's the most popular girl at school, and I don't have a death wish.

I shift awkwardly, feeling even more out of place now. If Max, Ruby and Cecelia are all main characters, Chiamaka is the protagonist. It makes sense seeing them up here.

But me? I feel like any moment now, guys with cameras are gonna run out and tell me I'm being pranked. That would make more sense than any of this.

I know things like Senior Prefects are popularity contests. Teachers vote for their favourites each year and it's always the same kind of person. Someone popular, and I am *not* popular. Maybe my music teacher put in a good word for me? I don't know.

"As all of you know, the roles of Senior Prefect and Head Prefect should not be taken lightly. With a lot of power comes great responsibility. It is not just about attending council meetings with me, or organizing the big events, or impressing a choice college. It is also being a model student all year round, which I am sure the five of these students here have been during their time at Niveus and will, hopefully, continue to be long after they leave Niveus behind." Headmaster Ward forces a tight smile.

"Please give another round of applause to our prefect council this year," Ward continues, triggering louder claps from the sea of pale in front of us.

I feel a few eyes on me, and I avoid them, trying to find an interest in the floor beneath my feet, rather than the fact that there are rows and rows of people watching me.

I hate the feeling of being watched.

"Now for the school values."

We all turn to face the giant screen behind us, like we always do, ready to watch the school values scroll down like credits at the end of a movie, while the national anthem plays in the background. In normal assemblies, we usually just pledge allegiance to the flag, but seeing as this is the first assembly of the year, Niveus does what it does best: amps up the drama.

The screen is enormous and black and covers most of the large, double-glazed window behind the stage. Niveus is a school made up of fancy, dark wooden walls, marble floors and huge glass windows. The exterior is old and haunted-looking and the interior is new and modern, reeking of excessive wealth. It's like it's tempting the outside world to peer in.

There's a loud click and a large picture fills the screen: a rectangular playing card with *As* in each corner and a huge spade symbol at the centre.

That's new.

I turn to find Jack in the audience, wanting to give him our *What the hell?* look, but he's staring at the screen as if the whole thing doesn't faze him. Everyone else in the audience looks just as unbothered by this as Jack. It's weird.

"Ah, there seems to be some kind of technical malfunction..." Mrs Blackburn, my old French teacher, announces from the back. A few more clicks, and all goes back to normal. The national anthem blares from the speakers and we sing along, with our palms placed on our chests as we watch the school values fly past: *Generosity, Grace, Determination, Integrity, Idealism, Nobility, Excellence, Respectfulness* and *Eloquence.*

Nine values most people at this school lack. Myself included.

"Now for a speech from our Head Prefect, Chiamaka." The student body goes wild at the mention of her name, clapping even louder than before and cheering like she's a god – which by Niveus standards, she basically is.

"Thank you, Headmaster Ward," Chiamaka says as she steps up to the podium. "Firstly, I would like to thank the teachers for selecting me as Senior Head Prefect – it's something I never imagined would happen."

Chiamaka's been Head Prefect three years in a row now: she was the Junior Head Prefect as well as the Sophomore Head Prefect – there's nothing remotely shocking about her selection. Mine, on the other hand…

She looks back at the teachers with her hand still placed over her heart from when we sang the national anthem, feigning surprise like she does every year.

My eyes really, *really* want to roll at her.

"As your Senior Head Prefect, I will work hard to ensure that our final year at Niveus is the best one yet. Starting with the Senior Snowflake Charity Ball at the end of the month. This year's prefect council and I will make sure it is a night everyone will talk about for many years to come."

People start to clap but Chiamaka doesn't back down, instead she drags the microphone forward, not yet done with her soliloquy.

"Above all else, I promise to make sure that the majority of the funding we get goes to the right departments. I'd hate to see all the generosity shown by our donors go to waste. As Senior Head Prefect, I will make sure the right people –

the students winning the Mathalons, competing at the science fairs, the ones *actually* contributing something to the school – are prioritized. Thank you."

Chiamaka finishes, flashing a wicked grin as the hall erupts in applause once again.

This time, I roll my eyes without a care, and I'm pretty sure the girl in the front row with the red bows in her hair looks at me with disdain for doing so.

The prefects all stay behind to get our badges, while everyone else marches out of assembly to their first period classes. I watch them all with their shiny new fitted uniforms, their purses made from alligator skin and faces made from plastic. Looking down at my battered sneakers and blazer with loose threads, I feel a sting inside.

There are many things I hate about Niveus, like how no one (besides Jack) is from my side of town and how everyone lives in huge houses with white-picket fences, cooks who make them breakfast, drivers who take them to school, and credit cards with no limit tucked away in their designer backpacks. Sometimes, being around all of that makes me feel like my insides are collapsing, cracking and breaking. I know no good comes from comparing what I have to what they have, but seeing all that money and privilege, and having none, hurts. I try to convince myself that being a scholarship kid doesn't matter, that I shouldn't care.

Sometimes it works.

The badges are all different colours. Mine is red and shiny, with *Devon* engraved under *Senior Prefect*. The prefects they choose in senior year are always immediately drafted as the top candidates for the valedictorian selection and while Chiamaka will probably get it, I'm still happy to even be considered. Who knows, if I can get Senior Prefect, what's stopping the universe from granting one more wish and making me valedictorian?

I don't usually allow myself to dream that much – disappointment is painful, and I like to control the things that seem more possible than not. But I've never been on the teachers' radars before, or anyone else's for that matter. I excel at being unknown, never being invited to parties and whatnot. Now that I'm here, and something like this is actually happening to me, I can't help but feel it is a sign that this year is gonna go well…or at least better than the last three. A sign that maybe I'm gonna get into college – make my ma proud.

Ward finally dismisses us and I rush out of the hall, weaving through a small crowd of students still hanging about, and into one of the emptier marble hallways with rows of dusky grey lockers. I only slow when a teacher turns the corner. She gives me a pointed look, her sleek bob giving her face the same scary judgemental appearance of Edna Mode from *The Incredibles*, then she passes and I can breathe normally again.

The sound of a locker door slamming hard grabs my attention, and my head whips around to find the source. A dark-haired guy with sharp, heavy make-up around his eyes and an expression that says *Fuck off* stares back at me. Josh?

Jared? ...I can't remember his name, but I know his face.

He's the guy who came out last year at Junior Prom, walking in holding his date's hand. *His guy-date's hand.* And it wasn't that big of a deal. People were happy for him. But all I remember was looking at him and his date, hand-in-hand, and feeling this overwhelming sense of jealousy.

Prom is one of Niveus's many compulsory and meaningless events, and so, like a masochist, I watched them all night, from the benches at the side of the hall. I watched them slow-dance, arms wrapped around each other like they were naturally safe there. Like nothing bad would happen to them. Like none of their friends outside of school would hurt or mock them. Like their parents wouldn't stop loving them – or leave them. Like they'd be okay.

My chest had squeezed as I'd held onto that thought. My vision blurred, the lights in the room becoming vibrant circles. I had blinked back the tears, quickly wiping them off my cheeks with the sleeve of the black tuxedo I'd rented, still watching them dance, like a class-A creep, looking away only when it got too painful.

"What?" A deep voice cuts into the memory like a blade. I blink to find the guy at the locker is staring at me, looking even more pissed off than before.

I turn quickly, walking the opposite way now, not daring to look back. Because, one, Jared? Jim? – *that guy* – scares the shit out of me, and two... My mind flashes back to prom, *their intertwined fingers, their smiles.* I screw my eyes shut, forcing myself to think of something else. Like music class.

I climb the steps to the first floor where my music classroom is, burning the depressing memory and tossing its ashes out of my skull.

My body tingles when I see the dark-oak door with a plate engraved *Music Room*, and the sadness melts away. This is my favourite classroom, the only place in school that's ever felt like home. There are other music rooms, mostly for recording or solo practice, but I like this one the most. It's more open, less lonely.

"Devon, welcome back and congrats on becoming a prefect!" Mr Taylor says as I step in. Mr Taylor is my favourite teacher; he's taught me music since freshman year and is the only teacher I ever really speak to outside of class. His face is always lit up, a smile permanently fixed to it. "You can get started on your senior project, along with the rest of the class."

My classmates are lost in the world of their own music, some on keyboards and others with pencils firmly gripped in their hands as they write down melodies on crisp white music sheets. We were meant to start planning our senior projects over the summer, ready to showcase when we got back. But I spent most of my summer occupied with my audition piece for college, as well as other not-so-academic things.

I spot my station at the back by one of the windows, with a keyboard on top of the desk and my initials, *DR*, engraved in gold into the wood. Not many people take music, so we all have our own stations. I've always loved this classroom because it reminds me of those music halls from the classical concerts online: oval-shaped, with brown-panelled walls. Being in this room makes me feel like I'm more than a scholarship kid. Like I belong here, in this life, around these people.

Even though I know that isn't true.

"Thanks," I say, before stepping towards the keyboard I've dreamed of all summer. I don't have a keyboard at home, because there's no space and they are a lot more expensive than they look. I'm sure my ma would get me one if I asked, but she already does so much for me and I feel like I burden her more than I should. Instead, when I'm not in school, I improvise; humming tunes, writing down notes and listening to and watching whatever I can. I'm more into the composition and songwriting aspect of music anyway, but it still feels good to have an actual instrument in front of me again.

I plug the keyboard into the wall and it comes alive, the small square monitor in the corner flashing. I put my headphones on, running my fingers over the black and white plastic keys, pressing a few, letting a messy melody slip out, before I sit back, close my eyes, and picture the ocean. Bluish green with fish swimming and bright sea plants. I jump in, and I'm immersed by the water.

The familiar sense of peace rises inside and my hands stretch towards the piano.

And then I play.

2

MONDAY

High school is like a kingdom, only instead of temperamental royals, golden thrones, and designer outfits flown in from Europe, the hallways are filled with loud postpubescent teens, the classrooms with rows of wooden desks, and students who are dressed in ugly plaid skirts, navy-coloured slacks and stiff blue blazers.

In this kingdom, the queen doesn't inherit the crown. To get to the top, she destroys whoever she needs to. Here, every moment is crucial; there are no do-overs. One mistake can have you sent to the bottom of the food chain with the girls who have imaginary boyfriends and wear polyester un-ironically. It sounds dramatic, but this is the way things are and the way they will always be.

The people at the top in high school get into the best colleges, get the best jobs, go on to run the country, and win Nobel prizes. The rest end up with dead-end jobs, heart failure, and then have to start an affair with their assistant to create some excitement in their otherwise dull lives.

And it's all because they weren't willing to put in the work to make it in high school.

Maintaining popularity at a place like Niveus is not about how many friends you have. It's about looking the part, having the best grades and dating the right people. You have to make everyone wish they were you, wish they had your life. I know to an outsider, it seems horrible – making people self-conscious, feeding off their envy, destroying anyone who gets in your way – but I learned early on that it's either kill or be killed. And if I had to stop and feel bad for every instance I've had to step on someone's toes to keep the crown, I'd be very bored.

Besides, regardless of whether it's me or someone else, there will always be a kingdom, a throne and a queen.

I stare down at the badge with *Senior Head Prefect, Chiamaka* engraved into the shiny, gold metal. It's weird that after three years of fighting my way up to the top of the ladder, it can all be summarized by something so small and seemingly insignificant. I find myself smiling as I run my thumb over the cold surface. Even though it's so minute in the grand scheme of things, it's what I've wanted since I was a freshman, and now I have it.

"Your badge is really pretty, Chi. Congrats," Ruby says, as I walk out of Lion. She and Ava, the other girl I hang out with most of the time, are outside by the door, waiting. The hallway is still filled with students, talking and biding their time before the warning bell rings. The new headmaster kept me back a little longer than the other prefects, wanting to introduce himself properly.

I'm hoping I made a good first impression on him. That

first image someone has of you is etched into their minds for ever, but the new head didn't seem that enthused by me. He just stared at me coldly, like I had insulted his tacky suit or told him his tie didn't match his shoes. I did none of that, I was polite. And yet…

I slip the badge into my blazer pocket and wipe the smile off my face with a shrug, not wanting to seem too eager.

"Thanks." I look down to Ruby's badge – dark-blue – pinned proudly to her chest. "You too."

She gives me a toothy, empty smile, her green eyes wide as she says, "Thank you, Chi."

I raise an eyebrow. Usually there's more from Ruby, a subtle jab that seems harmless to most but that I know isn't.

"I mean, it's such a shame they don't always give certain titles to the people who *deserve* them… But, you'll look great in the prefect photograph at the end of the year, Chi."

There it is.

I smile again as we walk through the hallway, heading towards my locker. "I know I will. I'm so glad you'll finally be in the photograph with me. It only took, what? Three years?"

Ruby's teeth are still bared as she nods. "That's right, three years."

Ava clears her throat. "What did you guys think of the new headmaster?" she asks as we get to my locker, clearly wanting to defuse the tension and stop the weird power-play Ruby has been trying with me since last year.

Some days it's like Ruby is praying for my downfall, other

days she seems satisfied with where she stands at school. Then again, that's Ruby. The catty, spoiled daughter of a senator. Even though I've known her since middle school, we only started speaking in high school, when I became someone worth speaking to, I guess. Anyway, she's always been a bitch, but maybe that's why we gravitated towards each other. Girls like us, unafraid to speak our minds, tend to do well together.

I met Ava in sophomore year, when she transferred to Niveus from some posh private school in England. She's this pretty, blonde bombshell who everyone immediately took a liking to with her British accent and her straightforward persona. I actually don't mind hanging around her that much. Unlike Ruby, she's nice and honest – most of the time.

"The new head is kind of scary. Where's he even from?" I ask, shoving my purse into my locker, glad to not have to continue playing this exhausting game with Ruby so early in the morning. I can't wait to go to class and get away from her snide remarks.

Most people think the three of us are friends, since we're almost always seen together.

But we're not friends.

Our relationship is a transaction. I need a close attractive circle. Small, because the smaller your group, the less people know about you – and the more they want to know. And, in return, Ava and Ruby like how powerful the three of us are together.

Ruby perks up, the way she always does whenever she has information that I don't. Her fiery curls light up as she beams, leaning in. "I hear he's from England, used to be the headmaster at some strict private boarding school."

"I didn't even know Headmaster Collins was stepping down," I say, annoyed that I have to restart all the work I've put in over the past three years with him. Especially given Headmaster Ward's unwelcoming, icy demeanour. I grab some chapstick from my pocket, just as someone taps my shoulder. I turn to face a familiar bright-eyed sophomore carrying a cup holder with two drinks.

"Morning, Chi. I got you a soy latte and a cinnamon latte on my way to school. Wasn't sure which you'd prefer… I remembered from last year that you liked them both, but if you change your mind, I can bring you something else tomorrow," she says, cheeks flushed as she rambles. I take the cinnamon one, relief spreading across her face.

"Thank you, Rachel," I say, taking a sip of the coffee and turning back to Ruby and Ava.

"Actually, it's Moll—"

"He seemed fine before summer," I continue.

"I heard Collins had some kind of nervous breakdown," Ava chimes in and I shoot her a look that makes her shrink back a little. I understand Ruby knowing things I don't; she always has her claws in other people's business. But Ava too? I've clearly been slacking over the summer.

Before I can pry further, my vision goes dark, hands clamped over my eyes. I don't have to see to know it's Jamie.

"Guess who," he says in a low voice. A part of me hopes the people in the hallway are watching. I can almost hear their thoughts... *Did Chiamaka and Jamie get together over the summer? They'd make the perfect couple. I'd kill to be Chiamaka...* All of them, drowning in envy. I smile at the possibility.

"Hmm... Tall, dark, handsome and missing billions of brain cells?" I say.

The hands slip away and I can see again; Ruby's face is unsurprised and Ava gives a sly smile.

"Correct," he says, before kissing my head and ruffling my hair like I'm his dog or his little sister. I hope no one saw *that*. I smooth my hair, avoiding Ruby and Ava's gazes.

"We should probably head to class," Ruby says, and I can hear the delight in her voice. She loves any moment of weakness she can find, and I guess my only weak spot, despite all the hard work I've put into being perfect, is the fact that Jamie is still my best friend and not my boyfriend.

For now, anyway.

I force a smile. "Ruby's right. Don't want to make a bad impression on the new headmaster, especially now that I've been made Senior Head Prefect – not that that was a surprise."

Jamie laughs, shaking his head. "You're too cocky. What made you so sure you were gonna get it this year?"

I shrug even though I know why I was so sure. Every year since sophomore year – freshmen can't be prefects – I've been Head Prefect. It's not luck, it's science. I deserve it, no

26

matter what anyone says.

I get straight As, and I'm the president of debate club, Young Medics, and Model UN. I can speak four languages, five if you count English, and I'm going to Yale for pre-med, or at least that's the plan. There's no one else who makes more sense for the role of Senior Head Prefect than I do – and there's no one else who's worked harder for it.

Head Prefect is the icing on the cake. It tells universities like Yale that I care about Niveus, which I do, and that I'm a leader, which I am. I'm more than qualified for Head Prefect. Even though I know I shouldn't care, it annoys me that when girls know what they want and how they're going to get it, they're seen as cocky. But guys who know what they want? They're confident or strong. The reason I should be Head Prefect is because I've earned it, and Jamie out of everyone should know that.

I know he probably didn't mean it that way though, so I brush off his comment as we head out of the crowded hallway. As I've come to expect over the past three years, the sea of blue parts; people move aside as we pass through, drinking in our faces, clothes and hair. I always opt for a simple look: today it's black thigh-high socks, a velvet Dolce jacket, and suede Jimmy Choo pumps. The more it looks like you didn't try, the better. I place my hand in my blazer pocket, feeling the badge again, the one thing to show for all my achievements. *Everything I've overcome.*

I feel this energy coursing through me, excitement bubbling inside. I'm not sure what it is – maybe it's finally being a senior, or maybe it is me being *cocky* – but something tells me that this year will be different from the others.

That this year will finally be the year everything falls into place, the year that will make all the blood, sweat and tears worthwhile.

3

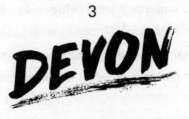

MONDAY

One of the only silver linings of being at Niveus is getting to miss some of my classes to work on my Juilliard audition piece.

Ever since I mentioned the possibility of applying to Juilliard, Mr Taylor has helped "fix" the problem of my attendance. Going to the best colleges is something of a priority for us Niveus students, and so it's not all that unusual to see upperclassmen miss classes for extra lessons in their chosen majors.

Like now. After first period ended, Mr Taylor let me move to one of the smaller practice rooms. I'm meant to be in fourth period math class, but instead I'm here poking random notes out of the keyboard. I swivel in my chair, reaching for more blank music sheets from the cabinet behind me, but when I tug the drawer, it doesn't give. I let out a sigh and drag myself out of the chair. I keep a large stack of music sheets in my locker for times when I need to scribble down ideas for new melodies.

I sprint down the steps and through the doors that lead to the hallway where my locker is, stopping short when the students there pause to stare at me. All of them. Some smile with teeth and others look at me with calculating glares. As if they know me. People usually look right through me, like my body is covered by some invisibility cloak. It's weird that they aren't in class, not that I can judge or anything, seeing as I'm not in class either.

I edge towards my locker, feeling a little confused and disorientated.

"*Is that the guy?*" someone whispers. I turn back to find some of their gazes are still fixed on me.

I try to focus on entering my combination, and not the sound of someone gasping, or what feel like judgemental stares digging into my back.

1...8...6— I start, but a tap on my shoulder interrupts me and I drop my hand. I'm met by Mindy Lion, a girl in my music class who I speak to sometimes, whose long purple hair and bright purple lipstick are impossible to ignore whether you want to or not.

"Hey, Devon…are you okay?" she asks, face filled with pity – which is really weird, because one, I don't suffer from resting bitch face, so I assume I look fine, and two, Mindy and I are acquaintances at most.

"Yeah, you?" I ask, because apparently we care about each other like that now.

"Yeah, of course. I just wanted to come over, because I know how hard it must be with the picture circulating and everything."

"What picture?"

Her mouth drops open.

"You haven't seen it?" she asks.

I shake my head, trying to look unbothered. I glance up; the people behind Mindy are blatantly rubbernecking at us now.

"What picture?" I repeat, my voice breaking a little. It's like my body knows before my mind that whatever she's talking about, it's not good.

Mindy fumbles around in her bright-red designer bag and pulls her phone out, tapping then presenting the screen to me.

I blink, looking at her phone closely. It's a picture of two guys. I glance back up at her, because what has this got to do with me? But then a weird thought pulls my eyes back down to the picture. It's not just two guys, it's two familiar figures – one with a bruised neck, and the other, a face I know all too well. I see it every day in the mirror. They are in a room, their lips locked.

My stomach flips and jerks out of my body, heartbeat stopping altogether.

Oh my fucking god.

4

MONDAY

I'm in pain.

Not the type of pain that hurts because it's bad, but the type that hurts from laughing so hard everything starts to ache.

I attempt to look away from Jamie, who is the cause of all this. The only downside to having my best friend as my lab partner is painful laughter and distraction from the task at hand.

He rips part of a page from his notebook and rolls it up into a thin cylinder before placing the end of it in the Bunsen burner's flame. He brings it up to his lips and pretends to take a drag.

"I'm so tortured. I listen to The 1975. I dyed my hair pink to be ironic since, you know, my soul is black, and my Christian name is Peter, but my clan call me Tortured Stone – because I'm obviously tortured but really badass."

I put my hand up.

"I'm requesting a different lab partner," I say, wiping my eyes with the sleeve of my white lab coat.

Jamie pushes my hand back down.

"Look at your options, Chi." He gestures to the other tables around us. "You could sit with Lance, who breaks every piece of equipment he's given, Clara, who eats the materials, or me: literal perfection."

I roll my eyes. None of that is true. Well, except maybe the last part.

Jamie quirks an eyebrow up at me, eyes a little narrowed like he's daring me to question him and his inflated ego. And he has the audacity to call *me* cocky. His golden freckles dance along his cheeks as his smile widens.

"I guess you're right," I say, giving in.

He looks triumphant.

"Good choice, Chi, good choice."

He changes the flame from orange to blue like the instructions say we should, his wrists covered with the colourful string bracelets his mom got him from her trip to India last summer.

I place my hand on my stomach, which is still aching from laughing so hard.

"Start packing up, five minutes until the end of class," Mr Peterson tells us.

Jamie groans, pouting at the Bunsen burner like a child.

I turn the gas off and load our equipment onto the white tray it came from – much to Jamie's annoyance. He loves controlling anything to do with fire in our experiments. I think his pyromania – his fire obsession – started in sophomore year, after a long summer at the camp a select few Niveus students get invited to annually, not that I care or anything. Everyone knows that legacy kids are the only ones who get invited to those events.

Legacy kid = Niveus students with super powerful parents and generations of family members who've attended Niveus Academy. Aka Jamie's entire family from the beginning of time. My parents aren't American and they don't have old American money, just old Italian money, so I don't get the same "privileges" as the legacy kids. Honestly, things would be a lot easier if I were one. My future would be more certain, and I wouldn't have to work so hard.

Jamie's known since he was in diapers that he'll get into any Ivy League school he wants, inherit his father's billion-dollar company, have connections in any important organization here in America and never really have to work a day in his life. I want my future to look as seamless as his, everything perfectly laid out. Money can only get you so far; you need power and influence to go with it, and the Fitzjohns – Jamie's family – have all three.

"I need to tell you something at lunch," Jamie whispers. The intensity of his voice makes me jump a little. I nod, his shoulder brushing against mine. Jamie thrives on attention. Every single touch – every hand graze, every elbow nudge, you name it – is purposeful. He knows how to make sure he's the *only* person you're focusing on. That plus his winning smile are what make him irresistible; I've seen him charm his way out of homework and parking tickets. I'm pretty sure he'd flirt with Death herself if there wasn't a possibility that he'd die and not be the centre of attention any more.

"Sure, Lola's?" I ask, trying to sound casual.

Lola's is this imaginary place we made up. Back when we were freshmen, we thought it sounded like a quirky coffee shop you might find in the middle of an old-fashioned town, where housewives meet up to gossip and smoke. As we got older, we realized *Lola's* actually sounds like the name of a sketchy strip club. Despite the connotations, we still use it. It's our way of saying: *Let's talk in private.*

Lola's can be any place we're alone together. In freshman year, the year we met, a teacher put us in pairs, Jamie introduced himself as *the guy who was going to ruin my life* and I responded that he thought too highly of himself. Back when we first met, Lola's was a corner in one of the empty classrooms. We would sit there during lunch and bitch about people in our year or talk about the people we wanted to be when we were seniors. I wanted to be the best. Best grades, best looks, best hair, best boyfriend…best everything – the person everyone envies. Jamie told me he wanted to be someone his parents respected.

Then, all through junior year, whenever we weren't in school, Lola's was his bedroom and his bed, under the covers—

"Yeah." He smiles, winking at me. "Lola's."

The sounds of text tones fill the air. My phone buzzes in my pocket. I take it out.

[one new message from unknown]

35

Hello, Niveus High. It's me. Who am I? That's not
important. All you need to know is...I'm here to
divide and conquer. Like all great tyrants do. – Aces

Divide and conquer...? Who even talks like that? And who
the hell is *Aces*?

My phone buzzes again.

This time a picture accompanies the message. Two guys,
kissing. One with a very, *very* bruised neck. Gasps and
giggles ripple around the room. I roll my eyes. It's the
twenty-first century, people, is this really something gasp-
worthy? But then I read the message beneath.

Just in, the picture says it all. Dramatic arts and
music do indeed mix well. – Aces

Is that...Scotty? With...Devon Richards?

Loud collective laughter pulls me away from the picture
momentarily. I look up at everyone else, as they stare at
their phones closely.

"Is that Scotty?" Jamie asks. I nod.

Scotty is one of my ex-boyfriends. I guess that's why he'd
ask, even though it's not Scotty I'm staring at. It's Devon.
He's not a person I care for, or talk to, but it's hard not to
notice the only other Black person at school. What's weirder
than this picture is that until today, I don't think I've ever
even heard Devon speak. Now, out of nowhere, he got made
a Senior Prefect...and then this?

Have I missed something?

"So...Scotty's gay? Can football players even be gay? Well, he does do drama too, so I guess—"

"Jamie, football players can be gay and drama kids can be straight. Don't be that straight white guy who sticks his foot in his mouth," I say. "Besides, Scotty could be bi."

"Just surprised, that's all," he says, which I get. I'm surprised too. I feel like such a hypocrite. Telling Jamie not to stereotype even though a part of me questions whether me being so shocked by Devon is because he's Black and kissing Scotty.

People finish packing up, eyes still glued to their screens. I'm the senior Science Rep, so I help the science technicians make sure all the equipment is returned safely and secured. It's not glamorous, but I'll do anything to make my Yale application the best. It just means I won't be walking to class with Jamie today.

"I'll see you at lunch?" I ask.

He nods, kissing my forehead. "Lola's."

His kiss is deliberate.

Jamie pulls away and looks down at me and we stare at each other for a brief moment. I smile, then look away first.

"See you," he tells me.

"See you," I say.

I watch him as he leaves the classroom. My head still warm where his mouth touched it, heart still beating erratically; his gaze that told me everything I needed to know.

I've got Jamie right where I want him.

We've been playing this game for years, but I think today's the day Jamie finally folds.

It's the period before Lola's and I'm in my English class. I can't concentrate on anything but the prospect of finally being Jamie Fitzjohn's girlfriend.

I've waited a long time – three years to be exact – for Jamie to see me as more than just his best friend. I've watched girls fawn all over him and I've listened to him drone on about his hypothetical perfect girlfriend, waiting for the moment he turns my way and realizes that his perfect girl could be me. And it's been frustrating; I'm not usually afraid of making the first move when it comes to the guys I date, but, with Jamie, it feels *different*.

Most boys are so predictable. I see right through them: their wants, desires, what makes them tick. My first boyfriend was a guy named Georgie Westerfield. He was the usual type girls like: tall, blond and the great-great-great-grandson of the guy who owns Westerfield Socks – so in short, swimming in billions of dollars. Most importantly for me as a freshman though, was that he was a junior and every girl wanted him. Being Georgie's girlfriend got me noticed, took me from being the invisible, unimportant, miserable girl I was in middle school. When I joined Niveus, I knew I wanted to make myself everything that I hadn't been. And being Georgie's girlfriend not only made me someone people wanted to *know*, but someone they wanted to be.

I discovered it wasn't hard to get close to Georgie; one, Jamie was his friend and mentee through football and two, Georgie liked that I was "different" – meaning me being Black made him look cool. I ignored that, as I knew there was only so long I could fake being into someone like Georgie anyway, and so I got to be Chiamaka, the girl who got the guy everyone wanted, and then the first to break his heart and move on to dating the next golden boy of Niveus.

I always study them before I strike. Their social currency. Each boy bringing something new. Georgie got me noticed and Scotty, the boy next door with ins to so many social circles, made me more likeable. Jamie is the only guy I've actually liked as a friend, the only one I didn't secretly hate. The only one who feels long term. It's hard to read someone like Jamie, though. We may be best friends, but I swear... most days I have no idea what that boy is thinking. Which is why I decided to wait, let him make the first move.

And like always, my plan worked.

Finally, at the start of last year – junior year – when I was still "seeing" Scotty but desperately wanting Jamie to *see me*, he did. He'd thrown what was meant to be the party of the year. We'd both gotten really drunk, so drunk I don't remember much of that night. But I do remember how Jamie finally looked at me and saw us as something more than platonic. He'd smiled down at me, tucked a piece of my hair behind my ear, and asked if I wanted to go upstairs.

And I said yes. He told me to meet him in his bedroom, and while that night we only made out, it was the catalyst for what happened the rest of the year. Jamie sneaking kisses, whispering things in my ear, asking me to come over…

I'm not naïve enough to think hooking up with someone means they like you. Things are just *different* between Jamie and me. I catch him looking at me sometimes, trying to rile me up on purpose, smiling widely whenever he succeeds. He makes me laugh…looks at me like I'm special.

I've spent the past three years building myself up to be the most popular girl at school, the girl who has it all, wanting to secure the *perfect* ending to my time at Niveus. And now that I'm Senior Head Prefect, all I need are the final pieces: the Snowflake Crown, a Yale acceptance letter, and Jamie.

I feel a nudge from Ava, who sits next to me in English class. Sometimes we poke fun at the conspiracies our teacher, Mrs Hawthorne, comes up with. Like the time she told us F. Scott Fitzgerald was really the reincarnation of William Shakespeare. To which Ava had said "and I'm the reincarnation of Jane Austen's arsehole". I'd laughed so hard Mrs Hawthorne had threatened to separate us. I admit, class is more entertaining with Ava around.

Perhaps if hierarchies weren't so important and people weren't constantly trying to take me down, maybe I'd be more trusting of people, and Ava and I would be more than just two girls using each other to survive high school. But the reality is, Niveus will always be Niveus. Besides, I didn't invent this twisted system that pits us against each other and makes us do crappy things for status – but I do know how to play it.

I have Jamie anyway, I don't need any more friends here.

"You don't even look like you're trying to listen," Ava whispers.

"I think Jamie's going to ask me out at lunch," I say, looking at her. Ava's eyes widen.

"Fucking hell, that's something. I always thought you guys were secretly dating anyway."

That makes me smile inside. It's one thing to convince Jamie that we are perfect for each other, it's another to make others believe it too.

"Well, soon it will be official – I hope."

Jamie always talks about looking for "the One". He's never dated because he says he's not yet found "her". People used to think he didn't like girls, but then he joined the football team – apparently that was confirmation enough he was straight.

I sort of believe in the One, that one person who makes your insides glow and makes you feel like you're losing control, but not in the same sappy way Jamie does. He acts like *the One* is this predetermined thing that God or Santa came up with when he was born.

I think we choose our own destiny. We choose who we befriend, kiss, and date, and I guess I choose Jamie.

The bell rings and I stand, throwing my notebook into

my bag and rushing out of the classroom, not wasting time by saying goodbye to Ava. I'll see her later in the cafeteria.

Jamie has history class, so I wait outside. Soon enough he's out, with a wide smile on his perfectly freckled face. His brown, floppy curls look like they are in need of a cut, but I like his hair this way. He looks like a member of a boy band I might pretend to dislike.

"Benches?" he asks, linking his arm through mine. I nod, trying to compose myself as we head out to the benches in the courtyard.

Jamie's told me how he plans to ask the One out. He said it'll be romantic, with chocolates and maybe a poem if he has the nerve – which I think is really cliché, but...I still want to see it play out.

The rest of the student body are spilling out of classrooms as we walk past them, some of them glancing at us like they know. First Senior Head Prefect and now this? The first day of school is only half over and I can already tell that this is going to be the best year of high school.

We take a seat on opposite sides of one of the wooden tables. I rest my chin on my hands and he does the same. Wherever we go for Lola's, however public, it always feels intimate.

"So," he starts.

"So," I reply.

"I think I've found the One."

"You have?" I say, sounding *way* too eager.

"I have indeed. She's clever, stunning, makes me laugh—"

"She sounds amazing," I interrupt, my heart banging at the walls of my chest.

"You might know her actually."

This is it.

"Her name is Belle Robinson..."

Wait...what?

"...I've seen her around school for years, and I always thought she was way out of my league..." He gives me a sheepish smile, face turning a little red. "But then we started talking and I knew she was special."

His words fade, going over my head as he speaks. This wasn't how this was supposed to go. I can feel cracks forming, my chest aching. I blink, angry tears falling. I quickly wipe my eyes, not wanting to smudge my make-up.

"I knew you'd be happy for me, but not this happy..." he jokes, despite the concern on his face.

I can't stop myself. "I thought you were going to tell me something else."

His eyebrows furrow together. "Like what?"

I feel stupid.

"That you liked me," I say quietly.

There are a few moments of complete silence, broken only by the wind and distant conversations from inside the building.

Jamie's face screws up, like the thought of us together is wrong. "You're my best friend, Chi. You know I don't see you in that way."

Images push their way into my brain: that night he asked

43

me to go to his bedroom at the beginning of junior year, all those nights since, the connection I thought we had. It was meant to be me and Jamie at the top of the school. We were meant to go to college together, get married, be wildly successful, have two wildly successful kids, then die.

"I'm dating Belle. I thought you would be happy for me."

Belle. Blonde-haired, blue-eyed fucking *Belle Robinson*.

I know her from some of my classes last year, and she's also on the girls' lacrosse team. She's semi-popular, not because she worked for it, but because she's pretty. People love to reward conventionally attractive people.

He takes my hand in his. "You're amazing," he starts. *But I'm not Belle*, I finish for him in my head. "I don't think you like me, Chi. I think you like the idea of me."

His words float above me once again, blurring into the background noise. He's used this line on so many girls; he lets them down easy, tells them their idea of being together is a fantasy. And I can't believe I fell for the fantasy myself. I'm so stupid. I tricked myself into believing I was above that. Better than girls like Belle. But apparently, I'm not.

I always thought Jamie turned these girls down because he wanted to be with me. I guess I was wrong.

Jamie's the best at talking people into believing him; he's the best at talking me into things. And he's the best at pretending nothing's wrong when things all go to shit. Leaving me to deal with the aftermath.

Suddenly, even though I don't want them to, memories start piling into my head. Junior year, winter break. The

night I've spent every moment since trying to forget...
Screeching tyres, louder than our singing voices moments
before as we yelled the lyrics to "Living on a Prayer". The
sound of a shrill scream making him swerve and slam into a
tree, jolting us forward. My head bashing against the
dashboard—

*"Fuck!" Jamie shouts. "Fuck, fuck, fuck...I think we hit
something."*

*My entire body trembles, chest squeezing as I try to
breathe but can't. The sound of the car unlocking sends a
sharp wave of nausea into my system as Jamie staggers
out into the road.*

*"FUCK!" Jamie screams. He stumbles back, tugging
at his hair. The sound of the radio drowns him out.
I desperately hit the off button.*

"Chiamaka, we hit a fucking girl!"

*I can hear her scream in my head again – I'm going to
throw up.*

*Jamie leans into the car, hair wet and sticking to his
pale forehead from the rain that's pouring down outside.
He's breathing fast, like he just finished a marathon. The
smell of the leather car seats mixed with Jamie's musky
cologne is overpowering, making my brain feel heavy.*

*"Chiamaka, we need to do something. My dad can't
find out!" His voice is pleading. Rain pounds the road as I
peer out the window at the body – her body. Through the
rivulets, I see her face. Blonde curls, pale skin, a dark pool*

forming a halo around her head. I gag, gripping onto the cold hard dashboard, closing my eyes.

I can't breathe – I can't breathe – I can't breathe.

I feel so sick.

I should get out – see if she's breathing. But I can't move; my limbs are stuck in place.

"W-we should check if she's breathing. And we need to call an ambulance, the police—" I say, as I take my phone out of my coat, fingers trembling. Jamie's eyes are desperate as he snatches my phone from my hands, shoving it into his pants pocket.

"We can't, my dad will kill me!" His voice rises. I jump in my seat as he kicks the side of his car, hard. "He's gonna fucking murder me."

Jamie hunches over, the rain pouring down his face, and places his hands on his knees, breathing harder than before.

I shake my head. Jamie's figure is getting hazy as tears blur my vision.

"We have to, she looks really hurt." My words clumsily spill from my lips. I need to get out.

"It's gonna be okay – no cops and it'll be fine," Jamie says, his voice cracking. "We can't go to prison, so no cops. We need to do something. My dad… He can't fucking find out about this."

Prison? I hadn't thought of prison.

The words stab at my chest, stopping my lungs from functioning the way they should. Each time I try to *breathe, there's not enough air; when I try to swallow, it's like there's something lodged in my throat.*

I can hear myself crying, but it's almost like it's someone else. I can't feel the tears, but I know it's me. The girl's doll-like face is scratched into a distorted image in my mind.

I should get out and make sure she's okay. I reach for the door handle. I have to see that she's still alive. She's not moving. The blood. We hit her really hard—

The next part happens so fast. I hear the loud slam of the car door as Jamie suddenly reappears next to me. The sound of tyres screeching on the wet road as he backs the car away. There's a pause and I look at him.

I have to get out—

There's a click as the doors lock. I rattle the handle uselessly.

"What are you doing?" I scream, banging on the window.

We can't leave her. We can't leave her.

Jamie looks at me briefly, eyes glazed over. Then in one quick motion, he swerves around the girl's body, illuminated suddenly in the headlights, and races forward, not looking back.

"Chi?" Jamie says, dragging me back into the present.

"You're right," I say, dizzy, gripping the bench as the sound of people talking in the distance fills my ears once again.

He smiles.

Jamie is good at rationalizing everything, making sense of the cracks in reality.

Especially when it's the things we need to forget.

My dreams, since the accident, always begin like this: water enters my body in every way it can, flooding my organs, squeezing and squeezing as I yell for help, which only makes more water seep through, burning my lungs, my throat, while my skin prickles on fire. I turn to the side and Jamie is there next to me in the car, frozen, staring blankly at the road ahead. I wave my arms to swim out, away, but I'm no longer in water. I'm dry and I'm back in the passenger's seat, watching her scream, eyes wide as we stop and she falls to the ground. In my dreams, I stumble out of Jamie's black car, palms stinging as I hit the gravel. I try to stand. But I can't. I drag myself towards the body, watching the blood seeping into the holes in the gravel, away from her blonde curls— Everything is silent. Her face is the last thing I see. The face I will never forget.

Then I'm gasping for breath, choking on air as I jerk myself awake.

I'm up like this every single night, in my dark bedroom, sweating and heaving. Some nights I have that dream more than once. Other nights, that dream is accompanied by another that is just as disturbing. Me trapped in a dark room, drunk, disorientated. Hundreds of blonde, bloodstained dolls surrounding me as the girl Jamie hit stands over me, a grin plastered to her pale face.

I get up, spots dancing in my vision as I run into my bathroom, my stomach rejecting all its contents.

In my dreams, I'm not a coward. I don't let us drive away, leaving her to die. I get out. I touch her. I see her blood on my hands. In my dreams, I don't help her either. I kneel on the ground, staring at her pale face, her eyes closed as blood oozes out until my mind can't take it any more.

At night when I'm alone, I'm reminded of the things I can't control. When I'm at school, I get to be someone else. Someone people like. But when I'm here sitting in the dark, shaking as that night replays over and over, her face a permanent bloodstain, I remember that the person I play at school isn't me, not in the slightest. The Chi who turns up at Niveus every day might not be afraid to hurt people's feelings, to do things to get what she wants. But she'd never do the things I've done.

She's a good person. Someone who deserves to be Head Prefect, to go to Yale and to become a doctor.

I clutch the toilet bowl, letting my body shudder and release quiet sobs.

And me...

I'm a monster.

5

DEVON

TUESDAY

I'm a few blocks from school, trying to prepare myself for the stares and whispers before I go inside.

It's no big deal.

It's no big deal.

Even though it is. I haven't even come out to Ma yet, and now everyone at school knows. I never planned on coming out at school. Not because I'm worried about being bullied, it's just… When I was dating Scotty he wanted to keep it a secret because he wasn't out and I figured he was worried about losing his friends from the football team. Then, when we weren't dating any more, I figured no one would care who I dated – not that it's their business anyway. If anything, I worried about the information somehow getting back to my neighbourhood, and then to Ma.

That's my biggest fear, her knowing. When I think of Ma finding out, I think about how disappointed she'd be. The thought keeps me up at night and makes me feel sick to my stomach. First she'd stop making eye contact, then she'd stop talking to me. After that, who knows. I remember when that guy from *Prison Break* came out and Ma had said,

"What a shame", shaking her head like being gay is something pitiful. I don't know what I hope for. Maybe that somehow she'll be okay with it, with me, even though she loves her Bible more than anything in the world.

I take a few steps forward, stop, walk back, then take a few steps forward again. The closer I get to school the more faint I feel, like I'm about to collapse. I thought I'd at least walk in with Jack today, like I usually do, but he didn't answer my texts. I even swung by his place before school, but his uncle said he'd already left.

I wouldn't feel this anxious if I had Jack next to me. I hope he's not avoiding me too.

I place my face in my hands, rubbing my eyes over and over before taking a deep breath.

No big deal.

The guys in my neighbourhood, the ones I used to go to school with before I got into Niveus, they'd kill me if they saw that picture. Toss my body into the garbage once they were done with me. These guys watch me on my walk home, staring me down, smirking. Sometimes they yell shit, other times they push me to the ground, then walk off laughing. The picture would make things in my neighbourhood ten times worse.

I know the likelihood of them seeing it is slim – Niveus is a world so separate from my home life – but I can't help feeling paranoid.

My stomach twists painfully, knotting, the longer I stand here thinking. I look up, inhale, then I walk, not stopping until I reach the big black iron gates that stand open for us in the morning. The two huge columns and double oak doors of the enormous white building loom ahead of me. I hesitate before climbing the steps, my heart beating so hard I can hear it. The footsteps of some students behind me get closer. If it's not me who opens the door, it'll be them, and I'd rather be the one to control when everyone sees me.

I hate this so much. I hate feeling like I'm gonna stop breathing any second now.

Without letting myself think much more, I push the door and walk in.

As expected, the crowded hallway quiets as they see me enter – sly smiles and whispers on pink lips. If it weren't for Scotty and that picture, I'd be uninteresting like any other day. When I went to bed last night, all I knew was that I had to find Scotty and ask him why he's doing this, leaking pictures of me after months of semi-harmony between us.

If I still had his number, I wouldn't have to see him face to face.

Note to self, don't delete numbers of the people you hate. They might come in handy someday.

I put my head down, moving as fast as I can towards the drama department. The drama kids usually hang out behind the stage there – in Crombie Auditorium, named after another rich donor. Crombie is my best shot at finding Scotty, seeing as I don't know his schedule by heart like I used to in freshman year. A few weeks before we started dating, when I still thought of him as the cute white guy who played the trumpet at the back of the school band, I learned his entire schedule, including where he went before and after classes. I wanted to make sure I kept bumping into him "by accident".

Later, after a toxic year-long relationship from the end of freshman year to the beginning of junior year, and a lot of tears and heartbreak, I used my knowledge of his schedule to avoid him as much as I could when things – us – didn't work out. And so, I hardly ever venture here any more. I even forgot how big Crombie is. Then again, everything in this school is unnecessarily huge.

I climb the steps of the spacious dark oak stage, slipping through a gap in the thick green curtains to find a circle of students on the other side. They're all seated on black metal chairs with white scripts in their laps. Apart from one girl who looks at me with an offended expression, no one else even glances my way. It's a weird change from the hallway earlier.

"This is a closed practice," the girl says, her plaid skirt the only item fitting the school's rule book. The rest of her is drenched in black – black leather jacket, black fishnet tights, black band T-shirt, black boots. The first day of school is the only time everyone follows the dress code. After that it becomes more of a suggestion than an enforced rule. I guess this is one of the many things you can get away with at Niveus, but I've never had the money to customize my uniform past the beat-up Vans I wear most of the time.

"I'm here to talk to Scotty," I say. We turn to where Scotty is sitting, flipping through his script like I'm not here. My heart jolts a little when I see his face, though not for any reason other than the fact that I haven't seen him since just before summer break, at prom. He'd brought some girl from the lacrosse team and spent most of the night obviously trying not to look at me. It's been even longer since we spoke – I actually think the last time I spoke to Scotty was to break up with him.

Scotty's hair is longer now, some of it tied up in a messy knot, while the rest sweeps his shoulders. Like the frowning girl, he's customized his uniform, and like always, it's fancy, his designer shoes screaming *rich kid*.

The more I look at him, the angrier I feel. He didn't even notice me walk in, distracted by his stupid script.

The girl looks at me again through squinted eyes, then realization smacks into her face.

"Shit, Scotty."

He finally looks up at her, then follows her gaze to me and his blue eyes widen.

"What the fuck, Scotty?" I grind out.

"Can we go outside?" he asks, abandoning the script on his chair as he stands.

Everyone else is staring at their scripts now, as if the text suddenly got more interesting – like they're not listening to every word. I push past the curtains and jump down from the stage to wait for Scotty. He scoots down a moment later and I shove him back.

"Woah!" He puts his hands up, shielding himself. "Before you kill me, you should know it wasn't me. I didn't send that picture to anyone," he says, straightening his blazer.

"You really expect me to believe that?"

Naturally I can't trust a word that Scotty says. Not after he cheated on both me and his SATs.

"I don't even have pictures of you any more, I got a new phone." He waves it at me. The latest model, of course. "Besides, why would I out myself? Especially at Niveus? You know how they take news like this. They're treating me like I'm some socialite now, keep asking me for details..." He smiles.

He's loving this, which is expected. Scotty loves being spoken about, and unlike when we were dating, when he was firmly in the closet, his sexuality is now an open secret amongst the arts students. Even I hear about his sex-capades from my corner of the school. Which is why that picture being released feels more aimed at me than him. And it's also why I think he might be the one behind it.

"It's embarrassing really – I don't even know how I'm gonna show my face at football practice without the guys wanting to know stuff."

I'm not even surprised that this is Scotty's only concern. He doesn't have to think about how the boys in his neighbourhood would react if they saw it.

I hate past-me for trusting him that much. I hate him for making me trust him that much. I already feel so exhausted and first period hasn't even started yet.

"I swear, Scotty, if you're lying to me about deleting all of it, I'll kill you."

"I'm not lying, wish I was though. We were quite photogenic, weren't we..." He moves towards me. "And video-genic, if my memory serves me right. It's a shame I don't have those files."

My ex is a psychopath. I always forget that part when I think about the other reasons we broke up. I squeeze my eyes shut, hoping the tears that desperately want to fall don't. Scotty seeing me cry would be another victory for him and a loss for me.

"Stay the fuck away from me, okay?" I move back. "Keep me out of your games."

Turning, I storm out of Crombie and go to Jack's locker. I feel weird not having seen him yet this morning. I usually see him by now, even on days when he goes to school early. I need someone to talk to about this.

Jack is always easy to find in a crowd. He's the only guy with a buzz cut at Niveus.

"Hey."

Jack stiffens at the sound of my voice. He pauses, then goes back to searching for whatever it is he needs from his locker.

"Hey," he says quietly.

"You weren't at your place this morning... Your uncle said you left for school early."

He nods, his pale skin tinted pink now.

"Yeah, had to talk to my math teacher."

"Okay," I say, feeling a little relieved. At least he wasn't avoiding me because of the picture.

I can feel eyes on us. He doesn't seem to notice.

"You good?" he asks, shoving papers into his bag.

I nod. "Yeah."

Someone snickers nearby and Jack slams his locker shut, turning to face them.

"Go and find a fucking hobby," he says to a random girl whose smile immediately disappears. He pulls his bag on, then turns without saying bye.

"Wait."

"What?" he asks, turning around without meeting my eyes. My stomach flips. Maybe he *is* avoiding me.

"What do you mean 'what'?"

"I mean, what do you want? I need to get to registration. It starts in ten."

He finally looks at me, and the realization hits. He's angry.

"Did you see that picture…going around?"

He doesn't say anything at first. Just stares at me, his brown eyes unreadable.

"They're gonna kill you. They won't let you deal for them like before."

My heart hasn't stopped beating this fast since yesterday.

"Who?" I ask, playing dumb.

"You know who."

I say nothing.

Jack sighs. "I don't know what you got yourself into, man,

but I want nothing to do with it. I can't have my brothers targeted."

I grab Jack's arm as he tries to turn. He pulls it back, looking around all uncomfortable.

"I can… I'll talk to Andre. I can tell him to sort this—"

"*'Course you can,*" he says, the disgusted look on his face unsurprising but still painful. I wish he wouldn't look at me like that whenever I mention Andre. "I can't do this right now." He moves back a bit, looking at me one last time. "I'm sorry."

And then he's gone.

I stand there, feeling worse than I did yesterday when I saw the picture.

I can still hear the whispers around me, because that's all anyone ever does here. Talk about people.

Jack's words echo in my head.

I can't do this right now.

I'm trying not to let it get to me. He has his brothers to think about, and the area we come from doesn't operate like Niveus. Here, they whisper about you. In our area… If they see or even hear about the picture, and Jack's seen with me, they could do things to him and his younger brothers, as well as me.

It wouldn't be the first time Jack has suffered because of my bullies. I just hope they don't know about the picture already.

As I turn, I'm met by three girls, all blonde-haired and

peach-faced, staring at me like they know me, even though I have no idea who they are.

"Is it true that Scotty cheated on you with Chiamaka?" the one in the middle asks. She has a huge blue bow in her hair, and a large rainbow-coloured lollipop in her hand. I know it's taboo to push a girl, but I want to. I dig my nails into my palms to stop myself from moving the girls out of the way.

I knew about Chiamaka, believe it or not. Scotty cheated on me with some other guys at parties he went to. His relationship with Chiamaka, he explained once, was a mutual popularity contract, not a real relationship. And I was stupid enough to accept that as an excuse.

"Excuse me," I say, before barging past them. I need the music room. I need to drown, I need to play. Jack once joked that music to me is like nicotine to a heavy smoker. I'm not a smoker, so I can't exactly say if that's true, but sometimes I feel like I'd die without music.

As I walk up the stairs to the music room, there's a buzz in my pocket. I stop walking, letting my eyes shut so that I can focus on calming my breathing – which is hard to do when your heart keeps hammering away like mine is. I slowly reach into my pocket, and beneath the old candy wrappers I'd forgotten to remove, I feel the warm smooth plastic of my phone.

It could be anything. It could be anyone.

It might be them…talking about me again.

Then again it might just be Andre texting or my ma…

[one new message from unknown]

My heart stops.

Just in...

I scan the screen.
And my nerves shatter when someone nearby says, "No fucking way."

6

TUESDAY

In my soon-to-be four years at Niveus, I've encountered many secrets, whisperings and rumours. While some of them have been about me, they were certainly never enough to ruin my reputation. The worst gossip was always about some other poor soul, who would either drop out from the weight of having to face their mistakes every day, or have a mental breakdown, leave school for a week, and come back with a new nose or handbag. And if I've learned anything during my time here, it's perfecting the art of making a rumour work in your favour – and coming out unscathed.

So it comes as a surprise when I walk through the double doors – later than usual because my straighteners were acting up – and everyone stares at me like I've got something to be ashamed of.

My stomach flips as I walk towards Ruby, who is by my locker, scrolling through her phone.

"Hi, Ruby."

She looks at me, a smile slowly forming, her ginger hair wrapped around her head in a braided crown.

"Hey, Chi." There's a playfulness in her eyes, like the look a wolf gets when it's hunting for prey.

I open my locker and push my bag inside. "Is there a reason, other than eternal jealousy, for all the stares this morning?" I joke, trying to seem unbothered. I pretend to search for something so that I don't have to look at her. "It's like I shaved my eyebrows off or something."

Her head cocks to the side. "It's probably just about the Jamie thing."

I close my locker and look her dead in her cold green eyes.

"What Jamie thing?" I ask. It could be anything—

Her smile widens. "Everyone's saying he rejected you yesterday at lunch?"

Oh.

"Well, you heard wrong, Rubes," I say, giving her a tight smile.

Her red-stained lips make an O shape.

"It must be people telling fibs," she says with a shrug.

My eyebrows furrow together. "Who?" I ask, because she clearly knows more than she's letting on.

"Well, you didn't hear this from me but –" she leans in – "Ava's been telling people you thought he'd ask you out even though everyone knows he's dating Belle now. Of course, I told people that it's just a rumour…"

Ava listened to me talk about Jamie while knowing all along he was dating Belle? I should have known better than to talk to anyone about anything personal. I feel really out of the loop, like there's so much going on that I should know about but don't. This past summer I was so caught up with Yale prep, I must've missed this. I must've missed everything.

"Did *you* know he was dating Belle?" I ask.

Ruby's smile fades a little. "Just found out."

I nod. Ruby's always been a terrible liar.

"Thank you, Ruby. I can always count on you," I say, thinking of ways to get back at Ava.

"You know I'll always have your back, Chi."

These girls are as loyal as scorpions. As I glance up, I see Ava walking towards us. She looks as white as a sheet, fear written all over her features. Sometimes the lingering threat of plotting to get someone back is better than actually carrying anything out. I smile at her and wave.

"Hi, Chi—" Ava starts, but I cut her off.

"Tell Sam I say hi," I sneer, before marching down the hallway towards Jamie's locker.

Ava has problems trusting her boyfriend Sam to keep his dick in his pants. Not only that, she's always been wary of the fact that Sam and I hooked up during freshman year, way before they started dating. I told her it was meaningless, but I know me bringing up Sam will eat away at her. I might even text him, knowing she'll be checking his phone all day now. It's not nice, but she tried to make me look desperate in front of everyone. So it's only fair.

"Hey, Jamie." I reach his locker as he turns around, revealing Belle behind him. They're holding hands.

"Hey, Chi."

My eyes linger on her. Her beauty is like a punch to the gut. I've seen her in some of my classes before, but never really *looked* at her...

I blink, crossing her out and ignoring the fact that she's here, with him.

"Why do people think I got rejected by you?" I throw in a playful smile, letting everyone listening in around us know I don't care and that I definitely wasn't rejected by *anyone*.

Jamie looks a bit confused, but I'm hoping he reads my mind through the best-friend telepathy channel and plays along. He's good at burying secrets, so what's one more to add to the pile?

"That anonymous texter, Aces, they...said you were," Belle answers.

Aces? The person who sent those messages about Devon and Scotty?

I stare at Belle again. Blonde hair held back by a blue headband that coordinates with our uniform, clear bright skin, pink lips. I hate how perfect she is, and how she's apparently the One.

"Oh...well it's a lie – isn't it, Jamie?"

"Yeah," Jamie confirms, his eyes twinkling with mischief.

"I'm sure it's just some lowlives spreading stories," Belle adds with a smile. I mentally roll my eyes at her. I don't need her input.

I wonder who this anonymous person – or people – is, sending messages to everyone. If they're smart, they won't say anything else about me.

"Hi, Chi," a girl says, holding out a tall Starbucks cup. "Here's your cinnamon latte." It's the sophomore from yesterday again.

"Thank you, Miranda," I say, bringing the drink up to my lips. She opens her mouth then closes it like a fish. I almost feel bad for not letting her know that all of this – the kissing-up, getting me coffee before school – is worthless. If you want to be known, you have to claw your own way up, not get people cold lattes every morning.

But who am I to turn down a cup of coffee? Especially after the stressful morning I've had.

The sophomore leaves just as the first warning bell sounds. Jamie leans in and kisses Belle. I look away; even if it makes me look like I *do* like him, I don't care.

"I'll see you later?" Jamie says to Belle.

"See you," she says softly, before leaving his side.

I force a smile, nudging him. "Someone's in like."

"I'm so much in like!" he shouts. I shush him, and he zips his mouth but grins.

"Let's go to class, *boy in like.*"

I've always been great at playing the role of best friend.

I pull on my clothes, I give him a smile, I leave his bedroom, his house and I come to school the next day and pretend with him. That was always my role. The best friend who pretends.

But this year I will get everything I want, and Belle will soon be a thing of the past. I just need a chance to show Jamie how wrong she is for him.

I take my phone out and scroll down my list of contacts, landing on Sam. I tap out a message, something about his new haircut suiting him.

Within seconds I get a response.

With a grin, I walk through the hallway with my head held high.

Like I said, I always get my way.

"Sweet and sour liquorice or sugar mushrooms?" Jamie asks, holding up the two packets.

It's after school and Jamie and I are in the candy store a few minutes' drive from Niveus grounds, where we always go on Tuesdays, before making a stop at the 24-hour Waffle Palace across the street. It's like yesterday at the benches never happened.

"Sugar mushrooms look weird…"

"And liquorice?"

"Liquorice is begging God for diabetes," I say without thinking.

He puts the liquorice down and silently moves towards another section of candies.

"Didn't mean it like that," I say.

"Yeah, I know." He pauses to survey what seem to be tiny candy pizzas.

I bite my lip, feeling bad. It's been a few months since his diagnosis, and I always forget to stop myself from saying insensitive things. He was really depressed when his doctor told him, thinking it meant no candy ever again – which was of course the thing that bothered him most. When he realized it didn't mean he had to stop it altogether, he went out and got this tacky tattoo of candy wrapped in red foil on his ankle.

Tuesdays have become the day when he allows himself to indulge a little.

"Don't feel bad or anything, I'm fine," he says, the smile returning to his face. "If you want to feel bad, feel bad that they've run out of candy canes."

"*What a shame*," I say, which he playfully swipes my head for.

I can't stand candy canes.

"I think I'm gonna get some liquorice and one of those tiny pizzas." He shows me his options like they are as important as college choices – which, knowing Jamie and his love of candy, it wouldn't be a surprise if they were.

"You do you," I say, just wanting to get out of here. The days of me craving candy all the time ended in sophomore year, but this tradition makes Jamie so happy, and I like it when he's happy.

I glance around the shop. It's mostly filled with parents and their kids and elderly people. I look up at the walls, bursting with jars of candies. Liquorice of all colours, glistening like jewels from the sugar that coats them, and others that appear dull in comparison. There are cola bottles, big and small, real and fake; egg-shaped candies, lollipops with bright wrappers.

"Let's pay," I say.

We walk up to the counter and Jamie places the packets on the surface in front of the shopkeeper who, rather than concerning himself with Jamie's candy and the twenty-dollar bill, stares at me, then my uniform and then my face again.

His lips curl as he shifts to grab something – his phone, placing it on the counter next to Jamie's unpurchased candy.

"What did you take?" he asks, and at first, I think I've misheard him.

"Sorry?"

"What did *you* take?" he repeats, pointing his index finger at me.

I glance behind me. Nobody's there.

He *is* talking to me.

"I didn't take anything—"

"I saw you!" he yells, which startles me. "What did you take?"

"I took nothing," I say, raising my voice too.

There's a pause, and then he's moving from behind the counter. My legs shake a little, ready for flight.

"Show me your pockets!" he shouts.

How dare he treat me like I'm a thief!

"I did not steal your fucking candy. If I wanted some, I would just *buy* it."

Jamie pulls at my arm and I turn to stare at him. His eyes look doubtful. My heart pulses faster, I can hear the sound of it in my ears.

"Just show him your pockets, Chi."

I swallow, shifting to look at the shopkeeper.

He moves forward, roughly reaching into my coat pocket.

"See—" I start, but I'm silenced by a crinkling sound and a packet of liquorice in his upturned hand.

"I'm calling the cops," he says, shaking his head as he makes his way back to the other side of the counter.

My eyes water.

"I didn't take it. I don't know how it got there," I say weakly, my voice breaking in a pathetic way I wish Jamie didn't have to hear. How did it get in there?

The guy presses nine.

"I didn't take it," I repeat.

One.

"I'll pay for it all, okay?" I hear Jamie say, pushing his twenty across the counter.

The man dials one again.

"Please, you can keep all the change," Jamie persists.

The guy pauses, looking between Jamie and me, before putting the phone down, and grabbing the twenty from the counter. The shop is silent now, the bystanders watching the scene unfold. My face feels hot as I watch the shopkeeper examine the bill.

"Thank you, sir," Jamie says.

The shopkeeper looks at me, and points again. "I'm tired of you people thinking you can get away with this shit. Don't come back here, you hear me?"

I nod, and rush out of the shop, followed by the sound of

the twinkly nursery-rhyme ringing as I open the door. Jamie pulls my shoulder as I run down the stone steps, and I turn to look at him, blinking away any tears that want to fall. What just happened?

"Let's go home," he tells me with a sigh. His face crumples as he shoves the candy into his pockets. "I'll just go to Waffle Palace another day with Belle."

I feel a blow to my chest.

"Okay," I answer.

"Okay," he replies.

I don't know why I say it again after saying it so many times in the store, but I feel compelled to. I didn't like the look on his face when the shopkeeper accused me.

"I didn't take the liquorice."

Jamie says nothing, just nods without making eye contact then walks ahead with his phone in his hand and his head down, typing into it.

Why is he acting like I did something wrong?

I take one look back at the candy store. The shopkeeper's still watching me through the glass window. Shadowy figures move around in the shop, faces I don't recognize. Someone must've put the liquorice in my pocket. I glance back up at Jamie who walks on slowly.

But who? *And why?*

7

WEDNESDAY

In this home of worn leather sofas, tabletops with cracked edges, mismatched chairs and exposed pipes, there is so much love.

Even if that love is for a version of me that isn't real.

I feel it whenever I stare at my ma in the morning, as I eat my toast and she gets ready for her first job down at the local school, where she cleans. I watch her confidently pray to God for answers, before warming her oatmeal in the microwave.

I finish my last piece of toast and I hug her from behind, hoping it tells her everything I think about her. I hope that if she finds out about the picture, this hug reminds her that I'm still me, still someone who loves her.

"I'm gonna go to school now, Ma," I tell her, moving back towards the chair I left my backpack on.

"This early?" she asks.

The microwave beeps.

I unzip my bag, pretending to put something inside, turning away from her before I lie. "Yeah, meeting Jack for some schoolwork."

She gives me a one-armed hug, kissing my forehead. "So proud of you. I'll see you later," she says, before sitting down on one of the lawn chairs that double as dining-room chairs. Ma's been telling me she's proud of me since I showed her my badge on Monday after she got back from work. I thought she was gonna cry, but she didn't. She wiped her face, and hugged me, whispering: "I'm so proud of you, Von."

"See you," I say, guilt weighing me down as I rush out, slamming the door behind me, then cringing when I think of how loud it was and how Ma will probably give me a lecture on that later.

But that's later, and this is now, where I have more important things to think about.

I walk past other homes like mine – crooked, paint peeling, doors barely hanging on their hinges – and into a part of my neighbourhood most people avoid. The part where a huge apartment block stands, with boys whose skin is as dark as mine chilling outside. Some have twists and cornrows in their hair – both styles I'm not allowed to wear at Niveus – and pants that hang off their backs effortlessly. A few are seated in the torn-up green car in front, some are on the roof of the car, and others lean against the outside walls of the block. I wonder when they sleep. They always seem to be up, waiting, whenever I come over, no matter the time of day.

I walk past all of them, legs shaky as I approach a big guy with cornrows and arms folded, leaning by the door. I can't tell if I know him from middle school or whether he's just a guy who I know works with Dre. I don't remember much from middle school, because the bullying was really bad towards the end, so Ma pulled me out. Plus, I visit Dre so much, the faces have started becoming more familiar as time passes.

"I'm here to see Andre," I tell him. Even though he's probably seen me before, the guys always act like I'm not here several times a week.

He stares me down, making me feel small, before kissing his teeth and pushing off the wall.

"Watch him," he tells some other guy, who nods and takes his place as he enters the block.

Behind the door I can hear his heavy footsteps, then the slam of another door inside. I try to stay still, not draw any attention to myself. A few moments later the guy yanks the front door open and tells me to enter. I walk into the low-lit hall and up the carpeted staircase to the second floor where Dre's apartment is.

Dre's apartment matches his personality: quiet and homey. It's spacious, decorated in browns, greens and reds. Like normal, I push open his door then walk through his living room and into his bedroom, where he's seated behind a desk. His head is tilted up and his eyes shut. For a moment I just watch him. His cropped black hair and shaved face surprise me. He had a beard last week. Without it, he looks like an actual eighteen year old. Like the boy I grew up with.

I close the door, loudly, and his eyes open up lazily. A smile creeps onto his face.

"Von," Dre mumbles, pushing himself out the chair and swaggering towards me slowly until we are centimetres away from each other.

In the silence, my palms sweat, and my heartbeat goes wild like it always does whenever I'm near him.

And then, like always, he kisses me. I wrap my arms around him and I feel him smile into the kiss, eagerly bringing his hand up to cup my face, moving me towards his bed. I ease my arms away and pull back, resting my head on his gently.

"I came to talk, Dre, not do *that*."

"But I like doing *that*," he says, kissing my forehead.

I try not to smile. "I have school and I needed to talk to you about something else."

He nods, moving back now. "The picture of you and that guy? Scotty, right?"

His words catch me off guard, making my heart stutter. Dre knows all about the rich kid from my school who broke my heart. But how did the photo travel so fast? It's barely been two days. I was going to ask him if he could try to bury it before anyone else saw it. He's good at burying skeletons. I think it's partly why no one bats an eyelid at the fact that I've been coming around three or four times a week for the past couple of months. He tells his boys to mind their business and they do.

I nod. "How did you find out?"

He doesn't say anything at first, just watches me.

"I got a message about it…"

What?

"From who?" I ask, my words tumbling out.

Dre shrugs. "I just got the picture with the text, nothing else. There was no ID."

I start panicking, thoughts spiralling. Is Dre the only person outside of school to get that message or does everyone in the neighbourhood know about it? Are they talking about me? Planning to get me like they did before—

Andre takes my hand and squeezes it, pulling me in again and away from the mental hole I was falling into.

"I think I'm the only person who got it. No one else is talking, so you're good."

I'm not convinced. News that can travel from Niveus to my neighbourhood this quickly could still reach people here. My ma could easily find out and I can't have that stress right now.

"I'll deal with it," he says.

"Deal with it how?"

"Deal with it" could mean anything. It could mean finding a way to get rid of problems – including Scotty, who for some reason I'm worried about now. Dre and his gang like sorting things out with their fists; it's how you get respect around here most of the time. You fight, someone films it, word spreads, then people back off – probably the reason I was such an easy target in middle school. I couldn't fight anyone, even if you paid me. My arms and legs are practically noodles.

I'm scared for the day Dre fights someone to prove a

point, and he's the one who gets hurt in the end.

He rolls his eyes. "Not gonna hurt your ex, don't worry," he says.

"Okay, thanks," I tell him, pulling back, but he stops me.

"Just—" He looks at me seriously. "Don't let anything else get out. I have a boss to answer to – he won't like you being here if he finds out."

I nod, wanting to reassure him even though I'm not exactly sure how I can stop something out of my control. His boss is this older guy in our area. A guy who trusts people like Dre to do things for him, no questions asked. I've only seen him a handful of times, but I've heard enough to know that he isn't a good person.

There's more silence.

My face naturally pulls into a smile. It's funny when Dre tries to be serious. It makes him look like he's got a stomach-ache or something.

I move closer, leaning in again to kiss him. I'd bet on my right hand (my instrument hand) that he's smiling now too. I miss the past summer when I was over at his place every other day, sharing moments like this. Moments when the world would fall away, all our problems would dissolve, and it would just be the two of us.

"Love you," he says quietly, pulling back.

I pause, looking up at him for a few moments, locking this memory away for later. For when I'm up at night and my brain is filled with worries and doubts and I need the reminder that someone loves me.

"Love you too," I tell him, feeling warm inside.

I'm hoping Aces doesn't take that away from me somehow.

Because I get to school early, there aren't many people around, so it isn't as bad as what felt like hundreds of faces judging and whispering in the crowded hallway yesterday.

Maybe I should start coming to school earlier all the time, especially as it seems I'm not walking with Jack at the moment.

I take some blank music sheets from my locker and head up to my first period music class, where Mr Taylor is, as usual, by his piano – which is basically his desk. Sometimes I come here instead of registration. Registration is all done electronically anyway, so Mr Taylor says it's fine and marks me in.

He nods at me with a friendly smile and I head off to my corner, switching the keyboard on, plugging my headphones in, then closing my eyes and picturing blue.

Bzzz.

My heart sinks as I reach into my pocket.

"Don't let anything else get out." Dre's words ring in my ears.

Just in. Looks like Chi's not so sweet. Sources say she got caught trying to steal candy. Careful, Chi, don't want a record Yale will see... – Aces

My heart settles a little.

Chiamaka Adebayo a thief? Why would she need to steal anything? Like almost everyone else at this school, she probably has enough money in her piggy bank to buy two sports cars and still have some left over to last several lifetimes.

Plus, she seems way too uptight to steal anything. But then again, I don't know her.

And I don't care…

I glance at the message again, then chuck my phone back in my pocket.

I check that my headphones are still in, then I breathe.

Drown.

And play.

8

CHIAMAKA

WEDNESDAY

"It's all over school," I whisper to Jamie during biology. Thank God there are only a few periods left after enduring people eyeballing and muttering about me all morning.

"It sucks," he replies, like I just told him the cafeteria is out of fries.

"But no one believes it's true. Doesn't take a genius to know you aren't that kind of person," Belle says.

I narrow my eyes at her. *What is your angle here, Belle?* She's probably trying to look good in front of Jamie, but I see through her.

Like yesterday, Jamie says nothing, and it makes me feel funny inside. Like I should feel guilty for an offence I didn't commit.

"I'm sure it will blow over," Belle reassures me.

Again, I ignore her.

"Yesterday evening, one of the science technicians noticed that the science resources storeroom was left open, and unfortunately some materials we need for today's experiment were taken," Ms Brown says.

That's... impossible. I *always* lock the resources storeroom.

"Fortunately, Niveus has plenty of back-up materials available. But the theft of these items and the carelessness demonstrated by our Science Rep will be dealt with, and there will be major repercussions." She pauses. "We want you all to know that we take this sort of thing very seriously," she finishes, briefly shooting me a severe look.

I feel my face burn as others glance at me too.

"Aren't you the Science Rep?" Jamie whispers, not so subtly.

I ignore him.

There's no way I didn't lock the storeroom. Someone else must have gotten the key and done this. I've been Science Rep for years, and not once have I left the room unlocked. I start to raise my hand, ready to clear my name, but I get interrupted by the slimy voice of Satan's child, Jeremy Hearst, in the corner.

"Well, we don't want Chiamaka near those spare materials either – you know, since they're so scarce. Wouldn't want those to go missing too," he says, triggering light, awkward laughter. Jeremy's an ass, that much is public knowledge. We've been in the same classes since freshmen year, and he's always thought of himself as the funniest guy in school. The funniest thing about him is his face.

It's going to take a lot more than fake news to shove me off the top. You'd think after three years he'd know that.

"You can all proceed with the experiment. Chiamaka, can you come up to the front, please," Ms Brown says.

I push myself out of my seat, shrugging off the nosy gazes that follow me.

"Chiamaka," Ms Brown starts when I get to her desk, her voice low and serious. "I'm only going to ask you once. Did you take the materials?"

I feel offended she'd even ask something like that.

"No, and I didn't leave the storeroom unlocked either."

Ms Brown nods, but, like Jamie, she looks at me as if I'm some crook.

"You of all people know how serious this is. I've had a word with some of the other teachers and they think it's best that you give the key back," Ms Brown says.

"But I didn't—"

"I've heard you. But unfortunately we just can't let a careless mistake like this fly. Some of those materials, if found in the wrong hands or in the wrong place, would be a real health and safety issue for the school. I'll still give you your reference for Yale, but I think it's best we find someone else to take over managing the resources storeroom. I'm sorry."

I bet she is.

I nod, not wanting to draw any more attention to myself by arguing back.

"I understand," I say.

"Good. Drop the key off before the end of the day. I'll either be in here or the science library."

Why not now, if I'm the criminal they claim I am?

She tells me to go back to my group and so I turn, trying

to make my face as expressionless as possible despite wanting to scream.

"Are you okay? Your face is red…" Belle says when I sit back down.

I look at her pretty heart-shaped face and kind eyes and then I look away, grabbing the instructions and focusing on them.

Jamie starts telling a bad joke and Belle laughs, and I really want to hit something.

She isn't even meant to be *here*. Jamie is my lab partner, but of course, given my luck so far these past few days, Belle was conveniently transferred to this class. Her old teacher has signed off for the semester, so the students in his class got divided up.

"Oxygen and potassium went on a date…"

Oh god, make it stop.

"Ask me how it went?"

"How?" Belle asks.

He told this same joke at my sixteenth. No one laughed.

"It went…OK." And then he's laughing and she's smiling, giving me a side glance.

I look down at my notebook, tracing over the words written on the experiment instructions sheet. I don't want to share mocking looks. I don't want to be friends. I already have a best friend.

I'm just waiting for them to break up, like I predict they will. I'm not sure how but it will happen, I'm certain. Belle is beautiful, but she's not me. She doesn't know Jamie like I do. He needs me just as much as I need him.

Their flirting continues for most of the class and it's like being slowly tortured to death. I'm relieved when the clock shows that it's almost time for the bell, as I've reached the end of my tether at this point.

"Jamie, are we taking your car or walking to my place later?" I ask, despite not really needing to. I just want it – them – to stop. "For our Marvel binge." Every second Wednesday of the month we go over to each other's houses, eat junk food, and watch superhero films.

Belle frowns. "I thought we were hanging out today."

I squint at her.

Jamie looks between the two of us, a torn expression on his face.

"Chi and I have this tradition... Sorry, babe."

Babe. That's new.

The bell rings. "Calculus with Mr Duncan or Mr Calhoun?" he asks her.

"Duncan," she says.

I smile.

"Calhoun for me and Chi."

What a pity.

They kiss and I look away again.

"See you at lunch?" Belle asks, looking at Jamie, then me.

"Sure."

I say nothing, studying my nails for imperfections. I find none.

"Look at you, all loved up," I say after Belle goes. We make our way down the marble hallway.

"Belle is great, isn't she?" I can literally see the hearts in Jamie's eyes as he says this. The way he's acting, you'd think they'd been dating longer than a few weeks.

"Great is an adjective, I guess."

Jamie wraps his arm around my shoulders, and I side-eye him.

What game are you playing, Jamie?

He kisses my forehead. I whack him.

He wipes his mouth. "Why's there water in your hair?"

I snort. "It's coconut oil."

"Smells good," he tells me, smirking.

I hold his gaze for a moment. A plan starts forming in my head. "Let's invite Belle today," I tell him.

His eyes go wide, eyebrows rising.

"Really?" He sounds so excited.

"Yeah, I would love for her to join."

"You're the best, Chi," he says, as we enter Mr Calhoun's classroom.

I know, I think to myself, even though I'm not sure how much I believe it. If I was the best, he would have chosen me first.

I learned a long time ago that the key is to make others think you know you're the best. But what happens when the cracks start to show? When those around you don't always believe what you feed them? And how can they, when you don't even believe it, not fully… You pretend that you don't cry sometimes when you see your reflection, that you don't stare at other girls and wonder what it would be like to be anyone else but yourself. The real Chiamaka. The person I'm always trying to run away from.

This year I was finally meant to have the perfect boyfriend. I was supposed to leave a lasting impression, make sure everyone at Niveus never forgets me, then move on to greater things.

But it's not too late. I won't let these small defeats get to me.

There is a chorus of buzzes and text sounds, and I scramble for my phone, fingers trembling as I clutch it. A text notification from *anonymous* appears on the screen.

It's a video.

Just in. Porn is easy to come by these days.
You either search for it online, or it falls right
in your lap when you least expect it to – Aces.

I don't click on the video. The thumbnail is enough to know this isn't about me. But I can hear the sounds of it playing from Jamie's phone.

"Can you turn that off?" I tell him, before pocketing my phone and moving to take my usual seat at the front of calc. class.

I listen to the sounds of people laughing, and feel agitated. Aces is clearly not holding back.

I'm a careful person, but I'm not perfect. There are things

I've done, things that could ruin me. *Blonde hair. So much blood.* And things I can't remember. A disjointed memory of the night I first kissed Jamie sears through my mind...

What else do they have on me?

#

9

WEDNESDAY

Since lunch, I've been getting stares.

It doesn't take a genius to figure out that the latest Aces blast was about me, but the question is, *what* about me? And why do I receive blasts about others only, and not myself?

It's probably this "Aces" person's twisted way of adding to the sick feeling in my stomach as much as they can.

"Hey, Richards!" some guy shouts as I walk down the hallway. I stop to look at him. He smirks before wrapping his arms around himself, kissing the air and making smooching noises.

It's not even been a full week and already senior year is sucking on a level I never imagined it could.

Exiting the double doors to the school brings me a sense of peace. Because at least now, the school day is over and I can go home.

A hand grabs my arm and jerks me into an alley by the main school building. I'm thrown against the brick wall and I hiss, my back throbbing in several places as I collide with the rough surface.

"Do you want to get killed?!" Jack shouts.

"No—"

"Then why the fuck is your fucking sex tape floating around the fucking school?"

My what?

Oh my god.

I might throw up. I can't breathe...my legs are shaking... my head is spinning.

"I need to find Scotty," I manage. *I need to kill Scotty.* A part of me wants to ask to see the video, see how bad it is, but I don't know if I can handle that.

Jack says nothing. His face is scrunched up, and he's breathing hard. I don't know what it is about his expression, but it makes me feel like I should be ashamed of myself.

Like I should feel dirty.

Before he knew I was gay, Jack didn't look at me like that. He was the first person I told, back when we were still in middle school. Before I came out, life was us having each other's back, sleepovers and video games while Ma was away at work, when we had no one but each other. Now it's this: Jack hating me for something I can't change. The both of us wishing things could go back to the way they were before I said those words.

We stare at each other. I have to stop myself from apologizing – because what would I even be sorry for? Existing too loud?

I break eye contact, pushing off the wall, my legs unsteady as I run back into the school, a place I'm starting to hate more than ever. Girls giggle when they see me and I get it now.

I get the mocking from earlier. It's all making sense.

I'm so embarrassed.

My sight blurs and I try to catch my breath, but I keep choking on air. I sniff, rushing forward, bursting into Crombie, high on adrenaline.

I'm gonna kill Scotty.

I jump onto the stage and tear through the curtain to where the girl from Tuesday is sitting next to Scotty's slumped figure, rubbing his back. His blue letterman jacket is draped over the back of his chair.

I try calming my breathing before I speak.

"Scotty," I say. No response.

The girl looks at me with an annoyed expression plastered onto her semi-plastic face. Her nose, which I now notice is a little slanted – I assume from a botched surgery, scrunches up at me.

"Scotty," she whispers, and he looks up and then looks away.

"My career is probably over," Scotty says.

My chest is still heaving.

"All the successful people these days have sex tapes. This is a step in your favour," says the girl. I want to hit her.

Scotty nods. "True."

I want to hit him.

"Scotty," I say again.

"Can't you see this is hard for him?" the girl tells me.

I want to laugh. "Hard for him? He's the one who made the video, and he was the *only* one who had that video."

"You're barely in the video, and Scotty said he deleted it. Besides, do you know how easy it is to hack into anyone's cloud?" she huffs.

"What?" I say, because I'm so confused. What the fuck is she going on about? I don't care if I'm barely in it. The fact that I am, and everyone saw it—

I scrunch that thought up like it's written on a mental sheet of paper. If this gets back home, if Ma sees this, she's going to be so disappointed in me; she'll see me differently. And Dre, he said...

"Well, I mean... I guess everyone *knows* it was you because we heard your voice and Scotty says your name, you guys are pretty vocal—"

"I know it's you doing this, Scotty," I say, face burning. "I know it's you sending the messages, leaking stuff."

Scotty stares at me, blond hair messy and covering his eyes as a smile slowly appears on his thin pink lips. The girl next to him watches us hungrily.

"You think *I'm* Aces?" he asks, feigning offence.

He's the only person I can think of with the motive to hurt me and maybe even Chiamaka. We both dumped him.

"It makes sense. You and I aren't friends any more and you're the only one who could have sent out that video..."

His smile falters a little. I must be imagining it, because surely someone as self-centred as Scotty couldn't care less about what I think of him.

"That's right, we aren't friends, or anything close to that – so why would I waste my time? Why bother with someone

90

no one here cares about? Chiamaka, maybe. People actually *want* to read about her, but why would I bother with *you*. What would I get out of that?" he asks.

There's a tiny pang as his words hit me.

Scotty looks down at his lap, pulling his phone out of his pocket and scrolling like I'm not here any more.

I used to be able to tell when Scotty was lying. When we were dating, I'd always get this twisting feeling in my gut, something telling me he wasn't being a hundred per cent honest. When he'd admit to cheating on me, what would hurt me most was the fact that I'd known deep down he wasn't being truthful. He'd confess, I'd cry, we'd kiss and make up. Until the day I broke the cycle and finally stopped letting myself be treated like that. Now, though, I can't tell. There's no twisting in my gut, nothing to tell me whether he means it. Whether he had anything to do with this.

"Could you go now? I told you I don't have any pictures or videos, so you have your answer. I'm not Aces. Laura and I are busy. I haven't got time to be speaking to nobodies."

Scotty's words hit again. He knows just how to use them. Repeating back to me the fears I fed him, while lying on his bed, in his arms, vulnerable but safe.

He uses his words instead of his fists – something I'm not as familiar with. Where I come from, words are nothing and actions are everything.

I know hurting me is something Scotty wants to do. Because, even though we haven't spoken properly in a while, I knew it hurt him that I stopped letting him get away with crap, like cheating on me and then lying about it. I know that because he also whispered dark monologues to me, about his fears and weaknesses. About how his family sees him as this huge fuck-up who'll never amount to anything. About how lost he constantly feels – something we had in common, despite the different worlds we come from.

The difference between him and me, however, is that I would *never* use his words to hurt him.

I watch him with a quiet disbelief. I know Scotty is a terrible person, so why am I so shocked? Why am I always shocked by people and their shitty behaviour? I blink back the tears that want to escape.

I feel stuck. I wanted Scotty to be Aces. His motive is so clear. He's the only connection I have to Chiamaka, and we're the only people Aces has talked about so far. If it was him, it would be so much easier to stop anything else coming out.

I can't imagine why anyone else would do this. I barely speak to people at school. But maybe there is someone else out there with a reason to want to hurt me…

A good reason.

I get this feeling sometimes that I'm forgetting stuff. Important stuff. It's like there's something in my memory that I can't quite focus on – my brain just goes fuzzy. Maybe whoever I hurt is lost in my messy sea of thoughts and memories.

"Scotty," I start, wanting so bad to tell him how glad I am now that I don't have to see his face all the time, or trust someone who is a compulsive liar, or feel that anxiety I used to feel that he was going to tell me something like, "*I'm sorry I did it, it won't happen again, I love you, Von.*"

Direct quote, FYI.

But I don't. Because I'm not that person. He is.

I squeeze my eyes shut now, pushing away the fears that won't stop intruding. Of what people might think of me – what Ma might think of me – hating myself for being with him for that long. I was so stupid, not realizing Scotty was a dick way sooner. I think I'll spend the rest of my life judging myself for ever thinking Scotty was even remotely attractive.

"Fuck you," I say instead, before turning around, ignoring his loud response.

"You already did!"

I leave Crombie, leave the building, leave the gates and go back to safety, where there is no Aces, no Scotty, no Jack, no annoying girls with crooked noses.

No memories that hurt to think about.

"How was school?" Ma asks as I take the potatoes and chicken out of the oven. I can barely hear her over the noise from my little brothers.

Elijah is singing some song he learned at school and James is yelling at Eli to stop.

Ma's question replays in my mind.

I think about her finding out, remembering the time this girl in my neighbourhood came out. I remember Ma telling me how her family kicked her out. Ma had looked disgusted, muttering, "I just don't understand." And I remember thinking that she would never understand me, either. I think about it and how this week has been so shit and it's only Wednesday and how I hate school and never want to go back.

But then I look at my ma, how tired she looks, how she'll be going out later for her night job, just so that we can live in this dump and I can go to a fancy school.

"Everything's good, Ma. Perfect," I say as I turn back, dishing the potatoes and chicken onto mismatched plates.

Everything's good.

Perfect.

10

CHIAMAKA

WEDNESDAY

Our superhero film tradition started by accident. We were fourteen, bored and uncultured. Jamie's mom had given him a superhero-themed gift basket one Christmas and we binge-watched everything. Soon enough it became our thing.

It's almost sacred now, so Belle's presence in my home cinema is basically blasphemy.

I sit here with the movie ready, resting on my lap, not wanting to disrupt the flow of Jamie telling his cow story from a few summers ago. I smile and nod even though I think the story is as pointless as it was when he told me the first time.

"...And so I'm trying to convince the maid that the udders are the cow's genitals—"

I don't know how Belle can genuinely be interested in this story. I watch her watch him, her annoying face keeping me occupied. She's curled up in the plush black-and-white cinema seat, neck elongated, rosy cheeks, long lashes, really pink lips – I get why so many guys like her. She's pretty – if you like girls like her, I mean. There's a weird rush in my stomach, like it's about to growl but doesn't.

I look away and it disappears, my body probably reminding me how much I can't stand their relationship.

"...I get in trouble because apparently we can eat cows but not chase them—"

I clear my throat, interrupting the strange direction his story is heading.

"Movie time." I get up and walk over to the projector at the back of the room and then place the movie in the player. I can hear Belle's light, irritating laughter behind me as the disc sinks into the machine. I don't want to turn back and see them acting all lovey-dovey, so I turn but shift my focus to the wall at the front, which is acting as a screen. The disc buffers then stops as the movie credits flash up.

"Why did Microsoft PowerPoint cross the road...? To get to the other slide—"

My first instinct is to grab the heaviest object I can find and lob it at Jamie, but instead I interrupt with a dry laugh. My eyes briefly catch Belle's and my stomach turns again, before I smile at Jamie.

"Good to see you're still recycling your dad's favourite jokes," I say. I press pause on the film, wanting their full attention before starting it, and move back into my place next to Jamie.

"You have a nice home cinema," Belle says. I can't read her face like I can read Ruby's and Ava's. *Is she mocking me or something?*

"Thanks," I reply without looking at her, my mind more focused on trying to see if the room is secretly ugly. This room is my safe space away from the loudness of the world. I sit here for hours sometimes, watching movies alone in the dark, clearing my head. Mom and Dad had this built for me years ago and I decorated it myself. The ceiling is black and filled with dozens of lights. It kind of looks like stars in the universe, which is what I was going for. There's a soft grey carpet and there are three rows of armchair-sized cinema seats.

I like this room and if Belle doesn't she can leave, the door is that way—

"You know, Chi used to have a massive Winnie-the-Pooh teddy, but threw it out because it clashed with the persona she was going for in sophomore year," Jamie says.

"Oh yeah? What persona was that?" Belle asks.

I smile tightly at the two of them. *Thank you, Jamie.*

"There was no persona, I just outgrew Winnie—"

"She told me herself, she needed to seem more like Blair Waldorf and less like Meg Griffin," he continues.

"I had a Winnie phase too... Outgrew it when I was seven though," Belle says.

Jamie laughs, and I'm tempted to kick them both out.

"I think we all outgrew it before high school, Chi's just special—"

"Movie's starting, time to shut up now," I say, pressing play abruptly. The hum of the characters' voices quickly fills the space between me and the lovebirds. I try to concentrate on the start of the film, but in the corner of my vision, I see their hands join, and her head drop to his shoulder, throwing me off.

"Should I get some blankets?" I ask.

Jamie nods, staring at the screen intently.

"Only two, Belle and I can share one."

My heart plummets to the bottom of my stomach as I stand to grab the two blankets from the back closet. All plans for a future with Jamie are disintegrating before me. This evening was meant to remind Jamie of how suited we are for each other, not make him fall further for Belle. Why can't he see that? I want to throw the blanket in his face.

"Here," I say, handing Jamie the blanket. He mutters a *Thanks*, already engrossed in the movie, so Belle reaches up for it. Our fingers brush together and I release the blanket quickly.

My heartbeat switches from faint to strong and present.

"Same time next month, and for ever?" Jamie asks at the door, like he always does. A younger, smilier Jamie had asked me that after our first day discovering Marvel and its wonders.

"Your place?" I ask. He bobs his head, his curls echoing the movement.

"Need a ride home?" my mom asks from behind us. I almost swear. I hate it when she creeps up on me like that.

He shakes his head. "I brought my car, but thanks, Mrs Adebayo."

My mom always smirks when he says our family name. I'm not even facing her, but I can feel her expression. It's because he says it wrong, like everyone always does, saying: "Ayda-bay-o" when really it's "Adeh-by-oh". But, oh well.

Jamie pulls me in for a hug, his arms wrapping around me, his nose brushing my forehead lightly. Usually this would excite me, but there is something so dull about it right now.

"See you," I say to him.

"See you, Chi, Mrs Adebayo." He says the last part with a nod.

"See you, Chiamaka and Chiamaka's mom," Belle echoes, as her hand joins Jamie's. They both walk off; I look away.

The door closes and I turn to my mom, surprised to see her braided hair done up in a bun and her face made up.

"Going somewhere fancy?" I ask.

She nods with a wink. "Date night with your dad before he leaves for Italy."

Dad goes to Italy once a month to visit Grandma – who loves to remind me of the weight I've gained each time I see her. He used to go a lot less, taking Mom and me with him whenever he did. My parents used to live there before they came here. It's where they met, in med school somewhere in Rome. I used to think it was the greatest love story of all time until Mom told me why we had to stop going. Dad's family aren't huge fans of Mom…or her dark skin. And by extension, me and my dark skin.

And that's fine. I hated going anyway.

"Was that Jamie's new girlfriend?" she asks.

My chest squeezes.

"Mm-hmm," I respond, focusing on the wall.

"She's pretty."

"Yeah, I guess so," I say.

The words *She's pretty* echo through the house and my mind. "I'm going to go upstairs now, Mom. Have a nice night."

Mom's smooth hand touches my arm before I leave, reminding me of so many years of being tucked in, and the tight, constricting hugs only Mom can give. I look back at her, her dark skin bright and her brows furrowed.

"Are you okay, Chiamaka?"

Of course I am, I want to say, but instead I say nothing.

"You seem a little down," she continues.

I shrug. "I'm fine."

She doesn't look all that convinced, and I'm not sure if I am either, but her shoulders relax, and she grabs her bag from where it's hanging on the coat-rack by the stairs.

"If you want pizza, I left you some cash," she says, as she kisses both my cheeks, then moves towards the door, a rush of her strong tangy perfume filling my nostrils. "Love you, Chi. See you later."

The door slams shut behind her, ringing in my ears moments after. I see her figure through the blurry rose-coloured glass panes and hear her heels click across the concrete path, until both disappear into the evening.

I sigh, then drag myself up the stairs and back into the cinema. I know it doesn't seem too bad – being falsely accused of stealing, twice, and having everyone think I got rejected by Jamie – especially since the revelations about Devon feel so much more personal. But being talked about is one thing and being mocked is another. I hate being mocked, it reminds me of middle school. Being the girl everyone liked to look down on, poke at, never the girl people wanted to be friends with.

Not that people want to be *friends* with me now – or before Aces – but they knew that they could never look down at me.

I start picking up some of the mess we made, kicking the blankets to the side to see if any trash is left underneath. I notice a crumpled-up piece of paper with something written in thick black sharpie. I bend down and pick it up, recognizing the writing as Jamie's – *1717*. He's always writing down his PINs and passwords on random pieces of paper.

I like to joke that one day he'll have to write down my name for when he finally forgets me. I remember him once saying, "*How could anyone at Niveus forget the great Chiamaka Adebayo?*" in his usual Jamie, over-the-top way.

I smile at the memory. Sometimes these moments creep into my mind and remind me that our friendship is real. And I need the reminder sometimes. Especially when he does things to get under my skin. Like getting a girlfriend.

I sit on one of the chairs, pulling out my phone and opening up the Notes app.

I title the new page: People who hate me.

Whoever is finding this information about me and sending these texts is doing it out of spite. It's someone who really hates me, Devon and Scotty. And I'm going to find out who, and *why*.

I stare at the blank screen, the cursor blinking, and before I can second guess it, I tap out Jeremy's, Ava's and Ruby's names in bold as my first suspects. Jeremy because I know for sure he'd love to take me down if he could; Ava because of how easily she spread the things about Jamie and me; and Ruby...well it's obvious, she's Ruby. I don't know if I actually believe that Ava or Jeremy are even capable of pulling off something like this, but I do know that whoever's doing this, they're not going to be doing it much longer. I'll find them and make them wish they'd never started this mess in the first place.

11

THURSDAY

It was raining heavily when I woke up this morning at six. I could hear the raindrops hitting the window, then spilling through the crack in the bottom. I would've closed it, but the window's permanently stuck that way.

Some mornings I sit in this half dreamlike state, letting the cold wrap around my body and hug me like the memory of my father sometimes does, despite the fact that he never hugged me when he was around. I haven't asked to visit him in years – Ma used to cry when I brought it up. So, I stopped asking.

My younger brother, Elijah, had cuddled up to me during the night, shivering more than I was, so I wrapped my school blazer around his skinny frame. Which is why my blazer currently smells of bananas, Elijah's ever-present scent.

As I rush past the blocks between my place and school, the rain hits my hood, dripping down my face and blurring my vision. I wipe it away but it just keeps falling, over and over again. Both the cold and the thought of who around here has seen the video make my body shudder. I keep my head down until I reach Jack's place. I knock on the door, hoping that he's gonna answer today.

Instead, Jack's uncle answers. He's a tall, tired-looking guy, and he always wears the same stained tank shirt and sweats. In the background I can hear Jack arguing with his brothers.

"Jack, your friend's here," his uncle yells. He never bothers with small talk – no hi, nothing. I think my longest conversation with him was the first time we met, after Jack's ma died. He asked, "Who are you?" I told him my name, and that was that.

Jack materializes, uniform wrinkled and tie slightly undone. I've been replaying what he said to me in the alley yesterday, picking apart his words. I don't know what brought me back here this morning. I guess I'm trying to hold onto my longest friendship, maybe, despite the obvious cracks in it. Or the sense of safety I get from the only face that means something to me at Niveus? I don't know.

Jack doesn't say anything, just walks next to me in an awkward silence. I know these silences well with Jack; but I keep holding on, knowing that on the other side of the silence there is still a friend, *my* friend. That's how it's always been. I know he still cares about me.

Niveus isn't so far from our neighbourhood. Our school lies between two worlds: the side of town where the rich people live, and then our side, where people can't afford food or healthcare. Usually I just keep my head down, regardless of where I am, but since the picture and the video got out, I feel even more uneasy in our neighbourhood. As we walk, I side-eye street corners, imagining boys in dark hoods with sharp shiny objects and fists ready to beat the crap out of me. The picture took less than forty-eight hours to reach Dre, so I can only imagine how many of them have seen the video, deduced it was me, and are waiting by the 7-Eleven. Ready to remind me that there is no space for me in this neighbourhood. Even though Dre said he'd deal with it, if it could get to him, it could get to anyone.

Having Jack here makes me feel a little safer, though.

I shudder and wipe my face again. I like the sound of rain, but actually being in it is the worst, so I'm happy – for the first time this week – to see the white bricks and giant black gates of Niveus.

Jack and I walk up the stairs and straight through the doors into the hallway, where the conversation was obviously very much alive before we entered. I suddenly feel hyper-aware of my oversized uniform, dripping water onto the marble floor.

"Gonna head to class," Jack says quietly, before leaving me by the entrance, alone. I watch him disappear down the hallway, feeling less safe now that he's gone.

The pulling in my stomach begins, like it has been doing all week, as I trek down the hallway. Aces has made me as noticeable as a guy with a face tattoo, and the annoying squelching of my sneakers against the marble doesn't help my case.

I rush up the stairs to the music rooms.

"Hey, Devon," Mr Taylor says with a smile as I enter.

This gets the attention of the other students and I get more disapproving stares.

"Hey, Mr Taylor," I say.

The toast I ate for breakfast wants to lurch out, as my stomach squeezes and squeezes.

I walk over to my station, feeling tired as I sit down heavily, then switch on my keyboard.

"Yo, Richards, what's up?" a voice says. I startle.

It's Daniel Johnson; quarterback, brown hair, brown eyes, typically "handsome" face. Daniel Johnson, who has never in his life spoken to me.

"Yo, Johnson. The sky," I respond.

He pauses, looking up, then realizes – sooner than I thought he would – and laughs.

"You're funny."

There's another pause and then he's sitting himself down next to me.

"So listen, it's the twenty-first century. No one hates gays no more."

I didn't get the memo.

"So, like, I'm cool with it – as long as you don't crush on me or anything, you dig?"

"*I dig*," I say.

He pats my back, then pauses with a wink. "No homo."

I want him to gather his things and bother someone else. But he seems determined to piss me off.

"So what's Scotty like? The guy acts like he's a *god*. But, like, trust me, I know what godly is. Girls tell me daily, you know?"

Daniel seems all philosophical about his dick game, shrugging in what I'm sure he thinks is a humble way.

"But none of his conquests tell me things. I tried asking Chiamaka – because even though he's gay, who wouldn't want to hit that?"

I wouldn't.

"So, what's Scotty like?"

For someone so big on *No homo*, he's really making me wonder…

I sit back, looking up like I'm thinking about it.

"Scotty *is* a god, Daniel," I say, realizing only after that he probably doesn't get any form of sarcasm.

He bobs his head slowly, processing my words carefully.

"Wow, maybe I shouldn't have doubted him," he says.

"Maybe."

Daniel turns and pats me on the back again.

"You're actually an okay dude, Devon."

I think that's meant to be a compliment but I'm not sure how complimented one can feel by Daniel. At last it seems my prayers are answered and Daniel moves away.

My phone buzzes. A text from *unknown*. Bold, bright text beaming at me.

Just in. Our favourite alleyway lurker,
Jack McConnel, has a drug problem. Let's just
hope his straight-A record doesn't suffer because
of it and his brand-new friends…

– Aces

The message creates this emptiness inside. Like all my organs have been removed and I am just this shell. Jack would *never* touch that stuff. His ma died because of drugs, his dad got incarcerated because of drugs, and he has brothers to look after.

He'd never do something that idiotic or risk his scholarship like that.

I go to my messages and hesitate.

Jack's name in all of this makes even less sense than Chiamaka's. At least with Chiamaka I could link us both back to Scotty, but now none of this makes sense.

I text: Are you ok? I know the rumours aren't true.

Within seconds, his reply vibrates in my palm.

Do you?

The hollowness gets deeper, like there's an invisible man digging a hole in my stomach.

I study his words, then reply:

The Jack I know wouldn't do something like that.

The Jack I know swore over his ma's grave that he'd never go near any of that shit. As they lowered her into the hole, tossed dirt on her wooden casket, he promised her dead body he'd stay away.

Maybe you don't know me that well.

I've known Jack for as long as I've known myself. The invisible man in my stomach stops digging and stabs my heart instead.

I look up again, turning to survey the class. A girl looks at me then covers her mouth and swivels back around in her chair, her shoulders vibrating as she lets out a quiet laugh. I feel eyes on me and I catch Mr Taylor staring. He gives me a smile.

My fingers are still wrapped around my phone, a part of me waiting for Jack to say he's joking, that Aces is wrong about him. The screen dulls, darkens, then locks. The other part of me knows the text is never coming and that despite how much I want to push the thought away, maybe I don't know Jack like I thought I did.

I sit and stare at my keyboard. The invisible man whispers in my mind, *Even your best friend doesn't care about you. He doesn't want you around; no one does.*

I'm alone, with no other friends at Niveus to confide in. Every day, I feel Jack pull away from me. It makes me feel like something is wrong with me. If Pa was here, he'd shut my thoughts up. Tell me things will work out with Jack. Or that I'll get other friends – eventually.

I dream about Pa coming home someday. We go out for pizza and he just tells me a bunch of life lessons. We catch up on missed time. I imagine talking to him about Aces, this anonymous bully who hates me for no reason, and he'll know the answers because that's what dads are for. They are meant to know all the stuff you don't. I dream about Ma not being so busy, having time to just listen, to talk, so I can tell her all the shit I've been hiding from her for years.

In my dreams she listens, and still loves me afterwards.

But I know dreams are dangerous, they give me too much false hope. I know, I fucking know that even if my pa wasn't in prison, he wouldn't be here for me anyway.

I close my eyes, squeezing them shut as my heart spasms. Dreams are toxic.

I know I'd still be alone.

I think about texting Dre, asking him if I can come over tonight or something, but I'm scared about what other things he's been told about me. What else could get out.

I wipe my eyes quickly and pocket my phone. I need to focus on something else.

I shakily play a note on the keyboard, starting my warm-up, letting the noise block more thoughts from spilling through the cracks.

12

CHIAMAKA

THURSDAY

"Malarkey."

"Watch your language, Chi," Jamie says with a grin.

"Seriously, that is malarkey."

Jamie bites into his sandwich, shaking his head. "It's not, trust me. Billy told Maggie who told *me* that Cecelia Wright and Mr Peterson are screwing."

I roll my eyes at him. When I told him I wanted to talk about "anything" I didn't mean this. I do question though why Aces reports random stuff about *me* and those boys but not this – which is *way* more interesting in my opinion.

We are at Lola's, in an empty classroom near the cafeteria. I came here mostly because I wanted an excuse to be away from everyone else. Especially people like Ruby, who would love to see the beginnings of my downfall play out.

And I wanted to talk about something more pressing – who Jamie thinks Aces is, for example.

I take my phone out, checking it for new alerts.

Zero. I sigh.

"Checking to see if Aces has exposed another secret?" Jamie asks, wrapping up the remains of his sandwich.

"No." *Yes.*

"I hear that if the secret is about you, you don't get the message."

I narrow my eyes at him a little.

"No shit, Sherlock. I kind of figured that out already... But are people talking about it? Like who it could be?"

Jamie shrugs. "I guess so. I don't really pay attention."

Usually I know everything going on in Niveus. Usually I'm in control. I've got ears in all classes, and people always tell me things. But this week there's been radio silence. I feel like everyone knows more than I do and for some reason, they are keeping me out of the loop. First there was Headmaster Collins's resignation, then there was everyone apparently knowing Jamie and Belle were a thing, and now, Aces. Not knowing who's next, *what's* next, has been making me really anxious.

"Let's head out of Lola's. Belle wanted to sit with us at lunch today."

I try not to let the annoyance show on my face. "Sure."

We exit the room, looking around to make sure no teachers see us leaving, and then we walk back into the cafeteria. Jamie heads straight over to Belle, who's sitting at the jock table in the centre with some of the girls from the lacrosse team and some guys from the football team. I follow, wrinkling my nose as I look at everyone eating what seems to be today's special. Green pasta. I notice Scotty sitting at the end, twirling the pasta with one hand while texting with the other. I'm surprised to see him here;

he usually hangs around the drama kids.

I wonder who he's texting.

Another reason I prefer eating lunch alone with Jamie is because the jock table is always so loud, filled with what are meant to be grown men in blue letterman jackets flinging food at each other.

I catch up to Jamie, wanting to tell him that Belle clearly seems busy eating *vomit*. But he's too fast, moving towards her like a magnet, kissing her softly. I look away, pulling a chair out and sitting opposite them.

"How was Lola's?" Belle asks. I take out my small tub of carrot sticks.

"Fascinating as always," Jamie says, mouth filled with sandwich again. He's somehow managed to unwrap it in the time between kissing Belle and sitting down.

There is silence between us, and I look up, noticing Belle staring at me with expectation.

I stick a carrot in my mouth, smiling wide as I chew. "It was great, I *always* love hanging out with Jamie."

Belle rolls her eyes, and I raise an eyebrow. *Did she just roll her eyes at me?*

I hear a text tone and my heart jolts. Belle takes her phone out, glancing at my face.

"That was just my sister," she says.

My heart starts beating steadily again, but I'm annoyed at myself that I let my insecurity show.

"What does she want?" I ask, a little too harshly, to cover it up.

Belle hesitates. "Just a joke about politics...can we watch another one of those mutant films?"

"What joke?" I push.

She squints at me.

"Does it really matter?" Jamie answers for her.

I open my mouth to tell him yes and make up a reason for why it matters, but he interrupts yet again.

"X-Men?" he asks, bringing the conversation back to mutants, because that's clearly more important.

"Yeah! I'm...really interested in them," Belle says.

Jamie looks at me.

I force a smile. "Sure. Not like it's already someone else's tradition or anything—"

This time my phone cuts me off as it buzzes. I scramble, quickly unlocking it and scanning the screen for signs of humiliation. But it's just my mom sending me another article on death-by-phone-charger.

"Thought it was Aces, didn't you?" Jamie asks with a loud laugh, clapping his hands like this is funny.

"No."

"Maybe Aces is really the boogeyman," Jamie says. I glare at him.

"It's not funny, Jamie," I say.

"It kind of is."

"It really isn't," Belle says, putting her fork down, annoyance pressed into her soft features.

"C'mon, I was just joking. Chiamaka is being sensitive."

Belle looks unimpressed. "Sensitive?"

Why is Belle acting like she suddenly cares about me? I need a break from this table and this conversation. I don't want to speak to Jamie when he's in asshole mode.

"I need fresh air," I say, standing abruptly and causing the chair to scrape loudly against the floor. Some of the guys look up, Scotty included. I lock eyes with him briefly, and – I swear I'm not imagining it – he smiles. Then without waiting for a response from Jamie, I leave.

I don't care about them, I tell myself. But I look at them again anyway – the texts from Aces. I rest my head against the wall of the bathroom stall I'm in, taking in the words. They're private. Really private. The type of rumours that could follow people after high school. The ones about Devon.

I wonder how Devon's coping. I think I'd die if stuff that personal came out about me. If I feel this sick all the time, *this* anxious, over trivial stuff, I can only imagine how he's feeling.

What if darker, more invasive secrets of mine were released? The stuff that could ruin everything...college... my career...my life.

The memory of blonde, bloodied hair stains the inside of my eyes as I shut them. The image is a constant reminder of how I just left her there to die.

Every evening for weeks after the accident, I'd call every hospital in the city, asking if a young woman with blonde hair had been admitted. I'd stayed up every night searching for news articles on every local news site, every message board – searching for a sign, a message about a hit and run; a girl left by cowards to bleed out and die.

The selfish part of me is terrified by the thought that she survived, and wants to find us, find me, and tell everyone our terrible secret.

What keeps me up more than anything though, is the night after. I'd visited the spot where it happened – this street cars barely pass through, about two hundred miles away from where I live, and the road was completely clear. I searched the entire stretch of it for signs of her. I drove up and down, convincing myself I'd memorized the place wrong. But there is no way I did. I have it permanently carved into my memory.

There was no body. No glass from the headlight that shattered when we crashed. No blood. Nothing. Like it was all a figment of my imagination.

But I know it happened. The tree we hit was proof enough. Bent out of shape with bark torn from where the car slammed against it. The tree told the truth while everything else from the crime scene was seemingly swept away.

I brought the accident up with Jamie weeks after it happened, when my insomnia had gotten particularly bad.

When I asked him, Jamie looked scared, lost even. Like he could cry. I could tell he wasn't sleeping much either. I remember how pale he got, like he could throw up.

But he changed the subject of course, then ignored me for an entire day.

Jamie doesn't even care about college, and the Fitzjohn family name would be enough to get him out of something this big. I'm pretty sure his family has ins with half the judges around here. But the Fitzjohn name is not only powerful, it's a heavy burden to carry and needs to be upheld. Jamie's always telling me how much his father's respect means to him, and I know he would lose it all if this came to light.

I tried mentioning it again, once, weeks after that. I still wasn't sleeping, and my panic attacks had gotten more and more frequent. I needed a friend. I needed to talk about it – what had happened, and what I'd seen.

He straight up denied it, asked me what I was going on about. Looked so confused, the fear I'd seen the first time I'd asked completely gone. After that I never brought it up again. Knowing who his dad is, and what would happen to Jamie, I figured it was something he fought to forget and this time had succeeded.

I've met Mr Fitzjohn a handful of times, at formal parties and in passing when I'm at Jamie's house; the tension in the air of that place is so constricting. Even his mother seems to crumple under the pressure of a loveless marriage and the perfect family image she's been upholding. I know from Jamie that they sleep in separate bedrooms, and she's always "taking something" to help her sleep and distract her from the man she's married to. Not that anyone would ever talk about that; it's all brushed under the marble flooring. To outsiders, the Fitzjohns seem perfect, but all of them are messed up in their own way. Jamie's more like his father than he realizes.

My family doesn't have any of this, though. No legacy here in America. If our secret comes to light, I have no way out. Everything is at stake, and while Jamie might appear calm on the outside, he *must* know that he could be next on Aces's list of victims.

Maybe outwardly seeming okay, rationalizing things, is how he copes with the possibility of being Aces's next target.

I wish I could be like that right now.

I sniff, but I can't hold back the stream of tears. I let myself cry uncontrollably now, let the aching from the tension in my brain ring, not caring about my mascara or the prospect of anyone in this bathroom hearing me.

Every single night I dream of her. The girl.

But now before those nightmares, I ask myself, *Who is doing this? What will they reveal next?*

"Chiamaka?" I hear a soft voice say, along with the subtle creak of the bathroom door.

I stay quiet, seated sideways on the ground of the stall, looking at my blue plaid skirt spread over my outstretched legs, the thick grey socks that cover most of my thighs, and my brown-heeled brogues pressing against the wall.

"It's Belle," she continues. The bathroom stall next to mine opens and my heart races a little. I hear a slight rattle as Belle pulls at my locked door. She raps at the door three

118

times. I can see her grey suede heels and white frilly socks.

"Are you in there?" she asks. I say nothing. I'm not sure why she's going to such great lengths to be nice. Maybe she's trying to prove a point to Jamie that she's the perfect girl. But I doubt Jamie would notice how Belle treats me, let alone care.

Belle is still and silent, and I almost think she's going to walk away, give up. But then I hear a scraping noise.

I watch the door as the lock slowly starts to turn. There's a sharp *clink* and the door opens.

Belle looks down at me, with wide eyes and a frown. She unzips her bag and hands me a folded tissue.

I don't take it.

"Silly question I know, but…" Her voice trails off. "Are you okay? You've been gone for a while… We still have five minutes until the first warning bell, so I thought I'd come and find you."

"I'm okay, thanks," I say quietly.

"Good, I'm glad." She smiles a little, then opens her mouth to speak again but stops herself. Chewing her bottom lip, Belle steps into the cubicle and leans back against the wall.

"Aces, whoever it is, is a coward hiding behind a screen. I think you're brave for not letting it get to you, coming to school and facing everyone. Really brave," she finishes.

I can't help but stare at her. Belle's eyes burn angrily, as though Aces is attacking her and not me.

Maybe she isn't doing this for Jamie.

"Thank you," I tell her. And I mean it. Jamie didn't care enough to look for me, but she did.

She cocks her head to the side, smile growing.

"I'm just glad you're okay," she says again. My heartbeat quickens.

I sniff, turning away from her and focusing on the wall in front of me.

"How did you get the door open?" I ask. As with the rest of Niveus, the bathrooms are all strong dark wood and the locks look pretty impenetrable.

"I'm really good at picking locks. I learned one year at camp," Belle tells me just as the first warning bell rings. She steps out from the cubicle. "Coming?"

I shake my head. Accepting her kindness, going along with it, makes me feel like I'm giving in.

To what? I'm not sure. But I know I don't want to be friends with her.

She nods, curls bouncing. "I'll see you later."

"Later," I say, hating myself for seeming weak and fragile. People take advantage when you're weak and fragile.

I reach up, tugging some paper from the dispenser in the cubicle, and dab my eyes. I hold the paper up between my fingers, looking at the black lines of mascara and patches of brown foundation.

I hate this out-of-control mess Aces is turning me into.

I've worked too hard for someone to try to make me into a disgrace and a laughing stock.

120

Jamie and I haven't spoken since lunch, and now it's last period chemistry. While our teacher, Mr Peterson, goes on about chemical reactions, all I can think of is Aces. Every time a phone goes off, my heart skips a beat and I feel like my insides could spill out if they wanted.

"…when certain chemicals are mixed together, the wrong reaction can take place. For example, we hear about celebrities overdosing all the time. But it's not necessarily because they take *too much* of a particular drug…"

Something slides towards me – a note. I open it, looking at Jamie's messy handwriting:

sorry for laughing about Aces.

I reply:

It's giving me anxiety. I don't know how you can find all of this funny.

I watch out of the corner of my eye as Jamie reads the note.

sorry – again.

He seems sorry enough. I take the note between my fingers and I hold my index finger out.

"Shake my hand and you will be forgiven."

He smiles and shakes my finger like it's a hand.

"...Sometimes it's a matter of mixing things that don't react well together. One popular example is alcohol and sleeping pills, which can trigger symptoms such as extreme drowsiness, memory loss and in some unfortunate cases, death."

I look up when Mr Peterson says that.

"Besides," Jamie continues, in a whisper, "I think Aces targeting other people is a sign. They know what your wrath looks like."

My mind is still spinning as Mr Peterson's words echo inside. "You're right," I say, trying to shake off the sudden strange feeling I got. This sense of déjà vu.

But as soon as I say that, I hear the wicked green laugh of the universe, and, like a switch being flicked, a reprise of phones go off.

I reach into my pocket, my heart hammering away against my shirt, and my stomach convulsing even more. I scan my phone. One notification from *unknown*. I hear the hubbub of chatter around me, as everyone starts to dissect the text.

[One picture attached]

We have a gangster among us, folks! Devon Richards, look at you. Hanging about on the wrong side of the tracks. What can be expected, when he makes frequent visits like these to very influential and, not to mention, good-looking drug dealers.

Be careful, Vonnie, Juilliard isn't too keen on
criminal records. I hope he's worth it. – Aces

There's a photo of Devon standing by some building.

I read the text over, drumming my nails on the table.
Who'd be that interested in Devon? This almost reads like
an angry or jealous ex…

I tap my screen, selecting a contact I haven't spoken to
in months.

Hey, Scotty, it's Chiamaka

I watch my screen, only looking up to check that
Peterson's focus is away from me. We are allowed to use our
phones in school – just not during class. Apparently, they
cause distractions. I bet the teachers never imagined
anything like *this*, though, when they made that rule. How
can anyone concentrate when there's a snake on the loose?

I drag my finger down the screen, tapping the table
impatiently.

"Who are you texting?" Jamie whispers, startling me.

I whack him lightly. "None of your business. Focus on
your work," I say, before tilting the phone a little to block
Jamie's prying eyes from seeing.

The three dots appear, indicating that Scotty's typing,
and I sit up.

Long time no speak.

Just texting to ask a question, and I want a direct answer.

I try to sound intimidating. I probably should have spoken to him at lunch since my intimidation works better in person. But I wasn't in the right head space.

Ask away.

I look up, catching the teacher's eyes, so I pick up my pencil and pretend to write with one hand whilst tapping a reply under the table with the other.

Are you Aces?

There is a short pause before the three dots appear again.

You're the second person to ask me that this week.
I thought we were friends?

I wouldn't call us friends... In fact the last time we spoke – sometime after our fake break-up at the beginning of junior year – he'd laughed at my shoes in the hallway and I'd threatened to cut off his stupid ponytail. But I thought we were on good enough terms too. He's friends with Jamie's friends, so we've always kind of been in the same circles anyway.

I thought we were too, yet you're the only connection

I can think of who'd have any dirt on both me
and Devon.

...

As I told the other person, why would I implicate
myself?

There's something inside me that knows it isn't Scotty.
That for all the shitty things he's done, he doesn't stand to
gain anything from this.

My phone buzzes again.

Scared that Aces will talk about that night?

Frozen, I stare down at the message, trying to figure out
what he means by *that night*. Does Scotty somehow know
about the girl we hit?

What night? I send.

Waiting for his reply feels like an eternity, but eventually
I feel my phone vibrate.

Jamie's party at the beginning of junior year. You
were wasted, remember? Kept telling people their
outfits sucked. It was funny, actually.

I only remember snippets of Jamie's party. I remember
the kiss... But the rest is a blur. I don't even remember
drinking that much, but I'm a lot more careful now if I do

drink around people. I want to be able to recall everything, keep their secrets in my bank rather than the other way around.

Why'd I be scared about that? The worst Aces could do is show everyone a video of me dancing badly on top of some table. I've been through worse attempts at people trying to embarrass me.

Is that all you remember? Scotty writes back, almost immediately.

I pause, trying to figure out what he means by that.

Yes, why?

I hardly remember that night and wanted to piece things together too in case Aces has anything on me. I do stupid things when I'm drunk. All I remember is talking to you, kissing some guy and throwing up in the rose bushes outside.

I don't remember speaking to Scotty that night. I close my eyes, trying to recall something, anything. And as if a bucket of ice water has been tossed over my head, a massive chill pulls me into a memory.

"Can I tell you a secret?" Scotty asks, his voice startling me. I'm in one of the guest bedrooms. The door was meant

to be locked... I'm not sure how Scotty got in. The music blaring from the party downstairs is making my head spin.

"It's about you..." he says, with a loopy smile.

"What secret?" I say, trying to sit up, panic rising inside.

He smirks a little, then takes a seat on the carpet next to me, almost spilling the concoction in his red Solo cup.

"I heard that Cecelia Wright isn't a natural blonde," Scotty says.

I blink at him.

"That's not about me?" I stare.

"No, of course it isn't... Your name is Chi, not CeCe." He wipes his mouth and leans in close. He smells like death, and that's the nice way of putting it.

"You know, I wasn't meant to be here tonight... Snuck away when Mom wasn't looking," Scotty says.

I want to sleep, but I feel so nauseous and shaky. And I want to know what Scotty has on me.

Scotty looks up and takes my face in his hands. "You're so pretty, Chi. Pretty as a doll."

I pull at his hands. "What's wrong with you?" I reach up to smooth my cheeks, but they feel wet. Was I crying? Why was I crying? I was...meant to meet Jamie in his room, but he wasn't—

"Why're you hiding up here in this room? It's a lot more fun downstairs." Scotty's voice slurs as he sways, knocking me a little. He completely ignored my question.

"I could ask you the same," I say.

"Came to look for my girlfriend," he says, laughing at the word "girlfriend" like it's the most hilarious thing in the world. I don't know if I should be offended or not.

"Well, she's fine, so…you can go now."

Scotty thrusts his hand out, this time spilling a bit of his drink, before concentrating hard on placing it down straight. When he does, he watches it suspiciously, holding his hands up like he has magical powers that will prevent his cup from defying gravity.

If it wasn't obvious before, the moment he starts singing the chorus of "Hit Me Baby One More Time" it is clear as day that he is way too drunk to deliver himself home.

"Did you come here with anyone?" I can ask Jamie if he minds Scotty crashing here. Jamie's friends will probably sleep in the guest rooms or one of the living rooms.

"No, but I might leave with someone… Let's see where the night takes me." He smiles sheepishly, and I hit him.

"You know, you are the worst boyfriend ever," I say. He and I are only fake dating since he's on the football team and is semi-popular and I'm on the verge of being very popular. We need each other. It's political.

"I know," he says, throwing his head back so hard it smashes against the wall, making me cringe. He groans, his fingers lost in the messiness of his hair as he cradles his skull.

"Are you okay?" I ask, as his head slumps forward. He sniffs and I lean in, noticing his wet cheeks now.

Is Scotty crying?

"Do you need an ice pack?"

He shakes his head before I can even finish asking the question. "I'm such a shitty boyfriend."

I don't say anything. Is that why he's crying? Because I don't care about the whole authenticity of this relationship behind closed doors—

"All I do is cheat and lie and drink and be a fucking disappointment to Von and my parents and Niveus..."

Maybe he's not talking about me after all.

He cries a little harder, picking his drink up again. I awkwardly pat his back.

I feel really sick. I've already thrown up in the bathroom but I'm probably going to puke up my entire digestive system and die next to Scotty in this bedroom, while everyone else adjusts normally to teenage life downstairs.

Scotty hugs his cup like it's a stuffed toy. There's a hole in his sock. His big pale toe sticks out and it's funny because he's nothing like this sober. He's always put together, in the finest clothes every legacy kid is expected to wear.

"You're not a disappointment, Scotty. Trust me," *I say, smoothing down my dress.* "And it's my duty as your fake girlfriend to not let you die from alcohol poisoning." *I tug the cup out of his hands. He slumps back.*

We are quiet for a while. I almost think he's fallen asleep.

The door to the guest room opens once again.

"There you are. I went in my room to look for you but you weren't there... Everything okay?" Jamie asks.

I nod, still shivering. Face dry from tears. I probably look like a mess. I force out a smile.

"Everything's great," I say.

"Good..." His eyes drift down to Scotty next to me, now fast asleep. "Wanna go somewhere to talk?" He says this with a smirk.

I start to get up, surprised by how painful it is to do so.

An image flashes suddenly in my mind, someone pushing me down, me falling hard, crying, screaming for help—

"I'd love to talk," I say, as his arms slip around my waist, brushing over the bruises on my hip...

There's a sharp pang in my head, the memory jolting my nervous system out of whack. I take a shaky breath, and smooth down my school skirt, feeling a little sick. I don't bother replying to Scotty's message. I got the answer I was looking for: he's not Aces.

Jamie taps my arm, his smile and eyes wide. "You're thinking too hard. I can literally hear your brain cells screaming, 'Help...there's only two of us left!'"

I roll my eyes. "My brain cells can manage," I reply in a whisper. Jamie quirks an eyebrow up with an *if you're sure* look, then turns back and continues defacing the instructions sheet we were given. He scrawls numbers and symbols all over it, like he usually does to pass time. I sometimes wonder how Jamie and I are in AP classes together when he literally never pays attention.

I tap his arm and he looks at me again.

"You forgot one of your passwords at my house the other day," I say, staring at his thick black marker pen.

He looks confused. "My password?"

"Yeah, the 1717 one."

His grin fades into a subtler expression. "Ah, *that* password. I don't need it any more," he says.

"How can you not need a password any more?" I ask.

He shrugs. "Needed it, then didn't."

I nod, not pressing further. Jamie is random like that sometimes. He goes back to writing on the page.

My head still throbs, so I try to focus on something else, hoping the pain subsides. My gaze drifts past Jamie, landing on Belle, sitting at one of the tables nearby. Her hair is falling over the side of her face, while her chin rests on her manicured hand, face flushed. I notice she's gripping the pencil so hard her knuckles are white.

I'd ask her if she's okay, but we aren't friends.

And so, I don't.

I imagine her blonde hair matted in red, blood dripping all over her uniform and forming a puddle on the ground.

Then I blink, and the image disappears.

13

DEVON

FRIDAY

We need to talk – Dre

Daniel, the weird quarterback in my music class who's taken a sudden interest in speaking to me, had the courtesy to show me the Aces text when I got to class this morning, before asking me what my "street name" is.

So I think I can guess why Dre messaged me. He wanted me to stay out of Aces's mouth, yet for some reason I'm basically *all* Aces seems to talk about. I want to find out who is behind this, so I can ask them how they know so much and why they won't leave me alone. It must be someone I accidentally pissed off.

My heart is thumping so hard that I hear it in my ears as I walk towards Dre's apartment. My school shirt is drenched and clinging to me, despite the chill of the afternoon air.

I grew up here. Right here, with the rest of these boys. We went to the same elementary school. We witnessed things no kid should see, like snitches getting stabbed and shot, fathers being handcuffed and taken away. We went to middle school together, too, until one day an older guy,

Malik, decided to beat me so hard after school that I had to drop out.

I remember everyone joining in – even the boys I thought were my friends.

They were shouting slurs, laughing as I screamed and bled.

The words "bitch boy" and "fairy" rang in my ears as they punched and kicked. Just like that, the boys I grew up with were no longer my boys. They were the boys I was made to be scared of.

If I could have fought back, like Dre, my life might have been so different. He's always been able to fit in here, it's like he has a handbook or knows unspoken rules that I don't.

I'm at Dre's apartment block now, staring at the guy at the door, Leon. Another boy from middle school. His brown curls nearly cover his eyes but his stony gaze is set on me. He's been close to Dre for years, never seemed to like me.

"It's Devon," I say, always holding my head high in front of them.

He disappears inside, coming back moments later with the confirmation.

The floorboards creak as I step inside. I walk through Dre's apartment, then into his room and there he is, with his back to me, hands in his pockets and his shoulder blades visible through the dark, clingy material of his T-shirt. I close the door behind me. "Hey."

He twitches.

There's a long silence; I can hear him breathing, and

sniffling. He brings his hand up to wipe his face then pushes it back into his pocket.

"We should stop seeing each other," he says abruptly, still not facing me.

I stay calm on the outside despite the fact that my chest aches like I've been stabbed.

"What?" I say, swallowing hard.

"We should stop seeing each other," he repeats. It stings. My eyes water slightly.

I heard you.

"Why?" I ask, even though I know.

He scratches his head, still refusing to look at me.

"Not everyone goes to your fancy school, Von. Not everyone has the privilege of not caring about their reputation. I have one – I *need* one. I have nothing else but this and I can't have you ruining it."

I step towards him.

"And how am I doing that, Dre?"

He turns to look at me now, eyes red, but I think it's a mix of whatever the fuck he's been taking and tears. I step even closer. He moves back like I'm gonna hurt him.

Dre tries to act all hard, but he's not. He's this teddy bear who needs to be hugged and kissed and loved.

I know this because I know him. I've known him for years, been friends with him for years – despite Ma's disapproval. We loved the same music. That's how this all started. Tupac, Biggie – they made our friendship. Rap, R&B, Soul, we love that shit.

We used to lie on his bed for hours, listening to the oldies till day was night, before his ma kicked him out when he was fourteen.

I remember the first time he kissed me – we kissed way too late if you ask me. I'd been dating Scotty for a few months at that point. I didn't even know Dre liked me until that moment, or that I liked him.

The memory clouds my brain.

"I'm sort of seeing someone," I tell him, despite my heart racing like I just ran a marathon and won.

Scotty, I'm seeing Scotty. I shouldn't feel like that's suddenly something I don't want.

He scoffs. "Rich white boy, huh?"

I want to kiss Dre again…

"Yeah, rich white boy," I whisper.

"Get out." Dre's deep voice cuts through my memories.

My eyes are watering as I shake my head.

He comes close to me now. "Get out. *Please*, get out."

Closer…

I shake my head again.

He presses his head against mine, digging into my skull, but I don't care. I grab him and he kisses me, long and deep, and I cry, tears tickling my chin as they leak down my face. I hold him and we kiss and kiss until he's pushing away and shouting.

"Get out." He shakes his head, moving back a little. "Get

the fuck out!" he yells, wiping his face roughly. I jump back as the doors burst open.

Two of his boys bust in. Leon is one of them.

"Want us to drag him, Dre?" Leon asks, his eyes avoiding mine.

I look back at Dre, who looks at me with red eyes that are glassed over with regret.

"Just get him out. Don't want him dealing my stash any more."

The knife in my chest turns and my heart crumbles. I close my eyes as they drag me away, pushing me down the stairs so I stumble. They shove me out so hard that I fall to the ground.

I can feel so many eyes on me. The boys outside – the boys I was made to be scared of – ready, waiting.

There is silence before it happens. The wind rustles through the trees nearby. A lighter clicks. Then footsteps.

And before it happens, I remember the first time Dre told me he loved me. It was days after we started dating and months after the first time we kissed. Only weeks after I'd ended things with Scotty. We were listening to music in his apartment, the place he was before here, arguing over senseless shit and he just said it. I remember thanking him for his honesty and we started laughing. I said *I love you* hours after, and everything was so light. Was that wrong? Us saying that so early on?

The first blow hits my side and I hiss.

"I love you."

The second blow hits harder. I think that this, paired with Dre's words, is as painful as a gunshot.

"*I love you.*"

The rest of the blows come at once, puncturing me over and over. Someone punches my eye and I scream.

"*I love you.*"

I feel it swell up. I can't see. I can't see. I can't—

"I love you," he tells me, straight after telling me I'm dumb for thinking Destiny's Child is better than TLC.

"Thank you for your honesty," I tell him, even though I'm dying inside. I look at him and he looks at me, eyebrows slit in a way that makes him look weirdly attractive, and eyes dark and lusty.

He smiles at me. "That all I get?"

I wrap my hand around his neck, bringing my head closer.

"I said thank you, though…"

There's a pause and then we are laughing for no reason.

He is smiling when he kisses me, leaning in and kissing me. And I feel so light.

God, I feel so light.

I don't know where I am. I was in front of Dre's, and now I'm here in a room, lying on what feels like a bed.

I let my fingers brush against the material beneath me.

"You're awake," a deep, invisible voice says. My heart skips a beat.

I spot the shimmer of a figure in the corner. Using my good eye, I squint, trying to see if it's someone I know or at least recognize. He's tall, with brown skin, eyeglasses, medium black dreads and shaved sides. He looks about my age. But that's all I can really see, my eye hurts so bad…

"It's Terrell," he starts. "Terrell Rosario – I saw how badly they hurt you and brought you back to my ma's place. Hope that's okay."

Terrell. Sounds familiar…I think.

My whole body throbs, like pins have been jabbed into the really sensitive spots. I can only imagine what my face looks like, when I can't even open my right eye.

I nod.

"I put some water on the bedside table," he says, pointing to my left side. I look over and there's a blue plastic cup.

"Thanks," I say.

I can feel his gaze on me, probably wondering what I did to get beaten up by them.

"I'm going to head home," I tell Terrell. Ma always warns me about people who try to do you favours.

He says nothing, watching me as I hold back tears. My arms shake violently as I try to push myself up. The pain isn't as bad as other wounds I've gotten before, but this hurts so much more because of Dre.

"I'll get you more ice packs."

I look at him again, his face becoming clearer as my vision focuses. He has this soft, worried expression on his face that makes me feel like this stranger and I are friends.

I watch him leave the room. Moments later he's back with a bag of what seems to be frozen vegetables. "We only had one of these," he says, holding up the bag.

He walks towards me cautiously. "Where does it hurt most?"

I point to my right side, and he climbs onto the bed, looking at me quizzically. I nod, figuring he wants consent or something, before he lifts my shirt a little and places the icy bag on the part I pointed out. I squeeze my eyes shut. It stings, but it's manageable.

The room goes silent as my side tingles and numbs. Terrell stands, observing me carefully, gazing across different parts of my body.

I can't help but notice his Spider-Man pyjama bottoms. My brothers both own similar pairs.

"I know the guys who beat you up," he starts nervously. *Most people know them.* "And...I don't know if me saying this makes you feel any better, but they went easy on you."

I guess that doesn't surprise me.

"I didn't see the fight happen. If I did I wouldn't have watched, trust me – I would have tried to help if it meant you being a little less hurt..." He bites his lip and looks away, his sentence feeling incomplete.

There's something about Terrell that feels so familiar.

"It's okay," I tell him.

Silence creeps in again, crawling into the bed and hugging me, trying not to graze itself against my cuts and bruises.

I slip away, Dre's face floating in my mind, the break-up replaying in a loop. I'm not that surprised by it, just hurt. I always get a little hurt when I lose parts of Dre. Like when he first started dealing after his ma and her boyfriend chucked him out. I lost another part of him when he started beating people up for popularity and respect. I lost another part of him when he moved up the ranks in his gang. I lose parts of him constantly. This was bound to happen someday.

I should have prepared better for the inevitable.

"Do you feel a little better?" Terrell asks.

I almost forget where I am again.

"Yeah I do, thanks," I say, just wanting to get home. He smiles at that, and dimples appear on his cheeks. They really suit him.

"Good, I was worried for you."

I pause, wanting a moment to go by before I have to tell him again that I'm going, but before I get the chance to, he's talking.

"Do you still play music?" he asks, a smile playing on his lips like he's daring me. I scrunch my eyebrows together in confusion.

"Music?"

He nods.

"I remember you played the piano."

I feel really freaked out all of a sudden. *Who is Terrell?*

I squint at him again, taking in all his features. I still can't figure it out.

"You're trying to remember me," he states.

"Sorry," I say feeling bad.

He shakes his head, pushing his glasses back up on his nose. "Nah, it's okay, memory is weird like that – I just find you really memorable..." He pauses, eyes drifting to my side. "It's probably melting now... I'll take that away for you." He lifts the frozen bag up and my side immediately misses the cold sting.

I wish he'd finish his sentence. I want to know why I can't remember him.

He leaves the room and I poke my side, the feel of my finger sending shocks to my chest.

I scan his room slowly. It's clean, but small and old like mine. Wallpaper peeling at the corners, and a torn-up desk chair with the foam spilling out.

Terrell walks back in and I see this as my chance.

"Where should I know you from?" I ask.

"Middle school," he starts, looking away. "We used to talk quite a bit before you left. I was new to the school in eighth grade and you were...nice to me. We also kissed once, I guess, and... It was my first kiss and you don't really forget those—"

"We kissed?" I splutter, not expecting that.

"Just once," he repeats, stopping himself like he wants to say more.

Why don't I remember him?

"And you remember me?" I ask.

He nods, like it's a weird thing for me to ask.

"I could never really forget you, Devon. Besides, when

you got into that fancy school you were the talk of the neighbourhood."

I remember the eggs thrown at my house when I got in. *Resentment breeds contempt.*

"I'm sorry. I don't remember much from around that time – it's like my memory is faulty." There's a twinge in my side.

"Memory is weird like that," he says again.

I knew something was familiar about him, but I feel like I would remember someone I kissed.

Maybe I don't know myself like I thought I did.

Memory *is* weird like that.

Terrell didn't really give me a choice in this – him walking me home – but I'm glad he is. I can't walk well without it hurting, and him helping me hop along makes the journey a little more bearable.

Plus, he doesn't talk too much.

We get to my front door about twenty minutes later – it would have been half the time if I wasn't injured. He finally lets go of my waist, letting me stand on my own.

"Thank you," I say, feeling like those two words are inadequate.

He shakes his head. "Don't sweat it. I'd do it for anyone in trouble."

I nod, moving to turn.

"Wait," he says, and I stop.

"Yeah?"

"I didn't give you a goodbye hug."

I can't help but smile slightly at the statement. "Goodbye hug?"

"I'm not sure when I'm gonna see you next, so I at least want a hug for the road."

A hug for the road. That's a first.

"Sure," I say, and his dimples appear again.

He moves towards me and gives me a hug, and even though it hurts, I try not to let it show.

"Thank you," I say again. It still doesn't feel adequate. With the week I've had it's hard to remember the last time someone has been this nice to me.

We pull away, and I can breathe again, my sides angry at me for letting an intruder touch them.

"I could give you my number," I suggest. "We could meet up or something."

My friendships are disappearing daily so I should find more of them before I become one of those *real* loners. At least before, I could pretend Jack and I were as close as we used to be in middle school, and I had Dre for company.

Terrell's face lights up as he digs into his hoodie for his phone. I give him my number, and he looks down at his phone like he's searching for something in it, then puts it back into his pocket.

"I'll see you, then?" he says.

I nod. "Yeah…and thanks again."

He starts walking backwards, and I watch him. He keeps

walking back and I keep watching him, and then he smiles and turns away, disappearing quickly in the direction we came from.

After a few moments lost in thought, I push our front door open to find Ma seated at the dining table in our dimly-lit kitchen reading through letters.

I can guess what they say, because they always say the same thing. I sometimes feel like I'm stuck in a loop, reliving the same day over and over. I come home, and Ma is always tired, always sorting through bills.

"How was school, *Mr Senior Prefect*," Ma says, not looking at me, just shuffling papers. She's been calling me that a lot since I told her. I'm glad it makes her happy. It makes me feel like I've really accomplished something.

I don't know how to answer her question. So I just say, "School was good, my music piece is coming together well, and I think I might have a decent shot at Juilliard – getting a scholarship too…"

She breathes out, wiping her eyes with the back of her hands. I take this chance to shuffle towards her, trying not to make my injuries obvious as I bend down to kiss her bowed head.

"I'll be back, lemme just grab something," I say in an almost-whisper, before abandoning my backpack and climbing the stairs as quickly as I can to my bedroom.

I hate seeing her look so broken all the time. She didn't want me to get a job, said it would distract me from school, and she's probably right. But I can't just sit back and let her struggle like this. Watch her cry like that.

When you grow up like this, whether it's in your nature or not, sometimes survival overpowers doing the right thing.

I search in my drawer for the envelope filled with twenties. I try not to make much noise, despite feeling like my ribs are cracking against each other. My brothers are already asleep and it's hard to get them both to sleep at the same time.

I close the drawer quietly, hobbling back down the stairs now. My thighs ache from the uneven pressure I'm placing on them. When I finally get to Ma, I place the envelope in front of her.

She looks up at me, eyes tired and glassy, and then she moves to stand, cradling my face in her wrinkled Black hands. She says nothing about my face and why it's beaten, she just strokes it.

We've been here before.

"I'll get you some ice for that…" she mumbles.

I shake my head, knowing we don't have any frozen food bags in the freezer this week.

"I'm fine," I tell her, my voice breaking, but not because of the injuries. My heart really hurts.

She nods, looking away from me and down at the money now.

"Vonnie, where did you get this kind of money?"

"Don't ask, Ma, please," I say.

We always have this conversation when money gets

really tight. She always wants to know where I get it from. Always.

And as I said, sometimes you have to do things that don't exactly align with your morals, and I did those things so that we can have a little cash when we need it. I try not to think about how I'm gonna get the money next time now that me and Dre—

I stop myself, pushing him down a hole in my mind where I keep all the things I don't want to talk about.

I go to school, I put on the costume the rich kids wear and I pretend for a few hours. I could act all high and mighty, I could think I'm the shit, lie to myself, but it doesn't change the fact that this is my reality.

Ma works three jobs for us. She does everything for us. And I do everything for her.

"Thank you, Vonnie," she says. "I love you more than words can tell you, you know that?"

I nod.

I know that.

14

CHIAMAKA

MONDAY

I wake up late.

Dad kept me up all night with stories from his trip to Italy to see Grandma, not that I minded much. I couldn't sleep anyway, with the guilt and worry weighing on me. I think it was three in the morning by the time I'd finally made it into bed.

When my brain registers the time, I'm already late, having to rush my morning routine as a result.

I pick up my straightener and hold it up to my curls, anxiously watching the time pass. The lights suddenly switch off, and my straightener beeps, indicating it's not heating up any more.

"Mom!" I shout.

She rushes into my room.

"What is it?"

"The electricity!"

"The builders have started the work downstairs. It'll come back on later."

"But I can't go to school like this."

"Why not?"

"My hair."

Mom gives me a confused look. "Your hair is fine."

I shake my head. "I can't go in like this."

There's a pause.

"You should love your hair, Chi," Mom says with a small frown.

"I know, I know and I do, I just…"

I don't want a repeat of elementary school. I don't want them to stare. Mom's eyes bore into me, like she's trying to work out what I'm thinking – something she's never really been good at. I don't want her thinking I dislike my hair or anything else that resembles her, because I don't.

I don't.

I look away from her, my curls brushing against my face, reminding me that they are there – for ever and always, whether I like it or not. Which I do. I do like it.

I force a smile.

"It's okay, I guess I'll go to school like this."

Mom nods. "And hurry, you're late."

I obviously know that.

It's only Monday and yet another week is starting to suck.

I comb my hair as much as I can and put coconut oil in it, before rushing out of the house.

I get to school, wishing I hadn't rushed so much this morning. Being here today is so different from last Monday. Last week I felt in control, like this year was going to be everything I've wished for. And now everything feels uncertain, like there is something dangerous lurking in the corner, ready to attack at any moment. My stomach squeezes into a ball as I walk. I keep my head up, making sure my body does not give off fear.

Bitches can smell fear.

I can't help but feel itchy as their stares dig into my skin. *Is it another Aces blast or is it my hair?*

I walk up to Jamie by his locker. The sound of everyone's voices deep in conversation rises to an unbearable level. He looks down at me briefly, flashing a smile as he searches through his locker, then his head whips back again and his eyes drift up to my hair, then down to my face. I can tell he wants to stare at it some more.

"Did you just get here? You missed registration," he says, shutting his locker.

I nod. "I know, I woke up late."

He looks surprised and I don't blame him. I've never once missed registration or woken up late for school before.

"Who are you and what have you done with my best friend?" He grins as we start walking towards our first period math class. I scan the hallway for signs of Ruby or Ava, but they aren't by my locker.

People move out the way as we walk through, their gazes fixed on my face, my clothes and my hair. I feel uncomfortable, but I am not going to let it show.

"Have there been any developments in the *Let's-ruin-Chiamaka's-life* show over the weekend?" I ask. "I didn't get any anonymous texts so…wasn't sure."

I didn't get any texts from anyone this weekend, for that matter. My phone might as well have been on silent.

"No…not since last week. I think Master Aces is done with you," he says with a wink.

Somehow, I know for certain that is not true. Why would they put out that stuff about Jamie, and the candy shop? It was like they were teasing. Letting me know there's more in store for me. There's someone behind this who has an agenda against me, and I have a body in my closet and a position at school that is always under attack. This feels like it's only the beginning.

"I doubt that," I mumble as we take our seats.

To prove my point, a swarm of buzzes fills the room. I don't feel one in my pocket. I want to cry. First the hair thing and now this. Aces is coming for me again, like I knew they would.

Someone says, "*Jesus Christ*," and my insides feel shaky as I look up.

No one is staring at me.

Weird.

"See," Jamie says, sliding his phone over.

Niveus High, it just keeps getting better…
Rumour has it, our favourite music student is doing more than just "visiting" his drug dealer. Oh, Dev, didn't anyone tell you ecstasy is a harmful drug?
– Aces

My heart is still pounding.

Why didn't I get the blast?

I reach into my pocket, taking my phone out.

It's dead. I must've forgotten to charge it last night, what with Dad and his never-ending stories.

I breathe out, my chest still aching.

"I'm not surprised," Jamie says, still looking down at the text. Something about the way he says that gets under my skin.

"How come?" I ask.

He shrugs. "He just seems like the type, right? I mean, he's from that neighbourhood—"

"Yeah, but still, he goes here," I say, not really liking his tone.

Jamie pauses, smiling at me. "You're right. He goes here."

His expression tells me he doesn't fully believe that Devon going here changes things. His expression tells me he doesn't think that Devon belongs here. And even though I belong, I don't look like my dad; I'm not white, and that becomes so apparent on days like this when my hair curls up and I have to brace against the stares and the confusion.

I don't straighten my hair because I hate it, I straighten it because everyone else hates it for me.

They ask me, "What are you?" And I want to be sarcastic and tell them *human*, but I don't. I tell them I'm Italian and Nigerian. They raise their eyebrows at the Italian part, like they are surprised whiteness can produce me. Some days, it really bothers me. And other days it doesn't.

It makes me wonder if my resemblance to my mother has anything to do with this – with Aces. Whether Devon and his Blackness and myself and mine are the reason this creep is picking on us. I feel sick at the thought of it.

"Chi, I don't want to sound paranoid or anything, but people are staring at us," Jamie whispers. I look up and they are. A wave of heat washes over me, my insides churning.

"It's probably nothing—"

He shakes his head. "Weren't you listening? I heard a bunch of phones go off again… Mine wasn't one of them."

I look around again, judgemental glares surrounding us.

I want to pretend people aren't staring. *Just be normal, feel normal.* But I can't, and it's driving me crazy.

Jamie and I have so many secrets together.

I grip the edge of the table, looking down, eyes blurring. I try to let the air in, but invisible hands wrap themselves around my neck, strangling me. They are cold and tough and beat at my chest, daring my heart to go faster. She shakes my head, dizzying me. The dead girl who haunts my sleep.

In the background I hear the teacher asking us to settle down.

I close my eyes and she's staring up at me with her mouth hung open, hair stained red—

"*Poor Belle,*" I hear someone say.

I stand, quickly marching over to a random guy in the class, trying to look calm as I hold my hand out. I can hear the teacher yelling at me to sit back down. The guy hesitantly hands his phone over.

> Belle Robinson, you have a problem. I'd ask your boyfriend and his bestie, Chiamaka, what they were doing this summer. Hint, it involves no clothes and a lot of heavy petting. Looks like Chi might have someone to take to the Snowflake Ball after all. Once a thief, always a thief. Sorry, Belle. – Aces

The gawping follows me into lunch. I haven't seen Belle all morning, and since first period, I haven't seen Jamie either.

Three freshman girls approach me, eyes excited and wild. It's scary.

"Yes?"

They look at each other.

"Is Jamie a good kisser?"

"I wouldn't know," I say.

All their eyebrows rise together.

"Aces never lies."

"Yeah," another says.

"They always tell the truth."

Is it wrong to hit a freshman?

"If Aces had the guts, they'd stop hiding behind a screen like a coward, and come and tell me what they need to say to my face. Anyway, whatever you read about Jamie and me, it's made up—"

"Is it?" A voice interrupts.

When I turn back around, Belle is standing there. She looks angry; her eyes squinted, her arms crossed.

"Is it really made up?" she asks.

"This is gonna be so good," I hear one freshman mutter.

"Yes," I answer, looking Belle in the eye, trying to seem confident.

"Oh? Because Jamie told me it's true."

My stomach drops. "What's true?"

She shakes her head, looking like she wants to hit me.

"The rumour that you liked him and kept trying to pursue him, even after he told you he wasn't interested."

What?

"That's not true—"

"So you didn't sleep with him? Or tell him you liked him, after he told you he was dating me?"

I become aware of people lingering, listening in on our conversation.

"Belle—"

"I came here to tell you this – this whole *Lola's* situation, you and him and your *traditions*… You and him, full stop, are over."

She can't do that.

"You can't do that."

Belle wipes her face harshly. "Oh, but I can! The girlfriend is way more important than the ex-best friend," she says, giving me one last look before storming back down the hall.

I feel numb. My arms are frozen.

"That was amazing…" I hear one of the girls say.

"She really showed her!"

I watch Belle – her head bowed, and her shoulders hunched – getting further away.

I *am* a horrible person. I didn't know about Belle and Jamie, but even if I had, that probably wouldn't have stopped anything from happening between us. I wouldn't have cared about her feelings. I just wanted him for myself, even if it meant hurting Belle in the process.

"What a bitch," I hear.

And maybe if it were another time, I would have thought of a smart comeback or walked off with my head held high or found a way to put them in their place. Instead I turn to face the three demons again, devious smiles on their cherubic faces, and my hand suddenly comes back to life. It whacks the middle one's face hard enough that it stings my own palm. She immediately covers her cheek, and her jaw hangs open.

I hear gasps around me as I stumble back. The girl's expression slowly transforms into a smirk, mischief dancing in her blue-green eyes.

She opens her mouth wide, an over-exaggerated scream erupting from it.

And in that moment, I know I'm screwed.

Headmaster Ward sits behind his desk across from me, staring into my soul with his small black eyes, his long wiry fingers crossed over one another.

"Headmaster Ward, it is not in my character to do something like that. I've never gotten into a fight before – things are just really hard lately. I feel like someone is out to get me."

I'm so over today.

"Miss Adebayo, there are countless witnesses, most with spotless records, who say you were bullying the girl. I thought you, as Head Prefect, would know better."

"That's not true!" I say, voice rising. "They are trying to make me look bad. They don't even know me!"

His thin lips turn inward. "And why would they do that?"

I hesitate. Would he even believe me if I told him about Aces? I've watched enough murder mystery shows to know nothing good comes from telling on the anonymous bully.

I sigh, then look down. "There's this person, or people, texting the entire student body, spreading rumours about me and a few other students, and making school very hard to be in right now."

I look up at him again, and his face hasn't changed. He doesn't even look surprised.

"I'll look into it," Headmaster Ward tells me. Even though it's not much, and he doesn't look like he cares, a tiny weight lifts. Something is happening.

Maybe I should have just told a teacher all along.

"We have a zero-tolerance policy for violence. You're lucky the girl's parents have decided not to press charges against you. As this is your first misdemeanour, I won't add it to your permanent record, but this is your first strike.

Another, and there will be serious consequences."

He dismisses me and I leave his office, passing through hallways where there are still people lurking, even though school finished half an hour ago.

I'm staring at my dead phone, not bothering to keep my head up and feign confidence. I feel too dejected to pretend. I knew Aces wasn't finished with me.

I bump into a soft figure. His cologne and the familiarity of his form make me look up.

"Oh, hi," I say, awkwardly. Jamie's hair is pushed back by a bright-red headband, which clashes with the light blue of his football uniform.

"Hey, Chi," he says, avoiding looking at me straight.

"We need to talk—"

"I think we should distance ourselves for now..." Jamie says, staring at a locker behind me. "I want to be friends, but I also love Belle and don't want to lose her."

Love. Wow.

"I'm gonna convince her that you don't even like me like that and that it didn't mean anything."

I laugh, mostly in disbelief. "Sure, after you told her otherwise."

He looks taken aback by the fact that I know. I raise an eyebrow at him, waiting to see what lie he'll tell next.

"She'll listen to me," he says matter-of-factly.

"You can't just say something and then convince someone you didn't say it or that it didn't happen."

This is what Jamie does. He talks about everything that

happened like it meant nothing. Rationalizes things, carves out new memories for you.

"*I like you a lot, Chi. For real,*" he'd said that night.

The past ripples between us, pulling me back in – the night of his party flashing by in broken fragments.

I remember arriving, meeting Jamie, feeling on top of the world. I remember Jamie handing me a drink, wrapping his arms around me, asking me to meet him in his bedroom. I remember thinking *He likes me* as he pulled away.

Then time winds forward. I remember stumbling, his arms wrapping around me, holding me close, and me thinking *He likes me*, us kissing, *He likes me*, my eyes still wet, heart beating fast for no reason.

My head stings and the memory pauses abruptly.

He's acting like he didn't tell me he liked me that night, and then every other night we slept together since. He told me before he left for camp too.

How will he rationalize that?

Maybe he'll say I misinterpreted what he meant. That he didn't mean he liked *me*. He meant he liked my body, my flesh, my bones – which he probably thought he could have, whether he saw us as platonic or not.

Silly me for misconstruing that.

Now everyone keeps looking at me like I have this giant red "A" embossed on my school sweatshirt like Hester in *The Scarlet Letter*.

Jamie thinks the world is his to control. That he can tell me, convince me, how to think and how to feel, like I'm some puppet. I used to believe it – get swept up in it. But it's getting harder and harder not to see past his lies; that he's anything other than selfish; that he cares.

"It did happen, Jamie. You can't just make it unhappen. Belle's smarter than you think. She won't believe you."

Jamie laughs. "That's ridiculous. Of course she will."

"It's not! And I'm so tired of you pretending things didn't happen!" My face heats up. I hate the way he looks at me, so unbothered by everything. "Things like the accident."

His eyes darken, eyebrows knitting together.

"What accident?" he asks, his tone changing, deeper than before.

That shuts me up.

He leans in close, whispering. "You should think before you open your mouth, Chi. People might start to think you're making things up for attention." His voice drips with venom.

We stare at each other for a few moments, his lips tugging up a little. Almost like he's smiling at me.

No.

Mocking me.

"See you around, Chiamaka," he says, as his voice slithers back to its neutral state.

Then he moves past and I watch his figure compress as he walks away, until it is no longer discernible. The cold in the hallway sweeps into my body.

There are moments when something happens, and puzzle pieces that didn't connect before now fit together perfectly. Maybe the piece I'd failed to connect was the one where I thought Jamie was any different to Ava or Ruby. That he ever really loved me or valued our friendship.

Nothing he ever told me was true. I was stupid not to have realized that sooner, blinded by the idea that someone could actually love a person like me.

Maybe what I thought was Jamie's love was never love at all.

They say love and hate are the same, just at different ends of the blade.

I hesitate, before drawing up the list of suspects in my mind and adding Jamie's name to the spot beneath Ruby's.

15

MONDAY

Home, lately, has been the highlight of my day.

Before Aces, I used to avoid it as much as I could. Despite how much I love my ma and my brothers, I wanted to avoid the reminders of all the bad that happened within those four walls, from my dad leaving, to my ma struggling, to having to live and sleep in the box I share with my brothers, constantly wishing for an out.

But now I run to the bad for comfort.

I walk out of the school, along the polished streets and past perfect homes until I reach the unpolished parts of town, where I can't afford to look down any more.

I cross the road and put my hood up, not wanting the boys in front of Dre's place to see me again. A lot of the pain and bruising from Friday has subsided. My eye still kills, but I can manage – plus I've been somewhat high on the pain meds Ma got from work. They numb everything.

Everything but Dre.

They can't distract or make me unlive Dre breaking up with me. It doesn't feel like we broke up – it feels like I've been banished. Like we can't be friends any more. I don't even need to kiss him or love him if he doesn't want me to, I just need to be his friend. But even that's not an option.

The pain meds can't stop me from caring about what people are saying in school either. What Aces will say next about me, and what it might do to my future.

A figure passes me and I look up to see a familiar shaved head, pink skin and a green backpack.

"Jack?" I say loudly, but he ignores me and crosses the street. I watch him fist bump one of Dre's boys, putting his backpack down as he leans against the parked car with them. I'd messaged him, asked if he wanted to walk home together. He didn't reply.

Jack never wanted to associate with them when I did, and now he does.

My phone beeps.

Want to hang out? – T

I haven't heard from Terrell since Friday night, when he asked if I was okay.

I look at Jack, who's taken a joint from one of the guys now, his eyes crinkled from laughing too hard at a joke one of them must have told. He turns, focusing on me. I pause, rooted to the ground as a chilling smile creeps onto his face, joint hanging from his lips. I think back to the message about him doing drugs and hanging out with Dre's boys, and how little Jack seemed to care. Maybe…it wasn't *him* Aces wanted to get a reaction out of.

What more does Aces want from me? I don't get it. They've successfully pushed away my only two friends, outed me at school and made me lose the only way I could get some extra money for Ma. And for what? Surely there's nothing else left? I'm just going to keep my head down, concentrate on my music and get the hell out of here.

I pull my focus away from Jack's face, texting Terrell back. Sure, I'm on my way.

I have a good memory. People, places, things. That's why I do well on exams. I got a really high score on my SATs, which I don't think proves whether or not I'm smart, just that I can remember a lot of basic shit, like how to get to Terrell's place. But apparently not the important things like *who* Terrell is. And when I kissed him.

His house is white, with a bright red door and 63 large at the top.

It has a white picket fence, but some of it has fallen over, and each panel is cracked and chipped.

There's a creak of hinges, followed by the slam of wood. I look up and Terrell is there, huge smile, circular eyeglasses, and medium dreads pulled back.

"You look tired," he tells me as I walk in and we go down his short hallway – wallpaper dark green, carpeted floors black – and straight into his living room. I didn't really get a good look at Terrell's place when I came here a few days ago. First thing I notice are the shelves; brown wood, filled with well-worn books and magazines. There's a bulky old TV in the centre, placed on top of a DVD player with DVDs cramming the little shelf space beneath.

"School's tiring," I say, still scanning the room.

Going to Niveus has afforded me the unwanted knowledge of what is good – *expensive* – and what is not. Despite the fact that the curtains are old and dark, the dining table and wooden chairs are scratched and worn, and nothing in here is remotely expensive, it feels like it is. It's nice and homey.

Nicer than I'm used to.

Terrell takes a seat on the green armchair and I settle on the bigger sofa. He watches me, and under his gaze I feel naked.

"Tell me about it?" he asks, and the way he does almost makes me think that he actually cares. People normally say this to further the conversation, not because they really care, but his face looks interested in my answer. Today was particularly crappy, though. Mr Taylor wasn't in, so I couldn't use the music rooms outside of class time.

"I don't like complaining about school usually, because I guess I'm lucky to even go there. I just..." I pause, trying to think whether it's even worth going into. I usually block out the bad and move on. I never really talk things through with people, just kind of hope things'll get better on their own, which they often don't.

"There're a lot of rumours spreading about me," I start.

Terrell nods. I wonder if he's heard them too, like Dre has. Or seen the pictures, or the video.

"Do you know who's spreading them? Why they might be doing it?"

I shrug. "No clue."

He nods again. We sit in silence, the conversation complete.

"How's music for you these days?" he asks, which reminds me that I'm meant to know who Terrell is.

"I'm applying to a few decent colleges for composition," I tell him.

He perks up, interested again.

"Like?"

I hesitate. "Juilliard is my first choice. And I'm trying to go for one of the scholarships."

He whistles. "That's tough."

I nod. "Yeah, it is, but my teacher, Mr Taylor, is helping me. He went there."

Terrell smiles at me. "Got a piece you're working on?"

"There's this one I'm going to send in for the audition, but I keep getting stuck on it. It was so clear in my mind over the summer."

I think everything going on at school is blocking the flow.

"Maybe you need another pair of ears on it," Terrell suggests. When I don't say anything, he pulls at his ears and smiles. "My ears are always available."

He lets go of them and I realize how big they are. It's kind of endearing.

Only Mr Taylor and Dre have really heard my piece, and Dre only did because I was lying next to him and started humming the tune.

I blink hard, erasing the memory.

"Thanks. That would be great."

There is a silence, where Terrell just stares at me like he's waiting for me to say something. It makes me nervous. I look around his living room again.

What if he's seen the video, a voice whispers. What difference would it make if he has? He's still talking to me, isn't he? Doesn't think I'm a burden because of it, like everyone else. I need to stop thinking about these possibilities.

"And you? What are you planning on doing after high school?" I ask, feeling really hot.

"Nothing too interesting, probably gonna try to find a job."

I haven't heard a response like that in so long. I used to think like that too.

"In an ideal world I'd maybe go to college." He shrugs. "The world's not ideal, though."

I nod, feeling awkward and privileged all of a sudden, even though I'm really not. I'm counting on scholarships, and if I don't get one then that's it for me and college.

"Want to watch a movie?" Terrell asks, now up from the chair, leaning beside his TV.

"Sure, I don't mind anything." All I watch are kid films because of my brothers. I stopped watching movies when I realized they were a magic trick. In real life, prom isn't the best night of your life. In real life, your first time is with a boy called Scotty in the back of his dad's Rolls-Royce.

In real life, parents aren't together. Not even close. In real life your dad, the only person who'd probably get your music struggles, is behind bars.

Terrell looks back at me. "*White Chicks* it is."

He puts the disc in, then stands, his big ears poking out, before climbing over the coffee table and taking a seat next to me, closer than I was expecting. I can smell his cologne; fruity but at the same time not. It's a hard scent to figure out.

"Ever watched this before?"

I shake my head.

"It's funny, one of my favourites."

My palms are sweaty. "I'll probably like it then, I'm quite easy."

Terrell laughs. "Easy, huh?"

My face burns.

"Didn't mean it like that," I say, smiling, leaning back now.

"Sure, either meaning is good for me."

I raise an eyebrow but say nothing.

I hadn't given it proper thought before, but now I can't stop thinking about it: the fact that Terrell seems to be open about his sexuality and so casual about it. It's not something you can be casual about around here.

The way he told me we'd kissed – that I was his first kiss – was so casual too. And weird. I know I couldn't have kissed Terrell. I'd remember something like that, especially in middle school. I always remember kisses because they always mean something.

My first girl-kiss was with Rhonda White in third grade. She was also my first girlfriend, and I really liked her. I thought her Afro was pretty cool. She ended up dumping me for some fifth grader, which I got completely. There were no hard feelings.

My first boy-kiss though was Scotty, and that wasn't until the end of freshman year, when I finally figured myself out. My first everything was with Scotty really. I don't regret it, though. I don't like regretting things, even things with bad endings.

A weight on my foot pulls me out of my thoughts, and I look down, jumping back when I see a tiny ball of fur with claws and a tail.

"Is that a rat?!" I shout, bringing my feet up onto the couch, looking away from whatever it was that violated my foot.

"That's Bullshit—"

"I felt something!"

Terrell looks amused by my discomfort.

"Yeah, I know." He bends over and lifts something up onto his lap. "It was my cat, Bullshit. Didn't know he was in here. Sorr—"

"Who the fuck names their cat Bullshit?" I ask, face warm as I try to distract from how much I embarrassed myself just now. The cat sits on Terrell's thighs, staring up at me with its honey-coloured eyes. It meows casually, like it didn't just give me a mini heart attack.

Terrell shrugs. "The name suits him."

He looks serious, stroking the cat with one hand. It's so small it could probably fit in Terrell's palm.

"Any more surprise pets you want to warn me about?" I ask, placing my feet on the floor again.

Terrell shakes his head. "What? You don't like animals?"

"They're…" I look at Bullshit, who stares back at me like he couldn't care less about my existence. He meows again. "…okay, I guess."

Bullshit hops off Terrell suddenly, and I jump again.

"I think you could grow to like him," he tells me, as the cat saunters off. I swear I see a smirk on its furry face.

Bullshit.

TUESDAY

The stares aren't as annoying as they usually are when I enter school. But that could also be because all the lights are off.

In fact, the majority of students hardly seem to notice me as I walk through the hallway. Most are distracted by the lack of light, and others are focused on Chiamaka standing next to my locker. She's holding this ugly green bag and a Starbucks cup, with her straight brown hair pushed back by a matching green headband.

When I get to her, the focus shifts to me. My heartbeat increases but I pull my shoulders back, trying to show them they can't get to me.

"Can I help you?" I ask Chiamaka, who still hasn't moved. The overhead lights suddenly blink back on. Chiamaka winces when she sees my face properly in the light. I can imagine how my face looks, what with all the bruising.

"I just wanted to tell you that I told Headmaster Ward about Aces and their lies and practical jokes...so this should all be over soon," she says quietly.

She looks up at me, her deep brown eyes filled with certainty.

I can't help but laugh. I haven't heard this much crap in such a long time.

"You think Headmaster Ward is really gonna help us?" I ask, because I'm genuinely perplexed. She looks at me strangely, and I think it's because I can't stop smiling.

"Yes, of course he will."

"Wow. Okay."

She shakes her head. "He only wants what's best for the student body, you'll see that in the prefect meeting today."

I've been trying not to think about that meeting. It means more time trapped in Caucasian-ville.

"Okay, Chiamaka," I say, purposely looking between her body and my locker, hoping she'll get the hint and move.

She stays staring at me for a while – I swear there's a flash of something I'd describe as almost human behind her eyes. Then she finally moves to go.

"Wait," I say.

She turns back. "What?"

"I think you need to be careful," I say, and I'm not sure

why. I just don't like how trusting she is of Headmaster Ward. This is the same guy who looks like he dismembers cats for fun.

"I don't need protection. You think lies can affect me, Richards?"

I think we both know they aren't lies.

Her eyes plead with me.

I shake my head instead. She looks relieved, probably because I didn't challenge that.

She gives me a tight smile. "Good. I think I've wasted enough time talking to you now. Goodbye."

And then she's gone.

I finally open my locker, rummaging through all my crap to find my notepad for AP English and my music sheets. I notice the glimmer of something at the back, purple and silver.

A USB stick?

I lift it out, noticing that it is taped to the back of a playing card. I flip it around. The Ace of Spades.

I look around the hallway as the crowd thins. I think the first warning bell has already gone off. Turning the card back round, I see the edge of a word peeking out from behind the USB. I rip off the flash drive, revealing a handwritten message.

Everything is on here — Aces

The second warning bell startles me, and I throw the

USB and card into my blazer pocket, before grabbing my sheets and book, and heading to registration.

As soon as the bell rings for lunch, I head to the library, an internal chain of what-ifs swirling through my thoughts as I quickly grab a free computer. I switch it on, then plug the USB in. The library is semi-crowded, with students mostly sitting around tables in the centre or getting on with their own work. Even though I picked a seat in the corner where no one can see my screen, I worry that someone somewhere is watching me, because they always seem to be lately. Who knows what might be on here?

I sigh, anxiously waiting for the USB to load, leg bouncing up and down.

I could just pull it out. I don't have a gun pointed at my head. There's no need for me to be scared.

It loads. My muscles tense up.

I click before I can overthink it.

There is only one folder: The Life and Crimes of Chiamaka Adebayo.

What the...

I let the cursor hover over the file.

Why do I feel guilty? Chiamaka and I aren't friends. I owe her nothing. In fact, she and I are the furthest away from *friendly* that you can get – if you discount earlier. We are basically strangers.

I click again and the screen flickers as a bunch of subfiles, all with different labels, descend the page. They are all time-stamped to last night.

One labelled *Two-timer* grabs my attention. I double click, ignoring the guilt. It's a picture of Chiamaka and that guy she's always with, kissing at some party. It's probably from when she was dating Scotty, which would explain the label. I got the message about her and some girl's boyfriend too.

She seems to have a thing for other people's boyfriends.

My cursor hovers over the other files, but my moral compass is screaming at me to stop.

I wonder if Aces sent files on us to everyone else they've spoken about. Does that mean Jack, Scotty, Chiamaka and her friend have a file on me? But then why don't I have a Scotty or Jack file?

My chest is heavy; dragging and achy. *Why us?* Chiamaka and me. We're at the centre of this, even if other people have been pulled in. I mean, there is the obvious thing… I catch a glimpse of my dark skin in the monitor, staring it down like it's gonna jump out at me. I shake my head. I've gone to this school for years, and I've never had anyone bother me before. Unlike in my middle school where I was everyone's favourite punching bag, because apparently my whole essence screams *gay easy target*. Even when I tried to hide it from everyone and myself.

I look at the list of files again, scrolling a little, stopping when I see one labelled *Murderer*.

What? I look at it closely, moving forward in my seat. A

murderer? Head Prefect and professional teachers'-ass-kisser, a killer?

If this is true, could I be implicated if I click on the file? Is that Aces's angle here? I shakily move away, closing the window instead.

I glance around the library. People are still lost in their own worlds, so unaware of the chaos in mine. I pull the USB out of the port, watching the files disappear from the screen one by one.

Who is Aces and what do they want? They're following me; getting into my neighbourhood, my home, my mind.

And I don't know how to stop it.

I have been watching the clock since I entered the meeting room after school.

I've managed not to say a word so far, thankful that the other prefects in here are such smart-asses that they take up most of the discussion with their thoughts and opinions.

We, or more like *they*, are discussing the legendary Senior Snowflake Charity Ball happening in two weeks. It's legendary because non-seniors are always told about the pranks pulled off at the ball. For most of the seniors, their biggest worries are what dress or suit to wear, and who they're going to prank – or be pranked by. All I can think about now is that the ball would be the perfect time for Aces to do something. The ball is compulsory – part of "Niveus's special school spirit", but I'm considering faking a serious illness.

Headmaster Ward looks at me all of a sudden, as if he can read my thoughts.

"Bringing the meeting to an end with a final point, we'll be closing parts of the school one day in the coming weeks to do a basic check of the electricity networks and facilities in the building. It was meant to be done over the summer, but wasn't, so this may affect events such as the homecoming football match. We will be discussing alternate locations for the match in the next meeting.

"Cecelia, thank you for taking the minutes. You're free to go. Can Devon and Chiamaka stay behind, please." Ward's eyes stay on mine as he drags out each syllable, every word bursting from his mouth like dark bubbles.

Chiamaka and I glance at each other. She has a small *I told you so* smile on her face.

I watch the other prefects leave. Headmaster Ward locks the door sharply behind them. Why does he have to do that?

He turns back.

"We have found the so-called 'Aces', if you will," he says.

What?

My heart jumps out from my chest.

Chiamaka sits up. "Thank you for looking into this, sir. Who are they?"

Ward says nothing at first. "Chiamaka," he starts, voice low. "When you came to me, I thought it was out of genuine concern. But your ill sabotage of each other proves to me that you are not serious and that you do not deserve your titles as Senior Prefect and Head Prefect."

The fuck?

I'm so confused. Is he trying to say that we did this to each other?

Chiamaka looks horrified.

"What?" she says.

He looks so bored.

"It has been brought to my attention that you have both been collecting defamatory information about each other. Information I discovered earlier today while looking through your personal school accounts. We do not tolerate this kind of uncivilized behaviour at Niveus and so, Devon, I'm revoking your badge for three weeks, since you have no prior record and good grades. You, Chiamaka, on the other hand, since this is your second misdemeanour this week alone, I'm afraid I will have to revoke your badge until further notice. You will both have detention every day after school – also until further notice – and that *will* go on your record—"

Shit.

"I'm not behind this, Headmaster—" Chiamaka starts.

"Quiet!" Ward shouts, which freaks me out because his voice changes completely.

"Detention starts tomorrow at four – please be prompt. You may leave."

Chiamaka looks sick.

I feel anger bubbling inside. Juilliard will see this and there's nothing I can do about it because Ward won't even let us defend ourselves. He's made his mind up, we're guilty. I just want to get home.

I take my backpack, unlock the door and walk out. Hands on my back push me forward and I turn quickly.

"So it was you!" Chiamaka shouts, eyes glassy.

"Chiamaka—"

"What type of lowlife spends their time trying to ruin—"

"*Chiamaka*—"

"This is going to go on my record, then Yale won't accept me, and I will be stuck at some community college where my efforts won't even matter, and I won't be able to go to med school." Tears are spilling down her face now.

I feel a pang in my chest. Remorse?

"I didn't do it," I tell her calmly.

She looks at me in disbelief.

"Why would I leak my own sex tape, call myself a drug dealer or out myself? Or bother you, for that matter? We don't even talk. How do I know you're not behind this?"

She says nothing, just stares at me as I stare back. I think it's the longest we have ever really looked at each other, and I'm not sure how long it lasts but it's long enough to be significant. Her face is round, pretty and wet. She's crying. Why is she crying?

I always assumed people like Chiamaka – people with money – could buy their way into college. Why is she acting like that is not an option? And even without college, she'll have a trust fund. They always do.

I watch her shoulders, which shudder like a cold breeze has passed through her. She reaches into her pocket and pulls out a red USB.

"Did you get one of these too?"

Why does it feel like I'm in a horror film?

"Yeah, I did," I say.

She looks up at the ceiling, wiping her face.

"Follow me," she says, walking down the hallway. I follow. The heels of her shoes click loudly against the marble, while mine squeak after each step. Every sound feels deafening. We finally turn into one of the smaller libraries.

She sits on a chair in front of one of the computers and I watch her type in her school login, throwing me a look when I'm still watching as she types her password in.

I sigh to myself. *Why would I want her password?*

She plugs the USB in.

"I didn't get to look at your file much since I had class, but it had a lot of folders. Maybe if you see them you can anticipate and prepare before they strike, or maybe we can show Headmaster Ward these with the notes—"

"So after he blamed us for doing this to each other, you seriously want to trust him again to catch the real culprits?"

Chiamaka ignores me, focusing on the screen instead. The computer makes a loud sound and the message *USB NOT RECOGNIZED* appears.

She takes it out and puts it back in. The same thing happens.

I think with everything going on and the rate at which my heart has been going, it seems natural causes could very well be the reason for my death.

"Give me yours," she says, holding her hand out. I take my bag off and reach inside, rummaging through books and papers, before feeling the cold metal of the USB. I grab it and give it to her.

She plugs mine in and it does the same.

"No no no no no!" I hear her mutter.

She hits the computer then puts her face in her hands.

"The USBs were a set-up," she says. "Aces planted them on us. There must be something in the coding that destroys the files once they've been viewed."

I swallow. "Why give us the information?"

"To confuse us? Or, I don't know, make us scared of what the other person has seen..." She squints at me a little, like she's searching my mind for what I saw.

I think back to the file labelled *Murderer*. I wonder if that has anything to do with it.

She stands, shutting the computer down. "I don't know why, or how, but..."

She pauses, lowering her voice now. "I think someone is trying to get us expelled."

"Scotty and Jack too," I add.

Chiamaka looks confused.

"Who's Jack?"

"The other guy Aces blasted," I say as I get my phone out, showing her the message. "Jack McConnel."

She shakes her head. "I didn't get that. I don't think anyone I know got that either."

That doesn't make sense... Thinking back, I don't remember there being the usual sea of text alerts when I got the message. Was I the only person who did? Why?

"So what do we do? How do we not get expelled?" I ask her. This is starting to feel *very* real. Even more real than before.

"I don't know." Chiamaka pinches her nose and sighs. "I need to go home and think. I'll be in touch," she says, then she moves past me and disappears through the dark-oak double doors, leaving me here with my thoughts.

Alone.

PART TWO:
X MARKS THE SPOT

16

TUESDAY

It's unexpected – Belle approaching me on my walk home.

I do a lot of that – walking. Since the accident, I haven't been able to drive without having a full-blown panic attack. It's funny; last year I begged my parents for a car, and now I can't even bring myself to drive it.

"Hi," she says, startling me out of my depressing thoughts about the USB I found in my locker and Ward taking my badge.

I don't say anything to her at first, because I feel like I'm hallucinating her being here. Why would she be talking to me? I extend my hand slightly, reaching out to touch her, make sure she's real. But I stop myself, in case she *is* real and thinks I'm weird for doing that.

"Hello," I say back.

"I was a bit harsh to you yesterday… I'm sorry," she says – which is even weirder, because it should be me apologizing. I mean, I did sleep with her boyfriend and then lie about it, even if I didn't know they were going out when Jamie and I were still sneaking around.

"I came to ask about your side of the story. I always told

myself that if there was 'another woman', I wouldn't do the basic thing and fight the girl and not the guy, but that's exactly what I did."

Belle's cheeks are dusted pink from the cold, her blonde curls trapped beneath a grey beret. Her eyes look so open and kind, but I can't help feeling strange about this. Why does she suddenly want to talk to me after everything? Especially now that someone is trying to get me kicked out, and *especially* since Belle is also applying to Yale, which, in the entire history of our school, has only accepted one applicant each year. I know it sounds stalkerish but I did some digging on my Yale competition months ago – I wasn't being creepy or anything, I just needed to know who I'm up against.

"Truthfully…" I start, stopping to think about whether telling her anything would make matters worse. "I did like Jamie, and it's silly because it should have been clear to me that it was just sex—"

Okay, way too truthful, reel it in a little.

"But he was my best friend. I should have known he didn't like me like that."

Belle shakes her head. "Then why would he sleep with you? I want to believe that this is one-sided and blame you, but I can't."

I don't know what she wants me to say.

"You should blame me and move on. It's easier that way. I can't explain anything Jamie ever does."

I try walking ahead but she catches up to me.

"Who initiated things between you two?"

"He did," I say, blinking fast. "But we both did it, and I wanted to. I can't tell you what his reasons were, but I wanted to be with him, so why would I say no? I felt like things could work out for us somehow...then he tells me he's with you now and that it meant nothing and I feel like I mean nothing and I—" Once I start I can't stop. There's a pressure in my chest, like I have had this weight here for ever. "That's just who Jamie is."

Belle looks at me, shocked.

"Jamie's a dickhead," she says.

I don't know why my first instinct is to defend him, but admitting all that out loud makes me stop and think.

I never really question whether Jamie doing bad things makes him a bad person. Everyone does bad things sometimes, makes poor choices. I know that more than anyone.

"He is," I say.

"I broke up with him," she says.

I'm shocked. She doesn't even look regretful.

"Why?"

"Because he's a dickhead."

There's a smile she's holding back, I can tell.

"And I had a gut feeling about this whole thing, so I ended it." She pauses, her hesitation making the atmosphere awkward. "I know it's weird...but I wanted to be your friend, Chiamaka. The whole time I was dating him, even... Except it seemed like you hated me – and I guess I know why – but as messed up as this is, you seem nicer than people say you are. Besides, we're both too good for Jamie," she says.

I say nothing. I do nothing. Don't even breathe. Belle's words are so confusing. One moment she's angry at me, the next she wants to be friends.

Jamie has been my only "real" friend in high school. Everyone else has been a chess piece in this popularity game. I don't know if I even want friends; all they seem to do is hurt you.

Belle is looking at me with expectation in her blue eyes, her face making my heart beat fast as I look away.

We *are* better than him.

"You're wrong in thinking I'm nice, by the way. Everyone was right. I am a bitch," I tell her which only makes her smile even more.

"I guess we all are sometimes."

My arms and legs are so cold, and the wind makes it worse. I really just want to go home.

I look back at her. The meeting is still weighing on my mind, as well as Aces.

"I was going to go home and watch Project Runway... if you want to join?" I ask, like my life isn't on the verge of collapse.

She nods. "I'd like that."

As we walk on, I think about the USBs again. I asked a tech guy I know about getting into Niveus's CCTV to look at who planted the USBs this morning, as well as tracking down the origin of Aces's blasts. Maybe I could ask him to recover the files from the USBs too, in which case I'll need to bring Devon into my plans. I can't have Aces taking any more from me – the deeper they dig, the harder it will be to come back.

And I refuse to let them bury me.

17

DEVON

WEDNESDAY

"Your school looks like Buckingham Palace," Terrell says, from the seat on his bright yellow bike.

I've finished with today's detention, after a whole hour scraping gum off the tables in a random classroom, alone. I think Ward separated Chiamaka and me on purpose. I'm not sure why. Maybe he thought we'd try to do more damage to each other, that I'd slit her throat with the edge of the scraper or something.

Ward was so quick to blame us. Make us out to be delinquents. If anything, I'd stab him first, before I'd even think of doing anything to Chiamaka. In reality though, someone like Ward could easily crush me like a bug. I can't fight to save my life. Not that he'd believe me if I told him that.

When I finally walked out of Niveus, hands raw and achy, Terrell was there, waiting for me outside. He'd texted me earlier with a mysterious message: I need to tell you something.

And now here we are; I'm on one of the swings and he's seated on his bike. I walked and he pedalled all the way to a park nearby. I avoid the big park in my neighbourhood, knowing that Dre and his friends hang there sometimes. My heart squeezes at the thought of Dre.

"Nothing royal about it, though," I say.

"Isn't it hella white and full of rich people? Sounds a lot like a palace to me." His dimples appear, which force me to smile back. I guess he has a point. Niveus is like this weird love child between America and England, from us calling our principal, "headmaster", to saying "registration" instead of homeroom, to the way the building looks. When I first came here, I thought it was really strange. It took some getting used to.

"Apart from that, it's hell."

"Are people still talking about you?"

I nod. "It's all because of Aces. People at school don't normally focus on me."

Terrell's eyebrows raise. "Aces?"

I forget Aces doesn't mean anything to anyone outside of Niveus.

"This anonymous texter. They've been bothering me and some girl, Chiamaka, a lot, spreading rumours about us."

Terrell nods to himself, like he's trying to figure something out.

"Is this Chikkaka girl Black too?" he asks. I want to laugh, but I stop myself. Why do I feel so loyal to her this week? It's pissing me off.

"Yeah."

I don't say anything else at first, thinking back to my

thoughts in the library about being Black and that maybe having something to do with it.

"And they only bother you guys?"

I nod slowly, hoping he doesn't go there – to the race thing.

Terrell shakes his head, squinting at me. "Are you guys blind or what?"

I sigh, turning away a little.

"What?"

"Are there any other Black people at your school?"

I suspect his question is more rhetorical than not, but I still shake my head.

"So, you go to a white school, in the white part of town, where bad things are happening to the *only* Black students…" he starts, like he's decoding a really complex math problem.

I want to interject and debunk his theory, but I can't bring myself to speak. I shiver as a gust of wind blows my way.

"I think it's racism." Terrell looks at me straight.

"Not all of them are bad, Terrell." And it's true. I may not be friends with any of the Niveus students, but most of them have been nice enough over the years.

He climbs off his bike and takes a seat on the swing next to me.

"Name three good people there, and I don't mean decent, I mean really good."

I'm not that social, so my circle really only ever included myself and Jack at school. Besides him, everyone else is okay – decent. Good. No, everyone else is good.

"My music teacher – Mr Taylor, Jack, and this guy, Daniel."

"Jack, as in the friend who abandoned you?"

I forgot I texted Terrell about that.

"He's from around our area, has a family to think about. He's just protecting himself while all those texts come out. They can hurt him too." And I've known Jack practically my entire life. If he was racist, why would he be my friend or pretend to care about me? It doesn't make any sense.

Terrell smiles at that. "I sense that it has nothing to do with his family."

What does he mean by that?

"Who's Daniel?" he continues, like he's not convinced by what I'm saying.

"This popular guy at school, he's weird and annoying but nice I guess."

"And Mr Taylor?"

I'm confident in him as an example of a good white person I know.

"He's the best music teacher I've ever had. Lets me stay in the practice room all day making music, and he really wants me to get into Juilliard."

"Does he now?" Terrell asks, voice dripping with sarcasm.

"Yeah."

He nods. "Okay, fair enough."

"You sound like you don't believe it."

He shrugs, nudging me. "I don't trust white people like

you do. I obviously don't think they are all murderers, but I think they are all racist."

"All?" I say, eyebrows raised.

"It sounds wild, I know, but racism is a spectrum and they all participate in it in some way. They don't all have white hoods or call us mean things, I know that. But racism isn't just about that – it's not about being nice or mean. Or good versus bad. It's bigger than that. We're all in this bubble being affected by the past. The moment they decided they got to be white and have all the power and we got to be Black and be at the bottom, everything changed. If we can't talk about it honestly, and I mean really talk about it, then what's the point? I read some Malcolm X last year, and I agree with him. Some might even treat you good, like an owner might treat a pet."

"That's wild," I say.

"Yeah, it is. I think anyone can be nice, but it's not about being nice. You can't escape a history like that and not be affected. Us Blacks, we start hating ourselves, and them whites start thinking they're all better than us. Even if they aren't thinking it constantly, it's in there somewhere."

I find myself smiling a little. He looks like one of those eccentric scientists after they explain a theory. His hair is wild too, sticking up in all directions. I don't know if I fully agree with him. I don't know if I *want* to fully agree with him. It's a sad way to look at things.

"You sound like someone who should go to college," I tell him. He looks like he'd major in politics or some other social science, writing articles and pissing people off whenever he speaks.

"World's not ideal," he reminds me.

"And if it was?" I ask, turning on the swing to look at him now.

"If it was, a lot of shit would be different." He looks at me. "I might go to college, major in business or something. I might do well and get out of here. I might do dangerous things like kiss boys I like and do all the things I've always wanted to do. But the world isn't ideal, so why poison my mind with thoughts that won't make a difference?"

I get that. Dreaming can be dangerous. It's hard to dream in a neighbourhood like ours. Ma always told me to dream, though, that the sky was my limit. I'm scared to dream *too* high in case I end up falling flat on my face. But I still do it.

It hurts to dream, but I dream regardless.

Ma has tried to create this ideal world for me. Despite my scholarship, she's still spending so much on this school, hoping a good college takes a chance on me. But what if none of that happens? What if I fail? Or get expelled? What if Aces ruins everything?

What if I just get stuck here, disappointing her, wasting her time and money, for nothing?

Terrell's hands are on my shoulders, and then they wrap around me as I try to breathe.

"S-sorry, was just overthinking… Worried about my ma and everything," I say, wiping my eyes.

"Is she okay?"

I nod. "I just worry about not getting into college, her wasting her money on me for nothing."

"It's not wasted on you, no matter what happens. I get worrying about money though. My sister's sick right now and money's tight. We can't help her with medical bills, so I get it. But don't let it take up too much space or make you feel sad."

His sister is sick?

"I'm sorry about your sister."

Terrell looks away. "No need to be sorry. Let's do something else."

I nod, taken aback by his abruptness. I should ask him if he's okay. I feel like all I do is talk about myself, never check to see if anything is bothering him. I need to be a better friend to Terrell, he's been so nice to me. But before I can say anything more, he's up and running towards the jungle gym. I push myself off the swing, which creaks as I stand, and follow him. Terrell climbs the neon green steps and crawls into the dark purple tube on top and doesn't come out.

I wait...

...and I wait.

What if he's stuck?

I survey the tube again. He seemed to fit fine when he was going in...

"Terrell?" I call out.

No reply.

I tiptoe, trying to see into the tube, but it curves up, blocking my vision. I sigh, moving to climb the steps slowly.

My body still hasn't fully recovered from when those boys beat me up, plus I'm pretty sure this was made for children and I don't want Ma to be charged money she doesn't have for my senselessness if I break it. When I get to the top, I lean into the tube and see Terrell in there, seated with his head ducked like he was waiting for me.

"Took you long enough," he says.

So, he *was* waiting for me.

"I'm not coming in there," I tell him, trying to sound serious despite the smile I'm holding back.

"Okay, I'll just sit in here until you do."

"That's cool with me."

He stares at me and me at him. I sit down, resting my back against the pole by the steps.

"It's pretty cold out," he says.

"Really? I can't feel it."

"Sure about that?"

"Very sure."

"Okay, if you're *very sure*."

He moves towards the entrance of the tube, climbing out and sitting on the slightly-lifted entryway.

"I think I can convince you to come inside," he tells me, running his hand over his miniature dreads.

I raise my eyebrows at his confidence.

"How?"

He smiles at me, eyes crinkling in the corners and dimples defined as he reaches into his jeans pocket, then takes his hand out with his fist closed.

"Come closer and I'll show you what's in my hand. Trust me, you'll come in when you see it."

I'm not sure what could convince me to do that, but I move forward, staring at the gaps in between his fingers, hoping to see a glimpse of whatever is hidden there.

"I'm closer, open it."

He looks ready to laugh.

I watch his hand again as it opens, revealing...nothing.

I stare at his empty palm and then back up at him.

"You're so full of shit," I say, which only makes his grin wider.

"And rice," he says, before moving back into the tube.

I pretend to hesitate before following him in, sitting closer to the entrance, still a bit worried I'll break it.

It's not as dark in the tube as I thought it would be, but it is smaller than I expected. I have to slide down slightly in order to fit.

Terrell, on the other hand, has to duck, seeing as he's taller. When I'm in, he moves closer to me, hitting his head, which makes me snort.

There's a shimmer on his hoodie that catches my eye. A metallic green alien print in the middle.

It's weird, the alien kind of looks like him.

"Told you I'd convince you to come in," he says in a low voice.

"I came in because I wanted to," I say, which isn't entirely true. A part of me probably likes being in such close proximity to Terrell. Besides, he was right, it was kind of cold outside the tube.

"Who's full of shit now?" he says.

"Still you," I tell him, shivering again.

We fall into a comfortable silence. I try not to think about bad things, like Aces or college or Andre. I try not to think about how this time two weeks ago I wasn't worried about being kicked out of school. I was probably at Dre's. Happy. Instead I block those thoughts. I think I've cried in front of Terrell one too many times today.

I glance at him. He's resting his chin on one of his knees now, looking up at me. When he catches me staring, he smiles.

"Are you cold?" he asks.

"Kind of," I finally admit.

He sits up, banging his head once again, which causes him to swear under his breath. I watch with warm cheeks as he pulls his hoodie off and tosses it to me.

"Wear this," he says.

I take the hoodie, pulling it on over my school shirt and tie. It's warm and comfortable, and feels like I have a big blanket wrapped around me.

"Thank you."

"No problem."

I move a little closer, away from the cold entrance.

"You know what's weird?" Terrell says softly.

"What?"

"I'm claustrophobic," he whispers.

I furrow my eyebrows together. "Then why did you want to come in here?"

"Didn't think it through," he says, looking a little anxious. I watch him lie back, sticking his head out the other end of the tube. It kind of reminds me of the way dogs stick their heads out of car windows.

"Freedom!" he says with an exaggerated tone.

Like earlier when I tried to ignore all the bad things, now I try to ignore the exposed skin on Terrell's torso. I focus on the ceiling of the tube.

Terrell decides he has had enough air and sits up, and I can focus on his face again. I notice some leaves stuck in his dreads and burst out laughing.

"You have leaves in your hair," I tell him.

He reaches up and tries to brush them off to no avail and so I reach forward and help.

"You're good now," I say, pulling away.

Terrell looks at me and I swallow. His eyes kind of remind me of the way Dre used to look at me just before we'd kiss or touch or do more than that. I feel myself placing my hand on Terrell's face, leaning in close. Something tells me to pull away, but then I feel Terrell wrap his arms around me and I ignore my brain and I kiss him.

I don't expect Terrell to kiss me back as quickly as he does, like he was waiting for it. For a few moments I forget that we are in this small purple tube – everything's quiet, I feel shaky, my heart won't stop ringing.

In the movies, kisses are all wrong. It's not fireworks or loud explosions. I used to think that every time I'd kiss a boy, the world would blow up. With Dre, kissing him felt like I was floating gently across a small cold lake. Right now it feels like I'm submerged in hot water, drifting deeper and deeper towards the bottom of the ocean.

I feel like I'm drowning, which is usually a feeling that makes me feel calm, but right now—

I pull away, breaking the kiss.

I need to leave.

I turn, scrambling out of the tube. I feel so warm, but I don't stop and think, I start climbing down the steps of the jungle gym but what I think is the last step isn't and I tumble to the ground.

"*Fuck,*" I whisper.

"Are you okay?" Terrell asks. I look back, a little horrified as his head pops out of the tube.

"I-I forgot something at home," I say, probably looking and sounding a mess. Terrell says something but I don't catch it.

I just run.

THURSDAY

Today, I don't care about the ogling. I need to get my composition sorted and finalized so that I can record it before the college applications open. I need it to be perfect. So perfect it wows them and they give me the scholarship I need to get out of here. I rush up the stairs to the music classroom.

"Mr Richards," Mr Taylor says as I enter, like he's been expecting me. Which he probably has since I'm in here a lot. It's weird, though, he usually calls me Devon.

"Morning, Mr Taylor... I just wanted to work on the final section of my admissions piece for a little while today."

"That's fine." He smiles. "Before you start, I just want to address a concern I have."

A concern?

"I don't normally listen to rumours...but I heard something and I wanted to check in with you."

Mr Taylor pauses, hesitant, like he's not sure how to phrase the next part of his sentence. My heart is in my throat. I swear if it's about Scotty I'll die—

"People are saying that you've been involved in drug transportation?" Mr Taylor looks confused, like I'm the last person he'd assume would be involved in any of that.

My stomach flips.

"I haven't," I lie.

He nods. "I just wanted to let you know – colleges are quite harsh about that sort of thing."

"I understand," I say, feeling sick. He looks at me like he can see straight through me and my lie. Then he turns away.

"Good, it would be a shame if something like that harmed your chances. We wouldn't want that to happen to one of our most promising students."

I nod, feeling bad for lying – but what other choice do I have?

I haven't dealt in nearly two weeks, for the obvious reason. The same reason that won't answer my calls or texts. I miss the familiar sound of the windchime text tone on my phone – I customized it so that I would know when it was Dre texting and not someone else. I push him back into the corner of my mind, and head to my usual seat at the back, blinking away the wetness in my eyes; I don't want to think about him right now.

I take a breath.

Then I close my eyes and drown.

Even though I didn't tell him to come, I'm not surprised to see Terrell outside Niveus after detention again. I didn't see Chiamaka today either, but I bet she rushed out as soon as she finished.

I knew I'd have to talk to Terrell about what happened yesterday in the park eventually, but I didn't think it would be *this* soon.

What am I even gonna say to him?

Sorry for kissing you – I'm not over Dre and I probably did that because I missed him.

I pretend to check a message on my phone, heart beating fast, knowing he's waiting for me to come out.

After a few moments of aimless scrolling, I pocket my phone and walk down the steps towards him.

I approach the gates and see him clearly, on his bike waiting, in a huge grey hoodie and sweats.

"Hey," he says, staring at me. I feel naked under his gaze. I think that's Terrell's superpower, making me nervous.

I wonder how long he's been out here.

Just as he says "Are you okay?", I'm saying "I'm sorry."

"For what?" he asks.

"Kissing you then running away. I just broke up with my boyfriend on Friday. I wasn't thinking and I probably made things really weird. I'm sorry."

Terrell looks at me, then down at his hoodie, which I'm wearing again. It's warmer than any hoodie I own.

"Can I walk you home?" he asks.

I wasn't expecting him to say that, but I nod anyway.

We start walking, Terrell dragging his yellow *wagon* along as I stroll next to him.

"Does he go to your school or something? The ex, I mean," Terrell asks suddenly.

"No." I look at Terrell now. "He's just a guy from our neighbourhood."

"What's his name? I might know him."

I hesitate. "Andre Johnson."

Terrell goes quiet again.

"So, he was the one who told them to do that to you?"

I shake my head.

"He got angry because the messages Aces was sending were making people start to suspect things about us, so he broke up with me."

"You don't deserve to be treated like that."

"I doubt Dre told them to."

Terrell shakes his head. "And so what if he didn't. Did he check on you?"

"It's not easy for him, he's had a hard life," I say, even though I doubt it'll make a difference in Terrell's mind.

"We've all had fucking hard lives – doesn't mean I'm gonna be an asshole about it."

"He has a boss who'd hurt him—"

"So if not him, you? Andre can sit there and be okay with them beating you, just because he doesn't want to deal with it himself – what a fucking pussy," Terrell says angrily.

"I've known him for years, okay? Maybe doing the right thing is easy for others, but he's always messing up and regretting it later. I don't want to be that person who makes excuses for people's shitty behaviour, but we all make bad decisions."

I don't want to talk about this any more. Talking about Dre hurts too much right now, like my heart's been stung by a wasp.

Terrell looks at me as if I'm unstable.

Then he looks away. "Has he texted you since?"

That question feels more rhetorical than anything. I haven't heard windchimes for days.

"Yes," I lie.

"That's good then."

I nod.

"Think you're gonna get back together?" he asks, his face a little pained.

I've been asking myself the same question. Dre seemed

pretty serious about not wanting to date me any more. I swallow the lump that knots in my throat.

"No, I don't think so. Andre's like family – I want to be his friend more than anything."

Andre and I have been friends since he was twelve and I was eleven. I've known him for almost seven years, though we only started dating last year. Before any of this, Andre was a friend, a really good one. On days like this I wish we'd just stayed friends, so that I could still speak to him and things weren't all broken and weird.

The silence grows a little awkward as we walk on. Terrell's probably thinking I'm pathetic.

"You know," he starts, "you're, like, *really* fast."

"What?"

He smiles, dimples appearing. "Yesterday, when you ran away from me. You should consider being an Olympic runner if you ever change your mind about music—"

I push him and he laughs.

"Shut up," I say, my face growing hotter.

"I'm going to start calling you Quick," Terrell says, looking very impressed with himself.

"Well I'm gonna start calling you Shit-talker," I reply.

"I'm cool with that."

We get to my place and Terrell walks me to my door. I feel bad for not inviting him in. I never invite anyone in.

I'm a bit embarrassed about the way my house looks inside, and scared he'll judge me even though I know he probably won't.

"Thanks for walking me home, and sorry again for yesterday." I say the last part quietly.

"I'm irresistible, so I get it," Terrell says.

"Sure," I say.

There's a pause and then he hugs me.

I don't think I've been hugged this much by a friend... ever. I have to admit, I like Terrell's goodbye hugs. They always feel nice and warm.

Later, when I'm in my room, as my brothers sleep and the world is quiet, I think about how nice it is to have someone who doesn't treat me like a burden.

I'd forgotten what that felt like.

FRIDAY

Last night, while I slept, the melody seized my dream and took over. It played on a loop until I woke up, jumped out of bed and rushed to school as fast as I could.

I finally know what my audition piece should sound like!

I'm so early that there are only a handful of people in the hallway as I rush in. I climb the stairs, pushing my way through the oak door of the music room. I look around the classroom. Mr Taylor hasn't even arrived yet, much to my sort-of relief – I really want to be alone right now, no distractions.

I sit at my desk, plug in the keyboard, watching it come alive with its usual zap sound, and then I close my eyes.

I decide not to use my headphones, since nobody else is in here.

I picture the sea, and the usual images filter through...

Me underwater... sinking...and then suddenly I'm on the beach, people are laughing and running across the sand. The sun is blinding, I run towards the water again to escape it. But bare arms trap me, holding me back from the sea. I struggle, but they won't budge, I turn to look at who it is—

My eyes flash open as I stumble off my chair, chest heaving. I look up and Jack is standing over me.

"What the fuck, Jack!"

"What the fuck? The fuck is I thought you were taking care of it?"

Taking care of what? Everything Jack had a problem with is solved. Dre already broke up with me, his brothers are safe. What the fuck is there to take care of? He doesn't even hang out with me any more.

"I did—"

"Taking care of it is laying low. Taking care of it is not fucking Terrell Mc-Creeper-son from middle school!"

I swear my heart stops beating.

I can't handle any more pictures or videos. I want to live my life without having to constantly look over my shoulder.

"You know Terrell?" I manage.

Jack shakes his head in disbelief at me.

"Of course I do. My brother told me he saw you guys

walking home together. Everyone knows Terrell's a fucking weirdo."

I didn't know he existed until last Friday.

My insides feel shaky and unstable. At least it's his brother telling him and not a school-wide blast about me.

"You do this to yourself, Devon. You do this all to yourself. We studied, we got into this place, we both had the chance to be *normal*. To leave middle-school habits in middle school – but nah. You come here, and you act as weird as Terrell. You deserve everything coming to you."

Jack moves back.

"Have a nice life, Devon," he spits.

Then he leaves.

I forget about trying to attempt the piece again, just stay seated on the ground and let my body do what it wants. I don't hold back, I don't shove things into corners or boxes. I can't any more.

I think about Ma and how she's struggling and how I'm so fucking helpless. How I need to do well and get a job and get a scholarship and get into college. I think about Dre and how he said he loved me then dumped me, like love doesn't mean anything. I think about how I love him so much it hurts, and how I can't make him drop everything for me like I would for him.

I think about Jack and how – despite the fact that we've been best friends for years, done everything together; despite the fact that I was there for him when he lost his parents, like so many of us do; despite the fact that he told me he'd always have my back when they took my dad away – as much as he doesn't want to admit it, he's always hated this part of me.

I remember when I first told Jack I liked guys, and the pained expression on his face. I remember the way he handed me his game controller and said he needed to go and check on the burgers on the grill. I remember feeling so shitty, but taking the controller and finishing the level he was on and not bringing it up again. Jack hated it when I started dating Scotty. He was never happy, and I told myself it was because Scotty was a dick, not because he *had* a dick. Jack would "joke" about girls that he knew with short haircuts and muscled arms who I could date, like who I'm attracted to is as trivial as appearance. And he would flinch when I spoke about Dre.

And on top of everything, there's Aces – this person, or people, hell-bent on ruining my life.

I feel so lost.

Maybe I'm just cursed or broken… Maybe this is unfixable.

I keep sniffing as my nose blocks. God, I hate crying. I can't breathe, and the more I gasp, the more tears fall, the more my chest hurts and squeezes.

The more I want to leave this place and never come back.

18

CHIAMAKA

FRIDAY

In all my years of school I've never gotten detention before. Now somehow I'm on my third.

Sure, I've done things that could have resulted in one, but I've never been caught for anything.

And now here I am, in the year it matters most, no longer Head Prefect and standing next to Richards, being given our labour tools.

Usually I don't see him in detention – or outside of it, for that matter. But today Ward took us both to the same classroom, handing Devon the litter-picker for outside and gave me the gum-scraper for inside. I almost feel sorry for Devon. It's raining pretty badly.

"No talking," Headmaster Ward says, giving us one last look before exiting the classroom.

Richards quickly moves towards the door, but I stop him, placing my hand on his shoulder before he can leave. I'm relieved that I've managed to catch him in time. I've tried to talk to him the past two days, but I barely see him at school. He hardly goes to his locker, doesn't hang out in the cafeteria either and when I do see him, it's like he can't wait to get away from me.

He gives me a *What?* look, but I press my finger to my lips, waiting for the sound of Headmaster Ward's office door.

Slam.

There it is.

"What?" he finally says.

I let go of him, walking up to the classroom door and shutting it gently.

I turn back to look at him.

"We're getting rid of Aces."

His eyebrows furrow together. "Getting rid?"

"Taking them down. I've been working on a plan, and this is what I know. One: Aces has to be a student here, because they know things only a Niveus student could, and have access to places a student most likely does. Two: They are following me, us, to watch what we do and document it. Three: They're clever. Very clever. Four: they seem to have a reason to want to take us both down."

"Yeah…I figured. I didn't know I was important enough to take down, though," Devon says.

Not going to lie, I was thinking the same thing. I'm being objective here: most people had no clue who Richards was before this all started.

"Apparently you are – I don't get it either."

I catch him rolling his eyes at me, which is surprising. Most people don't have the confidence to be rude to me – correction, *didn't* have the confidence to be rude to me. Since Aces started revealing my secrets, the other students have been getting braver and braver. I've barely seen or heard from Ava and Ruby, which I have no doubt is because of Aces and my steadily growing social pariah status.

The depressing fact about Aces is that they could literally be anyone. They could be people in my close circle, or people from the past, like Scotty, or anyone I used to get to where I am now. In the rise to the top, I've probably pissed off most people at Niveus. I just can't quite figure out how Devon fits into all of this.

"So, the entire student body is your suspect," he says with a tired sigh.

"Don't be so negative. I've drawn up a list of people it could be and I've spoken to a tech guy in my AP math class who might be able to help us solve this."

"You want a high-school tech guy to solve this."

Why is he so negative?

"Obviously not just any tech guy. Peter is a hacker. He is going to trace the messages and see who sent the texts, and he's already getting the CCTV to see who planted the USBs and to recover the files on them. I heard he even turned down early admission to MIT last year because some top-secret federal guy hired him to hack into a Russian database. He's really good. And at the moment, he's our best chance at getting closer to finding out who's doing this to us."

While I'm terrified about what might be on the USBs, I need to know what else Aces has on me – on us – so I can work out how to stop it getting out.

Devon stares at me for a little while, his expression

carrying no hope in it whatsoever. It's always nice to have a partner who has *zero* faith in your mission.

"Okay," he says, before walking past me and out of the classroom, the door slamming behind him.

I'm a practical person, which is why the sciences are the subjects I like most. I love that everything can be objectively proven, I love that there are formulas and methods that you can fall back on. I love the security.

I wish Richards would trust me on this one. He's an arts boy. They see everything as questionable, subjective.

I don't. I live in a world of facts and figures.

And I won't roll over and let someone else take my crown. Not in a million years.

I get home and can smell Mom's rice and efo riro cooking in the kitchen. With their busy schedules, it's rare for both Mom and Dad to be home, so I'm a little taken aback at first when I hear them talking in the distance. Whenever they are both home, they like cooking together and *bonding*, which is nice and all for them, but I'm not in the mood for rice or idle chit-chat.

"Mom, can I order pizza?" I ask, walking up to the door. Mom's standing, flipping the pages of some book she's reading while Dad's stirring the pot of white rice. He has his reading glasses on, which fog up as he stirs, and he's let his beard grow out recently, which he hardly ever does.

"Food is cooking," Dad answers, taking his glasses off to

wipe them against his apron. Which means no.

Starting an argument over this isn't worth it, so I go upstairs to my room, throw my bag down and throw myself onto my bed.

I'm about to text Peter to ask him if he's found anything yet when my phone buzzes.

Finished today's round of child labour yet? – B

I smile. Belle and I have been growing close since she confronted me on Tuesday. I wonder why I disliked her so much in the first place.

Thankfully! I'm now in the comfort of my bedroom, about to watch Pretty in Pink.

What's Pretty in Pink? – B

UHM...only one of the greatest movies made.

...Then why haven't I watched it? Chi, you are failing as a friend by not forcing me to watch it – B

Friend...

You should come over.

I should – B

See you soon.

Throwing my phone down, I hurry around my room, shoving clothes in my closet and looking around for imperfections before rushing downstairs to the kitchen where my mom is now chopping and my dad is next to her, blending.

"Belle's coming over," I tell them.

Dad looks up. "Who's Belle?"

"Pretty blonde who came over last week," Mom says before I can.

"Ah."

They glance at each other, doing that thing where they have their secret soulmate meeting without speaking.

Mom laughs. "So true."

"Mom, Dad, can you stop talking in each other's head for a moment? Am I allowed to order pizza now that my friend is coming over?"

"Why can't she just eat efo like we are?" Mom asks.

The truth is I don't want to make Belle uncomfortable – which I feel bad for even thinking, because it's not like I'm ashamed of being Nigerian…

"Honey, what if she can't handle the spice?" Dad says.

"Ah…she's an oyinbo. I forget not every oyinbo can handle spice like you."

"You bet I can." Dad wraps his arm around Mom and I look away, erasing this moment from my brain.

"Chiamaka, the efo is almost ready. I'm sure your friend will love it."

♠

"That was really nice, Mr and Mrs Adebayo," Belle says.

Dad looks at me, his thoughts seeping through his expression like, *see what we told you!*

I roll my eyes at him with a smile.

"Okay, so Mom and I will tidy up, you guys go and *hang* upstairs."

Dad is doing his *I'm a cool Dad, I promise* voice.

Belle follows me to my room, where she immediately takes a seat on my bed comfortably, like we've been friends for ever. I like that there isn't the need to be too weird around each other – even though I'm still scared my room isn't clean enough.

Her *Camp Niveus* shirt glimmers under the dull lighting of my room. It's burgundy and the silver ring of the camp logo stands out to me most, reminding me of the way Jamie's used to when he wore it, and her ripped jeans are frayed in an awkward way that distracts me from why she's here in the first place.

"So... *Pretty in Pink*..."

Belle's voice snaps me out of my thoughts and I realize I've been staring at her way too long.

I sit down on my bed, opening my laptop up. "Prepare to have your heart broken."

"And if it doesn't break?"

I raise an eyebrow at her.

"If it doesn't, you're not human and this friendship is over."

"Okay, but do you have enough tape to fix me if I am broken?"

My stomach flips and my heart does its thing.

Belle's face goes really red. "That was incredibly cheesy – sorry."

I shake my head. "I'm used to cheese. Every movie in my top ten – if you discount the Marvel films – should be renamed Cheesy Movies one through ten," I say.

She smiles at me, her cheeks still flushed – it is quite cold in here, I should probably offer to turn the heat up…

"I would never peg you as a romcom girl, Chi."

Jamie said the same thing to me once. I've spent so long building up an image of myself at school – an indestructible two-dimensional mask – that I forget sometimes it's only me who sees behind it, sees who I actually am.

I love chemistry, biology and physics so much I could marry the subjects and have this huge polygamous family, and I love all those criminal science investigation shows and films about mutants, but it doesn't mean I can't also like sappy things like *The Notebook* and *When Harry Met Sally*.

"I like happy endings," I tell her.

Her smile turns into a grin.

"Me too," she says.

19

DEVON

MONDAY

I'm lost.

Reason being, I decided to listen to Chiamaka fucking Adebayo.

After detention on Friday she attacked me *again* and forced her number into my phone, and then sent me a message this morning to meet her in lab 201 – wherever the fuck that is.

A hand grabs my arm and I almost scream. My heart's near to exploding as I swing around, only to see an annoyed-looking Chiamaka.

"You're late."

Think I don't know that?

"I didn't know where lab 201 was."

She doesn't seem impressed, and I don't think I really care. I want Aces to stop, I want Dre to speak to me again, and I just want to get into Juilliard and be done with Niveus.

She pulls me into a random room – lab 201, I guess – and I'm met with a lanky guy seated at a desk with a laptop opened up.

She hits my arm. "Give him your phone."

I look at her, hoping she feels the dagger I'm mentally throwing.

"Why my phone? Why not his or yours?"

Chiamaka gives me the look my ma gives me when I give her lip.

"Peter doesn't have a phone – which is shocking, especially for a tech guy, I know. He's already got my phone, but because I don't get the blasts about me, we need your phone too. Is that okay with you? Or do you need me to explain again, slowly?"

I should just leave; her condescending tone isn't worth it. But I don't. Like a zombie, I give the guy my phone and he plugs it into his computer.

"Were you able to get into the USB? I told Devon to bring his too—"

Peter shakes his head. "It's impossible. All the files are unusable. I could look at his too if you want, but the files on your USB seem to be deliberately corrupted, which I've never seen before…"

"We'll just see what comes up with tracing the messages back… How about the CCTV?" Chiamaka asks.

"I looked for the CCTV that covers the area by your lockers at the time you thought the USBs were planted, but there was a power cut just before. It killed the lights and the cameras and didn't restart until just before first period."

Aces always seems to be several steps ahead of us; they are very sophisticated too. I try to think of anyone I know

218

who might secretly be a tech genius and who might have something against me, but my mind goes blank.

Peter hands my phone back. A black screen with a bunch of code pops up on his laptop.

"It's done, everything I need is here," Peter says, which kind of makes me nervous.

It's not like I have anything too incriminating on there... just messages, and really what message can be worse than the damage Scotty's old phone archive has done?

"I'll work on tracing the locations these messages were sent from, shouldn't take me too long," Peter says.

"When can you have it done by?" Chiamaka asks.

"I have a lab report due, so maybe before the end of the week..."

She touches his shoulder.

"Peter," she starts, cocking her head to the side. "It's very urgent, I'm sure you understand that."

He nods, his face turning red.

"Good, so I can count on you to have it done by first thing tomorrow?"

Peter looks both terrified and turned on. That alone creeps me the hell out, enough to make me want to leave this lab, but I stay put for reasons unknown to my conscience.

"First thing tomorrow," Peter repeats.

Wow. Is that all the convincing straight boys need?

"Thank you, Peter." Chiamaka ruffles his hair, which he doesn't seem to like so much, and then she pulls me towards the exit.

I move to open the classroom door, but Chiamaka stops me, pressing her hand to my chest.

I swear, if she doesn't stop touching me—

"Let me go first, wait five minutes, then you leave. We don't need people thinking we are on to them, got it?"

I make the okay sign.

I don't know how surprised junior-year Devon would be by Chiamaka and me suddenly talking so frequently, but I know that he's judging me harder than senior-year Devon is.

Mr Taylor has my headphones in, listening to my piece. I finally managed to make an initial recording this morning and I have been watching him nervously for the last three minutes.

He finally takes them off and looks at me. "This is good, really good. I think you have something great here, Devon."

Great isn't amazing.

"I'm going to go and check Tabitha's piece. Good work, keep it up."

I sigh, looking down at my music. *Where did I go wrong?*

"'Sup, Devon," Daniel says, appearing at my desk.

I look at him. "Hey."

"So, I have something pretty big to tell you," he starts.

"Okay, sure."

With Daniel Johnson, something "big" could range from pizza on the lunch menu to *"There's a new headmaster, did you know that?"*

He looks around, his eyes darting all over then landing on me. "I know who's leaking your secrets."

I feel like I could throw up all over his Marc Jacobs shoes. "Who?"

"You have to promise not to tell anyone – this could get me in trouble."

Now I'm *really* scared.

I keep going over it in my head. Only someone I know – or someone who followed me – could have known about everything that came out. The only person I've trusted with all the information was Jack. Why would Jack do that? I don't know. And why would Jack know anything about Chiamaka?

"I won't tell a soul," I say, even though I'll definitely tell Terrell and Chiamaka.

He leans in, whispering, "The FBI."

I breathe out. I forgot that this is Daniel.

"Do you cover your laptop camera?" he continues.

I shake my head, trying to calm down and get rid of this feeling of dread.

He hits the table. "It's them. I'm telling you, man."

"Thank you, Daniel."

"It's okay, anything for my *main man*."

I blink at him a few times, unsure of how to react. Giving up on a reaction, I turn, facing my music, hoping Daniel gets the hint and leaves or shuts up.

221

It starts raining on my way back from detention. I carry my backpack above my head to try to keep from getting wet, but that doesn't do much. I can see home in the distance as I walk, but the closer I get the further it seems to be. I push through the drizzle and the wind until I finally reach our front door.

Ma's at the table reading letters. She puts them face down and smiles at me, but her eyes look sad. No matter what expression she has on her face, I can tell how bad things are when the light in her eyes dims like it has now.

"Hey, Von, how was school?"

"Good, Ma..." I look at the letter in front of her. "What's that?"

She shrugs. "I didn't pay electricity last month, so they're just writing about that."

"Ma—"

"No, Von, I don't want you involved. I'm your mother and I'm meant to take care of you, not the other way around." She drops her head, which she does when she doesn't want me to see her cry.

"Ma, please let me help you, okay? I can get the money."

She shakes her head. "I know what you want to do and I don't want you doing that ever. I want you off those streets, in that classroom – making your life better, not jeopardizing it."

I say nothing.

"I'll sort it out. Borrow money or something," she says weakly.

"The bank won't give you any more loans, Ma."

"It'll work itself out, Vonnie. God never falters."

I want to laugh. He never falters, huh? Isn't our life one big falter?

I stand here, watching her get dragged down by those papers, feeling as helpless as she is. Then I lean in, wrapping my arms around her.

I swear I will do well, Ma. I'll get you a house, and a life where you won't have to work.

I pull back, then head for my room, while weighing my options. I could listen to Ma and stay inside; hear her cries for guidance through the walls at night, hear her pleading to a figure who turns away when we need him most. Or I could go to Dre, ask him for help.

I walk into my bedroom, dumping my backpack onto the king bed I share with my brothers, who are watching cartoons on the small TV in the corner. I get lost for a moment, watching with them. Their eyes are wide and innocent. They don't have to worry about the world yet. They have no clue. *I hope they've eaten.*

Ma has her way of dealing with things – praying to someone who couldn't give a shit about us and working jobs that don't pay enough. She always tells me how much she wanted to go to college, but it's not something you can afford just like that, or something you can aspire to if your teachers – and therefore your grades – are shit.

We can barely afford Niveus, with my scholarship not covering all the tuition fees.

But she wants this for me; college, a degree...

I change into some sweats and get an umbrella from the closet.

"I'm gonna go to Jack's," I tell her when I step back into the kitchen. She and I share a look, one we share often. The *I don't believe you, but stay safe-Don't cause any trouble-Stay out of areas the police cars park in-Keep your head and hood down* look.

"Okay, Von." There's hesitance. "Stay safe."

Ma's always let me have freedom, as long as my grades were in check and I didn't get into trouble at school. But ever since her friend Maurice's Nathaniel got shot by that officer back in June, she's been looking at me weird, like she wants to take that freedom away to shield me from what's out there.

She lets me go, and I step back into the rain, now unaffected by its wrath as I rush towards Dre's apartment.

The guy at the door hesitates before going inside, coming back moments after with permission to let me in. My heart goes wild as I realize that I'm about to see Dre again for the first time in over a week. I know it's not important, but I wonder if I look okay.

I close my umbrella and slowly climb the steps, trying to gain some nerve before entering Dre's apartment. When I get to the top step, I breathe out.

Dre knows it's me coming. If he didn't want me to, he wouldn't have let me in.

I open the door. His living room is dim as I slowly walk

across it, worried I'll trip and bump into something, fingers vibrating against my sides. His bedroom door creaks loudly as I push it, stepping through.

Dre's at his desk, head tilted up, eyes closed like he's dreaming. He's wearing a green durag. His dark skin is bright despite the dullness of the lights, and his beard has grown out a little. He's trying to look like he's older than eighteen again, wants to be taken seriously. Meanwhile I'm scared of what growing up means.

I think, sometimes, we – boys from here – are dealt such a shitty hand that we forget we are minors, kids, in the eyes of the law. I guess technically eighteen is adult enough, but not when most of your childhood has been robbed, like Dre's was.

"Hey, Dre," I say. He doesn't move.

"What do you want?" he asks, his deep voice rattling my heart. I've missed that voice.

"To talk," I say. His eyes open and his head drops forward. His stare locks on me and I feel like uncooked meat hanging in the butcher's, surveyed and judged.

He pushes himself out of the chair, slowly walking over to me, though he's avoiding my gaze now.

"I don't want to talk to you," he says. The pounding in my chest only gets faster.

"If that were true, you'd have told that boy to not let me in. You wouldn't even respond."

"We were friends. I wasn't gonna turn you around, make you look like a fool," Dre says with a forced laugh.

We were friends.

"Just friends?" I ask. He looks at me now, his eyes are glassy. I feel a pang in my chest. "Do you kiss all your friends, Dre?"

He sniffs and shifts uncomfortably.

"Sleep with them too?" I continue, vision blurring. "Tell them you love them?"

I wipe my eyes. I need to focus. He's quiet, staring at me now, unwavering.

"You know that's not what I meant."

Don't lose focus.

"We have different paths," he starts, looking away from me again. "I'm a high-school dropout, I have no family, I live to survive. Your path is school, then a job and looking after your ma. You don't know how much I think about you, Von. I want to call you but I can't because this thing we have has an expiration date, whether it's when you go to some fancy college, or when you realize that you're too different from me."

I want to say that isn't true, but I have a feeling I can't be certain about that.

"You say you love me, yet *your boys* beat me—"

"'Cause you weren't gonna deal for me any more. Everyone gets an exit beating!" he says with his voice raised. This conversation is riling him up. Dre's usually a lot calmer, but everything about him seems on edge today.

I don't care for his excuses and I don't want to hear his gang's political bullshit.

"You could have stopped them, Dre, but you didn't. You knew what was gonna happen to me."

"I wanted to stop it, but then they'd ask questions—"

"Think they don't know what we do when I come here? Think they're senseless?"

He turns away from me, wiping his face with his sleeve. I feel another pang, but I ignore it. I can't let myself lose sight of what's important.

Cry, Dre, I'm not gonna judge you for crying.

"If that's what you do to the people you love, I'm glad this is done."

He shakes his head, still turned away. "I was thinking about surviving, and those people at your school saying things. If I lose this, I lose everything – but if you lose me, you still have everything."

Why doesn't he get that he's a huge chunk of everything?

I look around the room, how dark and cold it is – drugs on the table, some I know he's locked away in the drawers. I wish he didn't find comfort in temporary highs. I want to tell him that his path could be something different, but I'd be lying. He makes a lot doing this, it helps him survive.

He was so happy when he made enough to rent this place, and I just want him to be happy, even though I wish he was doing something less dangerous.

A draught of wind from an open window makes the room feel even colder. Dre and I are over, I knew that when he told me to get out last week, when his boys beat me up, and more so now that he can't even look at me, but I'm so used to being with him, it feels impossible to let go.

His tense shoulders drop then rise and he turns, the tears I saw earlier gone.

"Can I kiss you goodbye?" I say, thinking of Terrell and his goodbye hugs. Andre gives me a look like it's starting to dawn on him what goodbye means for us.

The wind pushes him towards me, only slightly.

"Yeah, of course," he says softly. I ignore my gut screaming at me to leave, to not kiss a boy who hurt me so badly, but my heart was always stronger than my gut. I inch forward with hesitation, my forehead resting against his as I breathe in his scent. I once asked Dre what cologne he used, and I remember how he smiled and told me "sweat", which was BS. I wish I knew now. I want to be surrounded by it after this kiss – I don't want to walk away from it. Dre's arms pull me in, our noses touching, then our lips. He's pulling me in so close it hurts, like he's trying to fuse our bodies together. My heart is steady somehow, but the rest of me is shaky.

We break apart, but I'm still trapped inside his arms. I rest my head on his shoulder, breathing slowly, trying not to think about when I'll have to move away, wave and leave. For good.

Don't lose focus.

But I did. I was going to leave without telling him that I need one or two small jobs, just to help Ma out. I look up.

His face, tear-stained and wet, surprises me. It surprises me even more that he lets me reach up and wipe the tears away.

"Really gonna miss your company, Devon," he tells me.

"Me too."

I still stand here in this cocoon, waiting for him to pull back. But he doesn't. I know I'm gonna regret this someday – maybe even moments from now – but I'm not ready to let go just yet, and I can feel him releasing his arms, and that scares the shit out of me, and so I kiss him again. He stops and pulls me close again and even though my heart is rattling like I just ran a mile, I let him guide me backwards slowly like he's done many times before.

Future Devon is shaking his head, watching as the back of my knees hit Dre's bed, then how I quickly scoot back towards the cold pillows, finally breaking the kiss to pull my hoodie over my head. But I ignore future-me's judgement.

Dre looks like he wants to speak, tell me to go home or say we shouldn't be doing something like this. I can hear his thoughts racing. He's overthinking this, like I would be if I didn't keep pushing the feeling back. His thoughts are screaming, but then as if swallowed by a vacuum, there is complete silence. All worry disappears and all that matters is right now, not the future versions of us that might regret this, just present Andre and me, who both want to do this, kiss the pain away for a little while.

Dre moves off the bed and goes over to the drawer in his desk, pulling out some condoms. I look away from him now and up at the ceiling, listening to the sound of the rain hitting the windows and the wind angrily crying out, letting it drown my thoughts.

His weight tilts the bed, as he leans over me and joins our lips together again.

I want this moment to last as long as it can; I want to be here with him for as long as I can.

Like always he's gentle, and considerate, making me feel special, kissing me all over. And then when we are finally done and I'm in his arms I let myself cry.

I'm aware that I completely lost focus on what I came here for. But he probably would've said no anyway.

He kisses my shoulder blades and hugs me close, and I know that soon I'll have to get up, put my clothes on and say goodbye – face my other issues, like Ma struggling and Aces. But for now, I want to close my eyes, listen to the sound of the rain and Dre's breathing, and drown.

20

TUESDAY

"You're late, again," I tell Richards as he enters the lab.

He says nothing, just blankly stares at me like he doesn't care. But I'm going to ignore that, because I need him to be invested in this, and hopefully after today, he will be.

I walk towards Peter, who is waiting with his laptop open in his lap. Devon is being annoyingly slow.

"What did you find?" I ask, cutting the niceties.

Peter smiles, leaning back against his chair.

"Probably everything you were looking for…but since I did this for you, could you do me a favour?"

It's like all the years I spent gaining respect have been washed away by the random appearance of Aces the cyber-bitch this year. But I guess since Peter *did* help, I could.

"Depends," I say.

"I heard Belle and Jamie broke up…and I hear that you and Belle are friendly now."

"Heard from who?"

Peter smiles with a shrug. "Around."

I'm sure people are surprised after the Aces blast about me and Jamie hooking up, that Belle and I are hanging out.

It's the opposite of what usually happens: boy is a massive dickhead to both girls, girls fight each other, boy is left unblamed as girls antagonize each other.

I'm glad it isn't like that with me and Belle.

"What about her?" I ask.

"Can you tell her about me, and how helpful I was to you?" Peter looks at me, desperate.

There's a flutter in my stomach. I don't like this, but I give a small nod.

Peter looks back at his laptop. "So, you'll be happy to know that only one device is used to send the messages, and that device is easy to locate."

"Where is it?" Devon asks, finally awake and interested.

"Right here, in the school. The Morgan Library, computer 17."

That's surprising. Why would Aces want to do it somewhere they could easily be caught?

"Can you get CCTV footage from Morgan?" I ask.

Peter shakes his head. "Morgan is one of the few places in the school that isn't covered. Perfect location to do a lot of *things*," Peter says, waggling his eyebrows.

I ignore the gross implication he's making because I know I'll throw up my breakfast if I pay it any mind.

I hardly go into Morgan Library. It's notorious as being hook-up central, plus there's a separate science library closer to the labs that I use.

"There's more though," Peter says. Richards and I both lean in. "Sundays and Mondays, at around ten o'clock, the details are entered and the messages scheduled to be sent out at specific moments during the week. They've hacked into the school's central administration system, so they can access the entire registry of student body phone numbers."

I remember how Headmaster Ward said he could trace what we were doing on our personal school accounts.

"Could you look at the personal school account of the student who logged in?"

Peter scratches his head. "Yes, actually. I attempted to as soon as I got in, and I'm afraid the personal account used wasn't registered to any student or staff member. On a normal account in the Niveus database, you'd have a unique name and passcode – yours, for example, is Chiamaka Adebayo, 5681—"

"Could you lower your voice? There's literally someone out to get me and you're here telling the whole lab what my password is," I interrupt.

Peter nods. "Sorry. What I meant was, I can see into anyone's account. This person, though, had no name and their password seems to be frequently changed. I imagine they use some sort of randomizer...but anyway, I can't identify who it is that sends the messages from this account nor can I access the files. There's a lot of encryption that would take me days to crack. I can only see what gets sent out from the computer and the times the texts are logged."

Aces is definitely way too smart to be any of the suspects

I currently have on my list. I don't think I've ever seen Ruby use a computer before.

"Can I have a copy of all the things you found?" I ask, my mind racing. Peter looks like he wants to refuse, but reluctantly nods anyway.

"Should I print it out?" he asks.

"Email, I'll be expecting it," I say, before turning, grabbing Richards's arm and pulling him towards the door.

Richards pulls his arm away and I turn to give him my death glare. Why is he being such a child?

"Whoever Aces is, from everything we know, it's clear they've plotted this – whatever *this* is – meticulously. We need to think ahead and pre-empt what they're going to do next," I say. I can't help but notice that Richards's eyes are tinted pink like he's been crying all morning.

"So what do we do?" he asks.

"A stake-out, this Sunday – we are going to catch Aces as they set their next messages."

"Then what?"

"We've got all their messages and Peter's data as evidence, and after pinning down who they are, we don't stop until they have nothing left. Expose them and everything they've done – to the school and every college they're applying to. I will ruin their future like they tried to ruin ours."

Devon nods. "I'm in."

234

I have chemistry and find my seat next to Jamie.

I sit down heavily, taking my notebook out. I remember the simpler days when I could just enjoy my favourite subject in peace. I should have treasured those moments.

"Pair up and follow the instructions on the sheet," Mr Peterson says.

I cringe inwardly. Now would be the perfect time for a change of partner. Anyone but Jamie. But partner changes don't happen easily, plus with me not talking to him and Ruby and Ava not speaking to me either, I'd rather not try my luck with anyone else.

I look over at one of the girls on the bench next to me: Clara. She's always hated my guts, and now she can do so openly. She gives me a smug look, before turning away.

I go up to the side tables, getting a Bunsen burner and the materials.

"Belle broke up with me," Jamie says, when I get back to our table.

"I'm sorry," I say, though I don't mean it.

He sniffs, and my heart feels heavy.

"I just *really* liked her."

There's silence as I unpack everything, but I can feel him staring at me.

"Sorry for leaving you behind, not being there when you needed me."

Why is he suddenly deciding to be all nice to me? I set the Bunsen up and separate the materials.

"It's okay," I tell him.

"It's not. I'm your best friend and I left you when things got tough."

I'm used to it, I want to say. I'm used to Jamie ignoring situations when things get tough or hard to speak about. Now I'm trying not to accept his crappy behaviour.

"Here's the list of elements we need to test," I say – without stuttering, which I'm so happy about because I can still feel Jamie's eyes on me and it's making me nervous.

"Okay," he says. I hear whispers behind me, and at first I'm confused, until I hear the voices more clearly.

"I don't know how Belle can hang out with someone like that..." someone says. I look up. Jeremy smiles at me and waves and I smile back, waving with my middle finger up. His smile falters and he turns away.

"What a bitch, no wonder nobody likes her."

Sometimes I really hate Niveus.

The best revenge right now is to not let my grades slip. I'm going to get into Yale, then med school and then I'm going to be the best doctor in the state, whether they like it or not.

Jamie and I work side by side for the rest of the class. He even lets me do most of the Bunsen burner work. After we're finished, he walks out with me.

"Do you want to come over to my place today, maybe go to the Waffle Palace or something?" he asks. I don't know why I'm surprised. Whenever something happens, he always wants us to forget and move on, go back to being best friends. I don't know if it's Aces, Belle, or something else, but I'm finally seeing through the cracks in Jamie's seemingly perfect demeanour.

I feel like I'm worth more than that.

"I'm busy," I tell him.

"Oh."

We walk and we get stared at but I keep my head up, heels clicking against the marble loudly. I imagine stomping on all of their glaring faces. I am not going to look weak.

"I could walk you home?"

I turn, "I have legs, Jamie. I can walk myself home, and I'm sure you can too." I give him a tight smile, and then I walk out of the school, down the steps and through the gate. Alone.

The house is empty when I get back.

I go upstairs immediately, opening my laptop and downloading everything Peter sent over.

The first sheet pops up. I scroll, watching as each message is traced back to the origin. Computer 17. Every message that was sent is there.

Just in. Looks like Chi's not so sweet. Sources say she got caught trying to steal candy. Careful, Chi, don't want a record Yale will see... – Aces

It's been two weeks since it happened. Two Tuesdays ago. And I still can't figure out how the candy ended up in my pocket. I wonder who these sources are. There were other people in the shop, but none I recognized as being Niveus students. Only Jamie. But it doesn't make sense that he'd ruin his relationship with Belle by posting the later messages about us. *None* of this makes sense.

The next downloaded page comes up on the screen – the dates and times of the logged texts.

Like Peter said, they all happened around ten o'clock.

22:06

22:13

21:57

All on a Sunday or Monday night. Who would have access to the school at that time? The janitor? The teachers? Anyone could steal a key…

My phone buzzes and I jump.

Is it weird that I've never watched The Notebook before? – B

I smile down at her message, feeling guilty for being happy that she texted when Jamie is still obviously upset. A good friend would try to fix his relationship with her… But I don't have to be a good friend to someone who isn't one to me.

Yes, really weird, you should change that soon.

I look down at my phone, waiting for her reply.
Maybe I was too forward.

I don't want her to think I was suggesting she come over and watch it, even though that's what I *was* suggesting.

I'm regretting sending it.

Are you free now? I have it on DVD. – B

I look at my laptop's screen, as another download pops up.

Logged at 22:04 on Sunday... That can't be right.

I scroll, zooming in on the page and details. My heart picks up.

How is it possible that Aces knew I would be accused of stealing candy on Tuesday, when they logged it on Sunday night at 10.04 p.m.?

My mom's making pancakes too... – B

I look down at her message. The sense of impending doom in my chest makes me feel like someone has wrapped their hands around my neck, blocking my air supply.

Blonde hair. Blood. Tarmac.

At any moment, Aces could release more lies or more truths. The police could come knocking on my front door, lock my wrists together in handcuffs and drag me away while the disappointment on my parents' faces burns into my mind for ever.

I need to go through all of what Peter has sent over, make sure I have an airtight plan to take back to Devon tomorrow.

Sorry, something came up.

I was just starting to have a real friend, and, like everything else, Aces is ruining that too.

21

DEVON

WEDNESDAY

"And?" I ask, as Chiamaka holds up sheets of paper with words and numbers I don't understand. Her bright pink Prada bag is a little distracting.

"This was logged before I was accused!" she whisper-shouts.

I look back at the pages, trying to understand her with absolutely no context. I can see rows of numbers – times, some before ten o'clock and some after.

"What was logged?"

She sighs loudly. "Oh my god, for someone up against me for valedictorian, you really *are* slow."

"Maybe if you explained yourself I'd understand," I spit back.

She gives me a tight sarcastic smile.

"Peter sent me the documents yesterday afternoon. I found the times linked with the messages sent, and the times they were scheduled and logged on this mysterious computer 17. The time *my supposed theft* was logged was *two* whole days before it happened – do you get it now?"

Shit.

"So, it was a set-up?" I ask.

She rolls her eyes. "Obviously."

I turn to face her properly now, moving away from my keyboard.

"Who would set you up?"

She shrugs, shaking her head like even the thought of it is making her distressed.

"My...friend Jamie was with me in the shop at the time."

"Would he do it?"

"No! Of course not," she says, not sounding convinced.

"Who else was in the shop?"

"I didn't see clearly – but we've got four days until Sunday, when we can catch them. Or at least catch whoever Aces got to do it. In the meantime, I'm going to ask the janitor about that power cut."

I nod. I've been able to breathe a little more, as Aces has been quiet for a few days. But I'm still on edge; I hate not knowing what might happen next – and I want to know who is behind this.

"I'll give you updates when I can." She pauses and gives my keyboard a look, like it's beneath her, which reminds me of why I don't like her. "Bye."

Chiamaka's clicking heels echo as she walks down the hallway. I turn back to my keyboard and grab the sheet of music I was writing on before she came in and disrupted my flow. I hope she doesn't make a habit of visiting me in my happy place. Too many people are ruining it lately.

I don't know what our regular chats make us, but I know

for sure that we are not friendly enough to ruin each other's happy places. I don't go into her labs without warning, but I guess she doesn't have the same courtesy. I almost mentioned Terrell's race theory but stopped myself because 1) I don't know if she'd buy it, and 2) the thought of some racist student doing this because I'm Black – we're Black – is too sickening to even make it a prime possibility.

I stare down at the sheet, and I touch the keys with my left hand, trying to make sense of the rhythm, trying to make it perfect. Right now it sounds so clunky and disjointed. Juilliard would reject it in a second.

I rub my eyes and move away from the keyboard once again. I can't work or play when I'm this frustrated so I text Terrell, hoping he doesn't find it weird that I'm texting him during school.

Want to hang after school?

My phone buzzes straight away.

Sure, how's your day going? – T

My lips stretch as I look down at the message. That's something I really like about Terrell – he always answers.

It's going… Trying to write and make this song better, but I can't. How's your day?

Buzz.

My ears are always available, so bring it with you
when you come later. My day is pretty chill, didn't
feel like school so I've just been at home. – T

I wish I could *not feel like school* without being all guilty
for wasting Ma's money. But my attendance is perfect, even
if I'm in the music practice room more than classes these
days. One day off from school won't ruin that, right?

I'll bring it over with me, thanks :)

See you later:) – T

I switch off the keyboard, shove all my things into my
bag, and rush out of the practice room, and down to the
school office.

"I'm ill and need to go home," I tell the woman at the
desk. She raises an eyebrow at me.

"Name?"

"Devon Richards."

Her long red-nailed fingers tap away on her computer
keyboard. She glances up at me, all haughty as she surveys
me, then back down at the screen. She stops typing as the
printer slides a form out.

The scratch of her signature permanently inking the
page makes me cringe.

"Sign here, and you're free to go."

Senior privileges mean parents aren't involved when it comes to calling in sick – which I don't ever do because for some reason I'm never sick – and when I used to try to pretend, Ma always knew I was faking. I sign the sheet, trying to push the guilt away.

I'm always in school, this is nothing.

I repeat it to myself over and over as I rush through the hallway, freeing myself from the prison behind the double doors and tall black metal gates.

I almost feel invincible.

I approach Terrell's bright front door, with a pounding in my chest and sweaty palms. I'm high on adrenaline and happy to step away from music, give my mind a break. I step over some of the weeds tangling by the entrance and smooth my uniform before knocking.

I don't need to overthink this. I don't know why I'm overthinking this.

Soon enough he answers, looking surprised and not exactly ecstatic.

"Hey, I was let out of school early so I just thought I'd come here," I say.

Terrell looks at me, then looks back in his house.

"I wasn't expecting you to be here for a few hours..." He pauses. "Now's not really a good time."

"Is everything okay?" I ask.

He nods. "Yeah, my sister is here. She's not doing so well so I'm just watching out for her while Ma's at work."

I see a black furball slink out of Terrell's doorway. It meows, then walks past me. Terrell glances at it briefly then looks back at me.

"Later?" he says, like his cat didn't just run away.

I nod, feeling like an idiot.

Unexpectedly, his arms wrap around me in a hug, and then the door's closed and I'm standing here, unsure of where to go now.

I walk away from his place, back towards Niveus – towards the side of town with unbroken picket fences, pretty front lawns, and happy families who never have to worry about their next meal or their college funds or their family being evicted.

I end up in the park Terrell and I went to. Dropping my bag on the ground, I climb the steps of the jungle gym and settle into the purple tube.

I close my eyes and at first all I see is darkness. I try to imagine waves, anything to calm me, make me forget everything that's going on, and soon enough I'm swimming, but then I feel warm hands. I feel *his* hands around me again. Kissing me, holding me, warm and soft, skin against skin, water hugging us, lungs on fire as our lips finally connect—

Then I open my eyes and I'm met with the darkness of the tube, out of breath and disorientated.

It's so quiet, I almost think I imagined it. The sound,

a click. Like a photo being taken.

I sit up quickly, noticing a hooded figure in the corner of the park, turned away from me. I watch them closely as I start moving slowly out of the tube, trying to climb down without them hearing me. The figure turns a little and I see the edge of something covering their face. *A mask?*

My gaze drops down to their hands. They are flicking through pictures on a large camera. My breaths turn shallow.

Aces?

I take a step forward, once again not realizing that there's nothing but air in front of me, and I stumble off the jungle gym, landing smack on my knees. I groan loudly, which alerts the figure and I hear them take off.

I get up quickly, dusting the dirt off my knees and running in the direction they went. But when I get through the park gates, I look out along the long road and no one is there.

There are no streets that they could have turned into that quickly, just rows and rows of giant gated houses.

It's as though the figure vanished into thin air.

22

CHIAMAKA

WEDNESDAY

It becomes apparent as Ward hands me my labour tools – a toothbrush and a bucket of soapy water – that Richards isn't coming to detention. As soon as Ward leaves, I text him.

Where are you?

A purple plastic tube – D

There's no time for sarcasm. We need to make sure our stake-out goes perfectly on Sunday, and I want to update Devon. The janitor said there wasn't a power cut, but that there have been a lot of "weird electrical issues" throughout the school of late, which is why they're having the maintenance day. It's not a coincidence, that much I know.

This time next week, I'll be able to focus on Yale and convince Headmaster Ward to restore my position as Head Prefect. This time next week, I'll be getting ready for the Senior Snowflake Charity Ball. At Niveus, the Snowflake Ball is the most important event of the year. And it's not just Niveus students; the headmaster invites the biggest donors and Niveus alumni to watch as they crown the Snowflake King and Queen – who'll be marked as the students that everyone needs to know as they graduate.

Last year's Snowflake Queen got into Harvard, with one alum's very powerful recommendation. That crown could be the thing that gets me a guaranteed spot at Yale.

Why aren't you in detention?

I got sick. – D

Sure he did.

Well when you're "better", we need to visit Morgan Library.

Okay. – D

Boys are infuriating.

The Sunday plan is not perfect yet. I'm still not sure whether coming in at nine in the evening is too early, nine-thirty is too close to when *they* might arrive or ten o'clock is too late. I'll pay the janitor, but then what – we roam around the school like people with no scheming bones in their bodies? We need an agreed place to hide that is close enough for us to enter the library soundlessly. We need an easy getaway. And I want proof – visual proof – of whoever sits at that computer. I can do most of it on my own, but I need to

249

know that Richards isn't going to mess up. Or lie about his health, again.

I jump as another text buzzes in.

By the way, I think Aces followed me. – D

What do you mean?

Someone in a mask followed me home, I think.
They were taking pictures. – D

Are they still following you?

No, I don't think so. I tried chasing them but they got away. – D

That makes me feel uneasy. If they are following us… then all the more reason we need a solid plan for Sunday.

He better be in tomorrow—

"Hey…" someone whispers. I look up to see Belle in the doorway, blonde curls packed up in a high ponytail and wearing her bright-blue lacrosse uniform. My eyes move down to her bare legs then away again as I turn, bend over, dip the toothbrush in the bucket filled with soapy water next to me and proceed to scrub at the non-existent dirt on a random table.

"Hi," I say.

Scrub. Scrub.

"Finished practice?" I ask.

"No, just on my way there actually… Wanted to see if you were here, say hey, maybe avoid Coach and her screaming for a few moments," she says.

I stop scrubbing, turning to face Belle and her apparently really long legs.

"Glad I can be your break from that." I watch the door carefully. "If Ward comes in, though, I'm going to tell him you were bothering me," I say with a smile.

She laughs. "You'd sell me out?"

I shrug. "Maybe, maybe not, depends on how I'm feeling."

I was sure that saying no to Belle's *The Notebook* invite would dampen our new friendship, but she's here, in front of me, making me all flustered and nervous. It's almost as if I like her or something, in a *more than friends* way. But that's absurd.

Is it?

"And how are you feeling?" she asks, head tilted to the side.

"Tired. It's like I'm scrubbing away at nothing," I say, gesturing to the tables.

"Why did you get such a long sentence anyway?"

That's kind of a funny way to describe it. It basically is a sentence. I'm surprised she doesn't know why. I assumed everyone would know about another position of lowliness I've been forced into.

"Ward thinks Devon and I have been spreading the rumours about each other. That *we're* Aces."

"Who do you think it is?" Belle asks. I pause, considering whether I should share my list of suspects.

"It could be anyone," I answer. *Anyone.* I look down. I keep going back to my list, but I just can't see how any of the people I thought it might be would be capable of doing all of this. "Who do you think it is?"

"Maybe someone jealous of your perfect looks and grades," she says. My skin burns.

I don't know how to respond to that, so I don't.

There's silence for a little while, which is only filled by my scrubbing and sighs, until I hear the sound of Belle's sneakers as she steps forward, taking a seat on one of the desks in the room.

"I'm kind of in the mood to ditch lacrosse and stay in here with you. Do you have a second brush?"

Why would someone want to clean on purpose?

"I haven't got a second one...but you can take mine," I say, holding it out with a smile.

She stares at me with a smirk on her pink lips. Then she places her lacrosse stick on the table and strides over to me, centimetres away. I'm taller than Belle, with or without these knitted Chloé sock boots, yet I feel small next to her.

Her eyes flick over to the door then back to me. She looks mischievous, like she wants to do something that could get us both in trouble. I feel the same way, but I'm not sure what she has in mind. She grabs the toothbrush out of my hand and takes the bucket in her other and I watch her.

My heart is going faster than it does when there's an Aces blast.

"So I just dunk it in, swish it about, then scrub the table?" she asks, turning.

I don't think I can form an answer with the noise in my mind. All I can think about is whether I should do this – test out this unstable theory I have.

Her head moves back when I don't answer. "Or am I wrong? Is there some profound way to clean a desk?"

Belle being nice to me could just be a symptom of wanting to strengthen this friendship that came out of nowhere. Or it could be something else, something that doesn't fit into the odds. You can't calculate emotion.

She steps closer. The soapy water swishes as she puts the bucket back down on the desk. She waves her hand in front of my face.

"Earth to Chiamaka."

Belle always smells of vanilla, with a hint of something even sweeter. It makes me want to drop everything and be unscientific about this.

I want to be unscientific about this...so bad.

But what if I test out this theory and it isn't correct? What then?

"Are you okay?" Belle asks, looking worried now.

"I'm confused, trying to work out whether we are friends or not." I surprise myself as the truth just slips out.

Belle looks a little hurt by the statement, but I didn't mean it the way it came out.

"I thought we were."

"What if I don't want to be friends?"

I don't want to say the rest out loud.

"You don't want to be friends?" Belle looks really hurt, which makes my body feel like heated explosions are going off all at once.

"I don't."

Belle nods, and puts the toothbrush down. "Okay, that's fine," she says quietly, before walking past me.

I think I want her to leave, stop confusing me, but at the same time I don't want her to go. I want her to stay and let me explain.

"I think I like you in a non-friend way... I-if that weirds you out, you can go," I say, stumbling over some of my words. I look down, and even though I can't see her, I know she's still in the room. I didn't hear the door close.

I keep going.

"I just don't think I can be friends with you if it weirds you out or if you don't feel the same way – for now at least. I was friends with Jamie for ages, and I always wanted more... I don't want to repeat that again," I say, without taking a breath.

This is embarrassing.

Closing my eyes, I add, "So leave, please, if that's not something you want too."

In the distance I can hear screams, from the gym or the grounds outside, but there's dead silence between us.

The sound of the door opening and then slamming shut

shatters something inside me. I breathe out raggedly, turning around to look at the empty room. Only I'm met, face to face, with the smell of vanilla and blonde hair and pink lips that smile at me.

Belle leans in, closing her eyes, and kisses me. And then, within nanoseconds, I'm kissing her too.

23

THURSDAY

I meet Chiamaka in Morgan Library during lunch.

Until today, I'd never really been in Morgan before, but like the other libraries it's huge and old, with dark brown shelves that reach the ceiling, books that carry this old dusty smell, and rows of computers. Computer 17 is tucked into the corner. Some guy's using it to watch videos, so all I can do is stare and wonder what's being kept on there. Hundreds of secrets, locked away on Aces's account.

Chiamaka's writing something down on a tiny notepad.

"If we hide behind the cart of books over there by the computer, we'll have the best view and best cover," she says in a whisper. I look over at the cart.

"What if it's not there on Sunday?"

She sighs, looking around. "The carts don't move, I've come here a few times this week to check and there's always a cart by the entrance. But if for whatever reason it isn't here on Sunday, then we hide behind the first bookshelf and wait for them to arrive." She flips the notepad shut as the first warning bell sounds, signalling the end of lunch. Despite Chiamaka's confidence, I still worry that something will go wrong.

We walk out of Morgan separately – Chiamaka a few steps ahead, so that it doesn't look like we were in there together – and I head towards my locker. The crowd divides us as people make their way down the hall.

There's a shift in the air as I near the senior lockers. Something feels different. For one, it is completely dark in the hallway. Two, people are slowing down, their mumbled voices growing louder, and at first I'm unsure what all the chaos is about.

Then the lights blink on and I see them.

Posters plastered to every single locker.

Posters of a passed-out Chiamaka in a short silver dress, black tights, black heeled boots, mascara dried on her cheeks and her hair a tangled mess. Some of the posters have *Bitch* written in big black bold text, others *Slut*.

I move closer to the posters. Surrounding her body are these weird identical blonde dolls.

I scan the crowd for Chiamaka, swallowing the lump in my throat when I see her in the centre of the hallway, frozen.

The quiet chaos is interrupted by pop music blaring from the school speakers, as a figure dressed head to toe in black, with a black hood and a terrifying Guy Fawkes mask, carrying hundreds of posters, appears out of nowhere and rushes forward.

The hairs on the back of my neck are raised and a chill runs through me unexpectedly. My mind flashes back to the park; the figure with the camera.

In one swift movement, they toss the papers they're

holding into the air. The sheets fall from the ceiling like giant snowflakes and people reach up, jumping to catch the paper, like it's some game. I block my face as the sheets rain down, but I glimpse the printed images. I reach down and pick one up.

It's my and Chiamaka's junior yearbook photos. Only, our eyes have been scratched out. It's like a punch to the gut.

Without thinking, I push through the crowd, walking towards the masked figure. They notice my sudden movement and look me dead in the eye before sprinting away, pushing through the crowd. They're fast, black sneakers carrying them quickly.

I start running but I'm quickly blocked by bodies, shoving me back as they grab at the posters that litter the floor. I fight my way through, not wanting to lose the person, but by the time I break out from the crowd, the figure has disappeared once again.

Aces?

Taking a shaky breath, I turn. My face is hot, limbs quaking as all eyes fix on me now. Some sneer, others stare blankly. I scan the hallway for Chiamaka, but she's disappeared. Her picture comes into view again, lined up along each locker. I run at the first one, tearing it down, moving to the next one, yanking it off, then the next, and the next, blood boiling. Whoever took this photo meant to do harm. She's passed out, unaware of the picture being taken. It's nasty; it's a violation.

I spot Mr Ward at the end of the hallway, holding one of

the posters. Then I watch as he crumples it up and throws it in the bin, before walking away.

The second warning bell rings, and the students around me abruptly start walking away, moving towards their classes. I stand in the centre of the hallway, the picture of Chiamaka clutched in my hand, the floor filled with copies of my defaced school photo.

Mr Taylor looks down at the crumpled posters of Chiamaka and me. His brow is furrowed and mouth twisted as he scans the page.

"I'm sorry, Devon. These were just in the hallway? You didn't see who put them up?" he asks.

I nod. "We didn't see who put them up, but there was a person throwing some of the posters around. They were wearing a mask so I didn't see who they were either."

Mr Taylor sighs and looks up at me.

"I'm going to find out who did this, Devon, okay?"

I feel relieved. "Thank you."

"Just go home, and try not to let this get you down."

I do exactly that – I go home and I try not to think about it. But it's impossible.

I'm at home, in my bedroom, knees bouncing like I've had too much coffee, seated on the edge of the bed trying to do homework, but I can't shake the image of those posters on the hallway floor; of the figure in a mask. It's like my mind can't comprehend what is going on.

I feel guilty that Chiamaka is probably on her own somewhere, dealing with this all by herself. I'm barely holding it together here, and the attack on me today wasn't half as personal. I couldn't find her after class, in the labs; she's not answering her phone, and I don't know where she lives. The posters made me feel sick; they were a threat to me and Chiamaka. Letting us know that someone is out for us and won't stop until they've destroyed us.

I feel a tap on my shoulder and I jump. My brother James is staring at me, a serious expression on his face as he holds up a drawing. My brothers have been watching cartoons all evening, like they usually do after they get back from school. Ma's in the kitchen making dinner. I normally help but I've been falling behind on everything lately, and I have to get my homework done.

I survey the picture, trying to look really impressed. Nine times out of ten, the picture is of an elephant – James's favourite animal – but this picture is pink and brown and lopsided.

"So cool, J. That an elephant?" I ask, pulling him onto my lap.

He shakes his head. "No…it's meant to be you," he says, sounding disappointed at my wrong guess.

I look at the picture again. The creature's face is big, the body small and crooked. James gave the creature two ears and two earrings, one that's a Christian cross and the other a normal stud, just like mine. The creature has a frown on its face and a tear drop under one of its eyes.

"I see it now, it looks just like me," I say, feeling a little offended, but it makes him smile. He crawls off my lap and joins Elijah again on the floor, by the small TV in the corner.

I watch the shapes move about on the screen for a moment, then I turn back to the shapes on my homework sheet. I feel my phone buzz next to me and I grab it quickly, hoping it's Chiamaka telling me she's okay, that the posters are fucked up, that everything is definitely directed at us and that we need to do something *now*, before Sunday.

But it's not her, it's Terrell.

You disappeared on me yesterday – T

He messaged me yesterday too, but I ignored it, hoping that if I pretended not to see the text I could erase how embarrassing the whole conversation at his house had been. After our exchange yesterday, I decided to go home. Facing him directly after that would have been too awkward.

Sorry for disappearing, hope your sister is doing better – D

Immediately he texts back.

She is – T

We've only been friends for a few days and already I'm being clingy and annoying. What the hell is wrong with me?

Want to come over now? You can bring me
your music – T

I look down at my homework, the sound of the cartoons
drowning out the yells from the good angel on my shoulder
as I slip my sneakers on and put my assignment sheets away.

I couldn't focus anyway, I reason, as I type back a response.

Will be over in 10 – D

Ten minutes later I'm lying back on Terrell's bed. It's really
comfortable, in a *don't have to share with nobody* way. I miss
the days when I was an only child and didn't have to share
a bed with my brothers.

Terrell is seated in front of me, listening to my audition
piece. I feel nauseous watching him.

What if he says my piece is bad and that I should scrap
it all?

Sometimes I feel like the time I'm spending perfecting
this audition piece is pointless. With the way things are
going, if this Aces bullshit reaches Juilliard, I don't think it
will matter how good my audition piece is. They won't want
a student who's been accused of all the things Aces has
accused me of.

Especially since none of the accusations were entirely
false.

Terrell's shoulders move under the black cotton of his

hoodie, and I watch them out of the corner of my eye. He almost seems to be dancing. I want to laugh, but I don't want to alarm him and disrupt whatever flow he has.

"I know what's missing," Terrell says, turning to face me now. His voice startles me, but I try not to show that it does.

"What?"

"Drums." He takes the headphones out of his ears and passes my player back to me.

Drums?

"Really?" I ask, because it seems so strange to me. I know how to play them – kind of – but I haven't had to since freshman-year band practice – which I quit as soon as I could. Working with others isn't something I like doing when it comes to music. I'm not even sure if the Juilliard composition faculty would like that.

"It's too soft without them, like that white-ass school you go to."

I nudge him. He nudges me back.

The piece has the keyboard and the clarinet. I guess I can see where he's coming from.

"You might be right…" I say, voice trailing off. My thoughts once again occupied by the posters in the hallway. My face. Chiamaka's face. It's hard to ignore the lack of white faces on the posters. It's hard to ignore the obvious thing tying Chiamaka and me together now: our Black skin.

There's so much cramming my mind. I don't feel safe at school, or anywhere really – like I'm constantly having to look over my shoulder.

I learned when I was younger to keep how I really felt buried, deal with feelings later, on my own. I'm good at burying things in deep boxes in my mind. I'm good at being okay most of the time. Until I'm not, and the boxes burst open and I explode.

"Hey…Terrell," I say quietly, fingers edging towards one of the boxes in my head.

"Yeah?" he says.

I close my eyes, feeling like I'm floating away, somewhere far from here. I sniff, thinking about what to say next. How to phrase it.

"Something weird happened at school today, something really, really fucked up."

"What happened?" Terrell says, already sounding worried, which is so Terrell. He cares.

I pull out my phone.

"The person who's been spreading stuff about me and that girl, they put these posters up today. I took some pictures," I say, showing Terrell.

He looks at my phone, eyebrows bunched up, expression growing more and more pissed.

"Have you told anyone?" he asks, tearing his eyes away from the screen and looking at me. I look down quickly, picking imaginary lint from my pants, trying not to make eye contact with him.

"I told Mr Taylor, my music teacher, today. He said he's gonna help us find out who put the posters up. Chiamaka and I are breaking into the school on Sunday to catch them in the act and stop them before it gets any worse – if that is even possible."

Terrell nods slowly. "Those pictures… They look scary…" His voice trails off. "Just be careful breaking in. Whoever's doing this could be dangerous. Are you sure you guys will be okay alone? I don't mind tagging along, if you want."

I nod. "We'll be okay," I tell him, even though I don't mean that at all. I just don't want to drag Terrell any deeper into this. But honestly? I'm terrified. This is our only option at this point, but the situation seems to be spinning out of control – it feels like suddenly everything is at stake. And we have no idea who our opponent is.

"It sounds like proper CSI work," he says, pointing his finger guns at me, coming close to my face with them. I turn his fingers towards himself but Terrell pushes them back towards me and I find myself smiling.

I bury things. It's how I cope. I don't face them head on like Chiamaka does. There's always the risk you'll get seriously hurt if you do that, dragging others down with you.

"Chiamaka even wants me to wear all black like we're gonna rob the school or something." I force out a laugh, but it feels strained.

He raises an eyebrow. "Well if you're gonna do it, you've gotta do it right."

I squint at him. "Are you trying to quote Wham?"

"Who's Wham?" Terrell asks.

"Old white band…"

Terrell *ahhs*. "I only concern myself with young, pretty brown boys, like me."

I laugh out loud at the statement. "You're not pretty," I tell him.

Dimples appear on both cheeks. "That's your opinion. I think I'm very pretty, not as pretty as you, but I think I'm okay."

"Whatever," I say, staring down at the picture of the posters on my phone until the screen goes black.

"Do you guys have any theories as to who might be behind this yet?" Terrell asks, taking one of his textbooks from his desk and onto his lap.

I shrug. "Chiamaka just says it has to be someone in our classes; someone who's watching us all the time."

"What if it's not?" Terrell says.

I scrunch my eyebrows up. What does he mean by that?

"What if it's a teacher? Are there any teachers who might be out to get you?" Terrell continues.

My mind flashes back to Headmaster Ward in the hallway, how he saw the posters of Chiamaka and me, but clearly didn't give a shit. I think about how quick he was to blame us for the USBs.

"The new headmaster... He seems to have some issue with Chiamaka and me. And it makes sense. Before he came, things were fine. There was no Aces; it all started as soon as he arrived at Niveus."

Terrell nods. "Maybe you guys have been looking for the wrong perpetrator. You should go to the school board, get him fired."

I remember in elementary school I had this white teacher. I couldn't understand it back then but she just felt evil. I always got this sense that she hated us – me and the other Black kids in my class. She'd be nice to Jack but would talk down to me like I did something wrong.

At the time I didn't understand it, but maybe this is what's really going on. Maybe Terrell is right.

It makes sense – Ward would have access to all our files, to the school on weekends. He'd be able to play with the CCTV, shut the lights off, create anonymous school accounts… But how do I even go about proving that type of thing?

"We probably need more concrete evidence, though. I'm hoping that on Sunday we'll get that. If all fingers point to Ward, we take him down," I say.

I swear I'm starting to sound just like Chiamaka.

FRIDAY

It's Friday, and I'm at school a little earlier than usual because Chiamaka finally wants to speak to me.

As I walk through the hallway, I can feel the glares of people, the patronizing smiles, shaking their heads like I give a fuck.

There are no more posters of Chiamaka up – the walls are blank, with the exception of the posters for that ball we're all required to go to next week.

I'm assuming the janitor probably took care of it, but the way everything is so spotless, it's like yesterday never happened.

I reach for my phone to check if Chiamaka's messaged again. I was at Terrell's place until really late; so I only remembered to charge my phone this morning, which is when Chiamaka texted.

As I walk into the music classroom we're meeting in, my screen flashes.

Okay, guys, this one's a biggie! Strap on your Gucci belts, and get your popcorn while I tell you a story about a girl who couldn't wash the blood off her hands. Because if she could, maybe I wouldn't know so much about it...

The fuck...

Our favourite mess... I mean Head Prefect, would KILL for some attention from Aces. It must be hard going from Queen status to pauper overnight, so I thought I'd help her climb up the ladder again.

So, the big question:

What's the sentence for murder? Ten years...fifteen... life? Who can help a girl out? More to come soon on this KILLER story – Aces.

My mind flashes back to the file on the USB.

The door of the music room bursts open and I jump back as Chiamaka storms in, tears running down her face.

"Devon, I think something bad is going to happen to me."

24

FRIDAY

[A FEW MINUTES BEFORE]

Whispers are like snakes; they slither into your ears and threaten to poison your sanity with their venom.

"*I heard Jamie knew…*"

"*I can't believe she hasn't been expelled yet…*"

"*I hope Jamie doesn't go down too, for being associated with her…*"

I spot Jamie with some of the football guys by his locker, laughing.

I approach him confidently, striding forward.

"Hi, Jamie," I say, patting his shoulder, which stiffens immediately. I notice some of his friends look at me like they are scared of what I might do to them. The fear in their eyes makes me feel a little unnerved. Even when I was on top no one looked at me with genuine fear, like they're doing right now.

Jamie turns, and when he sees me, his face darkens.

Then he swivels back and says, "I'll see you guys later," and they pat him on the back before rushing down the hallway.

"What?" he asks.

I fold my arms, to hide my shaking fingers. I haven't stopped shaking since yesterday.

"Thank you for what you did yesterday, with the posters," I say quietly.

I heard Jamie and some of the football team took the posters down. It was a nice but random gesture. He's still an ass, but I want to thank him.

"No problem. Is that all?" he replies coldly.

Why is he acting like I'm his enemy again, after his so-called apology on Tuesday?

"About the posters...I w-wanted to ask." I clear my throat. "That was from your party last year, wasn't it? I've only worn that dress once," I say.

He shrugs. "Maybe."

"Do you know what happened that night? The picture was really...weird... I don't remember a lot."

Some people enter the hall, glaring at us and walking away quickly, like they don't want to be too close.

"Nope," he says brusquely.

The picture from that night makes me feel strange. I've never seen it before, and I have no memory of it. Those dolls...they remind me of those dolls from my dreams, the ones that look like *her*.

Why would someone release this picture now, if they've had it for an entire year? What else happened that night?

"Are you done with your questions?" he asks.

I shake my head. "Has there been another blast? I might just be being paranoid but—"

"They're talking about you and the accident," Jamie says smoothly.

I feel a punch to my stomach.

"What!?" I squeak out.

"Aces is hinting at it, at least..."

"What about you?" If Aces is talking about it, they can't *only* be speaking about me.

"Why would they mention me, Chi?" Jamie says casually.

I can't breathe. The pain in my stomach worsens.

"What?" I say a little louder. "I didn't do anything!" Jamie was there. Jamie was driving the car, he was supposed to be watching the road, and he hit her—

"Didn't you hit her? Leave the body? That's called a hit and run, Chi... People go down for that." Jamie's voice burns my ears.

I see blood, I see her blonde matted curls, I see her wide eyes, I see her limp body— I want to cry.

"You knocked her down, Jamie, *you* did that! You drove away, you didn't let us call an ambulance or the cops—"

"Sure about that, Chi?" he asks with a smile, giving me a look that crumples everything inside. It was a look I always thought meant mischief. But now...it feels like hate.

The candy store... Aces knowing so much... The way Jamie is speaking. Before it seemed impossible, seeing as he claimed to love Belle, but maybe he would jeopardize their relationship just to hurt me. Like I said, love and hate are twisted versions of each other. Maybe his secret hatred of me outweighed whatever he felt for Belle.

Jamie turns, stopping in his tracks when I stammer:

"I-It's you, isn't it?" There's a slight tremor in my fingers as I tuck a piece of hair behind my ear. "You're Aces. You set me up in the candy store, you've been spreading my secrets around school. You're the only one who could have known all those things about me. *You*, for whatever reason, sabotaged your own relationship with Belle… But what did Devon ever do to you?"

Because Jamie is – was – my best friend. Sometimes best friends mess up; fall out. Sometimes we make each other so angry it turns into resentment, and from resentment, hate. The way he looks at me now, I can see it is definitely hate. For whatever reason, Jamie hates me…but Devon…

"Is it because we're Black?"

There is nothing except Jamie and me. No hallway. No whispers. Just us.

"Calling me a racist?" he asks.

Growing up, I realized quite quickly that people hate being called racist more than they hate racism itself. Which is why I'm not surprised when Jamie pauses, places a hand in his pocket and slowly swivels back around as he speaks. On his face, there is this unsettling smile that grows wider the longer I stare at it.

He steps forward. "Would I have *touched* you if I hated Black chicks?"

My body vibrates, anger boiling my blood, vision blurring. I push him, hard, and he stumbles back. Laughter escapes his grinning mouth as he catches himself.

Why the hell is he laughing?

"I'm not Aces...but I'm a bit confused here, Chi." He steps closer, the smirk replaced by furrowed eyebrows. "Isn't this what you wanted? Since freshman year?"

"What?" I ask. I can't stop staring at Jamie's face, at how easily he makes such drastically different emotions appear. It's like he's got a switch somewhere on his body.

"For people to know your name, for everyone to talk about you. Popularity?" His confused expression morphs into pity. "Now you have it, Chi." He moves forward again, so close to me I can smell his strong cologne. "How, after all of this –" he gestures around the now almost-full hallway, a grin plastered to his pasty face – "could anyone *ever* forget the great Chiamaka Adebayo?"

He reaches out and lightly touches my hair. I want to throw up, the tears in my throat making it worse. I look up at him. He's so focused on my hair, eyes concentrated the same way they are whenever we do work on the Bunsen burners. Like my hair is a...science experiment.

Abruptly, he lets my hair go, letting the strands that fall from his rough fingers brush against my face.

Then without another word, he turns, and leaves.

The girl who haunts my mind wraps her hand around my neck and starts squeezing, her scream echoing in my brain as I rush through the double doors, up the stairs, and into Devon's music class, where I told him I'd meet him. But when I get there, he's staring down at his phone.

He's seen it too.

"Devon, I think something bad is going to happen to me," I cry out, letting myself go, unable to stop.

The emotions pile up on top of one another – how scared I felt yesterday, how terrified I feel now. Everyone looking at my passed-out body, laughing at it. Jamie watching my body, using it, laughing at it.

"That's Yale gone – my future. I'm going to work in a fast-food restaurant, I can't be a doctor with this—"

"Chiamaka—"

I cry harder. "Everything's ruined—"

Richards's voice startles me as it rises. "Chiamaka!"

I look at him properly now. He doesn't even look like he's wearing a uniform, with that black alien hoodie and his sneakers.

"Chiamaka, we'll find them and stop this. Colleges probably don't care about petty gossip, okay?"

Devon is a bad liar. Of course they care, but I nod anyway.

Sunday needs to go off without a hitch; we need to be on top of our game. No one can know about what I did.

Before Aces hinted that I'm a murderer, I thought the whispers and the judgemental gazes were the worst feeling. I was wrong. The silence is much worse. Now whenever I walk into a hallway, or step into a class, everyone goes silent, even the teachers. The silence is a lot louder and more suffocating than their low voices.

I barely made it through today. It's hard trying to pretend

I'm okay when I'm not. I finish detention, after doing a double shift for missing yesterday's, and waiting for me outside is Belle. She has this huge smile on her face – like I haven't been accused of murder, like my whole life isn't falling apart, like someone isn't trying to ruin me. Belle hasn't seemed fazed by what Aces said; I don't know if that makes her naïve or perfect.

She hugs me, but I can only feel like this hug is a goodbye. I'm just waiting for the next message from Aces now; their story, their evidence. What are they going to say? That I was the one who drove the car, hit the girl, and left her there? In reality I'm an accomplice at most, but that doesn't matter. Aces has twisted everything. And who'd believe me over legacy kid Jamie Fitzjohn?

No one.

My power has only ever been in the hallways; in what people thought of me. How can that compete against someone whose parents are Niveus alumni and donors, people who hold actual power?

Belle links her arm through mine, and I hold on tightly as we start walking, leaving the school.

"Can I walk you home?" I say, hoping she says yes. I don't want to be left alone in my room.

"Sure, and on the way, I'll tell you about how Jamie tried to tell me he has *changed*. He even said you guys are on speaking terms." Sarcasm laces her words.

My stomach turns, and I remember our conversation from earlier. How Jamie looked at me like I was so beneath him.

How confident he seemed that he wouldn't be implicated in all of this. This whole time I was convincing myself that Jamie was as scared for his future as I am for mine, but truthfully he's a white man and *they* are able to get away with murder.

"He has a weird definition of 'speaking terms'."

Belle laughs. "I can't believe anyone would be best friends with someone like him for that long..." she says, side-eyeing me. I nudge her softly, laughing a little too.

"I know, right? And to the girl who dated him – *wow*, I could never."

"Lucky we aren't those people, right?" Belle asks, her fingers threading through mine naturally – which I try to act casual about.

"Right," I say.

"Anyway, I told Jamie that I have no interest in him, that there's another person I'm hoping to see."

My eyebrows raise but I try not to look hopeful.

"Did you tell him who?"

She shakes her head. "I didn't know if you'd want him to know."

I stop in my tracks and she stops with me.

On Wednesday we kissed and then Ward came in and I had to pretend Belle was giving me my homework, praying to God and all other gods that Ward hadn't seen us. Belle rushed out and we didn't get to speak about it, especially after yesterday when I just wanted to be alone.

Until now.

We start walking again.

"Sorry Wednesday got cut short. I wanted to talk after," Belle says.

"Me too."

I don't know exactly what it means or why Belle is the only girl I have ever thought about in that way, but I don't want to examine my feelings, I just want to like her and not think about my parents or the people at Niveus and their judgements and opinions.

"I'm bi," Belle tells me. "And I'm out, but I wasn't sure about you – I mean, everyone sort of knows all the things about you...like the guys you dated – and I didn't want to assume anything! But you pretty much hated me while I was with Jamie, so I thought the most we could ever be is good friends...until Wednesday."

She says "Wednesday" with a playful smile.

"I didn't realize I liked you until Wednesday... Well, I guess I was denying it," I say. "And for the record, I never hated you."

"Right..." she says after a long pause.

We've reached Belle's house now. We stand, looking at each other like it's a contest. I try not to blink, in case it *is* a contest. Then she blinks, and I win.

"Can I kiss you again? We never really got to finish, which I think is so unfair," Belle says, moving closer.

"Just to be fair," I say, and she kisses me again, this time uninterrupted.

From watching TV and reading books, I always got the

idea that a girl liking someone who isn't a guy is meant to be a big deal and that there should be this pressing self-hate that comes with it. I feel almost weird with being *this okay* with being attracted to Belle, but then again there's nothing weird about this in my mind, it feels right.

Belle says goodbye, closing her front door. I start to walk towards my place, a headache forming as I'm left alone with my worries. I can't imagine not following through the future I've dreamed about; I can't imagine going to jail; and I also can't imagine how disappointed my parents will be. I've only ever worked to make them proud. Now they'll think all their sacrifices were wasted on a monster.

I don't notice the black car following me until a few houses down. It moves steadily, stopping and slowing when I do, then speeding up when I pick up the pace. I swallow, walking faster.

I'm probably being paranoid, I tell myself, glancing at the car window. My heart stops. Though the reflections on the glass make it hard to see clearly, I spot a pair of black-gloved hands on the wheel and the same creepy mask from Thursday covering the person's face.

I start to run down the sidewalk, breathing hard now, eyes stinging as I try not to fall over.

What is this?

My toes feel numb in my heels as I try to outrun the car, the sound of the engine revving making my whole body tremble. I can see my gates in the distance and by the time I reach them, stumbling down the path, I can hardly breathe.

I'm hyperventilating. As I push the keycode into the pad and rush through, I hear the car engine switch off.

I unlock the front door and dive inside, slamming it shut, sliding both locks across.

I back away from the door like it's a bomb about to go off, trying to catch my breath but finding it hard to get air in. As I watch, there's a distant movement behind the blurry panes of the door.

They can't get through the gates. They can't get through the gates.

There's an angry beep of the keypad, before a figure approaches the door, and the distorted smile and pale skin of the mask come into view. I scream, backing further down the hallway.

"Mom! Dad!" I yell, sobbing as I watch the door.

No one answers. Not that I should be surprised. They're usually at the hospital when I get home at this time.

Hardly ever home at all.

"Someone help…please," I whisper the last part, voice breaking.

Again, no answer.

I watch as the figure stands there, watching me. Then I watch as the mail slot opens, heart rattling my ribcage as a gloved hand pushes an envelope in. It falls to the ground as the metal flap shuts.

I don't move.

After a few moments, the figure starts to back off, a single black line that thins as it gets further and further away.

I stand in silence for a few minutes, my tears drying up, fingers still shaking as I try to gather myself and work out what to do.

I move towards the door slowly, snatching the envelope up and opening it. It is filled with Polaroid shots.

The first picture is of my house from inside the gates…

The next is a zoomed-in photo of me through the window as I stand in my bedroom.

The next is of me again, tugging my shirt off.

The next I'm in my underwear, the photo taken through the gap in my curtains…

I shakily pick up the next Polaroid.

I'm in a towel, just out of the shower this time.

I already know what's coming.

I let out a breath as I pick up the final photo.

No photo. Just writing.

All will be revealed… I'm ready to have a ball, are you? — Aces

This isn't just texts and high-school pranks.

This is now all of my deepest secrets.

This is my house. My home. Where I thought I was safe.

Aces must have gotten my address from the central administration system. But I have no idea how they got through the gate. I look around my empty foyer.

I move towards the stairs.

It's so quiet, my footsteps echo.

If a tree drops in a forest and no one is there, does it make a sound?

If a girl, all alone in a big fishbowl, screams, and no one is there, can you hear her? Does she even make a sound?

My phone buzzes.

It feels like I'm reliving the same nightmare over and over, and it will never stop.

[one picture attached]
I see London, I see France, I see someone's underpants, past the swing, in the purple tunnel, our favourite music student likes to snuggle – Aces

Devon making out with some guy on a jungle gym.
My phone buzzes again.

There's more where all of this came from, Chiamaka. And I'm not afraid to share – Aces

What does Aces want from us? What is the end goal? It feels like everything is out of control; I am out of control. I can't shake the feeling that they're three steps ahead, and everything we're doing is playing right into their hands. Sunday feels so far away, but I don't know what else to do.

I go to my phone and watch as my fingers hover over the 9 and 1. But I can't call the police. However bad it gets. I can't call them knowing that Aces knows about the hit and run. Or at least, I can't call them before we catch who is behind this. So I open my contact list and scroll down. I hesitate for a heartbeat, before hitting the call button.

25

FRIDAY

"Do you think she actually killed someone?" Terrell asks.

I shrug. Chiamaka does scare most people, but an actual murderer? I don't know. She *has* been in denial about a lot of Aces stuff we both know is true, plus there was the stuff on the USB.

But I also know Aces is trying to twist everything against us, so who even knows if it's true or the entire truth. And after the masked figure in the hallway, those posters of Chiamaka and of me, and being followed, I'm scared about what they might be plotting next. It feels like the tone has changed this week. It was nasty before, but now it feels dangerous.

"Are you sure you don't want me to tag along on Sunday? I'm really good at fighting people. I've watched a lot of spy movies too," Terrell says.

"We'll be okay. I'll send you updates so you'll know we're alive," I say.

A ringtone startles me and I grab my phone out of my pocket.

Speaking of the devil…

"Hello?" I say.

"Devon?" I hear Chiamaka's voice ring out.

She sounds *off*.

"Is everything okay?" I ask.

There's a pause. I hear her sniff. "Someone, *Aces*, followed me home, practically chased me—"

"What? Did you see who it was?" I interrupt.

"No…they were masked, plus I was running for my life. Thanks for asking if I'm okay," she says.

"Sorry." Terrell looks at me with a puzzled expression, and I move off the bed. "Are you okay? Did they hurt you?" I ask.

"I'm fine," she says, but her voice wavers. "They pushed some pictures of me through my mail slot… They've been taking pictures of me, of us. They sent me a picture of you on some jungle gym… It looked private."

My mind flashes back to the park. Terrell. The kiss.

"Devon?"

"Sorry, I got lost there."

"That's fine. It's just…Sunday has to work out, okay?"

"Okay," I say, nodding.

She sounds really shaken up.

"Good. I'm going to go now. Stay safe and try not to do anything incriminating between now and Sunday," she says.

I'm confused. "What do you mean?"

She sighs. "Try to keep your dick in your pants, that's what I mean."

Oh.

"Oh…you too, I guess," I say.

"I will," she says.

"Okay."

And then the line goes dead.

"Who was it?" Terrell asks. I almost forgot he was here – somehow.

I don't want to tell him everything, make him worried. This is dangerous enough.

"Chiamaka, she just wanted to go over the plan again," I lie, climbing onto the bed and sitting next to him, avoiding looking him in the eye.

"Did you tell her about your headmaster possibly being behind this?" he asks.

I shake my head. "Not yet. It's just a theory. One I don't think she'll believe. She's so far up his ass. She's more concerned with getting her titles back. But if it is him, we'll know soon enough."

I anxiously watch Terrell's window, worried that someone is lurking outside. Watching, collecting secrets, plotting.

A cartoon plays in the background, the one Terrell somehow roped me into watching. I swear Terrell has the same taste as my kid brothers.

My eyes drift, landing on certificates and plastic medals hanging on Terrell's walls. I never looked at them properly until now. They all say *Star pupil* or *Highest achieved grade point average*, with different years marked on each.

Terrell is smart, so it isn't surprising. He doesn't seem to go to school much, though. I don't feel like going back either, I feel like running from Aces.

I wonder why Terrell doesn't go. I wonder what he's running from.

I feel myself getting sleepy. I've been at Terrell's for hours. I close my eyes for a moment, drifting off slowly.

I hear him say, "Promise me you won't die on Sunday."

And I can't tell if I dream that or if he really says it, but I answer anyway.

"I promise."

26

SATURDAY

I'm seated in between Mom's legs getting my hair cornrowed while we watch *Girlfriends* reruns and I eat ice cream, occasionally lifting my spoon up to her when I feel generous.

I love getting my hair plaited; it's relaxing – and somewhat painful but in a good way.

"How was school this week?" Mom asks casually, like it's a casual question to ask.

I think of the figure outside our door. The envelope stuffed through the letterbox. My body, exposed. Aces getting closer and closer and closer. I haven't opened my curtains all day, scared of who might be lurking outside in the shadows.

"Great," I say.

"High school feels a lot slower than it is, but trust me, it'll all be worth it when you're at college – whether that be Yale, or Stanford or NYU, it doesn't matter." Mom always loves to stress the fact that the college I go to doesn't matter – but why would she and Dad send me to private schools all my life, get me the best of everything and then expect me to give them mediocrity in return?

"And college is way more fun, less stressful; flies by like that." She snaps her fingers.

People are always telling me this about college, that it'll be better than high school. Given the way the last three weeks of school have been, anything could be better than high school at this point.

"I'm scared I won't get into college at all."

"Don't be silly – you have the grades, the attitude, the extracurriculars," she tells me, finishing up now.

All of that made me feel safe last year when Aces didn't exist.

Now I'm a thief, a liar, a murderer...

I look down at my knees, blinking back the tears.

"Done," Mom says, sighing loudly. I get up, knees clicking and aching from the long sit as I walk over to my full-length mirror.

In the reflection is a girl who looks like me, only different. Normal me has her hair whipped into straightness, a full face of make-up five days out of seven and the look of eternal confidence. Now I stare at myself, like I always do, confused by this thing my hair can do. It can go into this style and change me completely. I'm no longer Chi, but Chiamaka, daughter of a Nigerian mother who loves the hair on my head more than I ever could.

"Thanks, Mom, it's great." And I mean it. I love having my hair like this. But I never go outside like this *ever*. It's too risky. I'd rather straighten than get prodded and stared at, stroked like an animal and questioned. Like Jamie looking

289

at me yesterday as if I were some science experiment he's intrigued by.

I want to stand out for being the smartest and the best, not because my hair frizzes and fascinates.

Mom appears behind me in the mirror and I turn to face her. She smiles at me, like she's so proud. If only she knew all the things I've done. Who I really am.

"Did I ever tell you the meaning of your name?" Mom asks. I shake my head, I'd never really given it much thought.

Mom's eyes look sad. "Well, I named you after my mother. Like you, she was smart and beautiful, knew what she wanted – and what she didn't." Her smile widens. "Chiamaka means *God is beautiful* and Adebayo, from my father, means *she who came in a joyful time.*"

Mom never talks about her family; I've never even met them or been to Nigeria. But I know Mom loves them. Sometimes she'll cook something and say "this was my mom's favourite", or she'll tell me about her childhood and the busyness of Lagos – where she grew up: "Think New York is busy? Lagos is truly the city that never rests". But she never goes into detail, just gives me glimpses of her past life before she married Dad. I'm always left feeling unsatisfied, like I'd dreamed of eating a meal after being starved for a year, got to have a bite and then had it quickly snatched away before I could sate my hunger.

I sometimes wonder if Mom's family were as disappointed in her for marrying Dad as Dad's family were when he married Mom. I wonder, if they ever met me, whether they'd hate me for just existing like Dad's family does.

"Did your parents ever get to meet Dad?" I ask, treading carefully, wanting to get as much as I can out of her before she snatches it away for good.

Mom shakes her head.

"Although, like your dad and I, my parents came from different worlds. While they were both Nigerian, they were from different tribes. My mother was Igbo and my father was Yoruba. I felt lucky growing up to have that mix of such rich cultures, and I wanted you to feel that too. I wanted you to see your name and feel the richness of where you're from. I wanted you to know that when I call your name, Chiamaka, I'm saying, *my daughter is beautiful, and smart and brings me so much joy*." Her eyes are glassy as she takes my face into her hands and kisses my forehead.

I smile, feeling teary but not because I'm sad. I never thought to be proud of my name like that before, or knew that it had some special meaning.

"I have to go and get ready for work now," she says, wiping her eyes and pulling away.

I wish Mom would stay and tell me more. I wish she'd work less and spend longer telling me all about the world she grew up in, who she was before me. But instead I watch her move away.

"I love you," I tell her before she goes. Her eyebrows shoot up in surprise. I don't say it often, so I don't blame her for looking so shocked.

"Love you too, Chiamaka. There's rice and stew in the

kitchen for dinner, if you get hungry," she tells me and I nod, then she leaves me – like she always does – her footsteps echoing in the hallway.

A heaviness weighs me down as I watch the door silently. I sniff, letting my eyes blur and watching the now-quiet room disappear.

Two distinct buzzes sound, sharp and clear.

It doesn't sound possible, but I swear my brain rattles, like it's quivering in my head. I close my eyes, clutching my chest as my breaths gets shallow.

I walk towards my phone, the only thing in focus on my bed, and pick it up like it's an explosive.

I know this is kind of forward, but my house is empty.
– B

The feeling of dread slowly washes away. Its remains filter into the edges of my bones, another feeling taking its place.

I put on a beanie to cover my hair and rush over to Belle's place, knocking on her white door before she drags me inside.

"Want juice or something?" she asks. I nod and she gives me this green juice. We sit at her kitchen table and awkwardly sip in silence. Then she goes, "Nice hat. I don't think I've ever seen you wear a hat before…"

"I do…sometimes," I answer pathetically.

There's more silence, me drumming my fingers against the table. I put the empty cup down and she smiles at me. It's the first time I've been inside her house. It feels very cold and clinical, but not as cold as Jamie's house. His feels like a museum rather than a house, Belle's just feels more modern.

Out of the corner of my eye I catch a glimpse of a frame. A family photo. I notice it because it's the only one I've seen in her house so far. Usually people have photographs of themselves hanging all over, but Belle's walls are blank – there are no signs that tell me she lives here at all, just the fact that she has the key. I smile at her slyly, getting up and walking towards the frame. She gets up too and moves in front of me, covering the photo with her body – her eyes panicked.

"I want to see what a young Belle looked like!" I say, trying to peer over her shoulder, but she blocks me again.

"She's ugly and has no front teeth. Wanna go to my room?" she asks, her eyes lighting up, panic dissolving. "I have a bunch of movies I haven't watched yet, if you're interested."

I raise an eyebrow, trying to peer over again – everyone has photos of them as a kid that they're embarrassed about – but she places her hand on my cheek and kisses me. Then before I know it, we are in her room, lips locked, my fingers in her blonde curls and her arms wrapped tightly around my waist.

I kicked my shoes off when I entered her house earlier, so now I can feel her soft stringy rug through my socks, bunching up my toes then releasing. I can smell her perfume, rosy and light like her.

Suddenly, Belle's mouth is away from mine, and her face is pink. Her arms release from around me as she steps back, slowly, before sitting heavily on her bed, eyes glued to mine. It's not cold but something rushes through me, my hairs sticking up, goosebumps on my neck, my arms, my legs.

Belle is all I can think of, all I can see. I follow her path to the bed and place my hands on her pale cheeks, lifting her face up so that the blue stares into my brown. Placing my head on hers, I breathe her in again, her scent making me want to dissolve for ever and forget about everything. The mission tomorrow, how scared I am, how my future is hanging in the balance.

Our lips touch, and move, deeper and deeper, and I feel myself falling forward. I feel her falling, and then we collide, her back springing off the mattress.

I break our connection, when I feel her hands rub my scalp.

Where's my hat? I panic as I move away a bit.

"What?" she asks.

"My hat…" I say weakly.

"It's hot in here, you don't need it on…and besides, I like your hair, it's nice. I do my hair in French braids too, but I've never seen tiny French braids like those before," she says inspecting my hair.

French braids. I laugh.

"They aren't French braids, they're cornrows."

Pink dusts her cheeks again. "Ah…sorry, didn't know."

I shake my head. "It's okay, really." *I'm just glad you don't look at me like I'm other or something*, I think to myself, but I don't say it because I'm not sure if she'll get that completely.

Belle nods, a sly smile on her lips as she reaches up to her shirt, and starts to unbutton it.

"Want to continue not talking?" she asks, the yellow of her bra making everything inside tingle.

"Not talking is my favourite thing to do," I tell her.

27

SUNDAY

I knew she was serious when she said "Wear all black", but I never thought she meant *Dress like a criminal too.*

Chiamaka waves to me by the back entrance of our school, with a set of jangly keys in her hand and a balaclava covering her face. I got in through the back gate, usually left open for cleaners to come through. It's one of the rare places in Niveus without any CCTV. I kept watching my back on the way here, looking for scary masked figures with sharp knives ready to kill us both. But the streets were empty, with no sign of anyone following me at all.

I approach Chiamaka and her eyes survey my outfit critically, then she lifts the balaclava up slightly, revealing her unimpressed expression.

"That's the best you could do?" she whispers. I'm wearing all black, I don't understand why she's making a big deal about it.

We are basically wearing the same thing, except she's wearing black heeled red-bottom boots and I'm wearing Converse. At least my shoes aren't going to click loudly and alert Aces, and all the other anonymous people out to get us, that we are here.

"What?" I say.

She shakes her head, pulling the balaclava back down roughly. "Nothing, just come and watch the window with me."

"What does this see into?" I ask, walking up to the back door and the window next to it. I can barely see anything with Chiamaka's big head in the way.

"The library," she says.

Convenient.

"Anyone there yet?"

"Obviously not. Do you really think I wouldn't say anything and keep watching them play on the computers?"

I look up at the dark sky. *God, please give me eternal patience.*

"I thought we were going in and hiding behind the cart by computer 17."

She sighs loudly. "Let's go in."

She pushes the key into the hole – loudly, and opens it – loudly, and then steps in – loudly.

I'm no crook, but I know how not to get killed, or found out, and Chiamaka clearly doesn't. I follow her inside, watching her try to tiptoe and fail. We turn into the library. The room is cold, quiet and empty. I scan our surroundings, my eyes landing on computer 17, at the very edge, still. Untouched. Ominous.

"Hey, look," Chiamaka says. I follow her gaze to one of

the walls adorned with what feels like hundreds of black-and-white framed photographs, all with years labelled clearly on the frame. Freshman, sophomore, junior and senior years for each graduating class. It's kind of creepy, the school keeping all of these in *Morgan Library* of all places. Like the students make out while the Niveus alumni watch.

I'm almost positive the photos weren't here when we came on Thursday.

I scan the wall for the junior year photo for our graduating class, crouching a little to focus on it. There are so many of us. At any other school, my face would blur and blend in with the rest of the class, but I find myself easily. Dark skin as prominent as Chiamaka's; the sea of white making us stick out comically.

I spot a sophomore pic from 1963 out of the corner of my eye, where two Black straight-faced strangers stare back at me. I see the change in them in the next picture over – their junior year photograph – one of the girls seemingly taller in this one. It's weird seeing black-and-white photos of Black people sometimes. TV had me thinking we didn't exist until the 80s.

"We should probably go and hide until Aces comes… It's getting close to nine, and I don't want to be caught and have to die wearing polyester," Chiamaka says. I start walking towards the cart by computer 17, but I'm quickly pulled in the opposite direction, towards computers 6 and 7.

"Go under and drag the chair to hide your body," she whispers, completely abandoning the plan she was so adamant we follow. But I do what she says, taking a seat next to her on the ground, under the table, then dragging the chair forward to cover me.

I peek out slightly, computer 17 in my direct vision.

Maybe this plan is better.

We sit in silence for a while. I rub the sleep out of my eyes, leaning back against the wall, but hitting my head against the table in the process.

"Shh!" Chiamaka says, looking annoyed at the fact that I injured myself.

I don't trust myself with words right now, so I don't reply.

"That reminds me... What took you so long to get here?" she whispers, hitting me across the head, her balaclava now off and in her lap.

God, please...patience...thanks.

What took me so long? I was with Terrell actually, at an ice-cream joint near his place.

"I was eating dinner," I tell her, because ice cream technically is dinner.

I can feel her roll her eyes. Apparently now eating's a crime too.

"Next time, waste someone else's time with eating, we have a creep to catch."

"Sorry, I'll starve and faint right in front of Aces instead—"

She pinches my leg.

"What now?" I almost shout, looking at her. Her eyes widen, and she shoves her hand over my mouth quickly.

"I saw legs!" she whispers harshly, her head turning towards the figure. There's a pounding in my ears as I catch a glimpse of movement.

Holy shit.

Inching forward, I peer out through the gaps between the chair legs. I see a person dressed in black, an oversized hoodie covering their small frame, with black jeans and shiny Docs. Their footsteps are heavy, boots scratching against the carpet, gloved hands limp by their sides as they step towards computer 17.

This is it.

"Shit," I whisper without thinking, triggering an abrupt pause from the figure. I freeze for a moment, and I swear my heart stops, my body vibrating as I scooch back slowly. The figure turns towards us, scanning the room, and I see the scary smile of the mask from Thursday, the one that's been haunting me since, with its pale, vacant expression making it look so monstrous and terrifying. They stop looking round and continue heading towards the computer.

Through the small gap, I see Aces pull out the chair in front of computer 17, sit down, cross their legs and reach for the mouse.

My heart is beating so fast. Chiamaka's breathing turns shallow.

She sits back against the wall and curls into a ball. Her lips move but no words come out; she looks so freaked out.

I watch Aces's legs as they swivel gently in the chair.

Chiamaka sits up slowly, passing me the rope she somehow fit in her hoodie pocket. She's going to tackle them, and I am going to tie them up, then we're going to take a photo. Hard undeniable evidence. We'll also take pictures of the account and anything they have saved on there. We planned this, but somehow here, in the library, it feels like we're way ahead of ourselves.

Before I can even catch myself, she's up and charging towards them.

"Reveal yourself, bitch!" she screams, which I guess is my cue to stand.

Chiamaka pushes the figure onto the floor and tries to remove the mask from their face. A few blond curls slip out from their hood.

I move closer, only slightly. I don't want to get any blood on Terrell's hoodie. I hold the rope up, getting ready to jump in and tie their hands.

Chiamaka finally rips the mask off, but instead of holding what I quickly realize is a girl down, she stumbles off their body, visibly trembling. As Chiamaka stares at her, frozen, the girl stands, turns and rushes away from us.

What the actual fuck?

I throw down the rope and run to the library doors as they swing back towards me, hard, and then I race down the corridor. But there is nothing. No one. No sound of feet, or movement in the dark hallway. I can't even tell which way they went. I walk up to some of the doors of the nearby classrooms, and they're all locked from the outside.

I stand for a moment, watching and waiting, before I walk back to the library.

"What the fuck, Chiamaka? You let them get away!" I shout as I open the doors again, but she doesn't even seem to really hear me. She looks like she's seen a ghost. Her face is drained of colour, mouth hanging open.

Before I can say another word, she rushes out of the library too.

After all that talk of wanting to take "the bitch" down, Chiamaka bails when the mission needs her most.

As I bend to pick up the rope, my eyes catch the blaring bright screen of computer 17 instead.

I lean in. The girl left the computer logged into a page with black spade symbols decorating the border.

I sit down, and scroll to the top of the page.

ACE OF SPADES SECRET SOCIETY
Generosity, Grace, Determination, Integrity, Idealism, Nobility, Excellence, Respectfulness and Eloquence.

Aren't those our school values?

An animation of a smirking guy dealing cards grins at me in the corner. The words *Press enter for some fun!* appear across the screen, and even though I feel like I'm about to have a heart attack, I press enter. The school values dash across the screen, swirling and spinning, before arranging themselves in a line. *Press enter again!* the screen tells me, and I do. In a flash, most of the letters disappear, leaving the first letter of each word, like an acrostic.

N
I
G
G
E
R

D
I
E

Cold rushes through me; it feels like someone is walking over my grave.

Nigger die?

The fuck?

There's an arrow pointing down at the bottom of the screen, so I scroll, heart hammering. A folder comes up titled *Checkmate*. I double click and three more folders appear, labelled *Rook, Bishop* and *Knight*. Chess pieces? I click on *Rook* and a short table full of names loads on the page, some I recognize, some I don't. In one row I spot the name Jack McConnel, a sharp tick next it and next to that a short sentence that I have to re-read to make sense of.

Distribution of DR's messages.

Distribution of DR's messages.

DR... Devon Richards.

Messages... All the shit Aces has been sending to everyone. The screen blurs and I shut my eyes, squeezing the tears out. Jack's been sending the messages to people. Jack's the reason Dre found out about all of this. Jack's the reason Dre broke up with me. Jack's the reason I can't breathe whenever I enter the school.

I wipe my eyes and drag the mouse down, watching as more familiar names appear, unable to process. I'm numb as I click back and choose the *Bishop* folder. Like before there are rows of names, with short sentences detailing more *tasks* next to each one – all of them ticked off. The lists in the files aren't long enough to be the names of every single person at Niveus, but I recognize a lot of them as students. Anger bubbles inside as I read more familiar names like *Mindy Lion* and *Daniel Johnson* and other people I've shared conversations with, sat next to in classes for almost four years. All of them, in on this. *This.*

What is this?

I come out of *Bishop*, hovering over the next folder *Knight* now, scared of what I might see if I click. The files here seem to be lists of names and vague duties, nothing else. I decide to exit the *Checkmate* folder all together, wanting to find more than this. Something that will tell me what the hell is going on. There's another arrow underneath *Checkmate*. I scroll and I find two more folders beneath.

One labelled *The Girls*, the other *The Boys*. I select

The Girls first. A list of folders with names and old dates pops up:

Dianna Walker 1965, Patricia Jacobs 1975, Ashley Jenkins 1985… Each folder has a picture of a Black girl. At the end is Chiamaka's name and her yearbook picture. The same one that was on the posters on Thursday.

I click on *Dianna Walker 1965*, pressing the mouse again at a document labelled *Aces 1*. My hands are shaking.

Immediately, scanned photographs of handwritten letters appear.

Looks like our favourite negro has been up to no good
— Aces

What the fuck is this shit?

I wipe my eyes again, clicking onto *Aces 2* in Walker's file. There she is, sprawled out on a bed, no clothes, eyes closed; the photo is black-and-white and crinkled. There's something about the picture that feels like her body is being used, no consent. Something about the way this picture has been taken feels so wrong. It reminds me of the posters of Chiamaka, hung up on the lockers for everyone to see.

My stomach turns, and I close the file, feeling sick.

Suddenly, there's a zapping sound. The graphics on the screen slowly start to fizzle out. I reach into my pocket quickly, grabbing my phone to take pictures of everything I've seen. I scroll up and down, hands shaking, the screen getting darker, and before I can take any more, a loud bang makes me jump back.

I scramble away from the computer like it's an explosive ready to go off. Shielding my head, I frantically move backwards, breath shaky, heart wild. I hear more zaps, like the sounds in old video games, before the screen flashes. The Ace of Spades card appears then disappears, and the background turns a dazzling white.

The words *Ready to play?* materialize in bold black writing.

I push myself up from the floor, running back towards the door. My hands vibrate as I watch the screen, heart skipping several beats when it switches off with a final zap, returning to its dark, ominous state.

There's so much going through my mind right now. My face is wet, my body tense. This is bigger than we'd imagined. So much bigger. Aces isn't one person, or even a small group... It's so many people. And there were so many files I didn't see.

My mind is racing.

But the most prominent thought over all the noise is: *Who was that person in the mask?*

PART THREE:
BALLOT OR BULLET

28

SUNDAY

I don't stop running until I'm far enough away from school that I feel safe. Tears blur my vision, the cold stinging my face.

I look around the street. It's quiet and dark. It feels like I'm the only person left in the whole world. But I know I'm not, because I saw *her*. She was really here. I shakily pat my pockets, searching for my phone. I start panicking when I can't feel it.

I must have dropped it somewhere, but I didn't hear it fall – not that I was paying much attention to anything except getting away. I sniff, more tears falling. I shudder, as cold sweeps into my body. I squint my eyes and spot a payphone in the distance.

The fact that I know her number by heart already is a little embarrassing, but I've always had a good memory. When I get to the payphone, I push in some coins from my wallet, desperately press down on the worn numbers and listen to the sharp ring while looking through the glass, worried I'll see a mask – or worse that face, *her* face – watching me.

"Hello?" Belle's voice sounds uncertain, probably because I'm calling from an unknown number.

"Belle, it's Chiamaka. A-are you free right now?" I ask, sniffing again.

"Oh hey, what happened to your phone?"

I don't know if I'm ready to talk about what happened tonight yet.

"I can't find it," I say.

A dog barks in the distance and I jump a little, eyes darting again, waiting for her face to emerge.

"Are you outside?" Belle asks.

"Y-yeah, I went for a jog… C-can I see you?" I ask, teeth chattering.

"Are you okay?"

"Yes, I'm fine, I just…don't want to be alone right now," I say.

I have a feeling if I go home, *she*'ll be waiting for me there too. If she's the person who was driving the car that chased me home on Friday, then she knows where I live. Mom and Dad aren't home either, so it would just be me, all alone.

"Are you sure? You don't sound fine, Chi… You know you can tell me anything, right?" Belle says.

I nod, squeezing my eyes shut.

"I just—" My voice breaks. "I j-just can't be alone. Can I come over?" I ask.

There's a pause. I can hear her thinking.

"I've been…sick, so my room's a mess, but Waffle Palace

310

should still be open? I'll meet you there?" she says. I feel some relief.

"See you soon," I say, before hanging up and stepping out of the glass box. I look around once again, heart thrumming in my chest.

The girl's scream echoes in my head as my mind flashes between last year, when I was sure I saw her lying on the ground as we drove away, bleeding out, eyes wide, not moving at all... Then tonight, when I ripped that mask away, I saw the dead girl staring up at me.

Alive, grinning and with a thirst for vengeance in her blue eyes.

Half an hour later I'm in Waffle Palace, sitting back, watching the sky through the window as it shifts from dark blue and pitch-black, devoid of stars and light altogether. Trying to take my mind off tonight.

It's only just dawning on me that I left Devon alone back at school. I hope he's okay. I wish I could text him to check how he is. I look down at the dark brown of my hot chocolate, flecks of cream still visible on the surface. The cream is the only part I had an appetite for.

Belle sighs as she sits down, placing her wallet on the table. "Ordered us a huge ice-cream sundae to share. Thought all that sugar would cheer you up," she says with a smile, sounding stuffy. She's sick, but she still came out to see me. I try not to feel too bad about that.

"I don't need cheering up – I told you, I'm fine. Just wanted to hang out," I say, lying through my teeth.

"Could've fooled me." She takes my hand and squeezes. "You look like you haven't slept…or eaten in ages." There's concern riddling across her face. Her expression, however, quickly changes as the waiter places the huge glass bowl in front of us.

Belle claps her hands together, eyes lighting up. She's so happy that I smile a little too as I survey the dessert. Seven big scoops of ice cream, chocolate flakes in each corner, with sprinkles and deep-red strawberry syrup. My stomach twists and a wave of nausea hits.

Out of nowhere images of deep-red blood flash in my brain, and I feel dizzy as I look up at Belle, who's asking if I'm okay. Her face morphs into the girl's.

The girl Jamie and I left at the side of the road.

The girl who isn't dead.

Tears sting my eyes and I try to breathe deeply but I can't get enough oxygen. Belle is beside me suddenly, her arms wrapping around me.

"Is she okay?" I hear someone ask.

I don't know, I answer in my head, closing my eyes.

By the time I'm calm again, our ice cream has melted and been taken away and Belle is looking at me like I have a third head or something.

My chest aches as the images continue to flicker, blurring with reality. My nightmare is coming true, like I always suspected it would.

"I know it's been hard for you at school," Belle starts, "but I want you to know...you can trust me."

I look at her, and I feel like I can tell her anything. I'm so exhausted, these secrets weighing on my conscience. *I can trust her.* I squeeze my eyes shut.

"Aces was right about me. I'm a bad person and before you say I'm not, I am. I've done a lot of bad things, and it's all coming out now and I can't stop it."

Belle is silent for a few moments. I don't look at her at first, too scared that she'll look at me like I'm some monster. But when I open my eyes, she's weirdly calm.

"I'm scared," I say quietly, sniffing. "Of what's happening to me and what's going to happen."

"You're going to be fine," Belle says, taking my hands again. "We all have skeletons."

I feel hot, hoping my sweaty palms don't gross her out. Belle looks at me like I'm not the person I think I am. I wonder how many skeletons she has?

Every face in here flickers, morphing into the girl's. Is it a trick of the light? Or is it my brain playing games once again? I feel like I'm surrounded.

I look at Belle and see her hair matted with blood, as her face shifts. I feel like I'm losing it. The walls of what was left of my sanity are cracking and breaking away.

"Chi..." she says softly. "No matter what, you'll always have me, okay?"

There's a snap in my head, like someone clicking their fingers, and all the faces return to normal, including hers.

It's not much, but being here with Belle makes me feel better. And hearing her say those words makes me feel a little bit safer.

MONDAY

I'm surprised I slept at all last night. Rather than the usual dream sequence – that starts with me at the side of the road next to her dead body and ends with me in a dark room surrounded by blonde dolls – my brain finally let the dark consume me instead.

Coming back to Niveus feels like I've returned to the scene of a crime. Like those guilt-ridden criminals in investigator shows, I feel as if I'm walking into an open trap. One step in the wrong direction and it's over. Somehow a girl I'd never met before the accident is behind Aces and wants to ruin my life. But who is she? Why is she doing this? And how? Is this revenge for what happened that night last year? Has the girl found out who I am and wants me to suffer like she did?

On first thought, it might seem like a smart move for me to stay at home, but with Mom and Dad gone all day and knowing that girl could be coming for me – waiting until I'm alone to strike – I had no choice but to return to the safety of a crowded school of my peers who hate me.

I drag myself through the hallway, trying to keep my head up as I spot Ruby, Ava, and Cecelia Wright by Ruby's locker. I haven't spoken to them in a while. There hasn't been anything I've wanted to speak to them about.

I feel like there's a target on my back. I failed last night, failed to stop Aces like I'd planned, and today anything could happen.

Belle is at home with a cold, and I have no idea where my phone is so I can't even text her between breaks. I'm forced to go up to my "friends", to avoid looking like the loser I feel like.

Despite how tired I am, I force a smile as I approach them.

"Hi, girls," I say, eyes locking on Cecelia. CeCe's never liked me much; she made that clear when she told me once in sophomore year, *"Someday someone's going to knock you off your high horse."* I laughed and told her to keep wishing for the impossible.

CeCe gives me a once-over, eyes pausing at my feet. Today I'm wearing my dark-green crocodile leather Jimmy Choo pumps.

"Nice shoes," CeCe says, face as expressionless as her voice.

I smile. "Thanks, CeCe, they *are* nice." I don't bother to lie by complimenting her too.

Ava's looking down at her shoes and Ruby's looking at me.

"Haven't seen you in a few days. Wanted to check on you but I figured you'd be preoccupied," Ruby says, red brows furrowing together.

"It's been a pretty difficult few weeks, but it's just a blip. This whole thing will blow over and everything will go back to normal by next week," I say with a shrug.

This makes Ruby grin. I can see the fire behind her eyes, smoke wafting into my nose as it burns behind the green. "It's nice that you can remain positive after everything. I like that about you." Her gaze flickers to my shoes as well. "Are those Jimmy Choo?"

I nod slowly, trying to look for the double meaning.

"Hi, Ruby, CeCe and Ava," a voice chirps from behind, and I swivel slightly, met now by that sophomore...Miranda, I think she said her name was. "I dropped by Starbucks and got you three chai lattes, just how you like them. I know you're on a diet, CeCe, so I told them to put your order in a small cup and got grandes for Ava and Ruby."

"Thanks, Molly," Ruby says as they all take their drinks.

I feel a little crack inside, my heart racing as I try not to look bothered. The sophomore leaves and Ruby turns away from us, pushing her handbag into her locker. I feel stupid, standing here like I'm waiting on her or something.

Just as I'm about to tell them I'll see them around, make them think I have somewhere better to be, I hear someone call my name.

"Chiamaka, hey," Devon says, out of breath, looking a little shaken up. I'm glad to see him still alive. This morning I kept hoping nothing had happened. I couldn't check on him either – I had no way to. I wouldn't blame him if he was pissed at me.

"Hello, Richards," I reply as neutrally as I can, hoping he doesn't decide to strike up a conversation right now, *here* of all places. I already look stupid in front of the girls; he's only going to make it worse.

"You haven't been answering my texts. I need to talk to you, *in private. Now.*" He says the last part in a whisper. Devon looks so unbothered by the other three standing next to me.

CeCe sips her latte with her usual blank expression, but Ruby has now turned back around, her eyebrows raised, interest piqued.

Usually people stumble over their words when they speak to us, glancing up at us like they are in awe of the fact that we are breathing the same air. They don't wear the unimpressed expression Richards does. I know Ruby for sure won't like that, and I find it funny, loving that about him. Anyone who can make Ruby stop thinking she's better than the rest of us – particularly me – is someone I applaud.

I clear my throat, looking between him and the girls.

"What about?"

"Don't bullshit, Chiamaka. You know what about."

We stare at each other. For once, he looks determined. As determined as I am to end this. He's right, I do know what he wants to talk about – why I ran and left him alone. But I can't get my head around how I would even go about telling him what I saw. I have to tell him though, I know that – we're running out of time. Something tells me that the girl is dangerous, which means she could hurt us like

317

I hurt her. Last night might have been our only shot at stopping whatever plot she has, and I blew it.

I have to tell him, even if he thinks I've completely lost my mind.

Before I have a chance to respond, Devon steps closer. "I need to talk to you *now*."

Okay, who is he speaking to like that? I feel myself getting annoyed.

"Have you not heard of personal space?"

Ruby snorts, covering her mouth, and Devon looks like he wants to snap my neck. Something about the way he's looking at me makes me pause. Devon is never this forceful... I look down at his hands. He's shaking.

What happened last night?

"I'll meet you in five minutes, lab 201," I say quietly.

He looks a little taken aback, but he nods, then gives me one last lingering look, before turning and walking away.

"Wow, he's angry. I thought he was going to kill us or something," Ava says, watching as he walks through the double doors.

"Why? He's not violent," I reply matter-of-factly. Even though he looked like he wanted to snap my neck, I knew he wouldn't. Devon's not that kind of person.

"Didn't he make that sex tape with Scotty?" Ruby asks, and I shrug, not wanting to talk about him with them. "It was so bad, so obviously shot by a webcam. When I shoot mine I'll get a proper camera," she adds.

"Need to get going, but it was so nice catching up!"

I interject, not waiting for a response before turning away and walking down the hall.

A girl literally runs out of my way; probably scared I'll kill her in broad daylight with the sharp point of one of my heels.

I open my locker, pushing my handbag in slowly, letting my hair fall and hide my face as I blink, sniffing quietly.

I feel a tap on my shoulder and I jump, quickly wiping my face, ready to shout at whoever it is, stopping short when I see Jamie.

I haven't seen him since he went all Thanos on me on Friday.

"Yes?" I ask, stepping back a little. I don't feel safe around him any more, even in this hallway filled with people. Jamie looks pissed off, ready to beat me down like everyone else. What now? What has been said now? I'm so tired.

"Really, Chi?"

"What now?"

Silence.

"You and Belle? And you can't deny it, I've seen the pictures."

What pictures?

"And Aces don't really lie, do they?" he spits.

I narrow my eyes at him, a thought hammering through my mind. *I wonder if he knows the girl is really alive. I wonder if he knew all along...*

"Want me to apologize for kissing a girl you aren't even with? Want me to say I'm sorry for breaking the best-friend code? Oh wait, we aren't best friends. We aren't even friends.

319

Want me to beg for your forgiveness for liking someone without your fucking permission?"

His eyes widen, but before he speaks, I continue – because that's what happens when you hold so much back without release.

"You didn't like Scotty or Tanner. Didn't like Georgie or Paul. You hate it when I'm with someone else, because you think you can control me; control my body. Well you can't, Jamie."

How, after everything, can Jamie think he still has a say over anything I do?

He looks down at my feet, then back up at me. "You have toilet paper stuck to the bottom of your shoe."

I feel my neck burn, but I don't say anything. Instead, I slam my locker shut, making him jump back. Then I turn, walking away, not caring where.

People move away, the sea parting, fear written all over their pale faces.

When I enter lab 201, Devon is seated at the back waiting for me. I knew this lab would be empty, so we could speak alone. He looks so out of it, as though his own worst nightmare also rose from the dead and showed up last night.

I'm guessing he's angry I ran off and ruined everything. I'd be really pissed off if I were in his shoes. Which is why he deserves an explanation. I'm just going to come out and say it. No matter what his reaction is.

I sit opposite him, taking a deep breath before spilling my deepest darkest secret.

"I need to tell you something," Devon starts.

I nod. "Me first. I'm sorry for leaving you alone last night, messing up the stake-out. But I have a good reason," I say, glancing at him.

Devon doesn't seem like he cares all that much about what I have to say. I ignore his face and continue.

"What Aces said about me being a murderer wasn't a complete stretch..." His eyebrows raise. I knew he'd care about that. "About a year ago, Jamie and I were driving home from his parents' beach house when we hit someone. It was bad; there was blood everywhere; I thought she was dead. Jamie made us drive away, not tell anyone and I've lived with that guilt ever since. But then last night, when I tackled that girl to the ground and removed her mask, it was *her*. The girl I thought we'd killed."

Devon's mouth literally falls open. "Are you sure it was her?" he asks.

I nod. "Positive. I could never forget her face," I tell him.

"Fuck," he says.

"Yeah," I say. I sit up straight, leaning in a little.

"What do you think this means?" he asks.

I've been asking myself the same question.

"I have no idea," I say, feeling sick. "I don't know how she fits into all this; into Aces. But what did you want to tell me?"

He takes his phone out and unlocks it. "I tried messaging

you all night," he starts. "When the girl ran out, she left the page she was logged into open. So I went through the files."

Now it's my turn to be shocked.

"What did you find?"

He pauses, scrolling through his phone, and then he slides it over.

"I found a lot… There was a lot of scary shit. I don't know how the girl is connected though; if she doesn't go to Niveus I don't know what she would have been doing on the computer," he says as I scan the screen of his phone.

The picture I'm looking at is grainy, but I can still make out most of it. I spend the first few seconds trying to make sense of it all, but then I see an acrostic made up of the first letters from the school values. It feels like I've been punched in my stomach. I swipe and there's another picture. I see a list of names next to…tasks? *Watch CA during chemistry* and *place USB flashdrive in CA's locker* – with information on which class I'd be in on the specific date the task was due. It's creepy as hell. I scan the list a few times, searching for names I know. Names of people I didn't necessarily trust, but who I never thought could do something like this. I search for the names of my "friends", and as expected I see both Ruby and Ava and their tasks in bold. Both tasked with *collecting information on CA*. I blink. I knew Ruby wouldn't pass up the chance to hurt me, Ava too.

When I don't see Belle's name, I feel…relieved. I swipe. The final picture is a file labelled *Dianna Walker 1965*.

I look up at Devon again. "Was that all of it?" I ask, shivering.

He shakes his head. "There were so many files, I only saw some of them before the computer switched off, and I could only take those three pictures. It must have been on a timer or something. I don't know." He rubs his eyes. "Everything on that computer...it made it seem like everyone's in on it, that this extends past a couple of people targeting us because they want revenge, or they don't like us. It's...bigger."

I nod in agreement, feeling numb. Everything makes sense but at the same time doesn't. I look back down at the phone. "Who was Dianna Walker 1965?"

"Uh, there was a list of past students – students who I think Aces had targeted... Dianna must have been here in 1965? I didn't get to look at much of her file, but Aces seemed to have started with her," he says. "There was a photo...one that was like those...posters of you."

Wow.

"Have you looked Dianna Walker up? Where she is now?"

He shakes his head then takes his phone and types her name into the search engine. I watch him scroll for a while, clicking through into different sites, pictures, social media pages, companies, message boards. But there's nothing. No one who is even a close match to the scant details we have to go on.

"There was another name I saw..." Devon mutters. I look over at the screen as he types in *Patricia Jacobs 1975*. I watch him search through the results. Rows of text, rows of images scroll past. *Patricia Jacobs Niveus* he types next.

Patricia Jacobs Aces. Patricia Jacobs Bullying. Patricia Jacobs drop out.

"It's like they don't exist," I say, feeling a dull ache in my chest.

"Yeah," Devon replies, looking dejected, and anxious, as I imagine I do. I don't even know what to think any more.

The warning bell rings loudly.

"We're going to have to go to class, act normal. Let's meet up at lunch, Morgan Library, we can talk more then, maybe even gather more evidence," I tell him, trying not to sound as panicked as I feel. I hold back the rest of what I want to say, but I know he's probably thinking it too.

Aces is about race and someone powerful at the school has made it their mission to create a group to get rid of me and Devon.

And they're winning.

I have even more questions than answers, like who that girl really was and how she's connected to this racist plot. How many people are involved? How far does this go?

Are we safer here, where the masked figures lurk in corners wearing the faces of your former friends behind the plastic, or at home where it is so quiet, and anyone could do *anything*?

I have one final thought as we exit the lab separately.

This might be our last week at Niveus Private Academy.

29

MONDAY

The bell rings. I've done nothing for the whole of first period. I've just sat at my keyboard, staring at it blankly, head spinning. I didn't sleep last night, so I downed a cup of cheap coffee from one of the vending machines, but it just made me more jittery. More anxious.

Terrell called last night to ask how it went and I wanted to tell him, but I couldn't. I thought Chiamaka should be the first to hear it. It's messing me up. I feel shaky all the time, like there's a masked monster behind me, watching my every move.

"Devon?" Mr Taylor's voice cuts through my thoughts.

I turn to look at him. "I was just about to leave – I have this headache."

He nods, hesitating before saying, "I noticed you weren't playing; is everything okay?"

One of the unspoken laws I grew up with was *Don't be a snitch*. Even though every part of my body is fighting it, I say, "I feel like a lot's happening."

I can feel the hood-me slapping the private school boy seated in this chair around the face, threatening me.

Mr Taylor isn't like other teachers, I tell myself. I feel safe around him, and he's always wanted the best for me. I'd asked him on Friday if he'd found out who was behind the posters, and he'd told me that he hadn't but that he'd be keeping an eye out for me.

"What's up?" Mr Taylor pulls out a seat and leans in.

I rub my face. "I think I know who put up those posters. And the people who did that are still spreading rumours around about me and my…friend. I thought I could handle it, but it's only gotten worse. I think we're in danger, and I think we need someone to help us stop it before it's too late."

I shouldn't have come in today. What I saw told me that Niveus itself is somehow at the centre of this all, but Chiamaka wasn't answering her phone and I needed to tell her. I should have told her and left, taking her with me.

Instead of using my common sense, I found myself wandering off to music class, like a zombie. I even saw Daniel. He'd smiled his big handsome smile at me, but all I could see was his name on that list, and him pretending to be nice to me but ruining my life behind my back.

I can't "act normal" when I know something really fucked up and dangerous is going on. I shouldn't have listened to her. I shouldn't have stayed.

The wrinkles on Mr Taylor's face bunch up on his forehead. "I was once in high school too. Kids can be horrible, so I can imagine what you're going through." Something in his eyes changes, it's a small flicker but I notice it. Sympathy, I want to say, but it feels like something

326

different. "Especially with college applications coming up, I know how stressful it can be," he finishes.

I nod. "Juilliard is the only thing keeping me sane right now." This piece is coming together – kind of. I think Terrell was right about the drums. The drums will definitely make it better, but then what if it's still not good enough?

I look up at Mr Taylor, who is looking at me with a smile on his face. I'm not sure why.

"You're applying to Juilliard?" he asks. Which is so strange, because, *obviously*. He and I discussed it at length at the end of junior year. It's all I've been working towards.

I don't feel like I can give an answer to that, I'm so confused. But I nod slowly.

"Son—" A laugh jerks out of his mouth, then another and then he's full on laughing. "I'm sorry— I just— Seeing your face— I can't keep this up," he says between breaths, laughing like I told a *really* funny joke, slapping his knee with exaggeration, basically screaming. "Son, you're not going to Juilliard." He wipes his eyes and I feel something sink.

What the fuck? I know it's hard to get into and everything, but…Mr Taylor doesn't sound like Mr Taylor right now. He's the most optimistic person I know; he encourages all of us to do things we want to do – he's encouraged *me* since I joined.

"What?" I manage, my throat burning. "Why?"

He reaches forward and plays B-flat on my keyboard.

"They tend to only accept high achieving students…"

"I get straight As in all my classes," I say.

His voice lowers. "I wasn't finished." He stands, towering over me, and places his hand in his grey pants pocket. "They also tend to be pretty strict on class attendance – which, if my memory serves me right, is pretty poor for you."

What the actual fuck?

"I thought seniors were allowed to do that?" I say breathlessly.

"Of course they can…with sign-off from a teacher," he says, like that's not exactly what I did.

He gave me permission; he said I could; he told me it was okay, he—

"I-I thought you sorted it out?" I stammer.

"Son, you should never leave your fate in the hands of someone else," Mr Taylor says, stepping back now. His eyes, which were a light soft-blue, now look like a grey storm.

"You told me you sorted it out," I repeat like a broken record. *He told me he sorted it out.* "…that it was okay to practice whenever I needed to." My voice rises and the bile in my stomach itches to crawl through my throat and spew all over him and his suit.

Mr Taylor walks back over to his piano and strokes his fingers across the keys as a loud, discordant pattern of notes screeches out.

"That I did. But it's okay, it's okay…" He pats the air, like he's patting me from afar. "It's okay not to go to college, it's okay." Smiling wide. "Not all people are suited for higher education. Especially your kind. *Your kind* needn't have an education."

I want to scream for help, but he's suddenly up and by the door now, blocking the entrance. And anyway, who is going to help me?

Mr Taylor is one of them.

"Why?" I whisper. "Why are you doing this?"

Mr Taylor's face morphs, his expression confused. Like the answer is so obvious, and I can't see it. He leans back against the oak door-frame.

"Because I can."

He turns and leaves, and the door to the classroom closes behind him, slamming shut, *bang*, like a gun.

This doesn't feel real. This *can't* be real. Mr Taylor; Jack; Daniel…all these people I've known for years, trying to ruin my life. But I know it is. This is happening.

I shove my things into my bag and rush out, running down the stairs so fast that I almost trip and fall. I'm terrified of bumping into Mr Taylor. I'm terrified they're all watching me. I have to leave; I have to get out – but I need to take Chiamaka with me.

I dial her number, hoping she's found her phone by now. Voicemail.

I call her again. Nothing.

I run across the school, checking random rooms, the libraries, the girls' bathroom, even. Chiamaka's nowhere to be found. She's probably in class. We should have left sooner. Should have jumped to conclusions, should have pieced everything together.

I rub my eyes roughly. *I need to leave. I need to get help.*

I push through the big entrance doors, out into the open air.

"Hey! Stop right there!" a deep voice says. I feel spikes at the back of my neck. This feels like one of those nightmares I used to have when I was young, where I was trapped inside a cell of some kind, screaming for help, but no one would hear my pleas over the sound of the evil nightmare monster's laughter.

I run as fast as I can towards the black gates, slamming the exit button by the steps.

I need to get out.

The gates start to open, grinding slowly, until suddenly they stop.

I want to scream, I've got to run.

I stumble, looking back at Headmaster Ward, a remote control gripped in his bony fingers. I look at the gap in-between the gates; it's small, but I can make it. I jump through just as the gates start closing, wrenching my bag through as the metal clinks together.

I turn one last time. Ward is at the top of the stairs, expressionless as he watches me.

He takes a step forward and my heart jumps out of my chest as I run and run and keep running.

30

MONDAY

It feels weird being here in class, taking notes like nothing's happened. Eyeballs itch the back of my neck, and I dig the lead of the pencil into the page, gripping it hard as the teacher's words go over my head.

I tap my leg against the chair, desperately waiting for the bell to go off.

The bell rings.

I gather my things, as voices mesh together over the bell, chairs scrape the floor, tables move and people pad out of the classroom. I hear the sound of a few text tones, but I'm already out the door, head down, as I storm through the hallway towards Morgan Library. I need to see Devon and show him something I saw in the library on Sunday before I saw *her* – and I desperately want my phone back.

I push open the doors of Morgan, which creak loudly. My heart beats fast as they close behind me, cutting off the hubbub outside. I scan the room, bending and looking under the tables we sat under last night. I spot my silver phone-case and I sigh with relief.

"Thank *God*," I mutter, before reaching out to grab it.

Surprisingly it hasn't died yet, but I have one million and one messages from Devon and one from Belle.

Sorry I can't be with you today, will miss you
though x – B

I smile down at the message.

School sucks without you, get better soon so that
I have your face to look at when I feel down x – C

Ha, I'll try x – B

I stare at the message for a few moments before pocketing my phone. I feel like Belle is the only good thing in my life right now. I'm scared of Aces ruining that too somehow.

The bookshelves are filled with every book known to man – which isn't an over-exaggeration. I read once that Niveus gets sent a copy of any book published in the country, which is pretty impressive, I'll admit. My eyes fall on the books on the bottom row.

This section of the library is empty. No one at the computers. I stare at computer 17. It's watching me... like any moment it will transfigure into the girl, tackle me to the ground, lift its scary mask and smile.

A gentle laugh distracts me, my face heating up when I hear the familiar sound of people kissing. I inch forward, not wanting the couple to be alerted by my presence. Kneeling,

I reach out for one of the yearbooks – 1965 – and take a seat on the ground by the shelves as I run my fingers down its hard navy spine before I reach the sharply contrasting red of the flag at the bottom. The confederate flag.

I gaze up at the wall of creepy photos, hundreds of white faces watching me. And in the odd photo, Black faces stare out, wearing blank expressions, their hair beaten into submission like mine. The Black faces aren't always in the photos. That's to be expected. Most *good* schools didn't let people who looked like me in, and when they did, it wasn't many of us. I can't imagine what life would have been like for them, having protestors outside their schools every day, parents complaining about their existence there. Like they were these dangerous criminals, just because their skin was brown and not cream.

I look at all of them closely, tracing their faces in each photograph.

Wait a minute…

My eyes scan the pictures over and over, the thrumming in my ribcage making me feel jittery.

1965…1975…1985… The Black students; they all just… disappear. Their senior year.

Opening the yearbook, I search for their dark faces, eventually landing on a section titled "Camp Aces 1965". *One hundred years later, we proudly live up to our ancestors' legacy*, I read. A hundred years before would be 1865… the end of the Civil War. The war that preceded the abolition of slavery.

My heart racing, I scan the large photo of men in dated Niveus uniforms, staring at me. In each of their hands is the same playing card: the Ace of Spades.

A chill trickles down my spine. I stare at the men, pausing when I spot the face of a familiar student who grins at me in the corner of the page. Greasy hair – as black as the night – slicked back, face gaunt, and spindly, bony fingers wrapped around the same playing card.

It looks just like…

Headmaster Ward?

But that can't be…

I take my phone out, messaging Devon.

Hello?

You better show up.

Devon, this isn't the time to ghost me.

You have ten more minutes to show before
I get really mad.

I'm about to message him another threat when I feel my phone buzz.

A notification from Facebook.

[Belle Robinson has posted a new picture]

It's a throwback to her by some lake with a crocodile casually in the shot. I like it, scrolling to comment, but pause as a comment pops up from a Martha Robinson: *That croc would make a cute handbag.*

I click Martha's profile. The page loads slowly, her info appearing first. She's a few years older than us, and she and I have two mutual friends: *Jamie Fitzjohn* and *Belle Robinson*.

Belle hardly mentions her family, but then again I never mention mine – though at least she's met them.

A part of me wonders if Belle doesn't think I'm the sort of person you'd take to meet family. Jamie's clearly met Martha. Parents always like him, mine included. Like me, parents can't see through his façade; they can't see that his charm is manufactured and underneath it all lies a really terrifying person.

I refresh the page again, wanting to snoop some more. Martha must be her sister.

The page finally loads fully and the first picture pops up, Martha's photos appearing one by one.

Blonde hair. There are tremors in my head.

White skin. Searing pain in my stomach.

Her piercing scream. Numbness in my hands.

So much blood.

31

MONDAY

I'm sitting on Terrell's bed, chest aching, as he stares at me.

"So, let me get this straight." Terrell has his mad scientist look on his face. "Every ten years, you think they've been admitting two Black students, letting them settle in, then screwing them over and trying to ruin their lives?"

I nod.

"And who is Aces?"

"A whole bunch of people at school – students… I saw a list of names – names I recognize." The memory of Jack's name sends pangs all over my body. "And I think the teachers are involved too." Mr Taylor's laugh echoes hollowly in my memory. I'm still freaked out. "They all seem to have tasks. And they do this until we have no choice but to drop out, I guess, our futures ruined, or I don't know…worse."

"Fuck." Terrell moves off the bed and sits in front of his old battered computer screen. "Ever researched your school?" he asks, typing *Niveus* into the search engine. Bullshit is on the table next to the mouse, staring at me like I'm invading his space. Maybe I am.

"Well, yeah, kind of, when Ma put me up for the

scholarship, but not properly."

"Did you know Niveus means 'white' in Latin?"

I shake my head; of course it does.

Terrell types in *Niveus Private Academy* this time, then hits enter.

"These people are slick as fuck, but not that slick," he says, his voice quiet as he concentrates on the screen. "It's almost like they want you to find this shit. Like they're proud of it. I mean, right here it says that the school was founded by some of the biggest funders of slavery – popular plantation owners, merchants and bankers who financed operations. It's all here, you don't have to go looking too far."

My head swims and I zone out, the shock making it hard to process it all. Terrell goes on about the school's founders, but I close my eyes, thinking about the money Ma put into that school, just to get me through. All for nothing. We have struggled every day, every fucking day, and it won't mean a thing.

"Von."

I snap out of it and look at Terrell.

"Hmm?"

"The school was founded in 1717. Isn't it more than coincidence that the computer they use to do all this shit on is computer 17?"

Yeah...

Coincidence...

My heart beats fast as I look at Terrell, his hair jolting as he types, focused.

"Terrell," I say cautiously. "How did you know that?"

He looks at me. "What? That the school was founded in 1717? It says it right here."

I shake my head, organs shaking, mind shaking, everything shaking.

"How did you know about computer 17? I never told you about that."

He pauses, and then dimples appear as he shrugs. "You must have told me."

I didn't. I know I didn't.

I purposely left out details like that. I didn't want to involve him at all in the stake-out. I didn't want him to get hurt.

"Weird. I don't remember saying it to you."

"Strange how memory works, isn't it?" he says after a long pause, his voice faltering a little.

The only way Terrell could know that is if…is if he's in on it too. It's convenient that he showed up just when this all started, claiming to know me. Maybe he was placed to watch over me like I'm a lab rat, paid by Niveus to pretend to like me.

I've been so stupid. Trusted a complete stranger, who despite everything is probably working for Aces. The pictures of the purple tube. Pictures of me outside Dre's apartment. Everything about Dre. Maybe that's how Jack knows Terrell too… Maybe they were working together, trying to ruin my life, hurt me, for whatever reason.

Why can't I remember you, Terrell?

I take out my phone, trying not to look panicked. "Looks like my ma needs me home," I lie, which gets his attention. I move off his bed, standing up at the same time as he stands up from the chair.

"Want me to walk you home?" he asks.

I force a smile, shaking my head. "I think I need to be alone right now."

He nods. "Do you know what you want to do about Niveus?"

I don't say anything, I can't bring myself to. I can see him trying to understand my sudden shift in mood, looking at me, unblinking, like he wants to say something.

I just want to leave, so I say, "I'll see you, okay?" We lock eyes, his face confused and a little sad.

I'm breathless as I spin around, rushing out of his room, down the stairs and through the front door. He calls after me, but I don't stop or turn or listen, I just run – again.

When I get home, Ma is standing over the cooker, boiling potatoes. She looks at me, her eyes filled with love as she opens out her arms for a hug.

I put my bag down, throwing Terrell's hoodie down with it, and go to her, letting myself finally cry, knowing my ma is not a fraud like everyone else.

"Baby, what's wrong?" she asks, and I don't know what to tell her.

The school you have to work three jobs to keep me at is incredibly fucked up and racist.

No one asked for my permission before leaking my life to the world.

Me and the boyfriend you don't know about broke up... Oh yeah and, Ma, I'm gay and I don't want you to hate me for it because I love you so much and I can't live with you hating me so please don't.

That's what's wrong; all those things, and then some. But I can't speak; if I speak, I'll tell her everything, and then she'll hate me.

So I just cry and cling to her. The bubbles in the boiling pot grow louder.

"Vonnie, tell me what's up. You know you can tell me anything, right?"

I shake my head. That's what she says now, but she doesn't mean it. If I had girl problems, I could tell her everything, but not this.

"I don't want to lose you, Ma."

"Boy, I'm going nowhere. Jesus keeps me alive and well. Tell me what's wrong." She pulls away and forces me to look at her.

"I hate school." *What a fucking understatement.* "And you work hard so I can go." *I can't breathe, I can't look at her.* "I hate it so much. They look down on me, say things about me." I'm crying so hard it shakes my bones, rattling my ribcage. My nose blocks and I feel trapped in my own body.

"Vonnie, you only have a few months left...You should have said something ages ago, I would have pulled you out if I knew you'd be happier somewhere else."

"It's only gotten really bad now – they keep talking about me."

"Saying what?" she asks, eyes glassy and concerned.

I can't do it. I feel so fucking sick. I've known I'm gay for years. I have known and I got comfortable with it – but at times like this, when I know life could be easier without my sexuality, I wish I hadn't been born with the burden.

"Do you know a boy named Terrell?" I ask, because I don't want to have to tell Ma that the rumours detailing my sex life with a rich white kid from school and the dealer she told me not to be friends with are true. I don't want to weaken her heart, cause her pain.

Ma looks shocked. "You remember Terrell?" she asks.

Ma knows Terrell?

"I...know who he is, but I can't remember him."

She turns, putting the oven off, before moving towards our dining area and taking a seat on one of the lawn chairs. I stay where I am.

Ma looks at me. Straight at me. "I wanted you to come to me about your sexuality in your own time. After the Terrell incident, you couldn't remember, and I didn't want to bring it up."

My sexuality?

I rush over to the trash can in the corner and throw up. My body is finally doing what it's threatened to do this whole time. It's all water; I haven't eaten today. The lawn chair scrapes against the ground and then Ma's there, rubbing my back, over and over.

I hate this feeling so much. What does she remember that I can't?

"We don't have to talk if you're not ready, Von."

I shake my head.

It's out there now. No turning back.

The tears mix with my running nose as I bend over, hovering above the trash, trying to breathe.

"I'm gay," I choke out, daggers diving into my gut, shaking my entire being. I'm not sure if it was loud enough for her to hear.

"Yeah, I know," she says, and something washes through me. I'm not sure if it's relief. More tears mix with the nastiness that is snot. I stretch my hands out to the table next to the trash can for tissues, but Ma hands me some.

I wipe my face harshly.

"Ma, what happened with Terrell? Why c-can't I remember him?" I ask. My throat is achy and dry as I turn to face her. She avoids my eyes, walking over to the fridge to get a bottle of water and handing it to me.

"Most things I heard were from Jack." Ma wipes her face with her dry wrinkled hands. "What I know for certain is that you went to school, and you came back soaking wet, with a huge bump on your forehead and blood all over."

Goosebumps prickle my arms as the image of me engulfed by the water flashes: a little boy who looks like Terrell dragging me back, screaming that cracks the walls of my brain.

"I asked Jack – about what happened, why you were wet,

342

bloody, beaten. I don't usually ask, I know you don't like me to ask, but you're my child and you were hurt." Her voice breaks at the end, but she looks at me, hard-eyed, like she doesn't want to show weakness. Even her back is rigid.

"Jack told me about you and a boy. Terrell Rosario. And how you kissed and got caught by the wrong guys," she tells me. My chest squeezes.

An image appears again, all grainy in my mind, like an old home video… My middle-school playground; Terrell's face, his hair shorter, no dreads just curly kinks.

"Wait—" Terrell says.

I move back, scrunching my eyebrows up.

"What?" I say. I need to go home, help Ma with dinner.

He moves closer, eyes looking around cautiously.

"Remember how you told me that you sometimes think about guys – about holding their hands?" He reaches out and threads his fingers through mine. "Holding them." He moves closer, and my breath catches, heart unsteady. "Kissing them… I just wanted to tell you that I do too. I think about doing that with you. All the time," he finishes.

"I cried and prayed for you, Von." Ma's voice tears the memory apart, the brown plastic film from the video tape unravelling in my mind. "I prayed you would be okay," she continues. "But I knew this neighbourhood and I knew that school was too poisonous, especially if what Jack said

343

was true. After that, you didn't want to talk about it, hid away in your room and eventually, I assumed you forgot... blocked the memory."

I did forget.

She wipes my face. Wipes away the tears, the snot, and whatever else that sticks.

"You don't care that I'm gay?" I ask, because that's what scared me most. I feel a little light-headed as she shakes her head.

"Don't do drugs, stay out of trouble, do well in school, date whoever you like. That was the only thing I ever said to you."

I'm crying again, body jerking forward as the tears spill. Mama pulls me into her arms. I never thought the conversation would happen this way.

"I love you so much, I just want you to be happy," she says quietly.

You too, Ma. I want you to be so happy.

I check my text messages when I'm in my room, after I sat with my ma for what felt like hours. I'm seated on the bed with my brothers, who are watching some cartoon and arguing. The sound of slaps and yells agitates me.

I checked your messages when you were asleep, that's how I knew about computer 17. I'm sorry, I just wanted to help. – T

It's okay.

I'm not sure if it is okay, I'm not sure if I trust him any more or if that excuse is even real, but I'm too tired to be angry at him. Besides, he's my only real friend right now.

Sorry again. – T

The memory of us in the middle-school playground replays over and over in my mind, then the memory of us kissing, how nice it felt. Terrell holding my face, kissing me like kissing me was a good thing... Followed by blinding pain my brain won't even allow me to remember in full. But I see their fists, I hear them shout. And I know in that moment that kissing me is bad, very bad. I feel dirty. They made me feel so fucking dirty.

And then I'm on the beach, the sand getting in my sneakers, the waves calling out to me. The water crashing violently, with its arms wide open. The sea is so perfect to me, it makes me feel at peace – but it's nothing like that, not in the slightest. It's chaotic, it swallows lives and people. The waves scream, hit, beat the sand down, like the sand is an abomination. And even though the sea is this monster, I'm drawn to its chaos. I grew up on that shit. That chaotic shit. It's all I recognize.

My pa and his major fuck-up, my ma and her fuck-ups – with her messy, abusive boyfriends who left us when her clothes would burst from her swollen belly – to me and my fuck-ups. My everyday fuck-ups.

And so, I stepped into the sea, let it pull me in. Give me that familiar familial fucked-up embrace.

My phone dings and Chiamaka's name pops up.

Where are you? – C

I go off my and Terrell's chat screen and to Chiamaka's. I have so many messages from her.

My brothers jostle me as they begin to wrestle.

"If you guys don't stop, I'm gonna tell Ma, and you two will get your asses beat," I say, which immediately stills them, as always. Ma isn't even a scary person, she hardly beat me as a child, and she doesn't beat them. But Ma has this look, one that makes you think she could whoop your ass without hesitation.

I refocus my mind on texting Chiamaka back.

I left school early, I tried calling but you didn't answer. – D

Because I dropped my phone in Morgan last night, only just got it back at lunch. Anyway, I know how the girl I saw yesterday and Aces and Niveus are connected. I'm going to send you an address. Meet me there. I need to do something. And then we need to talk. – C

It's been a rough day and to be honest, I don't have the

energy to talk about this or anything right now, but I guess I have no choice. There isn't any time to waste. And I want to hear about the gaps in this crazy reality, how everything is connected.

Understanding what's going on is the only way to stop it.

Okay. – D

I text, forgetting to ask her when she wants me to arrive. I start tapping out another reply, but I'm interrupted again by the buzz of my phone, followed by a text tone that makes my heart skip and my brain fuzz.

Windchimes.

MONDAY

I storm all the way to Belle's house after school, skipping detention. Nothing matters any more, not school, not detention. I'm done, unofficially dropping out; I can't go back there, not after what I discovered today. It's what they wanted, us dropping out – disappearing. I have no idea what this means for my future, for college, but we need to deal with Aces…Niveus, now.

My face and chest are tight from my earlier tears, as I knock on Belle's front door.

She answers, giving me a huge smile and looking slightly confused by my unannounced presence here. I don't bother returning her smile because I'm not here to smile or laugh at her jokes or watch a romantic comedy and pretend.

I'm here for answers.

"Hey, I didn't know you were coming… Would have cleaned up a little," Belle says, still sounding stuffy. I notice she's wearing pink silk pyjamas, and she looks really awful. At least she wasn't lying about her illness. We walk through her foyer and into her kitchen. Hers is bigger than mine, with white marble everywhere and high-tech everything.

I remember how Dad complains about kitchens these days, and how technological they are. *"One can't even open a fridge normally any more,"* he always says. Which is an exaggeration – I mean, if he wants to open the fridge, he could always buy whatever model Richards probably has.

"I'm going to ask you a few questions, and I want the truth," I tell her. She pulls out a seat for me, but I remain standing.

Belle looks at me, then the seat, then me again.

"What questions?"

She says it like she hasn't got a clue. And I'd believe her too if I could *just* believe anything anyone ever says to me again.

How do I begin to explain the incoherent questions that have been circulating in my brain since last night? Things I have been trying to link up. Questions that slap me into consciousness, hold my eyes open, beat my chest so that it feels bruised and aching; questions that plague me like the familiar face of a dead girl.

"Do you think…" I stop. "Do you think that death is permanent?" I ask.

Belle's eyes widen. "Chiamaka, are you okay?"

"I'm fine," I say, sniffing. "Answer the question."

"What sort of question is that?"

"It's one I keep thinking about, and I know it doesn't make sense – not to an innocent person, but I think you can provide an answer for me."

We stare at each other, her face blank on purpose, her

eyes dull but deliberate. I can't believe I didn't see through it before.

I'm not as good as I used to be...

"I'll tell you a story I'm sure you already know. Almost a year ago, Jamie and I were in a car, driving back from his parents' beach house, when we hit someone." The images, clear as day, flash before me like they always do, as my head hits the dashboard and the worst night of my life begins once again. "Belle, on Sunday night, I went to school, waited in Morgan Library by computer 17 and knocked a dead girl to the ground. A girl I thought I'd hit and left to bleed out like an animal. So, I ask again –" my voice is shaky, face moist from tears that stain my skin –"do you think death is permanent? Or can corpses undie, roll out of graves, and find their way into Niveus?"

Belle sits there calmly, her legs crossed, like what I just told her is equivalent to announcing there will be rainy skies or that the time right now is a quarter to five. My whole body rattles.

The floorboards creak above us and I look up.

"Chiamaka, I can explain," she says, voice flat.

I'm not as good as I used to be, otherwise I would see through a bitch and a liar so easily, like I could before.

"Explain what? That your fucking *sister* is—"

"Chiamaka, please…" There are tears in her eyes.

The problem with compulsive liars is that unless you're up to their speed, it's so hard to tell if anything is true or not. The resemblance to her sister is striking. I can't believe I didn't see this before. Now when I look at her, I just see Martha.

"Since I saw Martha, I've come up with a hundred wild theories, blaming Jamie, thinking I was losing my mind – what's fascinating is that not *once* did I think you had anything to do with it."

Not once.

"Then I started to piece things together, and really it's my fault for not being more suspicious when you came and spoke to me that first day after school. So when I speak to Richards and he's telling me about Niveus being this evil institution, I start remembering things like how it's weird that there's this camp so many of you guys go to every summer. I never even really questioned why you'd go to a camp just to be with the same people from school, but then…then I stumble across 'Camp Aces' in some old yearbook and my theories start making sense. You'd need a camp for your sick games, you'd need a way – a place – to plan how you were going to ruin my life. Devon's life." My voice rises, which surprises me. I hate how vulnerable I feel right now.

"Me kissing you was real, Chiamaka," Belle says, with a catch of, what I'm now sure is, trained breath in between *real* and *Chiamaka*.

I shake my head. How could I be so irrational? Let myself *like* someone I don't even know. Then again, I thought I knew Jamie, but he showed his true colours too. They are as bad as each other.

"Why did you do it?" I ask. It's a question with a double meaning. *Why did you kiss me back? Why not just walk out of the classroom and never speak to me again – spare me the hurt.* And also, *Why are you a part of this? What is THIS?*

Belle looks away from me. "It's not that simple, I need to explain everything—"

"Why did you do it, Belle? What is the point of all of this? I have theories, but I don't want to believe them. Believe that people could be that sick. But all the evidence doesn't leave me with much choice. I want you to tell me now, *why?*"

The floorboards above creak once again. *Who else is here?* My heartbeat grows faster.

Belle looks up at the ceiling, wiping her eyes. "I didn't have a choice. It's been a family tradition for decades. My mom, my dad…my sister. They all went to Niveus. They are all invested in its…*traditions*, because it's what my family has always done. We go to camp, we learn more about the past…and about how the future could look just like it if we plan properly. It seemed harmless, get two kids to drop out, move on in life, forget…"

I'm dizzy.

Of course she had a choice. People always have a choice.

"…And it's not just Niveus, there are places all over the country, that…that do this."

She still can't look at me.

"What is 'this' exactly?" I ask, trying to sound as calm as I can.

Belle is pale, tears flowing down her face. I hate her lies and her fake weeping. She shouldn't be the one crying here.

This time the creaking comes from the staircase. I look towards it, body tense as I expect to see a masked figure emerge.

"They call it social eugenics," her voice stutters out.

The words puncture my chest.

Social eugenics.

"I didn't mean to hurt you," she sniffs. "I... As soon as I got to know you, I regretted everything. I wanted to change it, make things better for you, but the system is so complicated. There are so many people involved."

I wipe my eyes. "You'll be glad to know you didn't hurt me. I don't get hurt by people I don't care about."

Belle flinches at that.

"And you can't ruin my future either. It's in my hands, not Niveus's, not yours or your sick family's."

The doorbell rings. "That must be my ride," I tell her, moving away. Her chair scrapes against the floor and her hand grips my arm.

I turn to face her. "Get off me."

"Please, just trust me."

Her eyes look like crystals dipped in blue poison, her lower lip quivering, lashes blinking, face reddening.

A white cat is seated in the middle of the stairwell, watching the scene unfold. When it catches me staring, it hops back up the stairs, which creak from its sudden movement.

I look at Belle again.

"Trust you?" I'm breathing fast, chest billowing. "I never want to see you again."

I yank my arm away, opening the door.

Richards stands there waiting for me. His eyes move past me and over to Belle.

I don't want to be here any more. I just want to leave and never have to see or think about her again.

"Let's go. The smell of bitch-ass liar is nauseating."

When we get back to my house, I'm expecting it to be empty like it is at this time most days of the week, but when we walk through the door, Dad is in the kitchen making dinner.

"Chiamaka?" Dad calls out.

"Should I wait here?" Devon asks.

I shake my head. "Just follow me," I tell him.

"Coming, Dad!" I shout, walking into the kitchen where he's standing in an apron, stirring a pot.

"Come and taste this," he says, holding the spoon out at me.

I make a face. "I'm not hungry."

He raises an eyebrow but nods, lifting the spoon to his mouth instead. "It needs more salt," he mutters, pausing, then he looks past me at Devon standing behind me.

"You brought a new friend over," he says, sounding surprised. I don't usually bring over new people. He wipes his hands on his apron before moving towards Devon, who physically tenses up.

He holds his hand out and Devon timidly shakes it.

"Hi, I'm Chiamaka's bank account, occasionally known as Dad," he says, with a wide smile. Devon looks even more uncomfortable. Dad's humour is only funny to him. His glasses are fogged over and he looks a bit like a creepy scientist, what with all the smoke coming from the pots and everything.

"Anyway... Devon and I need to work on a school project tonight," I tell him, grabbing Devon's arm and pulling him towards the stairs.

"Okay, just keep your door open," Dad calls out as we leave.

"I will!" I shout, even though I'm pretty sure Dad has nothing to worry about.

We go up the stairs into my room, and I close the door behind us, leaving it only slightly ajar.

"So," I say, diving right in as Devon sits back on my bed. "When I went to the library I found this yearbook from 1965. I saw it on Sunday while we were hiding but didn't get the chance to check it out... There's this picture in it: 'Camp Aces'." I tap onto the photo I took earlier, shoving my phone into Devon's hands.

He scans the picture and looks unsurprised.

I zoom in on a young face. "Doesn't that look like Ward?" I ask.

His eyebrows bunch up. "Holy shit..."

"That's not all. I found out how the 'dead' girl is connected. She's the sister of a girl I was close with. Belle Robinson, whose house we were just at. Apparently her family all went to Niveus and are involved in Aces. Somehow they staged the car accident. Aces was set up to ruin our futures; to invite two Black students who showed exceptional promise to join the school, then break them down. Stop them from achieving what they should."

Devon just stares at my phone, a vacant expression on his face. It's like he's not fully here. He's still shaky, not as much as this morning, but it's like he's a human-sized Chihuahua.

I click my fingers in front of his face. "Hey, Devon?"

His head snaps up, his eyes glazed over. "Sorry... Yeah, this is fucked up," he says.

It's more than fucked up. These people are evil. But I can tell he's had to take in a lot in the last twenty-four hours, I can't expect him to be fully present. I don't think I'm even really here, or processing it.

I'm tired.

"Are you okay?" I ask.

He shrugs, looking away from me and handing me back my phone.

I take a seat next to him.

"Me too. I feel like crap," I reply to his silence.

We sit in the quiet for a few minutes. I need to know how to move forward from this, to not feel stuck.

I grew up in this world.

One where my hair was petted, tugged, laughed at,

pointed out, banned in school rule books. And so I straightened it to comply, to ensure they didn't probe me or touch me like I'm some pet.

I got the grades to look smart, because a part of me always feels dumb around them. I got the respect, acted *proper*, thought I was doing well. Thought I'd get into Yale, no problem.

Problem.

No matter what I do. No matter how much I iron down the hair that springs from my scalp, or work as hard as I can. I'm always going to be *other* to them. Not good enough for this place I've tried to call home all my life.

I can "fix" the kinks in my hair, but not the kinks in this whole system that hates me and Devon and everyone who looks like us.

A sniff breaks me out of my thoughts and I glance at Devon. He's trying to hide his face, but I see him wiping his eyes with the sleeve of his alien hoodie.

He's crying.

I pretend not to notice, wait until it's not so obvious before I speak again.

"Why don't we talk more tomorrow, when we're both well-rested. It's a lot to take in today. We can meet in the morning, think of a strategy to make those people realize we will not be derailed."

He looks at me, bleary-eyed. "What do you mean?"

"We didn't come this far to just come this far, right? We can't let them win, so tomorrow morning I'll meet you and we can think of ways to beat them. Neither of us are in the right head space tonight," I say.

He nods slowly. "Can we meet around twelve? I have to be somewhere in the morning," he says.

He can't be serious.

"Is it more important than Aces?" I ask.

"I have to see a friend tomorrow," he says, standing up now. I stand with him.

"Okay, we can meet at twelve... I can come over to your place?"

"Okay," he says. I was only asking to be polite; I've heard about the neighbourhood he's from. It's not a place I've ever been to, nor do I want to visit. I was hoping he'd say no.

We walk downstairs and Devon mutters a goodbye before leaving.

"Was that your friend leaving already?" Dad asks as I walk into the living room. He's reading a book and eating a bowl of soup, glasses edging towards the tip of his nose.

I nod. "Yeah, he didn't feel well so we're meeting up tomorrow instead," I say, thinking about how exhausted Devon looked.

"Everything okay at school?" Dad asks, flipping the page of the book.

I wish parents wouldn't ask that so much. Especially when the truth might hurt them and make them hate you. If I told him, "No, school is awful. In fact, I don't think I can go back, because the whole school is racist and they hate me, Dad," he wouldn't get that. He wouldn't understand anything I told him, because it's not something he's ever had to deal with. All he'd register is the fact that I've been accused of theft, murder and fornicating with random boys. And he'd think I was disgusting. I already hate me enough for the both of us.

Besides, even if I did tell him everything, I know he wouldn't do anything. Dad couldn't even defend me when his family would say racist things to me when I was a child. He'd just watch silently as Grandma would mock me and the way I looked. Said nothing when his family no longer wanted Mom and me to visit. Why would he defend me now?

So I say: "School's great, Dad."

And then I tell him another lie, that I'm tired, and I go to my room, and I try to sleep.

But all I see is her.

Images of Martha on the ground after we'd hit her. Dream sequences...or now maybe memories...of me drunk, stumbling into a room, music from the party playing in the background. I start panicking because I see these blonde little bloodied dolls everywhere and then I see a figure, which turns towards me and it's *her*.

I'm screaming but no one can hear me. I'm crying, I can't stop crying. The music is blasting. I'm shouting, "You're not real!" and she's laughing. I can see my reflection in the mirror behind her, my silver dress sparkling in the dark room, the straps hanging off my shoulders. I look like a mess.

I am a mess.

I'm screaming but no one can hear me.

I'm screaming so loud, but no one can help me.

For a year my subconscious has tormented me with a traumatic night that wasn't real. I haven't been able to sleep properly and none of it was real. People I knew, people I trusted, made me believe I was losing my mind. I feel angry and lost. How do you undo a fake memory?

My brain still can't let go, see it as anything but real.

At night when the world goes black, despite everything I've learned, the hazy dream/memory sequence of that night at Jamie's house, the party he threw in junior year, begins again.

33

TUESDAY

My first time in a prison was when I was ten.

I remember the exact date too: September 9th.

Even though the place was bleak, dark and grey, I was excited to be there. I don't think anyone in the history of life has been excited by a prison. But I was. I missed my pa, and after two years, he finally wanted to speak to me. Before then, he'd denied Ma's requests to let us see him. Then this time it was Ma, denying his request for her to visit him. She'd followed me all the way to the prison, but refused to come inside and see him.

He looked different from when I last saw him. For one, he was wearing a uniform. It was bright white against his dark skin. He had grown out his beard and hair. His chin was resting on his crossed-over hands, and behind the glass screen, he seemed so distant. I remember staring at him for a while, frozen, not sure why, but scared.

I eventually gathered the strength to shuffle forwards, sneakers way too big for me – Ma always bought them a few sizes up so they'd fit in the years to come. I took a seat in front of him and he finally looked up, like he hadn't sensed that I had arrived until that moment. His head jolted to the side, and I followed the direction to the grey payphone, noticing that there was one on my side too.

He picks his up.

I pick mine up too.

"Hello, son." His raspy voice sends a shiver down my spine. I haven't heard him speak in two years.

"Hi, Dad," I say.

He smiles, eyes crinkling in the corners the way old people's do. Dad isn't even that old, only thirty-two, and he looked his age before. He sure does look old now, though; grey hairs in his cornrows, and lines on his forehead.

"How's your ma?"

"She's good. Working as a lunch lady at school, so I get to see her all the time and she gives me extra servings," I tell him. When the men took Dad away I couldn't eat for days without feeling sick, but my appetite is back, and I'm so happy Ma gives me more pasta than anyone else.

He rubs his hand across his face and yawns a little.

"You tired, Dad?" I ask. His eyes are a little red, like Ma's get when she's tired too.

"Yeah, but I'm gonna get some good sleep tonight," he tells me. He stares at me through the glass. "How are you?"

I shrug; he's never asked me that before in my life. "I dunno."

Dad smiles. "Yes you do. Tell me what you want to tell me."

I'm not sure how to tell him exactly. It's not something I understand fully.

"Guys in my class keep talking about all the girls they like. Keep asking them out, keep talking about it," I start, pausing to see if he's still with me. Dad nods, and so I continue. "But I don't think about girls like that, I don't want to ask them out, or kiss them."

Dad nods again, then looks up at the ceiling a little, before returning his gaze to me.

"I was eleven when I started asking girls out. Takes time, don't worry; you'll be a heartbreaker like I was in no time. Did I tell you how your ma and I got together?"

I shake my head, even though Ma's already given me her side of the story. I want to hear it from him. Stories are cooler when you hear how everybody else experienced it.

He ahhs, then says, "We met in high school, senior year. Took me two years to notice her. I was busy working on my music, but when I finally put my sax down, I spotted her, and I knew she was the one for me. We kissed, had you and got married. So, you see, it wasn't until I was much older that I settled down with a girl. You don't worry about that, son. Your perfect girl is waiting for you to spot her too."

I nod, feeling a little better. It's just a matter of time.

"Dad, when are you coming out of this place? You

363

need to come home, Ma is sad without you."

Dad looks down now, silent. I almost think something is wrong with the line, but then I hear him breathing.

"I uh—" He wipes his face again. "I did something the state didn't like – something I don't regret. A real man never regrets, you hear?"

I nod.

"Feds don't agree with that sort of thing, so I'm here. Taking control over what matters is important. But you don't worry about that, or me being here, okay?"

I nod slowly, not really sure what he means. Ma refuses to explain it to me. Dad looks at me with this expression that makes me feel like nothing is right and he's hiding it. I want to tell him about my dreams of him coming home, us being a family again, but I don't think he'd want to hear that. Besides, we weren't really much of a family to start with. Dad was never home.

"Listen, Von, I'm happy you came," he says. That fills me up like one of those cartoon helium balloons they sell in the mall, all full and bright. I want to say that I'm happy he invited me, but he doesn't seem to have finished, and I don't want to be rude or anything.

"But I don't want you coming back here, again, ever. I don't want to see you after today," he says.

The balloon bursts, shattering everything.

What? Why doesn't he want to see me?

"Why?" I ask, just as the phone line cuts. A guard pats him on the shoulder, gesturing for him to stand, but my

364

heart is beating so fast. I need to know why, I need to convince him to let me come again.

"Dad!" I yell, but he's standing now, looking past me like I'm not there.

Then he turns and walks away. Through the green door behind him, which slams shut.

I stay, watching the door, waiting for him to run back and say he was kidding.

I thought it would be like one of those movies, where at the last minute there's a happy ending, people come back to each other and no one is crying. Those movies where the family – two parents, three kids and a dog – all go to the beach together. Just for the fun of it, splashing about in the water like it hugs them the way their parents do.

My dad's never hugged me before.

Tears rest heavily on my eyelashes, weighing them down, forcing me to blink, let them escape. My heart is racing and I feel a little dizzy.

I squeeze my eyes shut.

I picture the sea. The waves crashing but not in a violent way, in a nice way, like they are loud with purpose. I walk towards the sea, kneeling, touching it, breathing in the salt, then I lie down, let it carry me, hug me.

My heart stops racing. I'm calm again, but I refuse to open my eyes. I memorized the way from the entrance. I don't want to see this place again, I'm not excited any more.

So I walk on out, eyes closed, running one hand against the wall, as the waves pull me in.

The sound of a buzzer drags me out of that memory – the last memory I have with my pa. Ma told me she didn't want me seeing him either, so I never went back. But I get curious sometimes: how he's doing, whether he'd recognize me still.

I walk over to the chair in front of the glass screen as a familiar green door opens and Dre appears in an orange uniform. I almost gasp. His *face*.

I quickly take a seat, grabbing the phone. Dre stares at me for a bit, eyes drifting down a little to my uniform then back up to my face. He sits down heavily on the chair and then leans back, grabbing the grey phone sluggishly like it's not got a time limit.

"Dre, why the fuck are you in here – why'd you call me?" I whisper, because it has been playing on my mind ever since I received the text from Dre's phone yesterday, then the call. I glance at the uniformed guards a little, not sure if mentioning the calls from his phone will get him in trouble.

He shrugs. "Wanted a conjugal visit." His voice is worn out, like he's been yelling and it's broken or something.

I glare at him. "We haven't got much time, stop playing."

His eyes are so red, blueish purple on the edges, bags exaggerated.

He sniffs, wiping his arm over his nose. "Cops raided my place, found a lot of shit—"

"How?" I ask. None of his boys are snitches, or at least I didn't think they were.

"Someone must have called them, told them where to look."

Someone...

Aces...?

My heart races and I feel a little sick.

"Have you got bail?" I ask, swallowing the guilt. Bail can get him out, right?

"Too expensive."

"Did they give any info on how long they're keeping you in for?"

"Until the trial."

Trial?

I rest my head in my hand. Dre can't go to trial, let alone prison.

It's all my fault: if we'd read the signs earlier, dropped out sooner, did what they wanted us to do, Aces wouldn't have come for Andre.

I hear a knocking sound, and I look up a bit.

"It's fine, I'm fine," he says, eyebrows knitted together. He places his hand on the glass. I look at it at first, then him.

"You're not fine, Dre." I place my hand on the glass over his, our hands similar in size, but so different at the same time. I know his hands are rougher than mine, thicker.

"Your face is fucked up."

He looks at our hands. "My face is fine."

"Is fine slang for messed up? Dre, look at me, who did this to you?"

Andre looks at me, and my face goes warm, because he's *really* looking at me, not just my face, but my eyes, my mouth…eyes flickering.

He sighs heavily. "Just some guys, told me they'd heard of you and me, and—" Dre's face scrunches up as he starts silently crying. "They beat me every night, said they wanna knock sense into me."

I wish I could hug him, but this stupid glass separates us. He wipes his eyes harshly then puts his hand down and sits up.

"How've you been?" he asks, voice cracking a little.

Stressed is the first thing that comes to mind. Stressed and tired.

"Good," I say.

"Good," he repeats.

I feel like I'm gonna die from an overactive heart. It beats fast, ringing in my ears and in my mind, throat vibrating, hard to swallow, fingers moving like I had too much coffee again.

"You need to get out of here," I tell him. "You need a good lawyer."

He nods slowly. "My boys are working on it."

Working on it. That can mean so many things. One being, using drug money. But he's got to do whatever it takes to get out of here, so I won't judge him, especially since I did the same to help my ma.

He looks so small in his orange uniform, like he's drowning in his own clothes. It's all rumpled too. I remember Pa, and how he wore his uniform like it was a second skin almost. The white plastered to his bulky arms.

"I don't want to talk about this any more, just wanted to see you, catch up…" He looks around. We are the only people in here – other than the guards – despite there being other booths. "I just wanted to tell you that despite everything, I love you, always will."

My heart hammers away like there's no tomorrow. I'm breathless, and a little shocked. A huge part of me wants Dre to love me, but that same part of me didn't think he still did.

"What do you want to talk about?" I force out, trying to look unbothered, but I'm convinced he can hear my heartbeat.

He shrugs, eyes cutting through me. "Anything."

Anything?

I almost want to tell him about Aces, but I don't think we have enough time for that.

"Why's your uniform orange?" I ask instead. He looks down at it.

"All newbies wear them, different colours for your crime. It all depends."

I nod, looking in between his eyebrows now. Faking eye contact.

"What does white mean?"

Dre's eyebrows shoot up. "White?"

I nod. "Mm."

"Those are the death row guys," he says, and it's like

369

several shots bang in my direction, shooting me all in the same place, puncturing my vitals. I'm silent for a few moments, trying to find a response to that.

"Death row, are you sure?"

Dre's face scrunches up. "You're crying."

I wipe my eyes, shaking my head. "That can't be right."

Dre is silent, as I try to process what his words mean. Is Pa on death row?

How long does someone stay on death row before...? I've wasted so many years, listening to Ma, not visiting him, doing what he wanted. I was so angry at him when he told me he didn't want to see me any more that I didn't even try. God, how long does he have left? How can we stop it?

"You okay?" Dre asks. I nod.

"Just get sad thinking about that."

"I get it, it's s—" his voice disappears as the line disconnects. He stares at the phone in his hands. The look on his face is devastating.

Two guards come up behind him, tall, muscular and cold-looking. One taps his shoulder, and Dre stands.

The look he gives me before he disappears like my dad did makes me think he's about to cry, it's so pained, and lost.

I know if I was in this situation I'd have my ma, my brothers...Terrell.

But Dre has no one. No ma who cares what's happening to him, no pa.

I don't know how long I sit here for, but the guards don't tell me to leave.

I just let myself drift, aching as I think about Dre and how it hurts to see him here, where they beat him for being a boy who likes boys.

This world isn't ideal.

This world, our world, the one with houses as crooked as the people in them. Broken people, broken by the way the world works. No jobs, no money; sell drugs, get money. That's what this world is, that's how it works.

I don't want it to be like that for me. I don't want to stay here.

And I don't want Dre in here either. He has no one. His world is a lonely and miserable one.

After some time, when my cheeks feel stiff and the tears have dried up, I push myself out of the chair, not thinking as I walk up to the entrance and over to the reception.

There's a woman behind the desk, the same woman who signed me in earlier. She has deep-brown skin, red braids and thick glasses, and sits behind a glass that separates us. I wipe my face and knock on the glass, which makes her look up sharply.

"Yes?" she asks, an eyebrow raised. She looks a little annoyed, like I interrupted something important.

"S-sorry, I…I wanted to know if I could find out about an inmate here? It's m-my dad. I just wanted to know if he still accepts visitors? Whether I could see him today…or at some point this week or something," I say, voice cracking. I feel tears well up again. I desperately try to push away the overwhelming need to cry, but it's difficult.

She pauses, looking a bit more sympathetic now. "I'll see what I can find, okay? What's his name?"

I wipe my eyes. "Thank you. His name is Malcolm Richards," I say, watching her write on a piece of paper.

"Could you write down some information here to help me find him quicker? His date of birth, the year he came in…" She slides the paper under the glass and I nod, even though I don't know many details about him. He was practically a stranger to me. A stranger I've made into a father in my mind.

I feel bad going against what Ma said, wanting to see him anyway, but she lied to me and I don't know how much time I have left to speak to him, to stop this. A part of me has always hoped that one day Pa would come back and be the person I always painted him as being, and they can't take that away. I won't let them.

I only know the year they put him in here, not the exact date, which isn't so helpful, but at least I know his birthday. July 4th, like mine.

"Here," I say, passing the slip back.

She smiles and starts typing into the computer system. I focus on the sound of footsteps and doors slamming in the background.

The tapping stops, it's replaced by her clicking and then complete silence for a few long moments.

"Were you visiting anyone today?" she asks, drumming her long nails on the desk and looking up at me.

There goes my focus.

I nod. "Yeah, a friend."

"Good friend?" she asks.

The best, I think. "Yeah," I say instead, chest tightening.

I hate small talk, especially this kind of small talk. I just want to know when I can see my pa again.

"I'm sure it means a lot to him that you came to visit. You're a good kid," she says.

I nod slowly, watching her computer impatiently.

"Sorry, did you find anything?" I ask.

She looks visibly uncomfortable. "Yes…the Malcolm Richards that matches our records – he passed away quite a while ago. I'm sorry," she says.

Passed away?

"My pa is dead?" I ask, feeling numb when she nods. "When?" Not sure how asking this helps me.

She looks back at the screen. "About seven years ago; September 9th." She pauses and looks at me, as if trying to see what my reaction is before she continues.

That was the day I saw him. When I was ten years old. It was the last time I saw him.

I'm still, quiet. But my limbs feel like they could give out any moment now. My face feels hot and I feel like screaming, but I don't. If I start, I won't stop.

I'm in so much pain, but at the same time I feel nothing. Nothing at all.

"You knew he was on death row, right?" she says cautiously. "We usually try to inform family members beforehand, so they can come and speak to them on the day.

We usually give them a room…some time to say goodbye."

I didn't get that. I didn't get to know it would be the last interaction I'd ever have with him. I didn't get a room, I didn't get time. He was here, and then he was gone. If I knew, I wouldn't have spoken about me so much, would have asked him everything I needed to; asked him if he was okay, if he still loved Ma, if he loved me.

But I know the answer. Of course he didn't.

If he loved me he would have been there, wouldn't have gotten himself locked away. Wouldn't have let me think he didn't want to see me.

I wouldn't have spent all these years on him, thinking he was coming to rescue me from the bullies at school, and the bullies in my head. The ones that tell me I'm not enough, never will be. The ones that make me feel like drowning to be at peace; letting the ocean take me, for ever.

"Are you okay?" the receptionist asks.

I nod. "Thank you," I say.

"This must be really upsetting, I'm so sorr—"

I shake my head, cutting her off. "I'm good. Was never close to him anyway, didn't care about him. Was just curious," I tell her.

Everything hurts.

She nods, looking unconvinced. "Okay. Well, look after yourself," she starts, but I'm already walking out of the building, wanting to escape, disappear somewhere far, far away.

I'm walking so fast, it's almost like I'm running. I can feel the tears fall freely, as cries slip out and my chest gets tighter and I can't breathe.

I feel so lost and out of control.

Andre, my pa, Niveus, Aces. All of them, and the memories I have with them, strangling me.

"Hey!" someone shouts and I turn. It's the receptionist. I suddenly forget about being unable to breathe, the panic falling away a little.

She's holding my phone, my keys and the fake ID I used to get in here since I'm a minor. "You forgot your things…" she says, handing them over to me.

I can't bring myself to speak, so I just take them.

She looks like she wants to say something, so I wait.

"Look after yourself, okay?" she says.

I watch her walk back inside.

When I look down at my phone, I notice my fingers are trembling, so much it's like my phone is vibrating even though it's off. I turn it back on and I'm immediately met with messages from Chiamaka.

We're meant to go to my place and talk about next steps.

I'm not sure why I agreed to it. I never have anyone over. The only person I ever let inside was Jack, and he was basically family. With everyone else, I never felt comfortable enough showing them where I live.

Going to Niveus made me feel worse about it.

I text Terrell as I start walking out of the parking lot, heading towards the bus stop.

Hey, you at school today?

Everything is still aching, but I remember my promise to Chiamaka and myself to find a way to stop Niveus.

No – T

You mind if I come over and bring Chiamaka? I ask, selfishly hoping he's not with his sister.

Sure – T

Wiping my face with my sleeve again for the millionth time today, I pocket my phone and I sit down at the bus stop. I told Chiamaka to meet me at this ice-cream joint in my neighbourhood so she didn't just turn up at my house. I push away all the feelings that keep coming back, sealing them shut in one of the boxes in my mind for later, when I have the time to think about my pa and Dre.

Right now, what matters most is Niveus.

34

CHIAMAKA

TUESDAY

I meet Devon in a run-down ice-cream bar in his neighbourhood.

The place is practically deserted, apart from this random guy in the corner drinking coffee and reading a newspaper. Devon arrives after me, looking as tired as he did last night. Eyes red, hair messy, sullen expression on his face.

"Hey," I say.

"Hey," he replies.

I push myself up. "Still heading to your place?" I ask, slightly hopeful that he's changed his mind and doesn't mind walking all the way back to my house.

He nods, much to my disappointment, as we start walking out of the place.

I follow him down the path, taking in the surroundings. The houses are small and unkept, some with smashed-in windows and graffiti on the walls.

This place looks like the aftermath of an apocalypse.

We reach a house with a red door and a large 63 front and centre. I wait for Devon to take out his keys, but instead he knocks, and I raise an eyebrow.

Why would he knock on his own front door?

I hear a sound from inside the house, and I instinctively step back. There's a sharp turn of a lock and then the door swings open, revealing a smiley four-eyed stranger with brown skin and short dreads tied back, making his head look a bit like a pineapple. His gaze goes from Devon to me to Devon again.

There's an awkward tension in the air.

Devon steps in and disappears, walking past the stranger without another word.

There's definitely something I'm missing here. Several somethings.

"Hey, I'm Terrell!" the stranger says.

"Chiamaka…" I say.

He smiles wider. "I know, come on in."

The guy moves aside to let me in, and I pause, hoping Devon hasn't led me into a deathtrap. I step over some of the weeds by the entrance and walk in, through his hallway, and into a small living room. The TV is on silent and some cartoon is playing. The place makes me feel claustrophobic; there's hardly enough space to breathe properly.

Devon is sitting on one of the old-looking sofas. I take a seat next to him on the edge.

Terrell walks in and picks up the remote from the coffee table, turning the TV off.

"Welcome to my humble abode. You guys want anything? I went to the grocery store before you came, so there's a bunch of stuff if you want, kitchen's that way—"

"Wait, Devon, you said we were going to your place? Who is he and why are we having our meeting here?" I interrupt, growing more annoyed.

"Terrell's my friend, he knows everything and he's good at figuring stuff out. I thought it wouldn't hurt for him to help us plan. My house isn't really guest friendly anyway," Devon replies. Whatever that means.

If he'd just told me that, we could have gone back to my place.

"But you said we were going to your house—" I start.

"Well, I lied. Sorry," he interrupts, leaning back now. "Can we just move on? Decide what the hell we're doing next."

I sigh. "After you left, I was thinking of how to take Niveus down, but after speaking to Belle, I realize they're too powerful for us to do this alone."

"Who's Belle?" Terrell asks.

I really hate Devon for not consulting me on involving a complete stranger.

"She's a girl I know from school, she was in on it too... When I confronted her, she told me a bunch of things about how her family is involved, and this – Aces – is a tradition they call social eugenics. Some of the kids from our school, legacy kids, the ones with family that have old money and old power, they all go to this camp. It's where they plan to ruin our futures, and from what she told me...Niveus isn't the only school that does this."

Terrell's eyes are wide. "Eugenics?" he asks.

I nod.

"Woah," he says.

Woah indeed.

"Need me to fill you in on anything else before I go on?" I ask, hoping I don't sound too sarcastic. He's trying to help, I guess.

"So, from what I've gathered and what Devon's told me, your school accepts two Black students every ten years, then the immortal Aces targets them in their final year, spreading rumours, secrets and lies they've collected...until those Black students drop out. No college prospects, mentally traumatized, with their chances of achieving everything Caucasian-ville promised them, crushed," Terrell says.

So he does know everything.

"Yeah...that's pretty much what we think is going on. Which is why I think this is something that can't be fixed without outside help. So, I propose we go to the local news, tell them what we know, and offer an exposé on Niveus Academy. What do you think, Devon?" I ask him.

I think my plan is brilliant.

"I think your plan is stupid," Devon says. "How can we trust anyone but ourselves after this? This whole experience has taught me that we only have each other in this fight."

"How do you propose we go about taking them down, then? Since you want to be cynical and irrational."

I fold my arms, waiting to hear something better. He doesn't say anything. I smile triumphantly.

"Exactly. This is a good plan, you just need to trust me. I didn't get voted Head Prefect for no reason," I say.

"You got voted because you kiss teachers' asses – and I'm not irrational," Devon mutters.

"Oh? Says the boy who dated Scotty, literally the worst person anyone could *choose* to date, and a drug dealer!"

"You dated Scotty too, and you shouldn't talk about things you don't understand," Devon says, raising his voice.

"Who's Scotty?" Terrell asks.

I rub my temples. "You know what, we haven't got time to argue about this. You either trust me or you don't. I'll go to the journalist on my own if I have to. It's not only a good idea, it's our *only* option. Terrell, tell him it's a good idea."

Terrell looks between me and Devon, then nods. "She's got a point, Von. It is your only option...and the idea doesn't entirely suck..."

I smile. "So, are you in or are you going to continue throwing a tantrum?" I ask.

Devon wipes his eyes. "Whatever."

I feel a little bad that he's visibly upset, but we haven't got time for paranoia. We need to take Aces down before they hit back harder.

"I have the number for Central News 1 and US This Morning. I'll try Central News 1 first...see what they say," I tell him, taking my phone out to call.

I dial the number before looking up at the two of them. "Any objections? If so, speak now or for ever hold your peace."

"Just call the number," Devon says.

And so, I do.

35

WEDNESDAY

I didn't sleep at all last night. I was up thinking about everything.

My pa, how he's gone and how Ma knew that but didn't tell me. Andre sitting in that cold dark cell, alone and scared. How I don't have complete faith that this plan will work.

Chiamaka called Central News 1 yesterday and we got a meeting set up with a journalist for today. I'm meant to meet Chiamaka at her place, but I'm already dreading it. I'm tired of having faith things will work out, only for any hope I have to be violently crushed.

I hear a vibration that I don't register until I look at my bedside table and see the screen lit up, a spotlight illuminating my dark bedroom. I grab it. It's already five in the morning.

Time flies when your life is going downhill.

It's a text from Chiamaka.

Are you up? – C

Yeah, I'm up.

That feels like an understatement. Yeah, I'm up. Not because I'm an early riser, but because every time I try to close my eyes and dream, it gets twisted. The images become monstrous and violent. I'm scared to sleep. So, I'm here drowning, rain spilling outside, the open window making it louder, brothers snoring beside me. Up.

How are you? – C

I don't know.

I answer honestly. I just feel so lost and angry.

Same. – C

Then a moment later the phone buzzes again.

We'll be fine. This plan will work. Just going to print
out all our evidence. Make sure you bring the
posters. – C

Okay, I say, not believing her *We'll be fine*. We aren't and we probably won't be. And I'm tired of it, tired of living like this.

As the rain lightly hits the window, and the cold rushes in, I scan my cramped bedroom, and it's like I'm looking at my life through a new pair of eyes. Our weird floral-patterned green carpets that I never really minded before, making me feel itchy and sick, large dark closets with clothes that spill out, peeling bright-yellow wallpaper and that battered TV my brothers love so much. I look at this room now and it hurts to think that life might never get better than this. I feel destined to drop out of high school, stay here, in this house in this room, listening to Ma pray to a god who covers his ears when she chants.

I used to tell myself this wasn't permanent, that I'd live somewhere someday where I wouldn't have to share a bed with my brothers or sit in this home of mismatched things. But who was I kidding.

Boys like me don't get happy endings.

The stories I was fed about working hard and being able to achieve anything… That's all they are, stories. Lies. Dangerous dreams.

I close my chat with Chiamaka and find myself mindlessly scrolling, searching for a game, social media, something to get lost in before I have to get up, put on my uniform and play pretend with my ma. I've decided I can't tell her about this yet, but I will soon, once I've seen this plan through. To be honest, if it works, she'll see it for herself.

I scroll through Twitter, curling up in a ball and letting my thumb move up and down the glass screen. Then, as if smacked in the face, a thought occurs to me.

New tweet. The cursor blinks at me, waiting for me to write something. Amidst everything that's happened, I've let so many people tell the world who I am. I've let Chiamaka tell me what we should do. I just want, for once, to say something and for someone, anyone, to listen. I can do that on here.

But what would I even say? It's not as if I have many followers; I hardly use this account.

The screen shines bright, making my eyes hurt a little. I move my thumbs then read over my words one last time.

@DLikesTunes: #NiveusPrivateAcademy exposed: This school sabotages its Black students. Every Black student who has attended since 1965 has been targeted and forced to drop out. I was one of the most recent victims. Here's proof.

I attach the images I took of computer 17 – the acrostic, the names, the checklist, and then add the picture of me and Chiamaka's scratched-out yearbook photos.

I still feel sick looking at it, but I'm finally controlling something, even if it amounts to nothing.

I hit send and the tweet floats away.

I drag myself into the shower and then downstairs where my ma sits, eating toast, dressed in her work clothes like every morning.

"Morning, baby," Ma says when she sees me.

"Morning, Ma," I say, walking over to the counter to make myself some toast.

"How was your sleep?" she asks.

"Good," I say.

"Good."

There's silence as I wait for my toast.

It pops out and I butter both pieces up before taking a seat opposite her. There's more silence as I chew, spacing out as I try to block the thoughts that kept me up in the first place.

I watch her, wondering why she lied and did it so easily. I didn't think Ma lied to me, but I guess we all lie.

Is it selfish of me to be angry? To want answers? To tell her that while she was working hard to keep this roof over our heads, I was fantasizing about someone who never cared about us. And that his absence really hurts, even though I don't want it to.

Ma rises and puts her dish in the sink before walking over to me, and giving me a tight hug.

"Going to get Eli and James up for school now. Are you leaving early today?" she asks, still holding my face after the hug. I feel tears well up again for no reason.

I nod.

"Okay." She lets her hand drop and I immediately miss the warmth. "I love you," she says, as she moves towards the stairs. I watch her, until she's out of sight and I'm in our dark kitchen, alone again.

I arrive at Chiamaka's house at one o'clock on the dot. I ring the buzzer on the gates then walk through when they release. The sharp sound of heeled shoes and the front door slamming shut makes me focus on Chiamaka. I meet her halfway, where she startles me by forcing her bag into my arms.

"Hold this for a moment, I need to fix the strap on my shoes."

It literally seems like she just woke up and rushed out. Not that I know much about girls' hair or clothes and how they're meant to look, but hers definitely scream, *I woke up like this.*

"Thanks," she says, taking her bag back. "Get in the car. The news station isn't too far from here, half an hour drive tops," she tells me as she clicks towards this sleek black car like it's nothing. I watch her open the car door and throw her bag in.

I move towards the passenger side, only to be stopped by her hand on my arm.

"What?"

She shakes her head. "Nothing, I just think you should drive…" She hesitates before handing over her keys. "Here."

"You want me to drive your car?" I ask, dumbfounded.

"Yes," she says, like there is nothing weird about her suggesting that.

"I can't drive," I say, handing the keys back.

She looks annoyed. "And why is that?"

"I don't have a licence."

She sighs loudly. "But you *can* drive, right?"

I drove my first car when I was twelve. It was to get Ma to the hospital, back when we still had a car. She was giving birth to my littlest brother, Eli. Sometimes I'd drive Dre's car when I'd do drop-offs for him.

"Yeah I can—"

"Get in."

We have a miniature stare down. The bags under her eyes and her tangled hair are in hyper-focus now. She looks *really* tired.

I sigh. "Okay, fine."

She mutters "Thank God" before tossing the keys back at me, narrowly missing my face. I nearly make a comment about that, but I figure it isn't worth being insulted again and also she clearly isn't doing so good, so instead I silently unlock the doors and watch as she walks over to the passenger's side, slamming the door shut.

I get in, closing the door and clicking my seatbelt into place. I press a button and the engine bursts to life. If this was another time, another day, a different context, I might've commented on how cool her car is.

"Wait," she says. I look over, watching her chest move up and down rapidly. It calms after a few moments. "Okay, you can go."

I place my hands on the leather wheel of her car and my feet on the pedals.

Even though I have little faith in this plan, I can't help thinking, *This is it. This is finally it.*

I press down, and the car starts to move out from the front of her house. The gates open immediately and before I know it we're racing down her street, filled with white picket fences, large black gates and perfect rooftops with perfect families beneath them.

"Let's repeat the game plan," she tells me.

"We go to Central News 1—" I begin.

"We go to Central News 1, we speak to the person at the desk, telling them we have an appointment with that journalist I called yesterday," she interrupts. "We show the journalist the files, with the printouts, the picture of the yearbook and the posters, we show them the texts – wait, you *do* have the posters, right?"

In my backpack, safely stored away.

"Yep."

"Good, where was I… We show them everything, and then we plan our attack on the school with the journalist and we take it from there. Today is the last day that Niveus can control us," Chiamaka finishes.

"Right," I reply, trying to sound as convinced as she does.

From the corner of my eye, I see a police car.

"And what's the worst that can happen? Really…we're going to be just fine," Chiamaka says, I suspect, to herself rather than me.

"Yeah," I reply, eyes still focusing on the flashing lights of the car behind us. I hope they aren't flashing at us. The last thing I want is to speak to a cop right now.

"Even if Central News 1 doesn't want our story, we can go to any other station that wants it," she continues, oblivious to the car, oblivious to how agitated I am.

The flashing hasn't stopped.

I think they want me to pull over.

Sweat beads on my scalp. My hands are slippery. I haven't

got any other option – I have to pull over.

I could throw up all over the interior of this nice car.

"Chiamaka, I think I have to pull over, that police car has been flashing at us for a while."

Chiamaka turns around to look, then turns back.

"We need to switch seats," she says, unbuckling her seatbelt.

I follow suit, unbuckling mine.

I try remembering Ma's words.

If they ask you questions, answer politely. Don't go searching for your phone, don't touch your pockets! Don't, please don't, just do as they ask, put your hands where they can see them.

I love you.

"Pull in there, we need to switch before they see us. My windows are tinted so let's hope they can't," she says, as I pull over with shaky hands. She hits me, whispering, "*Hurry,*" as our limbs tangle. I finally get to her seat and I jump when I hear the tapping on the car window.

Chiamaka winds down the window, and says, "Good afternoon, Officer."

His eyes meet mine. I look away.

"Realize you were doing thirty-five in a twenty-five lane?"

Really?

"Sorry, Officer, *apparently I can't read properly,*" she says. I ignore the jab at me.

"Giving me lip?" the officer asks.

Chiamaka shakes her head. "No, sir," she says.

He looks at us, unimpressed. "Licence and registration, please," he says, getting out a notepad.

Chiamaka reaches up into the top section of her car and shows him something. He takes it, scanning it slowly. The guy is the stereotype of every cop we imagine when we picture how the gun pointed to our head could look in the all-too-normal narrative.

He's big, broad, with a blond beard, beady eyes.

"You two look like you should be in class, not out on the road," he says, still staring down at her details.

"We're in college," Chiamaka lies.

"Got any college ID on you?" he asks.

Why the fuck does it concern him?

"With all due respect, Officer, we are not obligated to show you that," Chiamaka says.

Clearly her parents didn't give her *the talk*. Her hands visibly shake from their position on the wheel.

Or maybe she just knows, because we all know, that the feds kill us all in their own game of social eugenics.

The officer stares at Chiamaka silently, his gaze cutting through her, frustration swirling in his eyes. My stomach flips.

He writes something down on his notepad then hands her back the papers.

I can finally breathe again when he moves away, but in the same breath he turns back and leans into the car. It feels like my nightmare. The monsters attack and chase me, but I can't run or hide because they just always seem to know where I am.

"Boy," he says sharply. I look up, chest pounding, aching.

"Yes, sir," I answer, hoping my hands are visible from their position in my lap.

"Do your seatbelt." His eyes scan my clothes. I look down with him.

"Yes, sir," I say, not wanting to move too much, give him a reason to "defend" himself.

My hands shake, my face heats and sweats, as I softly click it in, his gaze on me the entire time.

He finally taps the car and leaves to go back to his own and I can breathe again properly, even though everything aches.

I hate that these systems, all this institutional shit, can get to me. I hate how they have the power to kill my future, kill me. They treat my Black skin like a gun or a grenade or a knife that is dangerous and lethal, when really, it's them. The guys at the top powering everything.

If it isn't Niveus that does it, any one of them could get us.

The guys at the top are bombs and explosives, killing millions, getting away with it.

"Need a moment?" Chiamaka asks.

I nod, sniffling now, not able to hold back the tears that escape, or the cries that leak from my mouth. I place an arm over my face, and I let myself go.

Chiamaka's hand slides through mine and squeezes.

And even though I hate to admit it, I'm happy she's here.

We are in the parking lot, surrounded by a few cars, watching the Central News 1 building like we're waiting for it to come to us, not the other way around.

"I'm scared," Chiamaka admits.

Me too.

"Like you said, nothing to be scared of," I reply. This is the only option we have left.

"Exactly…nothing."

There's a lot to be scared of, though. Who knows what'll happen in there.

We sit in silence, waiting for the other to make the first move.

This is it.

Freedom.

36

WEDNESDAY

We walk into the building together. I take a deep breath, leading the two of us as we enter through the open double doors. *This is it.*

There's a woman at the front desk whose blue eyes pierce into us as she looks up.

"Hi, how can I help you?" she asks. Her rubbery skin makes me a little uncomfortable.

"We have a meeting with Ms Donovan."

"What are your names, please?" She types something into her computer.

"Chiamaka Adebayo and Devon Richards."

Her typing slows, and she glances up at us again.

"Okay, take a seat. Shouldn't be too long."

I sigh. Thank God. I was worried our meeting was cancelled or hadn't even been scheduled. I'm so used to everything going wrong lately.

We sit on the chairs on the opposite side of the front desk. I look at Richards. His eyes are closed, like he's sleeping. I wish I could drift off and relax. But all I can think about is getting this right.

I already messed up once, in the library when I ran out – I refuse to mess up again. We'll go in, show the journalist the facts, and she will write the story that will expose Niveus. She has to. What kind of person would see what's happened and not be outraged—

"Devon and Chiamaka?" a soft voice calls out and I snap my head up in the direction it came from.

There's a woman wearing tall cheap heels, a black pencil skirt and a frilly blouse. She gives us a smile, which is a little intimidating with her wide blue eyes, bouncy perfect blonde hair and red-stained lips.

She reminds me of the girls I've gone to school with all my life.

"Yes?" I say as Devon wakes up and looks in the same direction as me.

"Follow me, I'll show you to Alice's office," she says, which is Ms Donovan's first name. We stand, following the Barbie doll down the long hallway. The walls are mostly bare, white with areas where the wallpaper is peeling. It feels clinical, like the hospitals Mom and Dad work in.

We come to a stop and she knocks twice on a door labelled *Donovan*.

"Come in!" a low voice yells, and the woman pushes the door open, standing to the side to let us in. I walk in first and Devon follows. There is a woman behind a desk, typing something into her phone, not yet looking up at us. Unlike the woman who showed us in, the woman has thick brown hair, a tan and can't be a day younger than forty. The door slams shut behind us and I jump.

The sound pulls her away from her phone and she finally looks up at us.

"You must be Devon and Chiamaka! Sit, sit – just making a note of something in my diary," she says, typing some more before locking her phone and putting it on the desk, face down.

She leans in, chin resting on her folded hands as she smiles.

"So, how can I help you two today?"

Before I can speak, Devon answers her question.

"We spoke on the phone yesterday, or, well, you spoke to Chiamaka, but I was there too. Anyway, we have evidence that our school is trying to sabotage its Black students and we wanted to publish something about it," Devon says.

Her eyebrows shoot up.

"Yes, I remember talking with one of you. I get so many calls, sometimes I just need my memory jogged a little, but I remember. How could I forget such an *interesting* story? An anonymous racist bully, out to get the only two Black students at a private school…only to discover it's a plot that the whole school is in on. Quite the story," she says, then stares at us unblinking like she's waiting for something. "Do you have any physical evidence? I can't report anything without it…" she says, finally.

I nod. "Yes, we do." I unzip my bag, sliding over the folder of everything I could find to present to her, as Devon pulls everything from his backpack. Ms Donovan picks my folder up and flips through the pages, her eyes getting wider – hungrier.

If I were told about this story, I don't think I'd believe it. Even with the evidence. It seems too twisted to be true. But Niveus is that twisted, I know that now.

"This is…" the journalist starts, flipping another page.

I swallow, leg bouncing up and down, scared she'll say it's BS or that we're making this up.

"This is awful… I've never seen a story like it before," she says, looking back up at us. "You kids have gone through so much, I'm so sorry."

I feel relieved, my eyes water, but I blink away the tears. She believes us.

"Could you run a story? Get some coverage in the paper?" I ask.

She shakes her head and the sinking feeling returns. What does she mean, no?

"I can do something even better for you guys." Ms Donovan leans back, a serious expression on her face as she brings her fingers up to her chin. "People don't read papers these days, not the people who count for a story like this, anyway… You want to be heard? We need to broadcast this live on TV."

"Broadcast it live, how? We've dropped out. Going back just to get evidence of them in the act might get us killed," Devon says, sounding unimpressed by Ms Donovan's plan.

"We don't necessarily need to catch them in the act, just film a live exposé where you confront them. Have them cornered, unable to escape the truth about what they've done – what they're doing," Ms Donovan says.

She's right. We need to catch them off guard, expose the truth on camera for the world to see. I think it sounds great, even though Devon doesn't seem to yet.

"Do you have a school event coming up? A homecoming dance maybe, where we might be able to film?" she asks.

I nod. "We have an annual charity ball. The Senior Year Snowflake Charity Ball, it's tomorrow actually—"

"Perfect! Just perfect!" Ms Donovan says, writing something down on a notepad.

"You want us to go to the ball and do what exactly?" Devon asks. Still snippy, still rude. I wonder what's up with him. I know he wasn't entirely convinced that we should talk to this journalist, but he's here. He didn't have to come.

Ms Donovan remains unbothered by his tone.

"Give a speech, tell them how you feel, what they've done to you, let us catch it on camera and broadcast it on every TV in every state in America. We'll bring security of course, make sure you guys are safe. Sound like a good plan to you?" she asks.

I nod. It sounds like a brilliant plan.

The sort of explosive ending we need if we want to take Niveus down and restore any hope in becoming who we're meant to become.

"Good," Ms Donovan says, with a wide smile. "Let's talk strategy."

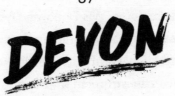

WEDNESDAY

We get to Terrell's at around four o'clock.

The entire drive back, Chiamaka wouldn't shut up about how excited she is about tomorrow and everything we now have in store for Niveus, with this new plan the journalist came up with.

A plan she has full confidence in. The meeting made her feel more secure in the idea that we stand a chance. It made my doubts even worse.

The plan is complicated and risky. I don't want to put my trust in something so dangerous. But even if I decide not to join in, she'll still go through with it.

And I can't let her do that alone. She might get herself killed. I don't think I could live with myself if I knew I could have prevented it in some way.

We were originally going to go back to Chiamaka's place, but I told her I wanted to be dropped off at Terrell's and she'd agreed, told me she wanted to tell him about the plan and how successful today was (in her opinion). Weirdly, they seem to get along.

Terrell's bright-red door looks gloomier in the rain. I can

hear Terrell moving about inside. The lock sounds and the door opens wide.

Terrell is standing there in his grey joggers, a *Black Panther* shirt and his signature dimples.

"Come in, we can go up to my room," Terrell says as Chiamaka steps in, immediately climbing the steps.

"Hey," Terrell says with a smile.

"Hi," I say, smiling back at him.

"Did it all go okay at the news station?" he asks.

I shrug. "Chiamaka's happy."

As if on cue, Chiamaka is shouting. "Are you guys coming or not?"

"We'd better go up," Terrell says, and I nod, following him up into his room. When we get inside, Chiamaka is seated on his bed, scrolling through her phone, and so I sit next to her. When Terrell walks in, he sits opposite us, on the chair next to his desk.

"How'd it go?" he asks.

"It went well, we have a solid plan. I know it's going to work, I can just feel it," she says.

She seems so certain. Almost naïvely so. But then again, she is smart, and she is apparently the rational one. So maybe I'm in the wrong.

"So, what's the plan?" Terrell asks, swivelling the chair side to side with his foot.

"Niveus has this Snowflake Ball they hold for seniors. They invite their donors, important representatives from top colleges, it's a chance to prove yourself..." Chiamaka says, trailing off at the end, voice growing quiet. "We're going to crash it," she adds after a moment's pause.

"Crash it? You're going back to Niveus, after everything?" Terrell asks, eyebrows raised.

Maybe he'll see how dangerous this plan sounds, and back me up for once.

"The journalist and her team will be crashing too, filming it all. I'm going to tell the cameras what Niveus has done, and it's going to be broadcast across America."

"Holy shit, that's genius," Terrell says.

"Right?" Chiamaka replies.

Okay, so they've both clearly lost their ability to summon common sense. There's no point in arguing, tomorrow is happening whether I think it makes sense or not.

"I need to get home and plan for the big event," Chiamaka says, pushing herself off the bed.

"Do you have a dress?" I ask.

She looks offended.

"What am I? Of course I have a dress. I picked my ballgown out before we broke up for summer last year. Do you have a tux?"

I shake my head.

"You can come over to my place before the ball tomorrow, my dad has tuxes he hasn't worn. You guys have a similar build... small, bony... Something in his closet should fit you."

"Thanks..." I say, not sure whether or not to be offended by that description of me.

"You sure you don't want to stay over? My ma's at my

401

sister's place until Saturday, I could build you a fort out of my spare sheets to sleep in or something?" Terrell says.

"That's so sweet of you, but in the nicest way possible... I'd rather die than sleep *here*...in a...fort? So, no thanks," Chiamaka says.

Terrell nods like she didn't just insult his home. "I'll walk you out."

"See you tomorrow," Chiamaka says. I mutter a goodbye and they both disappear through the door.

I can hear them shuffling downstairs. Chiamaka laughs at something Terrell says and then I hear the door slam shut.

Terrell's walking in again moments later.

"You good?" he asks, before falling back into the chair.

"I'm not sure," I say.

"Is it the plan tomorrow?"

"Partly, I think I'm just in shock. There's so much I'm trying to deal with at once."

"Like?" Terrell asks.

I sit back, feeling heavy. "I feel like I have no closure. Even if tomorrow goes well, there are people who I've known for years, been friendly with, who I still want answers from... I just— I'm so angry."

I'm not being completely honest. It isn't people, just one person who I'm angry with really.

"So, get your closure," Terrell says.

"How?" I ask.

Terrell slides forward in his desk chair, stopping centimetres away from me.

"If these people meant a lot to you, tell them how much they fucked up, let them hear how you feel," he says softly.

I nod. I need to confront Jack somehow.

"You give good advice," I tell him.

"Thank you, Quick," Terrell says.

Meow.

The sound startles me and my eyes dart around the room for the devil incarnate.

Meow, meow.

The cat crosses the floor of Terrell's bedroom, seemingly appearing from the shadows, and curls up next to his feet. I give it the evils.

"Hey, BS," Terrell says in a cutesy voice.

"I'm going to head home now I think," I say, standing.

Terrell looks up while stroking his cat with one hand. "Let me walk you out."

He walks me to the door and gives me a big goodbye hug. I hug him back tightly.

"Tell me how it goes tomorrow," he says, as he lets go.

I nod, promising him that I will.

Like this morning, I spend most of the evening in my room, zoned out, thinking about how shitty the world is. Thinking about Jack and how he was the one constant I had in my life.

I'm curled up on my bed, head buried in between my knees, trying to calm down; not feel so lost and out of control. I try to drown but it doesn't seem to work any more.

I can't get my head below the surface – something is keeping me afloat, forcing me to deal with the thoughts I usually keep locked away.

Someone with the key has broken in and unlocked Pandora's box.

I keep wondering why Jack would do this, why he joined in. Why, after everything we've been through, did he want to hurt me so bad?

Terrell is right. I need to go and get closure.

I sniff and reach out for my phone on my nightstand. It's only eleven.

I put my phone into the pocket of Terrell's alien hoodie. I don't know what I'm thinking, but I'm slipping into my sneakers, creeping out of my room, down the stairs and out of the house, making sure to close the door gently. Ma is a light sleeper, and on the rare occasions I sneak out, I need to make little to no noise.

Our neighbourhood is never all that quiet at night; there's always guys doing shady stuff in corners, loud music, and the occasional sound of firing into the sky.

Jack's uncle lives in the part of our neighbourhood Ma never liked me going to, but because it was Jack and I'd known him for ever, she allowed it. Sometimes when I couldn't sleep, or got bored at night and Dre was busy, I'd go to Jack's.

There's a gap at the side of his house, and if you walk through, you find yourself in his backyard. Jack's bedroom is on the ground floor and he has this huge glass door that you can see into.

Like I expected, the lights are on.

He's seated on the floor doing homework, eyes focused on the pages. I remember when we were trying to get into Niveus, Jack wanted to prove to himself and his brothers that they were more than this place, this neighbourhood, this life. I wanted to go somewhere I wouldn't get beat up all the time.

We'd stay up until three o'clock sometimes, testing each other, trying to get into this school that was meant to change everything for us. I think that was the closest we'd ever been. I feel tears tickle my chin as the memory floats above the noise, and I wipe my face with the back of my hand.

I used to come here, knock on Jack's door and he'd let me in. We'd play video games or talk about stuff we wouldn't say to other people. Sometimes we'd argue over stupid things like the world being flat. Jack would say, *"What if we've just been made to think it's not,"* and I'd tell him he was stupid, even planes flying around the earth proves the world isn't flat. Then he'd say, in all seriousness, *"Pac-Man theory! Maybe the planes just start again from the same point."* And I'd burst out laughing, tears streaming down my face, a stomach-aching kind of laughter.

Other times, we'd talk about serious stuff.

"Some days breathing is really fucking hard. I feel overwhelmed by it, you know?" Jack would say and I'd nod, because I did know. Jack hasn't exactly won the lottery in life either. His parents are gone, his uncle is a drunk, he practically raises his brothers. He'd shake his head, hitting

the buttons on the game controller, his eyes glassy as he breathed out, cheeks stained. "*But I have to keep going, for my brothers,*" he'd whisper. "*I don't have a choice.*"

Days like that I'd put down the game controller and pat his back. Sometimes he'd pause the game and we'd forget about the world and the unspoken rules about boys not being allowed to talk about things that bother us or hug each other, and he'd rest his head on my shoulder and cry.

This was all before things changed. Before I came out to him, before I started dating Scotty. There was a time when I thought we'd always be there for each other.

The words from computer 17 stab at my thoughts. His name in bold: *distribution of DR's messages.*

I sniff, looking up to the sky, trying to stop more tears from falling. I wipe my face with my sleeve and then, like I have done so many times before, I knock.

Jack's head whips around and he squints, recognition slowly bleeding into his features. His eyes widen, like he's seen a ghost. I watch him watch me for a few moments, unmoving, like he's waiting for me to break in and hurt him.

Then slowly, he stands. He's wearing a black shirt and shorts. I swallow the lump in my throat as he slides the door open.

I don't move, I look at him, not bothering to wipe the tears from my face any more.

"What do you want?" he asks, voice low.

"I know about Niveus."

Silence. His skin is pale and blotchy as he looks away.

"What about them?"

"You know what. I know about Aces, and all the shit you've done to me."

Jack shifts a little, eyes still avoiding mine. "I have work to do—"

He tries to close the door, but I block it with my body. "When you had no one, I was there for you, Jack. When you wanted to try and get into Niveus too, my ma paid for us to sit for those tests. She fed you, made sure you were okay, because she loves you like you are her own son. Then you stopped coming over, and that was okay, she was working all the time anyway, she hardly noticed..." I choke out a cry, and I can't stop. Jack's just staring at me blankly, like he wants to be anywhere but here right now. "What did I ever do to you for you to hate me this much?"

Jack sniffs, not saying anything at first. Then it pours out.

"I work hard for everything I get. You'd still get in with affirmative action or whatever scholarship they give to you guys, while I have to work twice as hard." He shakes his head, wiping his eyes. "I didn't ruin your life."

He says this like he's reciting some bigoted script that was fed to him. Says it like he's remembering lines he doesn't quite get but believes in anyway.

"That's not how life works, Jack. I don't just get given things – for you to say that is just— It just shows you don't know me at all."

I want to tell him that people like him, boys with white skin, they never work twice as hard. Boys like him don't

407

have to carry the weight of generations and generations of hate and discrimination.

But I don't know how to even begin explaining that. Me getting that scholarship doesn't mean I didn't work for it, it means I did, and I need it just to continue working twice as hard as everyone else. And anyway, the scholarship was a curse in disguise, it brought me in, made me think I could dream and actually break the cycle, but then destroyed everything in my life, bit by bit.

It was a poisoned chalice; good at first, but it slowly ate away at me until I was nothing but bits of flesh and marred bone.

"And you did ruin everything. I can't go back to high school, I can't graduate, I can't do anything. You *knew*, for God knows how long, and you fucking helped them," I shout. "What did I do to you that was so bad? You were my best friend… I love…I loved you."

Jack is looking away again, fingers gripping the glass, knuckles turning white.

"You should go," he says.

I shake my head. "No, you don't get to do that," I say, stepping forward as Jack tries to close the door again. I can feel the glass against my shoulder, crushing me. When he realizes I won't budge, he pushes me back and I stumble slightly, stunned for a few seconds before I push him back, stepping in now.

"Leave," he says, chest heaving.

I look at him and I think about how we don't know the

people we think we know at all. How people who are meant to love you, leave you – like Jack, my pa…Andre. I can feel my fingers shaking, insides rattling as I think of how many people leave and keep leaving. Like there is something wrong with me…like I'm not good enough.

Jack knew how much my ma struggled, and he watched, knowing this would all happen.

Before I can calm down and think about the consequences of what I want to do to him, I'm pushing him again and, again, he's staggering back. Now I'm punching him and he isn't fighting back, he's letting me hit him over and over, until my knuckles ache and his face is bleeding. My eyes blur as his face becomes splotches of white, purple and blue. We're both crying; Jack is on the floor and I am on top of him.

There's a knock on his door and I look up.

"Jack, everything good in there?" his uncle says. I quickly stand, shakily moving away from his body. Jack looks up at me, then turns away.

"Yeah," he croaks. "Everything's good."

Without saying anything else to him, I turn around and for the last time, slide his door open and stumble into the night.

THURSDAY

I'm woken up the next day by my phone ringing. It's bright outside, and my bed is empty, no sign of my brothers anywhere. My hand is sore, knuckles bruised. I'm a little surprised I slept at all.

It's like all I needed to get a good night's sleep was to finally confront Jack.

I reach out for my phone.

Three missed calls from Chiamaka.

Why the hell is she calling me? What time is it? I glance at the time and I bolt up.

It's already past two.

How long was I asleep for? Ma usually wakes me up if I look like I'm about to oversleep, especially on a school day. Why didn't she?

My phone rings again. I rub the sleep out of my eyes and accept the call from Chiamaka.

"Where are you? I've been texting you all morning!" she says, her voice only slightly raised.

"I overslept, sorry."

I expect her to shout at me or dish out an insult but instead she says: "That's okay, when will you get here? I've started getting ready, the event isn't for a few hours but it's best if you get here quickly so I can see if my dad's suits fit. If they don't, I'll have to call in an emergency tailor," she says.

Someone outside the Niveus bubble might have thought she was being sarcastic, but from dating Scotty, I know things like emergency tailors actually exist. And they are on speed dial after 911.

"I'll be there in an hour," I say, trying to hold back a yawn. How am I still tired?

"Okay, see you soon, then," she says.

"See you," I say before the line goes dead.

I scroll for any messages from my ma, explaining why for the first time in years she's let me stay home instead of going to school, but there are none. I decide to send her a message anyway.

I love you, Ma.

I know she won't see it until she's on her break, which should be any time now, but I need to tell her before this suicide mission.

I throw my phone down, shower and grab my backpack before leaving.

As I leave, I plug my headphones in and classical music fills my ears, one of Chopin's pieces, and I refresh mine and Ma's chat. Still nothing. I try not to feel guilty about keeping so much from her. I exit the chat and look for another app to get lost in while I walk to Chiamaka's. I click on Twitter, scrolling down the timeline slowly. I mostly follow college admissions pages and the odd celebrity, so there's not much to see until I see my tweet from yesterday.

I don't know what I was thinking posting it.

I scroll down, but stop short when I see the numbers underneath my tweet. I slow down my pace and click onto the tweet, just to double-check that the figures are right.

24,000 likes.

Holy shit.

There are people in the comments talking about how messed up it is, tagging other people, telling me I'm not alone.

I don't check my socials often, don't have my notifications on for them. They usually sit in my phone, taking up storage space, with no other purpose but to occasionally like a tweet from an admissions page.

I have messages from so many people. This is weird. I click on one of the messages.

@neenaK77: This is so fucked up, I hope you report them to someone

@ty_blm: You have my support, it's not right that this is happening at a time like this. Thought this type of shit only happened in the 1950s

There's more like these, packing my previously empty inbox.

If people saw this and believed me, maybe tonight they'll see what we have to say and believe us too.

@DLikesTunes: Thank you, we have, we're going back there tonight to stop them. I tweet at @neenaK77

Maybe Chiamaka was right.

Maybe we can defeat Niveus after all.

My phone buzzes and a message from my ma pops up.

Love you too, hope you had a good sleep – Ma

Why didn't you wake me up? I text back.

I know you haven't been going to school. We'll talk later, okay? Love you, Von.

...Ma knows I haven't been going in. Does she know about Niveus, or does she just have her special bullshit-detector turned up to full?

Either way, it means I'm going to have to come clean. If today goes well, it will be a lot easier to explain.

I hope it goes well.

CHIAMAKA

THURSDAY

Devon arrives in a timely manner at three-thirty, and I drag him inside and up the steps.

"Okay, so, we have five options that I think would fit you from Dad's closet. Pick the one you like most and I'll leave you in here to change," I tell him, when we get into my room.

I have the five suits laid out on my bed in front of him, all different in some way. One is made from velvet, another, laced in gold. I've laid out a range of styles for him to choose from seeing as I don't know Devon all that well, so I don't know what kind of suit he'd be into. Especially since his day-to-day fashion sense doesn't exactly make his tastes extremely obvious to me. He dresses like he's purposely trying to make some kind of statement about ugly garments. It's hard to gauge what someone who wears the same dreadful hoodie, pants and sneakers every day would wear when it comes to formal outfits.

He picks up the first one. It's the plainest one, with black lapels and a black bow. I should have seen that one coming.

"That's really...plain," I say.

"If you didn't want me to choose it, why make it an option?" he asks.

"It's not that I didn't want you to choose it, I just think it's a little boring... I mean, we're going to be on national television, in front of all the people who wronged us, so... thought you would want to dress nice for once."

He looks at me unblinking for a few moments, before chucking the suit back down and picking up the one next to it. This one is the flashiest.

The blazer is gold, with satin lapels, a black bow and black pants.

I smile and pat him on the shoulder. "Much better. Going to go change now, will be back in a few," I say, before walking out of my room and down the hallway, into my dressing room.

I've already done my make-up and put curlers in my hair. Usually when we have big events like this, I get someone else to do my hair and make-up, wanting to be perfect, how everyone expects. But what's the point any more? They don't expect anything from me. Maybe they never did. It was all a delusion.

My dress hangs in the centre of my closet. It's an Elie Saab original, flown in from Milan. I picked it out because it looks like it was made for a queen. Something I never was – just a social experiment, a chess piece in a sick game.

It is one of the prettiest dresses I have ever seen. It's sleeveless with a plunging sweetheart neckline and A-line silhouette, with golden embroidery raining down from the top and a plain rose-gold mesh at the bottom. I've stared at it all day, feeling like I'm a fraud for wanting to wear something so beautiful and perfect to the ball.

I slip out of my robe and wander over to the dress, hesitating before stroking the material.

It's not like I was ever truly someone worthy of this dress anyway. I'll just have to fake it like I always do. Only this time, it's not the students and teachers at Niveus who need to believe the persona. America needs to.

I pull the dress off the hook gently, unzipping the side before stepping into it for the first time since I got it this summer. I slowly zip it up, tugging a little harder in the middle where it gets stuck. It's always been a little snug on me – Elie Saab is not something you get tailored to fit you; either you're perfect or you aren't. *"You don't fix a Saab original, you fix yourself,"* Ruby once said to me when she was showing off her gown for prom last year, alongside her diet plan. It's a messed-up philosophy, I get that. I think these fashion labels do it on purpose though.

When it's zipped up, I push open a door on the side of the room where I keep my shoes. The walls are filled with my favourite pairs, from McQueen to Saint Laurent, all of them beautiful. But today isn't about just looking good, I need my battle shoes. The ones I will use to stomp on my enemies.

I bend down looking for a specific pair, my golden Jimmy Choos. You can never go wrong with Jimmy Choo. When I find them, I sit back on the chair in the middle and slip my feet into them, already feeling stronger than before.

Not that I have a choice. I have to be ready – to show Niveus that it has not defeated me, and never will.

Like Mom always says, *"By fire, by force"*. Tonight will be the last night Niveus gets to make people like us feel small and worthless.

When I get back into my room, Devon is dressed and sitting on my bed, scrolling through his phone.

He looks up when I walk in, and his eyebrows rise a little.

"You look nice," he says.

I take him in. His hair needs some brushing and other than the suit he looks a little plain. He's even wearing those godforsaken Vans he wears to school.

"Thanks… Where are your shoes?" I ask.

He looks down at his feet.

"On my feet," he says, matter-of-factly.

"You can't wear those."

"Why not?"

"They clash with your outfit."

He pauses, like he seems to a lot during our conversations. I always wonder what he's thinking, why his expression gets all intense. I assume he's realizing I'm right and thinking of ways to thank me for my wisdom.

"What size are you? I'll see if my dad has anything that might fit," I say. "He should have some simple loafers or—"

417

"I'm comfortable, I don't want to change into your dad's shoes," he says sharply.

Why is he so difficult?

At least one of us will look the part tonight, that's what counts.

"Can you at least let me do something to your hair?" I ask.

He nods. "Okay."

I go into my bathroom, getting out an unused brush, comb, and styling gel from my supply cabinet. In the corner I spot some black eyeliner, and so I grab it too, before going straight over to Richards on the bed. I start spreading some gel on his hair, combing it out the best I can.

I'm not exactly an expert on hair, but I do mine enough to know how to make it look half-decent. He literally looked like he had just rolled out of bed and come here, which wouldn't surprise me.

When I'm done with his hair, I take out the eyeliner and I go towards his eyelids. He jerks back a little with his hand up, like he's shielding his face.

"What the fuck are you doing?" he asks.

"Eyeliner," I say.

"Why?"

"You have nice eyes… I thought…I thought you'd look really nice with some on. I wouldn't lie to you," I say.

He looks really against the idea, and at first I think he is going to say no, but instead he lowers his hand and sits there with a straight face. I take this as my cue to continue, and I press the thick pencil onto his right lid.

"Is Terrell coming?" I ask, as I draw a line.

"No, why?" he says quietly.

I shrug. "Thought you'd bring him as your date or something... Guess I was wrong."

"Why would I bring him as my date?"

I give him a look, with an eyebrow raised. People think they are less obvious than they are. I see the way they look at each other.

"Aren't you guys dating...or at the very least hooking up?"

He's silent for a bit and I feel like I've crossed some line. Oh well.

"We're not dating," he says.

So they are just hooking up then.

"On to the next lid..." I tilt his head to the side slightly. His jaw is so tense, you'd think I was hurting him or something.

"I like Terrell. Wish you'd have brought him... He's much better company," I say.

Devon says nothing, so I just finish applying the eyeliner in silence.

"There," I say once I'm done, stepping back to admire my handiwork. I smile. He actually looks really good. Much better than before. I hand him a mirror and he looks at himself silently.

I can't really tell what Devon is thinking.

"Do you like it?" I ask.

He shrugs.

Which I take to mean yes.

"Before I forget, I got us masks. I figured it would be weird being the only ones without them," I say, reaching into one of my drawers and handing him a black mask. The Snowflake Ball has always been a masquerade. Another Niveus tradition.

I sit next to him now, checking the time on my phone. It's just turned four. The ball starts at six.

The journalist at Central News 1 told us to message her when we are about to leave so that they have time to arrive and set up their equipment. Devon and I will be going through the back entrance, the same one we used to get into Morgan Library on Sunday; no CCTV for anyone checking. We'll leave the entrance open for the journalist and her crew to come through.

Then we get up onstage and they hit record.

"I'm actually really excited for tonight," I tell Devon. "I can't wait to wake up tomorrow and not have to look over my shoulder, or feel like I'm losing my mind... I can't wait to go back to focusing on Yale and med school. I know you don't think this is going to work out, but I do. I really do."

Devon is silently looking down at his shoes, and then after a few moments he glances back up again.

"I didn't believe you at first, or the journalist woman... so I tweeted about Niveus and what they've done—"

"You what?"

"I tweet—"

"I heard you. If anyone at Niveus sees that tweet, they

might make things even worse for us. What were you thinking? Delete it!" I say, panic rising a little.

He looks at me, guiltily.

"What?" I say, because there's obviously something he's not telling me.

"I… It went viral. I was going to tell you, but I only just saw when I was coming here. It has over 24,000 likes. A lot of people believe us."

My eyes widen. *24,000?* Wow.

"Besides, didn't you confront that girl who told you about what they're doing? Don't you think she might have let Niveus know that we know everything already? Things are already worse for us," Devon says.

I swallow at the thought of Belle. I hadn't even considered that. Hadn't even thought about her, or the fact I'll be seeing her tonight. My chest squeezes a little.

I need a drink.

I stand quickly. "Do you want a drink?"

"Like alcohol?" Devon asks.

"Yes, like alcohol," I say.

He nods.

"Let's go to the basement," I say, and he follows me out of my room and down two flights of stairs into the basement. It's built like an underground bar, with stools and everything. I open up one of the wine fridges and take out a bottle of Chardonnay, placing it on the island.

I get out two glasses and pour some wine into each, before sliding one over to Devon.

I don't even really like the taste of it, but I know it will help me relax a little. I only poured half a glass so that we wouldn't be *too* relaxed or out of it, just enough to give us some liquid courage. I pick up the glass and raise it towards Devon.

"What should we drink to, Richards?" I ask.

He looks up for a moment before lifting his glass too.

"To destroying Niveus Academy," he says.

"To destroying Niveus," I repeat.

39

THURSDAY

We get to the back entrance of the school, our masks covering our faces.

In the distance there are people screaming, students laughing as they enter the building.

Chiamaka takes out the key for the back entrance, quickly unlocks the door, and we both step in. We'd agreed to go into Morgan Library and wait there for the journalist, Ms Donovan, and her camera crew. We chose Morgan both because Chiamaka wanted to grab the yearbook from 1965 to take in with us for physical proof and also the convenience of it having no cameras.

We turn into Morgan. Chiamaka walks up to the first bookcase and bends down, grabbing a blue hardcover book from the shelf.

"Got it," she says, opening it up and flipping through some of the pages. She has a small clutch tucked under her arm, holding the posters and print outs for later when we have to get up in front of everyone.

I swallow, feeling nervous as I scan the huge library.

I feel like someone is watching.

"Could you go and wait outside by the back-door entrance, be on the lookout for the journalist and her crew? She said they are almost here," Chiamaka says.

I nod.

When I get to the back door, the area smells like smoke. The fun and games are already beginning. People love to drink and smoke and pull pranks each year and then tell the lower years all about it, getting them excited for the day they'll become seniors and do the same. It's weird that this is what excites them, as if they don't already do this at home all the time; drinking, smoking, meddling with people's lives. But I guess there is something about doing it at school, right under the teachers' and donors' noses, that thrills them.

My phone vibrates in my pocket and I take it out.

Incoming call from Terrell

Why is Terrell calling me? He knows today is the day of the ball.

"Hello?"

"Are you at school yet?" Terrell asks.

"Yeah, I'm just waiting for the journalists to arrive, why?" I say, lowering my voice.

"I'm here," he says.

"What? Why?"

"Hey," Terrell says, but this time his voice isn't coming from my phone. I turn and he's standing there, dressed in black, like he's here for a funeral. Black shirt, black jeans,

424

black sneakers. I don't think I've seen Terrell wear so little colour before.

"What are you doing here?" I ask, still shocked.

It doesn't feel like he's real.

"I needed to tell you something… I thought about telling you after tonight, when everything calmed down or when you weren't as overwhelmed. But that's not fair to you. I won't blame you for hating me after this, okay? I just want you to know I'm so, so sorry—"

"Terrell? What are you talking about?" I ask, feeling breathless.

"I should have told you a long time ago but…I was scared." I look at him closely. His eyes are glassy, like he's about to cry.

"What is it?" I ask. My heart is racing.

Terrell looks away from me for a moment.

"I… I helped your school – I helped Niveus spy on you."

40

THURSDAY

Ms Donovan messages me that she's here and so I text Devon:

They're here

I push myself up from my seat and walk towards the door, but as I approach it, the door begins to open.

I step back, looking for somewhere to quickly hide myself. I pull one of the chairs out, ready to duck under the table, my mask falling off in the haste just as the door swings open and Jamie walks in.

There's a cold expression on his pretty face. His hair is shorter than when I last saw it; his suit is a crisp, dark blue, with a black bow strangling his neck.

"Hello, Chiamaka," he says, voice filled with venom. He takes his hand out from his pocket and brings out his favourite lighter. When he presses it down, a gentle flame appears, and then disappears.

"What are you doing here?" I ask, proud of myself for not stuttering or stepping back. I stand here, with my arms folded, staring him down in the same way he stares at me.

"Should be asking you that. You're not welcome here."

I laugh. "Who made you God? My parents pay my tuition – I'm more than welcome here," I say.

He steps forward, pressing the lighter down once again, letting the flame come as fast as it goes. The lighter has his name engraved into the gold exterior. His hands are wrapped around it tightly, like he's scared to lose it.

Jamie and his lighter remind me of a spoiled child and their favourite toy. I always thought his love for fire was born from camp, but I bet his twisted desire to watch things burn and become ash began before then. While other children played with dolls and trucks, Jamie probably played with this. Watched the flame swirl to life and then die, over and over until it became his obsession.

"You have no right to be here," he says, voice getting darker. "I don't understand you guys. Even after I chased you, even after showing you those pictures…" He clicks the lighter, the flame glows. "After Martha." *Click.* "After giving you so many chances to disappear…you keep pushing. Don't think I didn't see your friend's tweet. Think you're so clever? Little Miss Senior Head Prefect. I thought you'd at least have the sense not to show up here, but you just… can't seem to take a fucking hint."

He laughs a twisted sort of laugh, spinning the lighter again. It's a laugh that makes my insides shake.

"Are you in love with me? Is that it?"

I've come to realize that what I felt for Jamie was not love or even infatuation. I didn't care about how I truly felt about him. I just knew I wanted to be on top, by any means necessary. Even if it meant letting a sweaty brainless jock hold my hand and tell everyone he was my boyfriend, or letting a wicked boy like Jamie wrap his slimy hands around me whenever he wanted.

What I felt was a desperation to be powerful in a world that doesn't let girls be. Especially girls like me.

The only time I felt love or anything close to that was with Belle. I don't think any guy I've ever set my eyes on even came close to comparing to how I saw Belle.

So…love? Jamie can wish.

"I hate you," I tell him.

He smiles wider. "No, you don't." He steps even closer. I stand my ground. "You love me, but I don't love you. Who could? You're a whore. Everyone knows it. It's why I kissed you at my party. Why I knew you'd eventually sleep with me. You'd sleep with anyone…" He tilts his head and comes closer. "I never liked you. But I was curious. I had to try it, and I did…"

My heart is in my throat. I feel so disgusted. I'm trying not to cry.

"You were decent…Belle was better," he adds, clicking the lighter once again.

It is dangerously close to my face. I can feel the heat against my skin. I blink and a tear slips out. But I don't move. I don't dare move.

"I'm giving you this last chance to get out of this school where you aren't wanted, otherwise you'll really see what

I'm capable of." Jamie clicks one more time, so close my hair catches on fire. I stumble back a little and as I pat it out, Jamie's laughter rings through the library.

I'm not going to let what he said hurt me. I won't give him that power over me. I'm Chiamaka fucking Adebayo – I don't need some prick telling me who I am and who I should be.

"Are you done with your speech?" I ask, not waiting for a reply before continuing. "Call me a whore, I don't care. But *you*, Jamie, you bring it up because you do care."

He raises an eyebrow.

"You care that a girl like me can do what she wants, and not give a crap about what you or anyone has to say. You care that you liked it, and that your racist parents and this racist school gave you one job – to get close to me and then stab me in the back – but instead you liked it, every second of it. You liked kissing me—"

"Shut up," he growls.

"Liked the sex, the sneaking around—"

"I said shut up!" Jamie yells.

Which only gives me more energy.

"You care that I kissed your girlfriend." I smile, even though it hurts. "You care that we did more than kiss—"

He pushes me back against the wall hard, and I laugh in his face, more tears falling. But they aren't sad tears, it feels like I'm free. Like I'm flying.

"You're a loser, Jamie. A failure. A disappointment. You failed to bring me down to your lowly level and that *kills*

429

you—" I'm cut off by Jamie wrapping his hands around my neck and squeezing. He's shaking as he strangles me and I'm wheezing, laughing and gasping for air.

I can't breathe, but I can't stop smiling.

He keeps squeezing, his face red and vibrating with anger as he stares me down.

I don't want Jamie's face to be the last thing I see before I die, and so I summon all the remaining strength I have, and I kick him in his crotch.

Jamie staggers back, releasing me. I cough, throat hurting, chest aching. I don't give myself time to pause before I kick him again. This time he falls to the ground. Groaning loudly, his lighter falling with him.

"Fucking bitch," he wheezes.

I rub my neck, and I tilt my head to look at him. He's so pathetic, lying there, writhing around on the floor. I press my heel down where I know it will hurt him most and he screams.

I get a twisted sense of joy, seeing him cry.

I knew I picked the right shoes.

"Rot in hell, Jamie," I spit, before stepping away, grabbing my mask and striding towards the exit of the library.

When I get out, I notice my legs shaking, my heart beating in my ears. I touch the strand of my hair where he placed the flame. Crusty and burned.

I can still smell it, the smoke. I can still feel his hands wrapped around me.

But regardless, I feel some of that power returning.

The power I used to feel flood my body each morning when I'd walk into school and know I'd earned this position at the top. Now, I feel powerful because I've taken my voice back, stopped letting Jamie squash me into the image he has of me.

Of a weak girl he can push down and hurt without consequence.

That girl doesn't exist. She never did.

41

THURSDAY

"W-what the fuck do you mean?" I ask, moving away from Terrell.

"I didn't want to hurt you. I never would hurt you. Some old guy came into my school, told me he'd pay for my sister's medical bills if I watched over you, reported back to him."

I feel so dizzy. This can't be happening.

"This was after we first hung out, and at first I considered it. I just want my sister to get better. I was desperate, so I thought about doing it…did it for maybe a day, but quickly knew I couldn't. I told the guy I wouldn't do it. That I couldn't do that to you. Then you started talking about your school and I didn't tell you because I didn't want you to hate me, and the guy told me that if I mentioned him or our deal, things would get worse for you, so I just tried to help you guys out the best I could…"

My phone vibrates and I look away from Terrell and down at the message from Chiamaka.

She sent one a few minutes ago, saying the journalists had arrived.

They managed to come through the front entrance,
I'm with them at the back door to the ballroom.
Hurry. – C

"I have to go," I say, feeling too sick to even look at Terrell right now.

"Von—"

"Just, stop! Okay?" I shout, not wanting to ruin the make-up Chiamaka did around my eyes. So I blink back the tears and I turn around, walking into the building and leaving Terrell alone outside.

I become a shadow, walking quickly, head down, mask on, finally reaching the back of the ballroom where Chiamaka is standing.

"Where are they?" I ask.

"They've taken their positions." She lowers her mask. I notice bruising around her neck that looks like fingers. *Did something happen?*

There's no time for me to breathe, let alone ask questions. She threads her fingers through mine and opens the back door.

Before I know it, we're stepping through the doors and into the ballroom together.

42

THURSDAY

No one notices us slip through. There's a curtain by the back entrance, currently blocking us from being seen. Through a slit, I see everyone. They are all seated at large round tables, talking away to each other. The room is as beautiful as I'd always imagined it would be. High ceilings, diamond chandeliers, and tall picturesque windows looking out onto the ocean. It's perfect. Feels like I'm in a movie.

This ballroom was specifically built for this event and has been used for the Snowflake Ball for decades. They keep these doors locked throughout the year, except for today. I've dreamed of this since I joined Niveus.

I thought that when I finally got here, it would be a happy moment. Another marker of success.

I thought I'd be crowned Snowflake Queen. It's what I wanted the most after valedictorian and Head Prefect.

But as I look at the crowns sitting on deep red cushions at the front of the ballroom, I realize how stupid this all is. The prefect badge, the crown. Lumps of metal I'd tied so much of my self-worth to.

I take a breath and I step forward, through the curtain.

Voices get lower, whispers louder, as faces turn to stare at us.

I'm at the front now and I take in the room, trying not to shake. There are tables filled with familiar strangers, their faces covered by sparkly masks.

They hate me. Every person in this room hates me...and knowing that gives me the confidence to abandon any pride I have left, and march over to the cushions and grab one of the crowns. Devon gives me a weird look as I place the meaningless metal on my head.

People look surprised, amused, ready to see what I do next.

I see a figure slip in through one of the doors at the back. *Terrell?* Did Devon invite him after all?

It's good, he gets to see us take Niveus down. He was there helping us with the details, it seems right that he's here now. Plus, now I know that there is one person in the audience besides Devon who probably doesn't hate me.

I scan the hall for Ms Donovan, and her camera operator. They're both dressed as waiters, blending in with the rest of the servers at the back. I don't see the security, but I assume they are hidden somewhere in the room, waiting to jump in if necessary. Donovan starts counting down from five with her hands, the cameraman points the camera in our direction, then Donovan gives me a thumbs up and I begin, speaking clearly into the little microphone Donovan gave me to pin to my dress.

"My name is Chiamaka Adebayo and this is my friend

Devon Richards. And by design, we are the only Black students at Niveus Private Academy. Every ten years, Niveus accepts two Black students. Niveus waits until their senior year to really strike, to enhance its campaign of psychological and physical abuse. The aim? To force these students to drop out, ruining every hope they had for a future. It's a game Niveus calls social eugenics."

I open up the yearbook from 1965.

"Here is a picture of Camp Aces, a camp set up for legacy students at the school and their families to plot how they were going to destroy the lives of the Black students at Niveus. And, since this project was started, every single Black student has dropped out before graduation. There is no explanation for where they went. They just vanish. And they vanish because Niveus made them. But that's why we are here. We are going to break that cycle by telling everyone what is really going on at this school. We are here to expose Niveus, its students, teachers and donors for what they are."

I unfold the posters from my clutch, passing the one with our yearbook photo scratched out to Devon, and holding up one of the less incriminating photos that Aces had taken and shoved through my mail slot. I look away from the camera and stare them all down.

"We have had physical threats, we have been followed, we have been set up. We have had our privacy invaded and personal photos and information leaked across the school. And now we say NO MORE," I finish.

I'm standing here, like I always dreamed I would be.

At the front, the queen to them all. It's nothing like how I envisioned it. Not in the slightest. Yet I still feel powerful.

I turn to find the journalist again. But I furrow my eyebrows in confusion as I search the crowd. Where did she go? The cameraman is missing too.

There is movement across the crowd as people begin shuffling around in their seats. I soon realize what they are doing. They are swapping out their masks. Exchanging them for identical ones. The mask from the hallway. The mask that chased me home.

Everyone in the hall has one on.

They sit there.

I know it's silent, but all I can hear is the blood rushing in my ears.

This is *Aces*. Every person I have spent the past four years with. Every person who I have looked in the eye. Sat next to in class. Passed in the hallway. Every person who, all along, wanted to humiliate me, see me work to get to the top, only to tear me down. Every person who knew they could hide behind these *masks* – online or here, now; a cult, that wants nothing more than to see me and Devon fail.

"Is your performance over?" a deep, dark voice says from behind me. I turn sharply and I am met by familiar jet-black hair, a wrinkled, expressionless face and eyes devoid of light, staring down at me.

"We gave you the chance to leave with some of your dignity intact, but instead you two clearly want the Dianna Walker treatment," Headmaster Ward says.

"What did you do to Dianna?" Devon says, sounding terrified.

I feel like I'm in a nightmare.

"You don't scare us, we've recorded it all and it's being broadcast across America," I say.

"Is that so...? Where are the cameras?" Headmaster Ward asks.

I glance back out into the sea of Aces. There's still no sign of Ms Donovan or her cameraman. What is going on?

"Alice, is that true? Are these two heretics going to destroy us all?" Headmaster Ward continues, turning to the crowd as one of the masked people removes the scary white mask from their face, revealing a smiling Ms Donovan underneath.

No.

"Fuck..." Devon whispers.

Fuck, I think.

This can't be happening. How is this possible? How is she involved?

I remember Belle's words, when I'd confronted her on Monday.

"*...it's not just Niveus, there are places all over the US that... that do this.*"

Central News 1 is a part of it.

God knows who else.

We need to get out of here, I think, just as I hear a low rumbling sound. Footsteps and people yelling.

I step back, as the doors of the hall burst open and all

of a sudden a rush of people swarms in. Outsiders. They're chanting something, but I can't make it out from the stage.

Some climb on the tables, kicking the expensive china. Others are simply screaming and blasting music from phones and speakers in their hands.

Protestors?

I finally make out what they are saying. "*No justice, no peace*". Over and over again.

So many brown faces, disrupting the ocean of white.

They are all so angry.

I think they are fighting for us.

I look at Devon and his eyes are wide.

Before I can do anything else, I feel a large hand grab me, dragging me away through the curtains. I glance back, trying to break out of this powerful grip, and that's when I feel cold metal pressed to my forehead.

A gun.

THURSDAY

There are protestors everywhere. Loud music breaking up the quiet. People screaming.

It's chaos. But even stranger, I don't think I have ever seen this many Black people, ever, outside of my neighbourhood.

I've definitely never seen this many Black people in Niveus. All these years, it was just me and Chiamaka.

People are here fighting…and they seem to be fighting for us.

I didn't want to be right about Central News 1, I wanted them to be good. But something I've realized is that very few things in this world are good.

I turn, expecting to see Chiamaka next to me, but there's no one there. I feel a little panic, the same panic as when you lose your ma in the supermarket when you're a kid. I hear a noise behind me and I turn, walking towards the entrance we came through. I see two figures. As I get closer, I see clearly.

Standing by the doors is Chiamaka. She looks horrified, frozen in place as Headmaster Ward presses a gun to her head.

I freeze, watching my ex-headmaster, who's moments away from shooting Chiamaka.

I shakily step towards the thick curtain, trying to draw it back without him noticing. If I act quickly, maybe I can push him off, grab the gun, stop him from doing anything.

A part of me wonders if this is what happened to Dianna Walker. The first girl Aces targeted, back in 1965. What if... they killed her?

Ward starts saying something to Chiamaka, but I only make out the words *classroom* and *move*. Chiamaka looks terrified. I have to stop him. He moves her towards the door, his hands gripping her arm tightly.

I swallow, pushing the curtain a little, only stepping through halfway. Chiamaka looks at me briefly.

He backs her up a little more, then reaches out to touch the door handle but quickly jolts back.

I take this moment to charge towards Ward, barging into him, hoping it makes him tumble. Only I didn't expect him to be this strong. He stumbles but doesn't fall.

He turns to look at me, disgust written across his features. There are screams in the background and people chanting.

I notice Chiamaka edging towards Ward.

"What did you do to Dianna?" I ask, breathing hard. "Did you guys kill her?"

Chiamaka takes something out from her bag.

Ward raises an eyebrow. "Why don't we see for ourselves?" he says, raising his gun to me now, just as Chiamaka sticks something in Ward's neck. He freezes up and falls to the ground, the gun dropping with him.

Chiamaka grabs his gun with a handkerchief and slides it away from him.

I'm breathless.

In her hand she's holding some kind of stun gun.

"Are you okay?" I ask, partly wondering where she got that from.

She wipes her eyes. "Yeah. We need to get out of here."

I nod and we walk through the curtains, jumping back when a loud boom sounds.

I look up. Smoke spills from the ceiling.

Wait...smoke?

People are looking around too, searching for where it came from.

My heart beats fast, and just as I grab Chiamaka's hand, there is another explosion.

I instinctively duck.

Then, as if we are in some disaster movie, parts of the ceiling break apart, wood falling from the sky.

Holy shit.

Screams start to fill the air. Chiamaka grabs my arm, pulling me towards the exit. We push through crowds as everyone attempts to escape, the smoke wrapping around the ballroom.

When we finally stumble through the doors at the front of the room, there is even more smoke in the hallway. People are covering their mouths, coughing, running, desperate for any escape.

We're running so fast, I almost fall a few times, tripping over Chiamaka's long dress. More explosions sound as we burst out through the entrance to the school, racing down the steps and into the cold fresh air of the evening. I cough, feeling out of breath and disorientated.

My breath looks like a ghost as wisps swirl out of my mouth, before disintegrating into the air.

I look up at Niveus, once this tall, looming building, now crumbling before me, scorched by angry red flames.

It's weird, I don't think about it until this moment. But when it does register, when everything finally sinks in, the most obvious thought occurs to me.

The school is on fire…

Niveus Academy is burning.

44

THURSDAY

We finally get outside and watch as Niveus goes up in flames.

There are sirens in the back, firefighters rushing inside the collapsing building. It sounds awful, but a part of me wants to laugh.

Even the most powerful can be brought down. And we're all witnessing it.

We can all see the *great* Niveus Academy fall. At last.

"There are people in there...There's no way they'll make it out okay," someone says tearfully nearby.

I wonder how the fire started...if it was an accident. Who started it?

I feel my chest tighten.

I wonder if any of the protestors got stuck.

I chew my bottom lip, freezing when a thought crosses my mind. Terrell standing there in the audience.

Was he real?

Did I imagine him?

I hope I did... God, I hope I did.

I look at Devon. He looks out of it – in this trance, staring up at our old school.

"Devon," I say quietly but loud enough for him to hear.

"Yeah?" he replies monotonously.

"Where is Terrell?"

"What?" he asks, turning to face me now, looking sick.

"I saw him inside…I think… Did he come? Was he here?" I ask, hoping he says no.

But before he can reply, another explosion erupts and a large chunk of the roof collapses.

45

THURSDAY

My mind flashes back to Terrell telling me about his involvement in this.

Terrell's here.

He's in there.

I feel sick.

I have to go to him.

I don't know what is carrying me, but I find myself running towards the building.

It's my fault. It's all my fault. I shouldn't have left him.

I feel Chiamaka dragging me back and I start calling his name, like he'll hear me inside there.

The flames grow, eating Niveus alive and I want to scream.

"Terrell," I yell.

No answer, as expected.

I can't lose him too… I can't lose any more people. I feel weak, like I'm about to fall—

"Devon?" someone says. I'm almost positive it's in my head.

I turn back and Terrell's there. Right there in front of me, with a matching worried expression on his face. I feel so relieved, I run over to him and pull him in for a hug. Forgetting everything that's happened. Just hugging him tight, so happy he's okay. He holds me close and I bury my face in his shoulder, tears falling.

I really thought I'd lost him there. *Thank God you're okay, Terrell*, my thoughts whisper.

I can feel his heart hammering.

After a few moments I pull away, wiping the tears from my cheeks. "I thought you were inside," I tell him.

"I'm okay," he says, his eyes focused on Chiamaka and not me. "Glad you guys both are too."

"Really thought you were gone," Chiamaka says, wiping her eyes. I'm surprised by that. She hardly knows him, yet she's crying like she was about to lose her good friend. What surprises me even more is her hugging him now.

Sirens wail in the distance and I turn towards the sound. Ambulances are parking next to the fire trucks.

"We should head back before the police arrive," Terrell says.

I nod.

"You're right."

The last thing I want to deal with is any police officers.

We end up in Terrell's bedroom soon after.

He sets up a makeshift sheet-fort and gives us something to change into. I'm wearing one of his Superman shirts and

447

sweats. Chiamaka told her parents that she's okay and she's staying at a friend's. She's now wearing a plaid PJ set Terrell apparently owns even though I've never seen him wear anything so normal – other than his outfit from earlier tonight.

We all sit in the fort talking about tonight – the protestors and the fire and the shady journalist. I refrain from saying *I told you so*. I knew it was too good to be true, too easy. I knew we shouldn't have trusted another stranger. Niveus can buy anyone, of course they can.

We should have known that. But at least we do now.

At least there's that.

I'm just so exhausted. I'm ready to sleep for ever, but we stay up till one talking. We conclude that the protestors were probably there because of my tweet, and the message I sent about the ball. I hope none of them got hurt. Without them, I don't know if we'd be here right now.

Maybe Ward would have finished what he started.

"What do you think started the fire?" Chiamaka asks.

It looked serious. They'll need to rebuild a lot of the buildings.

I shrug. "Could have been anything," I say.

"Does this mean it'll be closed down?" Terrell asks.

"Probably," Chiamaka says.

We sit in a sombre silence for a few moments.

My mind turns over what might happen to everyone now… What happens to Mr Ward… *Aces*. Whether this will all get buried in the aftermath.

As if Chiamaka is reading my mind, she murmurs, "Well, I'm tired. Going to head to bed… Where is your bathroom, please?"

"Down the hall, to the left," Terrell says.

She steps out of the fort, leaving us alone.

Silence.

"Can we talk?" Terrell asks.

I nod, because with Terrell there is no getting out of talks. He's upfront, he seems to like to confront everything in the moment. Or so I thought. Because he hid this well for weeks.

"I'm sorry. The last thing I'd want to do is hurt you. I was never going to completely go through with it. I would never hurt you, ever. I told the guy that."

"Okay," I say.

He looks nervous. "Do you hate me?"

I look at him. As much as I want to be mad, it's like there's something about Terrell that prevents me from being mad at him. I feel hurt, but I don't hate him. I don't think I could.

I shake my head. "I don't hate you," I say.

"Thank you for not hating me," he says.

"It's okay," I reply.

I don't know if things will be okay right away, but I can tell they will be eventually.

There's a weird sound in the distance and at first I think it's Chiamaka, but then Terrell pushes himself up.

"I need to feed Bullshit, he gets cranky when I delay his meals."

"I don't think your cat likes me," I say, leaning back a little.

Terrell raises an eyebrow. "I think he doesn't like sharing me. He'll warm up to you."

I find that hard to believe. His cat looks at me like he wants me dead. If it wasn't completely impossible, I'd be convinced that Bullshit was in on the whole Aces thing too.

"Doubt that," I mutter.

Terrell smiles, which makes me smile back and then we just stare at each other in silence for a few moments. Terrell breaks eye contact first, pushing his glasses up as he stands and moves out of the fort. I can hear him speaking to Bullshit, scolding him for interrupting his conversation.

I take out my phone, searching for reports of the fire, worried about who might have been caught up in it. I wonder if Jack came.

I scroll. The reports don't say much. Just that there was a fire at the school, an unknown cause.

I look up again, at Terrell in the hallway pouring food into a bowl. I watch him, stroking his cat as it eats the food.

He moves away and ducks back into the fort again, sitting opposite me.

"Cat food smells like crap," I say, wrinkling my nose.

Terrell laughs. "Thank God we don't have to eat that, right?"

Chiamaka returns with a scowl and her arms crossed as she walks towards us.

"What?" I ask.

"Where am I sleeping?" she asks.

"You can have my bed. I don't mind sleeping with Devon here," Terrell says.

I feel really hot, but I ignore the way his sentence sounded.

Chiamaka smiles. "Thank you, Terrell," she says, before climbing into his bed like she probably intended on doing anyway, whether Terrell said yes or not.

"Guess that leaves us with the fort. Want me to get any more pillows or blankets?" Terrell asks.

I shake my head. I'm good.

I lie back first, staring up at the sheets strung above me, ignoring Terrell and his proximity when he lies down too.

We lie there in silence and I start to feel a little drowsy. From the combination of today's stress from the ball and just being emotionally drained anyway, I find myself drifting a little.

"Stargazing?" Terrell asks.

I turn to him, looking confused. "What?"

"You're looking up pretty intensely – thought you were searching for stars in my sheets," he says.

I nod. "I was… Millions of stars in the sky tonight," I say pointing up at nothing.

"I see them… I know some of the names for them too, you know."

"Enlighten me," I say, watching as Terrell gets comfortable and looks up.

"That one there is called Tupac, named after the legend

451

of course. Scientists were like…that star is mad bright, let's name it Tupac—"

I burst out laughing and Terrell smiles at me.

"Maybe you should consider a career in teaching people how to BS," I say.

"Maybe I should," he replies.

We spend the rest of the night like this. Talking, Terrell joking, making me laugh.

The last thing I think before sleep catches up with me is:

No more Niveus…

No more Aces.

46

FRIDAY

The news has been playing on Terrell's TV since I woke up this morning.

Terrell is seated on the floor, drinking coffee next to a sleepy-looking Devon. They're both watching in silence as the screen shows the remains of Niveus, as well as footage from last night's fire.

They report that a faulty electrical circuit caused it, that it was an inevitable tragedy.

It all feels like a really messed-up dream, but it really happened.

Our school burned down.

I sit now, with my own cup of coffee made by my new friend, Terrell, watching the news with them.

I feel a lot of relief seeing that building go up in flames. It feels like the perfect ending to this saga.

Niveus Academy reduced to ashes.

Bold graphics flash frantically up on the screen.

CASUALTIES CONFIRMED AS THE BODIES OF
THREE STUDENTS FOUND AT THE SCENE

People died?

That news makes me feel a little sick. People at Niveus were all part of this racist machine, but I knew them. It's hard to not feel a little sad for people you knew and interacted with for years.

The first face pops up, a photo from the school yearbook. I feel a punch in my gut.

"CeCe…" I say quietly.

"You knew her?" Terrell asks.

I nod.

"She was a popular girl at school," Devon adds.

A popular girl.

"I wasn't that close to her. Honestly, she was kind of a bitch to me," I say. Though it's not like I was ever that nice to her either, and it doesn't make me feel any less sick to my stomach.

CeCe and I were one and the same. Both smart, willing to do a lot to protect our titles, wanting to be on top.

And now she's dead, for ever resigned to being *a popular girl at school* and nothing more.

Another face pops up, and it's someone else I've seen around.

I feel sick.

"Did you know him?" Terrell asks.

I shake my head.

"He was in my music class," Devon says.

"I'm sorry," I say.

We sit in more silence, waiting for the third face. I feel

454

anxious all of a sudden. I'm not sure why. These people wanted to ruin my life – our lives. They didn't care about us, whether we lived or died.

So why do I feel so bad?

"Another guy," Terrell says, as the third graphic goes up.

I freeze.

I feel Devon glance at me, but say nothing.

The edges of my vision start to crumble. I don't know how I'm meant to feel about this, or react, so I don't think, I just sit here and let it happen.

My face is wet and I hate myself for crying. He doesn't deserve it.

"I need some fresh air," I say, placing my mug on the ground before getting up and leaving Terrell's room.

I feel more tears gather as I rush down the stairs and head outside.

The morning chill wraps around me, and I feel faint.

I can't believe it.

I bring my wrist up, wiping my eyes again, as more tears spill.

I can't believe Jamie's dead.

"Chiamaka?" a voice says from behind. I turn back, quickly wiping my eyes.

"Yes?" I say, as I turn to face Richards.

He looks sorry for me.

He shouldn't. There's nothing to be sorry for. Just a girl here crying over her awful dead ex-best friend.

"Wanna get out of here?" he asks.

I raise an eyebrow. *Yes, please.* "Where are you thinking of going?"

"Some place quieter than here."

I nod. Sounds like the sort of place I need.

We get to the beach nearby a while later. We decided to walk, since neither of us are exactly fit to drive right now.

I got changed into a nicer-looking shirt of Terrell's, one without any graphics of weird superheroes, and Devon stayed in his PJs from last night. Terrell stayed behind, said he'd make some breakfast.

When we get to the beach I take in how quiet it is. Like truly quiet. Like the whole world has disappeared.

The waves crash against the sand and Devon takes a seat on the ground.

I've lived in this town most of my life, but never been here. I don't think I even knew of its existence.

"How did you find out about this place?" I ask him, taking a seat next to him now.

"Used to come here a lot when I was younger, when things at home and at school got too much," he says.

I nod.

I can see why. It's really peaceful here. I sit up, crossing my legs. I'm about to tell him how nice it is here, but he's speaking again.

"I tried to kill myself here, years ago," he says.

I look at him. That's...surprising.

"Oh," I say. Because that's all I can think to say in response to that.

"I think I thought it would be nice… to just die – drown, in my favourite place. Now I find other ways to drown and cope," he says.

"What stopped you?" I ask.

He doesn't respond at first.

"Someone followed me here…pulled me out, didn't let me do it," he says quietly.

"Sounds like a good person."

"He is," Devon says.

We sit in silence, just watching the waves.

"You're not a bad person you know…for grieving him."

I'm guessing he's talking about Jamie.

"I'm not grieving him," I say.

Devon nods.

"Well even if you wanted to be sad about it…you're not a bad person. Just human," he says.

"Okay," I reply, wanting to end the conversation about Jamie there.

It's hard to detach the Jamie I liked, my best friend since I was fourteen, from the real Jamie. The one who was a racist coward, who never really liked me, who always had this plan in mind to screw with my life like this.

But I'm going to have to let go of the fake Jamie somehow. I refuse to grieve over someone who probably would have celebrated my death if the roles were reversed.

It's unexpected, but I feel a weight on my hand as Devon

slips his fingers through mine and squeezes. I give him a weird look, but he doesn't notice.

And I don't take my hand away.

I've felt alone a lot in this world, filled with people and faces that don't look like me. My parents always working. My friends all back-stabbing actors. My relationships never real.

But right now, with Devon, I don't feel alone at all.

Not one bit.

47

FRIDAY

Later, when I'm alone, I look at my tweet again.

The support has doubled since I last saw it. People are talking about the protest and my tweet that sparked it. So many people are supporting us and the truth.

I hope things work out, and the truth remains in the open, unburied. I hope we get to be okay after all this.

I go to my messages and see my inbox filled once again. A message from a verified account catches my eye and so I click on the message.

It's from a Black journalist.

@CindyIsHere47: I saw your tweet and I'd love to speak with you. Let me know if that is something you're interested in.
– Cindy

I don't want to trust anyone from any institution that can be paid off easily by Niveus. But then I click on her profile, eyes widening when I see the company she works for.

They are big. Known for their unapologetic articles and

fearless takes. All detailing the lives of people like us, wronged by the systems.

I'll show Chiamaka the message. Show her who it's from, see what she thinks.

But for now, I close out of Twitter.

I'm back in my room now, in my house.

I close my eyes, pretending it's already the future, and I'm somewhere else, living a completely different life.

Dreaming is dangerous. But I allow myself to this time.

I think we deserve a happy ending.

EPILOGUE: THE FIRE NEXT TIME

SIXTEEN YEARS LATER

A letter from *The Underground Society*

Dear Mrs Johnson,

It has come to our attention that you are planning on enrolling your son, Rhys Johnson, at Pollards Private Academy. We are writing to warn and advise you against sending Rhys to this school, as Pollards Private Academy systematically targets its Black students, practising a form of social eugenics. Attached to this letter is evidence dating back to 1965, when the first case of social eugenics took place at the now-closed institution, Niveus Private Academy, tragically costing the first Black victim there her life, as detailed in the documents. From 1965, the school caused undue trauma to all enrolled Black students, including, but not limited to, emotional and physical harassment and severe mental trauma as well as attempts to sabotage academic records, college applications and employment possibilities.

To guarantee your son's protection from having a similar experience at Pollards, we would love to invite him to join the Ruby Bridges Academy. This is a school set up by The Underground Society – a society founded to tackle the systemic inequality in schools across the country.

Niveus was not the only institution practising social eugenics, and we are still working to find those connected to Niveus, while also providing an alternative solution for students we identify as being targets of any of these institutions. Our aim is to reform all the systems, starting with education.

We hope you consider our offer.

Yours sincerely,

Dr Chiamaka Adebayo and Professor Devon Richards

Co-founders of The Underground Society

DEVON

I watch him sleep soundlessly, chest rising and falling, rising again. Beard overgrown, scruffy, head clean-shaven – always. The room is dark, despite it being early in the afternoon, and I have somewhere to be, but I get sucked into his beauty and find myself trapped.

I let my eyes fall to his bare back, where my favourite tattoo of his is, the one with numbers. I run my fingers over the date written on his back, then I lean in and kiss it.

"If you're gonna touch me, at least touch me somewhere it counts," his sleepy voice mutters.

"You'd love that so much, wouldn't you, T?"

His dimples pop out and he laughs.

"Why are you up so early?" he moans.

"Firstly, it's twelve thirty, and secondly, I have a doctor's appointment at one."

"You just want an excuse to see her," he says, turning to face me now, squinting. "God, I'll never get tired of looking at your face," he muses out loud.

My heart is beating fast but steadily.

"I'll never get tired of looking at me too," I reply, leaning in, giving him a quick kiss.

"That so?' he says, wrapping his arms around my shoulders, trapping me.

"Mm-hmm…" I kiss him again.

When I'm with him, I feel like I'm falling in love all over again. I'll never get tired of him. It's one of the only things I'm sure of.

I know that if I don't move away, I'll end up skipping the whole day, and so I stand before he can pull me back down again.

"Ma made you breakfast," I tell him, pulling my jacket on now.

He grins. "I love her more than anything in the world."

"Marry her instead, then," I tell him, walking out of our bedroom. I run down the stairs into the foyer, then I turn to the kitchen. Grey coils are springing out of Ma's bun and there's a smile on her face as she sits on a stool doing sudoku puzzles – Ma has an addiction to those – while whatever's in the pot bubbles in front of her. There was a time when it felt like this wasn't enough. A time where I resented her so much for hiding what she did about my pa; I didn't pick up her calls, I didn't check in on her. It's hard to forgive when you're hurting so much. But I hurt no more. Now I know she was all the family I needed. And if I can wake up every day to Terrell's face and ma doing her puzzles, I think that would be everything to me.

"Gonna go to the doctor's, Ma," I tell her, hugging her from behind, before kissing her forehead.

"Is Terrell awake yet?"

I nod. "I told him you made breakfast."

"Have a nice trip," she says.

I leave, rushing out the front door, down the steps of our home and straight into my car.

It doesn't take me long to get to the hospital, where I walk past the receptionist – much to her obvious dislike – up the stairs and straight to her office, with her name on a plate outside the chestnut-coloured door.

I knock and she yells "Come in" and so I open the doors to find her behind her desk, sifting through papers. She throws me a quick glance and I smile, moving towards her and hugging her from behind.

"Richards, unless your heart is failing, you need to wait in line."

I roll my eyes. "No time, I have a music class to teach. Just wanted to swing by and say hello."

She raises an eyebrow. "Did you get me coffee?"

I sit down on the chair opposite her desk. "I'm not your intern."

Her eyes squint behind her glasses, hair packed up in a bun, coat dazzling and tailored.

"Couldn't tell, you definitely dress like one," she mutters to herself, a small smile playing on her lips.

Most days I drop by. When she's not busy, we go out to lunch. Today's clearly not one of those days. She goes back to staring down at her papers like a mindless zombie, occasionally signing things in black ink. Her phone chimes and she briefly looks at it, then looks away.

"How's Mia?" I ask with a smile.

"She's good, very pregnant, but good…" she replies, still not looking up at me. "I actually wanted to tell you something," she adds, still shuffling through papers. "I found out that this Black student, Rhys Johnson, is applying to Pollards. I got members of the society to speak with his family, get them to reconsider, but they want the best for him and the best in that town is Pollards."

"So what, we just let them enrol him?" I ask.

Chiamaka nods. "We'll keep an eye on them, have people watching out for him. Plant someone on the inside. Anything to make sure we never let another Black kid get hurt by places like Niveus again."

CHIAMAKA

It's late when I leave my office to check up on my final patient.

I nod at a nurse wheeling in a pregnant woman, smiling as the bleach-like, sanitary smell of the hospital fills my nostrils.

My shoes squeak against the floor, and curls from my bun loosen, falling and blocking my sight a little. But I can still see the room number in the distance.

I think about the boy, Rhys. How much unwarranted suffering he could face at that school. Like we did. Like our ancestors did.

I think about how many Black spirits have been killed by white supremacy and lies. How many of us were experiments. Worthless bodies in some *game*.

I think about Henrietta Lacks, whose body they used, mistreated, and tossed away but who changed medicine for ever. Who never got her revenge for the way they stole her cells, as if they were entitled to her body. Because she was Black and a woman, and in that combination, she, to them, meant nothing.

To me, she and all the other spirits broken by this world and its systems, are the reason I get up and do this every day.

I walk into the room.

There he is, my final patient. Face hollow and sickly. Green and blue veins all over his arms and neck. Lying back, eyes peering up at me.

He's dying.

I close the door behind me and I smile.

We lock eyes and I move forward, approaching his bed, glancing at his heart rate through the monitor.

I can hear the sound of the beeping from the machine as the lines zig and zag slowly.

I drum my fingers on the machine, turning to face him now. He moves his mouth to speak, but no words come out.

And they don't have to.

The shock in his eyes is evident.

"Hello, Headmaster Ward," I say.

THE END

TURN THE PAGE FOR AN
EXCLUSIVE EXTRA CHAPTER,
FEATURING A PRIDE PICNIC WITH
DEVON, CHIAMAKA
AND TERRELL

PRIDE & PROMISES

NINE MONTHS AFTER THE FIRE, DEVON,
CHIAMAKA AND TERRELL GET TOGETHER FOR
A PRIDE PICNIC IN THE PARK.

DEVON

It's been a while since I dreamed of drowning.

A while since I dreamed of anything at all, really.

Which I guess is why it caught me by surprise.

One minute I was on the sand, the next being carried out by a gentle current, and then I was enveloped in it all, tugged through the fabric of the ocean, split in half, squeezed so hard I gasped for air—

And then I wake up in the dark, body springing upright like I've just been electrocuted back to life.

As my PJs cling to my skin and I try to steady my breathing, I consider how fucked up it is that dreaming of dying is the only time I actually feel alive.

I know my subconscious wants me to think of *him*, of today, and remember the significance of it all.

And how could I forget?

I have been not-so-subtly counting down the days, the minutes and the seconds.

It's been so bad that even Chiamaka's noticed. Last week she caught me staring blankly at the countdown app on my phone. She didn't say anything, but I could hear her thoughts, loud and clear, judging me for being this pathetic boy who pines after things he shouldn't.

I hear the soft sounds of my brothers sleeping next to me, and I grab a hold of my phone, squinting down at the time on the screen.

5.43 a.m.

And then the date.

June 9th.

Almost time.

I wonder if sending a text right now would be weird, or premature.

I should probably wait. Right? That's what normal people do.

But I guess this year has shown me that I'm anything but normal.

I hold my breath as I click onto our chat, hesitating once more before tapping out the message I have waited months to send.

Hey, I know you're probably busy today, I just wanted to say I miss you

I sigh, deleting the message and starting again.

Hi, this is Devon. I just wanted to see if you were okay

Delete. Way too formal.

Last night I had a dream that I was dying and you
didn't save me. I'm not sure if you were even in the
dream. Not that I dream about you a lot or
anything…but I guess I wish I did…dream of you
more. Maybe then I'd know what to say to you now

Delete. Way too dark.

I throw my phone down on the bed and put my face in
my hands, rubbing my eyes to wake myself up properly
before attempting this again.

Why is this so hard? It doesn't have to be. I just need to
write a message and send it. Why do I overthink everything?

I pick up my phone again, and I type.

Hey, Andre – I missed you

And then I finally hit send.

I don't wait for regret to settle in. I don't let myself think
about his response. Instead I shove my phone in my bedside
drawer, bury my head in the pillows and attempt to fall back
to sleep.

I still have a few hours before I have to meet Terrell and
Chiamaka, and so I make a promise to myself that I won't
think about him any more.

A promise to enjoy the day and not worry about whether
he'll ever want to see me again.

CHIAMAKA

I'm going to kill him.

The him in question being Terrell.

"Stop singing, you're going to crash my car!" I yell.

Which only prompts him to sing louder.

We have been on the road for thirty minutes, and every minute has been spent listening to Terrell's disturbing playlist and even more disturbing voice.

"Is this even music?" I ask him, lowering my Chanel sunglasses to judge him properly.

"Yes! The best music," he replies with a grin that makes me want to hit him.

I roll my eyes and push my sunglasses back up my face before crossing my legs and staring out the window.

I'm not even sure why I agreed to this trip. Well, actually, that's a lie. I know why.

Ever since the events of last year, things haven't been so great at home. Especially with my dad. It wasn't anything he did in particular, I guess. It was all the things he didn't do.

The resentment I had all those years spilled over and exploded one day when I asked myself, *What is the point of a dad who doesn't even try to protect you against your own racist family?* And when the answer to that question was clearly, *Nothing*, it changed everything for us.

I can tell he feels guilty. We haven't gone this long without talking, ever. And I worry sometimes that my resentment will never go away and will only evolve into hate.

And so I avoid him and the possibility of such a bleak future.

Which, of course, has its consequences. Including this one: that when Devon suggested we go to Pride in another city, I took the chance without even thinking.

I sigh, staring in the rear-view mirror at Devon sitting in the back of the car, looking blankly down at his phone like he's been doing a lot lately.

It hasn't taken much to figure out that it has something to do with that drug dealer he was dating.

Adam? Or something.

A part of me wants to tell him to get over it, to let go of love and the idea of relying on people to be there and not hurt you so badly.

But the other part of me understands what it's like to *really* like someone, and for it to implode in the worst way.

That was what it was like with Belle.

If I hadn't blocked her number months ago, I wonder if I'd also be glued to my phone, torturing myself about whether she'd ever text me again. Wondering if she ever even cared.

But I don't let myself wallow in that.

Instead, I focus on the here and now. Not on the future, like I used to. The future is so unpredictable. The present is the only thing that can be controlled.

And right now, I'm controlling this.

I place my finger on the stop button and Terrell's playlist abruptly pauses, cutting him off mid-screech.

He looks at me, offended, and I smile at him.

"So much better, wouldn't you say, Devon?"

Devon looks up, confused, like he forgot he was here.

"Uh, yeah, I guess."

Terrell is silent for a few moments and I feel myself begin to relax, but then I hear him yell, "Acapella it is!" And then he proceeds to sing at the top of his voice without the soundtrack to help mask the noise.

Devon looks shocked and amused by it.

Terrell seems unfazed by the number of daggers I am mentally throwing.

He continues the tuneless yelling for the rest of the journey to the city and I have to stop myself from taking off my shoes and hitting him with them.

He's lucky that I'm distracted by the thoughts that I can't stop from appearing in my mind throughout the journey.

Thoughts of my dad and how much I miss him and resent him at the same time.

Thoughts of how I was meant to be starting college in three months, but am not now. Instead, I'm waiting for the next cycle of school to begin this September, when I will be home-schooled in the hope I might have a shot at grasping back some semblance of the life I once desperately wanted.

Thoughts about Belle Robinson…and what she's doing now. Will she be at Pride back in our hometown? Is she hoping I'll be there? Did she ever care about me?

I'm thankful once we arrive at our destination that I no longer have to swim in my own thoughts or be tortured by Terrell's vocal inabilities.

As we get out of the car and Devon grabs the picnic his mom packed for us, I look up at the scene before me.

Pride in the Park.

There are what seems like thousands of people gathered on the grass.

A band plays music in the distance, and everything is rainbow-coloured and bright.

It's like the gates of the park are the doors to Narnia – if Narnia was a Pride event, that is.

I am awestruck by how welcoming it all looks.

This time last year, I hadn't even considered the idea that I liked girls. But now that I know, it feels like it was something that should have always been apparent to me.

Especially now that I look around at the event, see the couples walking hand in hand. Arms trapped around waists. Friends in large groups, laughing. Two girls kissing, one wearing a Valentino rainbow dress. And it looks so much like home.

I decide to erase all the negative thoughts I had in the car from my mind and focus on the present again. Like I promised myself months ago – to only live life in the present tense.

"Chiamaka, can you help me with the stuff in the trunk?" Devon asks, clearly struggling with it all.

"Sure," I say, tearing my eyes away from it all, and I walk over to him.

Present tense. I remind myself, again and again until it sticks.

Present tense.

DEVON

We have been at Pride in the Park for a few hours now, and Terrell and Chiamaka, who had been squabbling in the car all afternoon, are now up on their bare feet, dancing and singing to the band playing on the main stage.

It is a weird sight to see.

Drunk Chiamaka is a lot bubblier than sober Chiamaka.

"Devon, get up and dance with us!" she yells as she twirls Terrell around.

I shake my head. No way am I dancing.

She rolls her eyes at me and holds her hand out. "Present tense!" she yells, and I'm not sure what she means.

"What?"

"Stop moping and staring at your phone. Yes, it sucks to love someone and for them to not see that, but we can't live life trapped in the past! You have to live now, Devon. Present tense!"

I raise an eyebrow at that.

I hate to admit it, but drunk Chiamaka is right.

I made a promise to myself, one I broke within minutes of starting our road trip.

I wasn't going to focus on him.

I was going to enjoy myself.

I sigh, putting my phone on the ground and taking a swig of the drink I have been nursing, before I finally take her hand.

This makes her grin widely and as the song switches to something more upbeat, she takes my other hand and swings both together, forcing me to move.

I watch Terrell doing the Macarena.

Present tense, I repeat to myself inside.

And then I bounce my knees and let go.

Chiamaka cheers me on and I don't think, I just move, feeling myself relax.

I know I will regret this in the morning.

But right now, that doesn't matter.

I dance and forget about the world and all my problems, letting myself disappear into the moment.

I'm not sure when it happened – I was too far gone in the joy of the present to hear it or see it come through. But sometime, during this whole embarrassing sequence, my phone buzzed on the ground.

Gently vibrating as the soft sound of the windchime tone rang out.

[1 new message from Dre]

TERRELL'S
PRIDE PLAYLIST

SCREWED
JANELLE MONÁE (FEAT. ZOË KRAVITZ)

DID IT ON'EM
NICKI MINAJ

GENGHIS KHAN
MIIKE SNOW

CHERRY
RINA SAWAYAMA

NEED TO KNOW
DOJA CAT

DISTURBIA
RIHANNA

APPLAUSE
LADY GAGA

LOCO
ITZY

HIT 'EM UP
2PAC, OUTLAWZ

AIN'T IT FUN
PARAMORE

AUTHOR'S NOTE

Dear Reader,

I am so pleased to be writing this author's note, nine months after *Ace of Spades* was first published in June 2021. And what a year this has been!

When I first started writing *Ace of Spades*, I was in my first year of university in Scotland, ten hours from my home in London. I was scared about the prospect of being away from my family for the first time, and I didn't feel like I really fitted in.

At university, it seemed as if almost everyone was interested in parties and drinking, and as I wasn't, I found myself stuck in my room a lot of the time with not much to do.

And so I wrote a story.

When I wasn't in lectures or seminars, I was writing *Ace of Spades* (and if I'm being honest, sometimes I was writing it *in* those lectures and seminars too). It became something that felt like my own personal safe space. I could spend time with my fictional friends, Devon and Chiamaka, and they'd keep me company during the long cold days in Scotland. Sometimes I'd be writing in the library and find myself laughing at a particular scene or sentence, which probably didn't help me on the friendship front. Then one day, sometime in the spring of my first year, I had a finished manuscript. One that I would go on to revise and submit to agents. One that would finally get me an agent, after hundreds of rejections with older projects. One that would get me my very first book deal with my dream publisher, Usborne, and my dream editor, Becky Walker.

I already felt like the luckiest person alive, but I could not have imagined in one million years what was to come.

As I'm writing this, I'm happy to share that in just nine months since *Ace of Spades* published, it has sold more than 100,000 copies in the English language. It has been nominated for so many exciting awards and has even won a bunch of them. The Books Are My Bag Readers Awards 2021 was my first award win ever in November of 2021, and since then there have only been more and more amazing award wins and nominations. *Ace of Spades* also became an international bestselling book, topping charts all over the world, including the US, with the *New York Times* and National Indie bestsellers lists, the UK, where it debuted at no. 2 on the Nielsen Bookscan bestsellers chart, and the Portuguese bestsellers chart. It is often so hard to believe that so many amazing things have happened in just nine months.

And they have all happened because of you, reader.

In this year, so many of you have welcomed Devon and Chiamaka into your hearts. These characters that kept me company during some of the hardest times in my life are no longer just mine. You have all embraced them fully, showing the world that stories about queer Black kids matter and, in turn, showing sixteen-year-old Faridah, who dreamed of becoming an author and seeing herself in the pages of stories, that she matters too.

Thank you for all of the wonderful messages, the incredible fan art, cosplay and edits. Thank you to all of the amazing booksellers and librarians, who have sold and championed and supported my book!

And thank you so much to all the readers, new and old, for picking up my book and sharing this journey with me.

Warmest wishes,

FARIDAH ÀBÍKÉ-ÍYÍMÍDÉ
MARCH 2022

LOOK OUT FOR
FARIDAH ÀBÍKÉ-ÍYÍMÍDÉ'S
BRAND-NEW
YA THRILLER...

COMING SOON

ACKNOWLEDGEMENTS

There are so many people to thank and not enough trees in the world to express my gratitude, but still, I will try my hardest – using as little bark as I can.

I want to first thank my mum for all that she has done for me. She always encouraged me to be creative, abandoning the classic Nigerian saying, "If you're not a doctor, lawyer, or engineer, you are a disappointment." And instead, she valued my happiness above all else. With my mum by my side, I never felt like a disappointment. Growing up, life was difficult at times, and she always made things better with a story. At bedtime she'd recite Nigerian folklore or make up a cool adventure, and so I learned to love storytelling from her.

Thank you to my sisters, Maliha and Tamera, for being so supportive and for listening to my ideas (with very little bribing).

Thank you to Hannah Sheppard for being one of the first people to believe in this story when many people didn't.

A special thank you to everyone at The Bent Agency for making me feel so welcome.

A huge thank you to my wonderful agent, Zoë Plant, who took me in and has championed me and my books ever since – also thank you for answering all my random late-night emails.

Thank you to Molly Ker Hawn for supporting me and this book during a very difficult time.

A massive thank you to my editor Becky Walker who I have called my book's soulmate – from the moment I spoke to Becky on the phone almost three years ago I knew she was who I wanted to work with. It has been such a pleasure working on stories with Becky and *Ace of Spades* would not be what it is without her.

Thank you to everyone at Usborne for championing *Ace of Spades* and being such an amazing publisher to work with! Thank you to Rebecca Hill, Sarah Stewart, Alice Moloney, Gareth Collinson, Katharine Millichope, Sarah Cronin, Hannah Reardon-Steward, Stevie Hopwood, Christian Herisson, Arfana Islam, Lizzie Whittern, Laura Lawrence, Sharon Afutu and Natalie Bunch.

A huge thanks to Amy Dobson and Ronke Lawal for everything!

Thank you to Kingsley Nebechi for illustrating such a stunning cover! Thank you for bringing my characters to life with your incredible art work and design.

Thank you to my cousin Ade for lifting me out of the sunken place. Without her this book would not have been written, and I'd probably still be in a very bad place.

Thank you to Aleema for all of the late night calls and

for helping me get unstuck/out of my occasional writer's block.

Thank you to everyone who has supported me throughout this journey. You know who you are. If I start listing names I literally won't stop, and as I said in my intro, not enough bark.

And lastly, thank you to the kettle I keep in my bedroom. I have named him Steve. I have boiled many a tea, and you have supported me through very tough times.

Thank you.